PUFFIN BOOKS

DAGGERS OF DARKNESS

As one of Segrek's Select you could be the heir to the Great Throne of Kazan. But the ancient system of succession in this strange and wild kingdom is under threat from the forces of evil in the guise of the murderous vizier Chingiz. Time is running out for you already. Following an assassin's attempt on your life, your body is infected with poison from a Death Spell Dagger forged by Chingiz himself. Unless you reach the Great Throne in time and hand back the dagger to its maker, you will perish and Chingiz and his dark creatures will rule the land.

Who knows what evil will pour out of Kazan if you fail in your quest? The destiny of the Great Throne depends on YOU.

Two dice, a pencil and an eraser are all you need to embark on this thrilling adventure, which is complete with its elaborate combat system and a score sheet to record your gains and losses.

Many dangers lie ahead and your success is by no means certain. YOU decide which routes to follow, which dangers to risk and which adversaries to fight!

Fighting Fantasy Gamebooks

Steve Jackson and Ian Livingstone
present:

Daggers of Darkness

Luke Sharp

Illustrated by Martin McKenna

PUFFIN BOOKS

PUFFIN BOOKS

Published by the Penguin Group
27 Wrights Lane, London W8 5TZ, England
Viking Penguin Inc., 40 West 23rd Street, New York, New York 10010, USA
Penguin Books Australia Ltd, Ringwood, Victoria, Australia
Penguin Books Canada Ltd, 2801 John Street, Markham, Ontario, Canada L3R 1B4
Penguin Books (NZ) Ltd, 182–190 Wairau Road, Auckland 10, New Zealand

Penguin Books Ltd, Registered Offices: Harmondsworth, Middlesex, England

First published 1988
3 5 7 9 10 8 6 4 2

Concept copyright © Steve Jackson and Ian Livingstone, 1988
Text copyright © Luke Sharp, 1988
Illustrations copyright © Martin McKenna, 1988
Map copyright © Leo Hartas, 1988
All rights reserved

Printed and bound in Great Britain by
Cox & Wyman Ltd, Reading
Set in 11/13pt Linotron Palatino by
Rowland Phototypesetting Ltd
Bury St Edmunds, Suffolk

*To the Return of the Hero
with help from
Colin Meikle
Michael Bishop
Karl Johan Durr Sorenson
and A.I.B.*

CONTENTS

HOW TO FIGHT THE CREATURES OF KAZAN

Before embarking on your adventure, you must first determine your own strengths and weaknesses. You must work out your initial LUCK, SKILL and STAMINA scores. You may use the *Adventure Sheet* on pages 18–19 to record all the details of an adventure. Here you will find boxes for recording your SKILL, STAMINA and LUCK scores. If it is possible to make a photocopy of this page, do so. Otherwise record all details in pencil.

Skill, Stamina and Luck

Roll one die. Add 6 to this number and enter the total in the SKILL box on the *Adventure Sheet*.

Roll both dice. Add 12 to the number rolled and enter this number in the STAMINA box.

Roll one die. Add 6 to this number and enter this total in the LUCK box.

For reasons that will be explained below, SKILL, STAMINA and LUCK scores change constantly during an adventure. You must keep an accurate record of these scores and for this reason you are advised either to write small in the boxes or to keep an eraser handy. But never rub out your *Initial* scores.

Your SKILL score reflects your swordsmanship and

general fighting expertise; the higher the better. Your SKILL score reflects your general constitution, your will to survive, your determination and overall fitness; the higher your STAMINA score, the longer you will be able to survive. Your LUCK score indicates how naturally lucky a person you are. Luck – and magic – are facts of life in the fantasy kingdom you are about to explore.

Battles

You will often come across paragraphs in the book which instruct you to fight a creature of some sort. An option to flee may be given, but if not – or if you choose to attack the creature anyway – you must resolve the battle as described below.

First record the creature's SKILL and STAMINA scores in the first vacant Encounter Box on your *Adventure Sheet*. The scores for each creature are given in the book each time you have an encounter.

The sequence of combat is then:

1. Roll both dice once for the creature. Add its SKILL score. This total is the creature's Attack Strength.
2. Roll both dice once for yourself. Add the number rolled to your current SKILL score. This total is your Attack Strength.
3. If your Attack Strength is higher than that of your opponent, you have wounded it: proceed to step 4. If the creature's Attack Strength is higher than

yours, it has wounded you: proceed to step 5. If both Attack Strength totals are the same, you have avoided each other's blows – start the next Attack Round from step 1 above.

4. You have wounded the creature, so subtract 2 points from its STAMINA score. You may use your LUCK here to do additional damage (see below).
5. Your opponent has wounded you, so subtract 2 points from your own STAMINA score. Again you may use LUCK at this stage (see below).
6. Make the appropriate adjustments to either the creature's or your own STAMINA score (and your LUCK score if you used LUCK – see below).
7. Begin the next Attack Round by repeating steps 1 to 6. This sequence continues until the STAMINA score of either you or the creature you are fighting has been reduced to zero (death).

Fighting More Than One Creature

If you come across more than one creature in a particular encounter, the instructions on that page will tell you how to handle the battle. Usually you will fight each one in turn.

Luck

At various times during your adventure, either in battles or when you find yourself in a situation in which you could be either Lucky or Unlucky (details are given on the relevant pages), you may call on your LUCK to make the outcome more favourable. But beware! Using LUCK is a risky business and if you are Unlucky, the results could be disastrous.

The procedure for using your LUCK is as follows: roll two dice. If the number rolled is equal to or less than your current LUCK score, you have been Lucky and the result will go in your favour. If the number rolled is higher than your current LUCK score, you have been Unlucky and you will be penalized.

This procedure is known as *Testing your Luck*. Each time you *Test your Luck*, you must subtract 1 point from your current LUCK score. Thus you will soon realize that the more you rely on your LUCK, the more risky this will become.

Using Luck in Battles

On certain pages of the book you will be told to *Test your Luck* and will be told the consequences of your being Lucky or Unlucky. However, in battles, you always have the *option* of using your LUCK, either to inflict a more serious wound on a creature you have just wounded or to minimize the effects of a wound the creature has just inflicted on you.

If you have just wounded the creature, you may *Test your Luck* as described above. If you are Lucky, you have inflicted a severe wound and may subtract an *extra* 2 points from the creature's STAMINA score. However, if you are Unlucky, the wound was a mere graze and you must restore 1 point to the creature's STAMINA (i.e. instead of scoring the normal 2 points of damage, you have now scored only 1).

If the creature has just wounded you, you may *Test your Luck* to try to minimize the wound. If you are Lucky, you have managed to avoid the full damage of the blow. Restore 1 point of STAMINA (i.e. instead of doing 2 points of damage it has done only 1). If you are Unlucky, you have taken a more serious blow. Subtract 1 *extra* STAMINA point.

Remember that you must subtract 1 point from your own LUCK score each time you *Test your Luck*.

Restoring Skill, Stamina and Luck

Skill

Your SKILL score will not change much during your adventure. Occasionally a paragraph may give you instructions to increase or decrease your SKILL score. Your SKILL score can never exceed its *Initial* value unless specifically instructed. Drinking the Potion of Skill (see below) will restore your SKILL to its *Initial* level at any time.

Stamina and Provisions

Your STAMINA score will change a lot during your adventure as you fight and undertake arduous tasks. As you near your goal, your STAMINA level may become dangerously low and battles may be particularly risky, so be careful!

Your backpack contains enough Provisions for ten meals. You may rest and eat at any time except when engaged in a battle. Eating a meal restores 4 STAMINA points. When you eat a meal, add 4 points to your STAMINA score and deduct 1 point from your Provisions. A separate Provisions Remaining box is provided on the *Adventure Sheet* for recording details of Provisions. Remember that you have a long way to go, so use your Provisions wisely! Remember also that your STAMINA score may never exceed its *Initial* value unless specifically instructed on a page. Drinking the Potion of Strength (see below) will restore your STAMINA to its *Initial* level at any time.

Luck

Additions to your LUCK score are awarded during the adventure when you have been particularly lucky. Details are given in the appropriate paragraphs of the book. Remember that, as with SKILL and STAMINA, your LUCK score may never exceed its *Initial* value, unless specifically instructed in a paragraph. Drinking the Potion of Fortune (see below) will restore your LUCK to its *Initial* level at any time, and will increase your *Initial* LUCK by 1 point.

Equipment and Potions

You will start your adventure with a bare minimum of equipment, but you may find or buy other items during your travels. You are armed with a sword and are dressed in leather armour. You have a backpack to hold Provisions and any treasures you may come across.

In addition, you may take a bottle of magical potion which will aid you on your quest. You may choose to take one bottle from the following:

Potion of Skill – restores SKILL points
Potion of Strength – restores STAMINA points
Potion of Fortune – restores LUCK points and increases *Initial* LUCK by 1

These potions may be taken at any time during your adventure (except when engaged in a battle). Taking a measure of potion will restore SKILL, STAMINA or LUCK scores to their *Initial* level (and the Potion of Fortune will add 1 point to your *Initial* LUCK score before LUCK is restored).

Each bottle of potion contains *one* measure, i.e. the characteristic may be restored only once during an adventure. Make a note on your *Adventure Sheet* when you have consumed the potion.

Remember also that you may choose only *one* of the three potions to take on your trip, so choose wisely!

Poison

Unfortunately, you will find that poison is spreading through your body. At various times, especially after you have exerted yourself, you will be asked to mark off Poison units on the *Adventure Sheet*. If this occurs, you must shade in one area of the outline figure provided on the *Adventure Sheet*. The poison will spread as you progress through the adventure, so you must always shade in an area next to one that has already been infected. If you find that the figure is completely covered by the poison (all the areas in the outline are shaded in), then your adventure is over. The poison has completed its fell task.

Medallions and Mazes

There are six regions in Kazan and each region contains a Medallion. (The clans that rule the regions are listed on the *Adventure Sheet*.) Traditionally, the Medallions are kept in huge mazes full of untold dangers. If you succeed in obtaining a Medallion, make a note of the fact in the box provided. The Medallions possess great power; each one enables the holder to walk away from three lost combats: even if you lose a fight, you may restore your STAMINA to 4 and act as though you have defeated your opponent. If you choose to use this power, however, you must at the same time reduce your SKILL by 1 point, your LUCK by 1 point and mark off 3 Poison units on the *Adventure Sheet*.

Gold

You will discover that Kazan is a very mercenary land. The currency is Gold Coin. You will possess 6 gold coins when you begin your adventure. One of these will be sewn into your boot; this is your lucky piece, and you must not use it unless specifically instructed. You will also carry a small purse of iron coins of very little value. Mark any additions or deductions carefully in the Gold box on the *Adventure Sheet*.

ADVENTURE SHEET

SKILL 12	STAMINA 24	LUCK 12	GOLD 31
INITIAL SKILL=	*INITIAL STAMINA=* 23 22	*INITIAL LUCK=* 11 12	

POISON UNITS

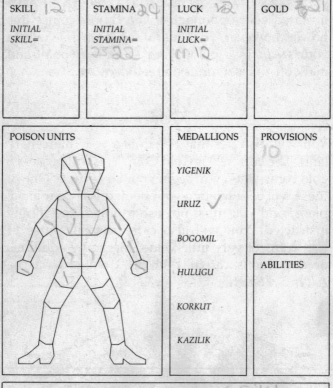

MEDALLIONS

YIGENIK

URUZ ✓

BOGOMIL

HULUGU

KORKUT

KAZILIK

PROVISIONS

10

ABILITIES

CLUES, SPELLS, OBJECTS FOUND & NOTES

Tidfilli

9880   1000
-641   -874
 359   126

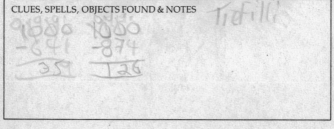

ENCOUNTER BOXES

SKILL=	SKILL=	SKILL=	SKILL=
STAMINA=	STAMINA=	STAMINA=	STAMINA=
SKILL=	SKILL=	SKILL=	SKILL=
STAMINA=	STAMINA=	STAMINA=	STAMINA=
SKILL=	SKILL=	SKILL=	SKILL=
STAMINA=	STAMINA=	STAMINA=	STAMINA=
SKILL=	SKILL=	SKILL=	SKILL=
STAMINA=	STAMINA=	STAMINA=	STAMINA=

BACKGROUND

You open your eyes. Above you stands a creature swathed in a dark cloak. He is holding a long dagger which he is about to plunge into your body. You try to move but cannot; you are transfixed by his staring, unblinking assassin's eyes. The blade gleams in the moonlight as it flashes down towards your throat.

'Begone, creature of the night!' a familiar voice cries. 'Homrath Deis Blichneth Vaqua!' The dagger falls with no power and grazes your shoulder. Just before you swoon at the fiery torment, you catch a glimpse of the departing figure of the would-be assassin, then you turn your head and see Gally's gentle eyes, before you black out.

When you awake, the pain in your shoulder is a dull throb. Gally is bathing the wound and chanting in a strange tongue. He sees that you are watching him, and says: 'Welcome back. I feared the dagger held a greater evil, beyond even my powers. But you are quickly recovered. Well met, brave Kazanid, one of Segrek's Select.'

'But how do you . . .?' you begin to ask.

'This inn is dangerous now,' he says. 'I will take you to a safer place and then all will be explained.'

The drinking companion you knew as Gally leads you into the Keep at Gorak, up a spiral staircase and into a large room full of dusty books, jars and bottles, small furry creatures and birds. Suddenly you realize that 'Gally' is none other than Astragal the Wizard. He explains that there is little time. Only recently has he learnt that Segrek, ruler of Kazan, died the previous year and that the vizier, Chingiz, suppressed the news and sent out the Mamlik Assassins to kill all the Select before they could undertake their journey to the Throne at Sharrabbas. He tells you to sit and rest, for there is much to be done. As he leaves the room, you hear him ordering the guards to let no one in. You sit back, rubbing your shoulder, and watch the birds flutter in and out of the window. By your side, a small book lies open; you pick it up, to read a very familiar story.

Kazan – Very little is known of this strange, wild land. It is situated to the west of **Gorak** (see above) and south of the Swordflow, in the extreme south-west corner of Khul. The capital city is Sharrabbas, where sits the Throne of Kazan. The remainder of the land is divided into six tribal regions, each fiercely independent and warlike. The Kazanids are renowned for their bravery and their acceptance of any creature or being that can stand up to their hard and, some would say, savage tests. There have always been rumours of the presence of gold in the Greater Ilkhans, the range of mountains to the south of Sharrabbas, but no prospector has ever returned with firm evidence. Kazan has a very strange ritual of succession to the throne. But the system has meant that every ruler of Kazan has been very brave, strong and quick-witted. Those parents who choose to nominate their children as Heirs to Ushun Koja (or the Select) bring their babies to Sharrabbas, where they have to undergo a series of tests. The parents of those children who pass the tests are given money to bring up the infant in the approved manner. At the age of nine the child is exiled from Kazan and must roam the lands of **Khul**, making his or her own way and surviving the rigours of loneliness and fear. When a ruler dies, the Select are summoned by messengers who travel the countryside, leaving secret symbols in traditional locations. They must make their way to Kazan, enter the great Mazes and obtain as many of the Clan Medallions as possible. They then have to reach Sharrabbas, where they must be the first to sit upon the Throne. The Kazanids are a very secretive people and the mystery of what happens in Sharrabbas has never been revealed.

Suddenly your reading is interrupted by Astragal rushing back into the room, clutching the evil dagger of the Mamlik Assassin. 'This dagger was forged by Chingiz with a very strong Death Spell. There is no way to recovery but to hand it back to its maker, Chingiz. You must hurry!' You secure the dagger in the lining of your boots.

So begins your journey to the Throne of Kazan. You must make your way through the wild lands, take the test of the Clans, enter the Mazes and carry as many of their Medallions as you can to Sharrabbas. Once there, you must find the Great Throne. All the while you will be sought out by the Mamlik Assassins who serve the evil Vizier Chingiz. Caution must be your watchword! You may encounter Necromancers, undead beings of no physical substance but possessing great powers of evil magic. Avoid them if you can.

Unfortunately, as Astragal explained, you have been scratched by a Death Spell Dagger: your body has been infected by the evil of Chingiz. The poison will spread slowly through your body, but it will have no real effect until it has travelled through every part – and then death will be sudden and violent.

Now, turn to 1.

1

Astragal leads you to the boundary of the lands of Gorak, shakes you by the hand and wishes you good luck. By order of the Mage Council he cannot enter Kazan – but he hints that he will make attempts to contact you from time to time. He waves farewell as you begin the climb up into the mountains that divide the two lands. Your shoulder starts to ache and you know that the poison is beginning to work its way through your body (mark off 2 Poison units on the *Adventure Sheet*).

You climb for many hours, passing from green fields to the cold land up above the snowline. The snow underfoot gets thicker and the going gets harder. You are exhausted but know that you cannot stop (deduct 1 point from your STAMINA). Eventually you come to the mountain pass known as Drago's Gate; an ancient stone obelisk marks the Kazanid frontier. On the rock a body sprawls, a dagger planted in its chest. You notice an open backpack lying on the snow by the obelisk. Do you wish to take any of the objects that you see scattered around by the backpack (turn to **233**), or do you want to inspect the body first (turn to **89**)?

2

The Eagle holds an iron rod in its talons and Geronicus invites you to grasp it. The huge bird flaps its wings and lifts you effortlessly. It flies fast and high. Suddenly, you see three large Grypfalcons bearing down on you. The Eagle cannot manoeuvre because of your weight. It tries to climb up into the mountains but the Grypfalcons follow, harassing it. The bird eventually swoops down close to the ground and drops you. *Test your Luck.* If you are Unlucky, you land badly: deduct 4 points from your STAMINA. If you are Lucky, you land in a soft patch of snow. Turn to **275**.

3

You find yourself in a chamber that is pitch-black. Something slithers underfoot and wraps itself around your ankle. Before you, you see two red eyes and you hear the sound of a sword being drawn from its scabbard. If you have the Ability of Darkfight, fight as normal; if not, then deduct 2 points from your SKILL for this combat only.

DARK MONSTER   SKILL 6   STAMINA 8

If you win (mark off 1 Poison unit on the *Adventure Sheet*), return to **160**, throw the magic die and mark your new position.

4

The track you are following becomes a well-constructed, cobbled road. At frequent intervals along the side of the road, you see small obelisks. An occasional cart passes by. You have just stopped to take a stone out of your boot when a man on horseback, swathed in a large brown cloak, trots past, leading a spare horse; he stops and offers you a ride into Sharrabbas at the price of 2 gold coins. While you are considering his offer, you notice the name 'Wolfsbane' etched on his saddle. Do you accept the offer (turn to 352) or refuse and walk on (turn to 23)? If you do not have enough gold to pay him the amount he demands, you must refuse.

5

Mandrake is very difficult to follow; he seems to melt into the crowd. He leads you through small, winding lanes, made dark by tall buildings. Eventually you lose him at the meeting of the three lanes. Which do you approach:

Street of the Forty Guilds?	Turn to 98
Street of the Stonemasons?	Turn to 164
Street of the Swordsmiths?	Turn to 328

6

You chase after the Orc and catch up with him when he has the Dwarf trapped in a blind alley, his sword raised to cleave the unfortunate's head in two. You draw your own sword.

EXECUTIONER ORC   SKILL 7   STAMINA 6

If you win (add 1 point to your LUCK), the Dwarf thanks you and takes you under his wing. He sets off at a fast pace through the twisting streets until you reach the Dwarf quarter of the city, where he enters a house and disguises himself by exchanging his green cloak for a red one. He explains that his master, one of Segrek's Select, was killed by the Mamliks when they entered the city. He suddenly stops and stares at you, as though he can sense something about you. 'You are in great danger,' he then says urgently, 'you must contact Mandrake Wolfsbane.' He tells you to go to the sign of the Cross Keys in the Street of the Forty Guilds. You cannot travel through the main streets, he tells you, but you should be safe if you follow one of these two routes: via the perimeter walls (turn to **129**), or through the thieves' quarter (turn to **306**). Which way do you choose?

7

You stumble down the path for many hours. Then you find yourself overtaking a figure ahead of you. This person is hardly moving – just shuffling along – but is well wrapped up against the weather. Just as you are approaching the figure it topples over. Do you rush over to help (turn to **267**) or would you prefer to pass by in safety and carry on down the valley (turn to **81**)?

8

You charge into the bushes and encounter two more Trolls who are waiting with swords drawn. Fight each in turn.

	SKILL	STAMINA
First TROLL	8	9
Second TROLL	9	9

If you survive (mark off 2 Poison units on the *Adventure Sheet*), you climb into one of the tall trees, where you hide as best you can. Turn to **391**.

9

You hand over some iron coins and his eyes light up. He unshoulders the instrument and turns the handle, and a sweetly melodious tune flows out. It begins to captivate you, until it is all that you can hear. The hurdy-gurdy man laughs; you begin to feel numb and realize that the tune is Spellbinding. You struggle against the spell as the would-be Assassin pulls out a dagger and raises it, aiming for your chest. Have you the strength to break the spell before the dagger strikes? Throw 2 dice for the power of the spell, then compare this with your STAMINA. If your STAMINA is equal to or greater than the power of the spell, you break free (turn to **108**). If not, then the Assassin plunges the dagger into you; its poison works very quickly and you die in great agony.

10

The Treffilli vibrates. You take two sprigs and whisper the Spell: 'By Ash and Bird and Crust.' At once you disappear. Remove the sprigs from your *Adventure Sheet* and deduct 4 points from your STAMINA. The Necromancer cannot detect you as you take to the rough country. Turn to **88**.

11

You trot your mount towards the sound on the left. The noises you can hear are indistinct and come from behind a bushy ridge. Suddenly your horse rears up and throws you. *Test your Luck*. If you are Unlucky, you fall badly: deduct 3 points from your STAMINA. If you are Lucky, you land on soft turf, unscathed. Whatever the outcome, your horse gallops off into the dark. You stand up and look around you but can see nothing. You are aware of something moving very close to you. You hear the sound of a sword being unsheathed and then footsteps approaching you. Do you decide to stand and fight in utter darkness (turn to **317**) or do you prefer to run away (turn to **214**)?

You push open the door. Inside, there is a room full of goods for sale. Two Trolls are arguing with the Kazanid owner. 'There's nothing wrong with these skins,' scowls one of the Trolls. 'That's as may be, but there's no market nowadays for wart-covered Goblin skins. Anyhow, I won't ask you how you came by them.' One of the two Trolls thumps the counter and mutters. Then they go over to a corner, sit down and start drinking from a bottle inscribed with a scimitar. There are other traders in the room whose eyes never leave you as you place the gem on the counter. Gimcrak weighs the stone and offers you 10 gold coins for it. If you accept, add the gold to your *Adventure Sheet* and remove the gem. As soon as you set foot outside the trading post you are attacked by three Kazanid Ruffians. You must fight each in turn.

	SKILL	STAMINA
First RUFFIAN	5	8
Second RUFFIAN	6	7
Third RUFFIAN	6	6

If you survive (mark off 2 Poison units on the *Adventure Sheet*), the fight has attracted a crowd from inside, but no one lifts a finger to help you. You stride off. Turn to **391**.

13

The driver is an old man, but he looks very strong.
He carries a fine blade close to hand, and he looks as
if he knows how to use it. When you ask him for a
ride, at first he is silent; he looks you up and down
and then agrees to take you for the price of your
company. He warns you that you will be crossing
wild bandit lands – and you may even meet some
Kalamites; however, he does not explain who these
creatures are. When the cart passes through one of
the town gates, you are stopped by a one-legged
hurdy-gurdy man who also asks for a ride. The
driver, Drukkah, looks steadfastly at the beggar and
shakes his head. 'Don't like the look or the smell of
that one – he's no more a hurdy-gurdy man than I'm
the Vizier of Kazan.' Turn to **286**.

14

You hear a sudden creak and then a crash as the bench collapses and you are tipped into an underground stream. You stand up in the waist-deep water and your hand, stretched out in front of you, finds a dead body floating past. Just then a Mamlik appears from behind a small waterfall, dagger in hand. You grab his wrist and drag him down.

MAMLIK   SKILL 8   STAMINA 10

If you survive (mark off 1 Poison unit on the *Adventure Sheet*), you cannot get out of the water and have to swim along with the stream. You emerge in the deep water of the harbour just as a ship is bearing down on you. You have no option but to grab a loose rope. You climb up and collapse on the deck (deduct 2 points from your STAMINA). When you recover, you find the captain standing over you; he tells you that you are on your way to Kazilik. The price of passage on his vessel is 25 gold coins. If you have this much, deduct it from your *Adventure Sheet*; otherwise, you will have to work your passage. Deduct all the gold coins you do have left, and then deduct 2 points from your STAMINA for every 5 gold coins you have to make up to the total of 25. Turn to **189**.

15

You feel sure that a short rest will do you a lot of good, so you sit down in the snow. The gentle figure you saw in front of you begins to laugh and its face transforms into one of extreme evil. It screams at you, 'Segrek's Select, you will die here in the snow.' You cannot rise, and the effort to do so makes you feel weaker, while the poison throbs in your shoulder (deduct 2 points from your STAMINA and mark off 2 Poison units on the *Adventure Sheet*).

Just then, you seem to see the face of Astragal the wizard; it spurs you on to combat the evil. Throw 2 dice for the Evil Power of the storm and compare the total with your STAMINA. If your STAMINA is equal to or greater than the power of the storm, then gradually you manage to get up and walk on. Turn to **169**. If it is less than the Evil Power of the storm, then you cannot resist. You are covered by the snow and will soon die.

16

The first Dragon falls into the sea with a steamy splash. However, fire has broken out amidships, due to the attack of the second Dragon. Flames and sparks leap up and suddenly there is a great explosion. The ship shudders and begins to sink fast. Leaping overboard, you grab some driftwood and float gently to the shore. Turn to **348**.

17

You are in a well-lit chamber. Torches blaze on the walls and in the middle of the room is a forge with several small Medallion moulds. Sparks shoot out and some hit you. Deduct 1 point from your STAMINA. Return to **160** and throw the magic die for your next position.

18

You carry on along the sloping path. The mountain pass is very bleak and the chill wind cuts through you. Ahead you observe a perfect spot for an ambush. Pulling out your sword and tightening the straps of your armour, you steal from boulder to boulder. Suddenly an arrow strikes you in the chest, glances off the leather and plants itself in the ground. As its force sends you tumbling over, you hear a scream heralding the attack of two Bandits. They leap out, wearing face-masks and clutching scimitars. Fight each in turn.

	SKILL	STAMINA
First BANDIT	7	8
Second BANDIT	6	6

If you win (mark off 2 Poison units on the *Adventure Sheet*), you are just recovering your breath when a large band of rogues emerges from among the rocks. Do you decide to run (turn to **326**) or do you choose to surrender (turn to **127**)?

19

You land badly on your sword-arm. Deduct 1 point from your SKILL. Furthermore, you lose consciousness and have a nightmare about Black Bulls, Daggers of Darkness and Mamlik Assassins. Deduct 1 point from your STAMINA and mark off 1 Poison unit. Turn to **176**.

20

The gates of the Bogomil Maze open. Inside, you are confronted by two huge stone statues of rearing horses. You see the image of a woman with long white hair. She speaks in formal tones. 'You have been granted the honour of entering the Maze. Seek the Medallion and prove your worth as one of Segrek's Select. There is one true path through the maze and many dangers.' To the blast of trumpets, you stride forward. You find yourself in a series of torchlit tunnels. You can choose to go west (turn to **165**), east (turn to **281**), or north (turn to **236**). Which way do you decide to go?

21

You creep along past the guardian Orc, up a hillside and into some broken scrubland. When at last you feel that you are safe, you stop to check behind you. Dismayed, you see three shapes, each holding a blazing torch. From time to time one of them bends down as though to sniff the ground. These are the legendary Sniffer Orcs which, if rumour is to be believed, can follow any track or trail, across rocks, through water, over any terrain. At that moment you look up into the dawn's light and see a large flying creature that is part human, part eagle . . . a Boulyanthrop. If you possess the Grey Talon of Sakar, turn to **345**. Otherwise, you will have to turn and face your pursuers, for they will never relent (turn to **171**).

When you agree to her request, she rubs her hands with glee and leads you up a small hill to a blasted oak. She explains that some Fiends have robbed her and have concealed her precious treasure-chest in the depths of the hollow tree. 'Can you get it for me, my lovely?' she begs. You climb the oak and find at the top a large dark hole; climbing in, you drop down and find yourself in a large cavern encircled by tree-roots. In the gloom you can make out a metal chest, surrounded by whitened bones and odd bits of armour. Suddenly two Hellhounds appear from out of the dark, barking, howling and frothing at the mouth. You must fight each Hellhound in turn.

	SKILL	STAMINA
First HELLHOUND	7	6
Second HELLHOUND	7	6

If you survive (mark off 2 Poison units on the *Adventure Sheet*), you manage to drag the chest up out of the tree, and you climb down with it. Before the old woman can reach it, you force open the lid – it is full of gold coins. Do you help yourself (turn to **105**) or let the old hag get her hands on the chest and pay you your due (turn to **241**)?

23

You walk on for a while. Eventually, you find yourself catching up with a cart that is creaking and rumbling over the cobbled road in front of you. The land is too flat for you to get off the road and still avoid suspicion. Up ahead in the distance, you can see two Trolls wearing the panther livery of Chingiz and collecting some sort of toll. They stop the cart in front of you and charge the driver an exorbitant 3 gold coins before allowing him to pass. You guess that the Trolls are pocketing most of the money for themselves. There is no way of circling around the Trollish toll-gatherers without being noticed, so you try to pass. 'Not so fast, friend, we've been told to pick up any lone strangers passing through . . . unless you make it worth our while.' If you do not wish to encourage their venality, turn to **274**. It's up to you how much to give them. If you decide to offer them a bribe, first deduct the amount you think will be adequate from your *Adventure Sheet*, then throw 2 dice for the amount *they* would regard as sufficient. If the amount you have chosen is equal to or greater than the amount they demand, turn to **106**. If it is less, turn to **274**.

24

You put on the smile of a simpleton and stand there while the Orcs try to spit a pip on to your hat. Suddenly they both leap to attention; you turn round, to see a black-cloaked figure holding a staff on which is carved a panther. She doesn't speak to the Orcs but they scuttle off. She then steps close to you and your gaze is held by the bright-red eyes of a Necromancer. She raises her staff. Do you have the ability to fight a Necromancer? If you do, you pull out your sword (turn to 99); if not, then you are Spellbound and cannot move (turn to 334).

25

You encounter a figure gazing at one of the walls. She looks strong and confident, and she smiles as she speaks to you. 'So you are one of the Select also. You know that by ancient lore we must fight; only one may claim the Medallion of Uruz.' She pulls out a scimitar, salutes you and attacks.

BOLLEMA   SKILL 9   STAMINA 10

If you win, two mysterious shrouded figures emerge from the walls and take the body away. You look at the wall and see upon it an inscription of three Medallions. You pass through the next door, which seals shut behind you. Turn to 207.

26

You are in an eating-house patronized by several Dwarfs, Elves and Kazanids, who look at you suspiciously. You walk out into the street again. Turn to **98**.

27

Cautiously you step out on to the perilous bridge. Throw 2 dice for the strength of the bridge and then throw 2 dice for your weight. If your weight is greater than the strength of the bridge, it collapses when you are in the middle, and you fall to your death in the chasm. If your weight is equal to or less than the strength of the bridge, you cross safely. Turn to **310**.

28

You are taken to the Maze entrance. As you stand in front of it Aggellatha proclaims formally, 'Seek the Medallion of the ancient and noble tribes of Uruz. The dangers are many but the True Path exists for the heart not tainted by evil.' You are looking at the entrance and the Minotaurs guarding it, when suddenly a Gryphawk lands at one side of the door, cocks its head and gazes levelly at you. If you possess the Grey Talon of Sakar, whisper its Spell, note the numbers in sequence and turn to that paragraph; otherwise, turn to 366.

29

A Giant Spider drops down from the recesses of the roof. You push Saxifragus behind you and pull out your sword. You chop at the beast's hairy legs while the wizard stands in the background, giving you helpful advice.

GIANT SPIDER   SKILL 7   STAMINA 10

If you survive, you now have time to cut laboriously through the web. Mark off 1 Poison unit on the *Adventure Sheet*. Turn to 76.

30

You are dubious about the chances of finding a good hiding-place in the snow – especially when the riders could easily pick up your tracks. You stand your ground as they approach. They notice you and one of them releases a large Gryphawk. It comes fluttering towards you but, when you pull out your sword, it veers away, back to its owner. The riders approach close to you and draw up. Turn to **250**.

31

As if from nowhere, a rider appears in the circle and most of the Kazanids bow their heads in deference. He looks at you very carefully, examining your Gorak armour closely. He announces that his name is Zaranj and that he is the leader of this group. He dismounts and takes you to one side. Next, he asks you if you are one of Segrek's Select and you decide that you have to trust him. 'Tell no one else here,' he replies. 'Chingiz has bought many souls with his stolen gold. In Korkut, traditions bind me to put you to the test so that you may enter the Maze to seek the Medallion – but there are many in this land who do not wish to see a True Monarch on the throne. Come.' He leads you to where a horse stands tethered. Turn to **287**.

32

You just manage to keep your head above water without having to swim. The weight of your pack, cloak and sword stops you from moving quickly. As you set out for the opposite bank, you feel something tug at your ankle. Then it encircles your boot and stops you moving. You chop down into the water with your sword, and blood rises to the surface and your foot is released. Then something grabs you again and stings you (deduct 1 point from your STAMINA). You plunge your sword into the water once more. *Test your Luck*. If you are Unlucky, then something pulls you under and you drown, thus ending your quest. If you are Lucky, you sever the vital tentacle and, freed, stumble across to the other bank. Turn to **294**.

33

You run across the ground with your boots in your hand (deduct 2 points from your STAMINA). Just then, a branch from the old gnarled oak reaches out towards you. You look up, to see the heads and bodies of warriors attached to the tree. Keeping well away from the oak, you put your boots back on. Add 1 point to your LUCK. You realize that you are now hopelessly lost but you are sure you can hear Impish laughter in the dark gloom. You look around and decide you have to make a choice between two possible routes. Do you head left (turn to **311**) or do you choose to try the right-hand path (turn to **257**)?

34

You emerge from the cave. The Orcs' commander has disappeared. You feel slightly sick and realize that the poison of the Mamlik Death Spell Dagger spreads quickly if you exert yourself (mark off 2 Poison units on the *Adventure Sheet*). You retrace your way to the track and find that the horses have all bolted. You continue in what you hope is the right direction.

After several hours the snow eases and you can discern a dark figure outlined against the gleaming white. Do you approach this figure (turn to **387**) or does discretion prompt you to pass it carefully by (turn to **18**)?

35

You are in a room with a large curved snake in the middle. Suddenly a stairway appears and you feel compelled to climb it. Turn to **157** and mark your new position on the chart.

36

You follow the west corridor. The screams get louder, but you can see nothing. Suddenly a bone drops on to your shoulder! You look up and see a skeleton, spreadeagled on the roof, with long metal stakes impaling it there. You shudder as you see a metal spike shoot out of the ground ahead of you and slam into the roof. Throw 1 die for your position, then throw 1 die again for the place where another stake shoots out. If the two die-rolls match, you are speared to the ceiling and killed. Repeat this procedure twice more. If you survive, you rush through another door which shuts behind you. Turn to **153**.

37

The path climbs and climbs until you begin to encounter patches of ice and snow. You feel very tired (deduct 1 point from your STAMINA and mark off 2 Poison units on the *Adventure Sheet*). Just then you hear what can only be the sound of a Dwarf singing. It is coming from a newly worked tunnel that leads into the mountainside. Do you wish to enter the tunnel and investigate (turn to **112**) or would you rather press on up the path (turn to **245**)?

38

You creep out carefully, shutting the doors behind you. Suddenly a dagger is plunged into your neck and a Mamlik laughs as you stagger away. 'I knew I could smell you close by,' he murmurs. The poison has got into all of your body. Mark off all remaining Poison units on the *Adventure Sheet*. Your quest is over.

39

Instinctively, you flatten yourself against the wall. The horse gallops past – but large wooden stakes suddenly spring out of the wall behind you. *Test your Luck*. If you are Unlucky, two spikes have pierced your armour (deduct 4 points from your STAMINA and mark off 2 Poison units). If you are Lucky, the spikes miss. If you survive, you go through another door. Turn to **349**.

40

The chamber is very gloomy. You walk about, stepping into soft, squishy muck. Looking up, you see horizontal ridges carved into the scummy walls. You think you may be able to clamber up from ridge to ridge. If you do not want to do this, then return to the other chamber (turn to 265).

Throw 2 dice for the distance you will have to leap to the top. Compare this with your STAMINA score. If your STAMINA is equal to or greater than the distance, then you have made it. If not, you fall: deduct 1 point from your STAMINA and try again. If you try and fail three times, return to the other chamber (turn to 265).

When you reach the top, you find a tunnel running north and south. Which way do you choose to go: north (turn to 390) or south (turn to 360)?

41

The mare you have chosen is a placid animal that will give you a good restful ride. The Yigeniks are supreme horsemen; they always ride at great speed, leaping over or across anything that might otherwise divert them. The mare is sure-footed and needs no real effort to control, so by the time the Yigeniks stop you are quite rested. Add 2 points to your STAMINA. Turn to 372.

42

The Yigenik knights clap you on the back and make it clear that you will benefit if you do well at the tournament. The jousting field is packed with people, you see as you look around while donning the unlucky knight's armour and mounting his horse. You are handed a lance and then are made to wait for several hours. Eventually your turn comes, however, and you take your place on the field.

You charge at your opponent. Throw 1 die for your opponent then 1 die for yourself. If your throw is the greater, you have unhorsed your opponent; you win a prize purse of 5 gold coins. If your opponent's throw is the greater, you are knocked from your horse (deduct 4 points from your STAMINA and 1 point from your SKILL), and you may not enter another contest. If you have been successful, you may choose to joust with another opponent (the prize in every case is a purse of 5 gold coins). You may continue until you are defeated or choose to stop. Turn to **4**.

43

You clutch the Talon in your fingers as you are thrown over the wall of the tower, desperately willing some sort of help. Almost immediately, a large bird appears and sinks its huge talons into your shoulder armour. Not strong enough to hold you up, nevertheless it slows your rapid descent and carries you close enough to the tower wall for you to be able to grasp an overhanging stone block. Turn to **381**.

44

You stumble deeper into the cave, which begins to slope upwards; you can feel a cool breeze and see a brightness through the gloom. You look up, to see a hole in the roof of the cave, covered with a thin broken layer of snow. You disturb the snow with your sword and find that a bush is covering the hole. Gradually you heave yourself up and force your way out.

Suddenly a scream assails your ears and a Mamlik Assassin leaps at you wielding a dagger. *Test your Luck.* If you are Unlucky, the dagger grazes your leg (deduct 2 points from your STAMINA and mark off 2 Poison units on the *Adventure Sheet*. Henceforth whenever you are instructed to mark the progress of the poison, you must double the number of Poison units sustained.) If you are Lucky, the Mamlik misses and his blade snaps. He rushes away and then you hear his snorting steed galloping off. You walk in the direction that you believe will take you down to the plain. Turn to **18**.

The voice echoes in your mind: 'You are in the Chamber of Ancient Magical Spells. Here is where the power of the kings and queens of Kazan is determined.' You see a table with a row of three bottles and another row of three jars on it. The ghostly voice speaks again. 'True monarchs of Kazan are able to face the dangers of Gnossis. You must now choose the contents of one bottle and one jar; mix the materials from the two and drink the resultant brew. Beware, for three of the mixtures are deadly. You must perform this feat *twice*. Choose now.'

	Volcano Dust	1000-Fathom Seawater	Mist from the Mithrir Forest
Eye of Newt	63	93	142
Viper's Tongue	166	284	330
Ground Dragon's Claw	356	376	384

Make your choice and go to the paragraph indicated to discover the result of dabbling in alchemy.

46

You rush after the Orc. The stone stairs wind up towards a tower. Suddenly three Goblins appear on the stairs; they are all heavily armed and attack you immediately. The stairs are narrow, so you will have to fight each in turn.

	SKILL	STAMINA
First GOBLIN	5	5
Second GOBLIN	5	5
Third GOBLIN	6	6

If you survive, you feel the poison throbbing in your body (mark off 2 Poison units on the *Adventure Sheet*). You rush up the stairs and are faced by two wooden doors. Which do you enter, the one on the left (turn to **212**) or the one on the right (turn to **187**)?

47

You summon a great storm of thunder and forked lightning which crashes through the window and makes the Dungeon Beasts scuttle off into the distance. You pass unhindered into a richly furnished part of the Fortress; you must be nearing the inner sanctum. The passage ends in two doors, one marked with the sign of Segrek (turn to **158**) and the other with the sign of a panther (turn to **325**). Which do you choose to enter?

48

'I, Omorphina, announce the Run of the Arrow!' A group of huntresses, all dressed in black leather, quickly form a line. Your bonds are removed as one of them shoots an arrow into the forest. They motion for you to start running and you set off, slowly at first, then picking up speed. You see the arrow stuck into a tree trunk, and when you pass it you hear a whoop as the huntresses set off in pursuit of you. Throw 3 dice and add up their total. If this is greater than your current STAMINA, then the huntresses have caught you. You are immediately beheaded. Your quest is over.

If your STAMINA is equal to or greater than the throw, then you outdistance the huntresses. Turn to **368**.

49

Her name, she tells you, is Adana-Broussah, a member of the nomadic clan of mercenaries known as Beshbalik's Marauders; they are also known in southern Khul as the Scavengers of Slaughter. Her voice lowers and becomes conspiratorial: 'Greetings from Astragal. I am a link in one of his chains of information. I am bidden to look out for you and to pass on this message: all the Medallions are taken. Now, by fair means or foul, you must enter the Fortress at Sharrabbas and get to the throne. If you have a Medallion, the task will be easier, for Chingiz and his Necromancers have yet to break into the Heart of the Throne.' Now you must decide: do you wish to accompany Adana-Broussah to Beshbalik's camp (turn to **200**) or do you prefer a lonely path (turn to **116**)?

50

You dash into the tunnel leading to the south as the herd of bulls crashes on eastwards. At the end of this southerly passage is a metal door but on this side of it you can see a bubbling fountain made of stone. Carved on it is a bull drinking from the water, with an arrow sticking out of its back. Do you drink some of the water (turn to **238**) or make straight for the door and go through it (turn to **292**)?

51

You lower yourself into the boat. The painter unties itself and the craft floats across to the other side of the river. Turn to **294**.

52

You look around the trading-post. Tacked up on the walls are signs proclaiming that 'We buy anything'. You will probably need gold in a city like Sharrabbas. Do you have anything to trade? You read one of the signs:

Yellow Gem	2 gold coins
Red Gem	5 gold coins
Green Gem	10 gold coins
Blue Gem	15 gold coins
Any ring	5 gold coins

If you decide to do any deals at these prices, mark the changes on your *Adventure Sheet*. You come out of the trading-post and bump into a small bedraggled boy. He offers his services as a guide for 2 gold coins. Do you accept (turn to **182**)? If you refuse his offer (or if you have no gold), then turn to **318**.

53

You reckon that the road is the easiest and quickest way to travel. You walk along for a long time until you are overtaken by a horse and cart being driven by a Dwarf. You stop him and ask him for a ride. He agrees and doesn't charge you anything. It's good to ride for a change (add 2 points to your STAMINA). You are beginning to doze when, suddenly, the cart stops. 'Now, what's this?' the Dwarf grumbles. Ahead, there is a road-block. 'Chingiz's creatures – he thinks he owns this land.' You leap off the cart. Do you run to the left-hand side of the road and hide (turn to 261) or do you prefer to go to the right (turn to 300)?

54

You have to expend a lot of effort to smash open the door (deduct 4 points from your STAMINA). When finally you do enter the room, you come face to face with a woman holding a dagger. On seeing you, she rushes away through another door. You are just dashing after her when you spot a small statue of Segrek, lying in a corner of the room. You stoop to pick it up . . . and you hear the voice from the Heart of the Throne: 'Brave adventurer, you have fought hard – but remember that it is not just the power of the sword that holds a kingdom together. Remember this when you mount the throne.' You hurry on through the gleaming gold door in front of you. Turn to 363.

55

You draw your sword as the girl comes running, screaming, up to you – but then she runs off and the Gryphawk flies off after her. You look at your hands; they are covered in red dye. You quickly pat your pockets. She has taken half your gold coins (if you have any), plus any phials, potions, rings or gems you may have had. If you are carrying a Medallion, that is untouched. (Make the appropriate adjustments to your *Adventure Sheet*.) You are wary of any more thievish tricks and quickly make your way to the Street of the Forty Guilds. Turn to **98**.

The figure disappears – and you find yourself in a dungeon cell, looking at the Medallion of Yigenik which is guarded by two panthers. Inside your head you hear the hoarse voice of the Necromancer: 'Although an illusion, these creatures are real in your mind. If their claws rip your flesh, you will suffer all the agonies.' The panthers snarl and attack; you must fight each in turn.

	SKILL	STAMINA
First PANTHER	5	6
Second PANTHER	6	7

If you win (mark off 2 Poison units on the *Adventure Sheet*), the scene fades and you are back in the room below the stairs. In front of you are two dead rats, and there is no sign of the Necromancer. You realize that you have wasted time and that the Medallion has been taken. You go back out into the street and head out of town. Do you make for the forested valley (turn to 257) or for the mountains (turn to 275)?

57

You climb up a long way until you arrive at a greasy ledge from where you look over into a banqueting room, its tables covered with dirty plates and bottles. You drop down into the room and head for a door – when it is suddenly pushed open and before you stand four Mamliks. One slinks away immediately while the others prepare to attack. Fight each in turn.

	SKILL	STAMINA
First MAMLIK	7	10
Second MAMLIK	6	8
Third MAMLIK	7	9

If you survive, mark off 2 Poison units on the *Adventure Sheet*. The other Mamlik has raised the alarm while you were fighting, and you now hear footsteps outside. You jump back into the chute, down the ladder, and through the giant rat-hole. A rat is waiting there for you. Turn to 378.

58

You poke with your sword at the bundle which, you discover, is made of leathery skin. You pull it aside, to reveal a crouching Goblin, holding a vicious-looking Gryphawk. He screams, the bird squawks and they both attack. Fight each in turn.

	SKILL	STAMINA
GRYPHAWK	5	4
GOBLIN	5	5

If you win, you feel a little dizzy and realize that the poison is working its way through your body (mark off 2 Poison units on the *Adventure Sheet*). However, you stagger on and, after some time, you can make out a dark figure outlined in the snowscape. Do you approach this figure (turn to **387**) or do you prefer to hide and let it pass before carrying on (turn to **18**)?

59

You decide that it's safer to stay there; after all, you do not know what lurks below. You hide behind one of the snowbanks. Just then a Kazanid appears and looks at the planks. 'Huh, one's missing,' he grunts. 'He's been here for sure: I'll call the others.' As he disappears you get up to run. *Test your Luck.* If you are Lucky, you slip on a sheet of ice but recover your balance and run off (turn to **252**). If you are Unlucky, you slip, fall on to one of the planks and go tearing off, head first, down the ice-track. Deduct 4 points from your STAMINA and turn to **234**.

You ride off hard and fast, to get a good start. Soon you can hear the rumble of pursuit, and after a short time you turn round to see if anyone is catching up. You can see only Beshbalik astride his Fangtigers, his Grypfalcon standing on his mailed shoulder and flapping its great wings. You know you cannot outdistance the Fangtigers so, after crossing a wide, shallow river, you dismount and prepare to fight. Beshbalik sends first the Grypfalcon, then the Fangtigers, to attack. Fight each in turn.

	SKILL	STAMINA
GRYPFALCON	6	6
First FANGTIGER	7	6
Second FANGTIGER	6	8

If you win (mark off 2 Poison units on the *Adventure Sheet*), Beshbalik does not approach. He nods to you, calls your horse to him, mounts it and rides off. You know that he will not pursue you any further. Add 1 point to your LUCK. Turn to **88**.

61

You hear a deep booming voice. 'Your path will be hard, you must be brave and have faith in your true purpose.' Torches suddenly flare up, to reveal a large circular room with two doors on the far side. Between you and them, however, stands a very large black bull. It snorts and stamps, then lowers its head and charges. You pull off your cloak and hold your sword ready.

BLACK BULL   SKILL 7   STAMINA 8

If you survive, do you leave by the left-hand door (turn to **223**) or would you prefer to go out through the right-hand door (turn to **152**)?

62

You trust the Sensewarrior, so you tell him all about your quest. His blank eyes betray no emotion at your words. 'So the Assassins are roaming the land . . . What next, the mad Necr– . . . no, Chingiz would not dare. Come.' He leads you across the bridge. When you are safely across, you see the ropes supporting it break, one by one, and the structure collapses. He mutters, 'Goblin Spellcasting,' and betrays a wry smile. For the remainder of the descent into the valley, he is silent, until he chooses to stop by a large oak. 'Here,' he announces, 'I will teach you the Darkfight.' Mark this ability on your *Adventure Sheet*. In any combat held in darkness you will retain your normal SKILL.

You continue down the valley until you reach a lone tavern, the Snorting Stallion. You enter and Alkis bids you order something to quench both your thirsts while he sniffs around. The Kazanid behind the bar has two barrels set up. Which do you decide to ask for: the one marked with a Scimitar (turn to 357) or the Dragon brand (turn to 149)?

63

You have drunk the mixture that will bring madness and death. Chance has intervened in your quest for the throne of Kazan. Your mission is over.

64

You are faced with two sealed doors to the south and east, a tunnel leading north and one leading west. To the north there is a gleam of daylight through a partly open door, and you can also see two statues of rearing stallions. Which way do you choose: the tunnel to the north (turn to **133**) or the tunnel leading west (turn to **196**)?

65

You find yourself in an open space with a clear view of the Fortress. Suddenly, your eye is caught by a spy-glass lens glinting in the sunshine; someone is watching *you*. Just then you spot two Grypvultures carrying Khomatads, flapping out of the tower then dropping down towards you. You run but cannot escape them. They trap you in a narrow street and attack from either side. Fight each in turn.

	SKILL	STAMINA
First KHOMATAD	7	8
Second KHOMATAD	8	9

If you survive (mark off 2 Poison units on the *Adventure Sheet*), you know that time is not on your side. You duck into another street. Turn to **276**.

66

The crashing noise gets nearer and nearer as you make your way down the tunnel. By the light of a blazing torch you can see a carving of three Medallions. Suddenly there is a very loud crash, one of the floor-slabs is lifted and up pops the head of a Goblin. You slide into the shadows as the Goblin shouts, 'We're in! Now, where's the gold?' He gets out, followed by a Mamlik. The Mamlik dusts himself down, points to the carvings, and then stabs the Goblin in the back. The Mamlik walks over to the door and goes through it. Do you wish to follow him through the door (turn to **324**) or do you prefer to drop down into the tunnel (turn to **141**)?

67

You think that you'll be better off mingling with the crowd. In the middle of the group you see Beshbalik dispensing gold coins to the Marauders – then suddenly, close to him, you spot a Mamlik who is standing staring at you. He pushes his way through the mob towards you and the poison in your blood throbs (mark off 1 Poison unit). Do you turn and rush into a nearby hut (turn to **135**) or just stay where you are in the crowd (turn to **251**)?

68

Vetch is easy to follow; he seems to command great respect from the native Kazanids. At one point he makes a swaggering Orc step aside and into a puddle; this pleases the crowd in the streets no end. You catch up with him and confide to him the nature of your quest. 'You've come to the right person,' he replies. 'Tell no one else, for there are many spies here. Follow me!' He leads you to a ramshackle building, takes you inside and tells you to wait in a room. Do you sit and wait patiently (turn to **216**) or do you follow him to see where he has gone (turn to **259**)?

69

A door opens in your mind. You blink as you find yourself standing outside the fortress of Korkut. In front of you is a cobbled lane that leads down to the harbour. You stand there, dazed. Do you walk down to the port (turn to **239**) or would you prefer to enter a tavern that you see across the street (turn to **117**)?

70

The track opens out on to a bleak, flat plain with occasional rocky outcrops. Out of the corner of your eye you see a large bird, flying high overhead. It circles closer, and you can see that it is supporting an armed creature. Suddenly, the bird swoops down and the rider lunges at you.

KHOMATAD   SKILL 8   STAMINA 8

If you survive (mark off 1 Poison unit on the *Adventure Sheet*), turn to **4**.

71

'Yes, I was happy under Segrek's benevolent rule, I was important then,' the Elf sighs. He is lost in thought for a moment, then he remembers the gold. 'I believe that most of the Select are dead or captured, and Chingiz is feeling confident – but until he kills all the Select, he cannot claim the Heart of the Throne of Kazan that bequeaths true kingship. You must seek help from Bithymian Vetch or Mandrake Wolfsbane. Sharrabbas is now a city of intrigue and deception; Mamliks, Necromancers and creatures of the dark abound. Good luck and, if you succeed, remember me, "Lightfinger" Greel, if you need a chancellor.' Turn to **23**.

72

You have the choice of following a corridor to the north, where you can see a small obelisk, or one to the west, which also has an obelisk. The door you have come through will not open again. Do you go north (turn to **235**) or west (turn to **389**)?

73

You are in a room containing three stone statues of Trolls. They begin to come to life. *Test your Luck*. If you are Unlucky, they all come to life and attack you one by one. Fight each in turn. If you are Lucky, good fortune slows down their metamorphosis and only one comes to life, so you have to fight the first Troll only.

	SKILL	STAMINA
First STONE TROLL	8	9
Second STONE TROLL	7	10
Third STONE TROLL	7	10

If you survive (mark off 2 Poison units on the *Adventure Sheet*), return to **160** and throw a die for your next position.

74

You stand in front of a wall of green shimmering smoke and a voice announces, 'You have passed through the Heart of the Throne and have no rival. You have proved your bravery; walk forth and complete the ascent to the throne, for you will be greeted, paraded and adulated.' The mist clears and a metal door opens.

You step out and are met by two Mamliks holding longswords. One of them stabs you before you can move. If you have the Power of Invulnerability to Sword-Strike, you are not harmed; otherwise deduct 4 points from your STAMINA and mark off 1 Poison unit on the *Adventure Sheet*. The Mamliks rush off in opposite directions, sounding the alarm. Do you now go to the left (turn to **269**) or to the right (turn to **369**)?

75

You continue westwards, then turn a corner and head north. There you see a black horse standing stock still, blocking the whole tunnel. Cautiously you walk closer – but it suddenly comes to life, paws the ground and charges at you. Do you stand in front of it, sword at the ready (turn to **194**) or flatten yourself against the wall (turn to **39**)?

76

You trudge along the dusty tunnel. The wizard begins to recite incantations, then, in a commanding voice, tells you to stop. You put him down and he tells you to throw the claws on to the ground. 'By the evil of the panther master, be broken, allow the Select of Segrek entry to your Heart that no other may enter.' The claws sink into the ground and the stone floor is shattered. 'Inxus Askath Loth Begammus Krac . . . quick, now jump!' The hole shimmers as though it is about to close again. You leap down. Turn to **332**.

77

You are placed in a chamber the floor of which consists of 49 separate raised blocks. You must get from point A to point B, using the throw of 1 die. You may throw the die as many times as it takes. Several blocks (marked with an S) have vicious snakes resting on them, which will bite you if you land on their block (deduct 3 points from your STAMINA if this occurs). Three bites and you are dead.

A throw of 5–6: you may move one block up or down

A throw of 3–4: you may move one block to the left or right

A throw of 1–2: no move; stay on your block and deduct 1 point from your STAMINA.

There is only one rule: you cannot return to any block you have already stepped on. If you are unable to move, deduct 1 point from your STAMINA and throw the die again. Mark your path lightly in pencil.

If you get to B, turn to **160**.

78

You squeeze out through the small hole. Outside, you can hear the clamour of battle. You duck down out of sight when you see a Necromancer standing with his back to you and directing operations. A troop of mounted Orcs ride past through the thick smoke – but they do not see you (add 1 point to your LUCK). You set off carefully, slowly and painfully over the rocky terrain. In the distance you spot an Orc guarding some horses, but he looks too strong for you to tackle in your present condition. Turn to **21**.

79

Circling around, you put your weight on something that gives under you. You fall and land in a pit full of sharp stakes. *Test your Luck*. If you are Unlucky, you are speared in the thigh (deduct 1 point from your SKILL and 4 points from your STAMINA and mark off 1 Poison unit). If you are Lucky, you manage to fall between the stakes and are merely winded.

You stand up and see the Troll peering at you from above. 'Yes, I was wondering how to get past that trap,' he murmurs. He obligingly throws down a length of creeper and hauls you out. Somewhat shamefacedly, you thank him. Turn to **263**.

80

'No, he's not one of Chingiz's spies,' says the Mamlik. 'Take him by the secret way into the Fortress.' This renegade Mamlik is obviously the leader of the rascals and thieves who haunt this dive. They take your gold coins. (Deduct 25 gold coins from your *Adventure Sheet*.)

You are led through small back-streets to the south-western side of the Fortress at the base of which, under the cover of some bushes, caves, all blocked by iron bars, are revealed to you. Your companions push open one of the grilles and one of them is about to explain something to you, when there is a yell and a stone gargoyle comes crashing down from one of the towers. They all run away and you throw yourself into the cave. In the darkness you feel your way ahead and find two chamber entrances: one to the left (turn to **265**) and one to the right (turn to **40**). Which do you take?

81

The path drops down steeply and then flattens out. After passing a large rock quarry, the land begins to open out. The path then forks; both directions seem feasible. Do you choose the left fork (turn to **379**) or the right fork (turn to **122**)?

82

There are steps going up the side of the chimney. You climb a long way, only to find yourself eventually up against a metal grille. Then smoke begins to waft up from the fireplace below and you start to choke. Suddenly, you notice faint chinks of light coming from between some of the stone blocks. You have got to kick those blocks out. Throw 2 dice for the strength of the wall, then compare this number to your STAMINA. If your STAMINA is equal to or greater than the strength of the wall, you have broken through. Turn to **140**. If not, then you choke to death in the smoke and your quest is over.

83

You plummet down from the tower. *Test your Luck.* If you are Lucky, you land on some bushes growing from an overhang (deduct 4 points from your STAMINA, 1 point from your SKILL and mark off 1 Poison unit): turn to **381**. If you are Unlucky, you fall all the way to the ground and are killed instantly on impact. Your quest is over.

84

You settle down to rest and fall asleep quite quickly (add 2 points to your STAMINA). You are awakened abruptly by the noise of someone screaming, and the first thing you see is the dagger of a Mamlik Assassin about to plunge into your chest. What is your first reaction: to roll away (turn to **131**), or to raise your hand and try to hold off the dagger by main force (turn to **301**)?

85

You wrap your cloak around you in an attempt to look more like a beggar than an adventurer. Just then someone calls out to you. You look across a small hollow, to see four knights trying to replace a wheel on a cart. Do you go over to help them (turn to **180**) or ignore their call and carry on (turn to **122**)?

86

You stop to rest and eat some of your Provisions (add 4 points to your STAMINA). After some time your suspicion that you can hear something moving in the undergrowth becomes a certainty. You are just pulling out your sword when suddenly an arrow is fired from behind a tree to your left. You move quickly. *Test your Luck.* If you are Unlucky, it hits you and passes through your shoulder (deduct 1 point from your SKILL and 4 points from your STAMINA. Mark off 1 Poison unit on the *Adventure Sheet*). If you are Lucky, the arrow misses.

A black-robed figure drops down to the ground. A second glance reveals that this is a woman with long black hair and evil-looking eyes. Before you can do anything to defend yourself, you are surrounded by six similar figures. You are helpless. Turn to **395**.

87

You take a tight grip on your sword and follow the tracks. They seem to be made by a two-legged creature with large goat-like hoofs. The tracks suddenly disappear into a wall where there is no door visible. You carry on, turn a corner and head west – to stop in astonishment when you see two hoofed feet and a scimitar appearing out of the solid wall! When the body follows, you realize that you are facing a Horned Devil, which is blocking the corridor. If you wish to run back and go the other way, deduct 2 points from your STAMINA and turn to 36. If you prefer to fight the creature, you approach it carefully.

HORNED DEVIL   SKILL 8   STAMINA 6

If you survive, you rush through another door. Turn to 221.

88

After a long descent, your path leads into a dense forest. You are not at all sure which is the correct direction for Sharrabbas, but cart-tracks are visible on the path, so you guess this must lead to some town or other. Occasionally your route passes large black pools which seem to be throbbing with fish. One pool has a fishing rod held up by a forked stick and a line hanging down into the water, and almost at once you see that the line is being tugged from below. Do you grab the rod (turn to 270) or do you leave it alone and continue your journey (turn to 167)?

89

You go over to the body: the dagger protruding from it is exactly the same as the one that wounded you and infected you with its poison. Suddenly you realize that the man is not quite dead: his eyes open, he looks at you and speaks. 'The Mamliks . . . no . . . they left me here . . . yes, for dead, got on their evil black steeds and rode off on the path to the left . . . ha . . .' The Death Spell Dagger begins to hiss, the body wastes away to a skeleton, and the possessions surrounding it dissolve in smoke. You decide not to hang around, so you take the right-hand path. After a short time, you come to another fork in the track. Do you choose the left path (turn to **314**) or the right (turn to **120**)?

90

Luckily, you land well, with only minor cuts and bruises (deduct 1 point from your STAMINA and add 1 point to your LUCK). However, when you get up you find yourself surrounded by large black bulls. You make a dash for a nearby tree as one of them charges. Throw 2 dice for its speed and compare this with your STAMINA. If your STAMINA is equal to or greater than the speed of the bull, then you outdistance it. If not, then it overtakes you and gores you (deduct 4 points from your STAMINA and mark off 2 Poison units).

You manage to climb up into the tree – but you are stuck there as the bulls gather and start to butt the trunk with their huge horns. All at once a rider appears; she shouts at the bulls and makes them back off. She stares at you for a moment, then suddenly throws a small dagger which hits a branch close to you. A cloud of blue smoke is emitted that knocks you out. Turn to **176**.

You tell the horsemen that you are one of Segrek's Select. This makes the riders sit up and look at you with greater interest. Bhoriss walks his horse around you and then speaks. 'You follow a difficult path, for now traditions are being flouted.' He looks pointedly at the Orc, who scowls and spits. 'We are to test you. Do you agree to the test of the Bogomil?' You cannot refuse.

They lay you on the ground and tie your arms and legs to wooden stakes. A wild stallion is then brought in. It stamps, snorts and kicks, then rushes to where you are trapped. Throw 1 die for the position of your right arm, then throw 1 die for where the horse's hoofs hit. If the two numbers thrown match, then you have been hit (deduct 4 points from your STAMINA and mark off 2 Poison units). Repeat this procedure for your left arm and for both your legs. If you are hit twice, you die and your quest is over. If you survive, you are released and pronounced worthy to take the second test of the Bogomil. You are given a mount and you all gallop off in a group. Turn to 123.

92

Luckily, there is no Mamlik around. You know the Orcs can have no idea of your mission or status and, being particularly slow-witted, they are at a loss as to what to do with you. 'Wait till the Mamlik returns,' growls one of them. If you possess a Mamlik ring, you may show it to them and bluff your way out of trouble (turn to **255**). If you have no ring, then you know that you must make good your escape before the Mamlik Assassin returns. You dive for your sword. Fight each opponent in turn.

	SKILL	STAMINA
First ORC	7	6
Second ORC	6	5
Third ORC	6	5

If you win (mark off 2 Poison units on the *Adventure Sheet*), you run off into the undergrowth just as you hear approaching hoofbeats. For many hours you have to move fast and silently, until at last you find yourself on the edge of a mountain slope. Turn to **397**.

93
INVULNERABLE TO SWORD-STRIKE
You have drunk the mixture that gives you this Power. Make a note on your *Adventure Sheet*. If this is your second Spell potion, turn to **74**; otherwise, return to **45** and choose your second mixture.

94

The Orc is within grabbing distance on the top of the tower. You leap across and make a snatch for his feet, but as he falls he reaches up and puts the Medallion into the beak of a Grypfalcon. You let go of the Orc and jump up to catch the talons of the bird. It lifts you up and out of the tower; then it swoops down over a tree and tries to shake and brush you off. You hold on as it flies up into the mountains and finally slams you into a cliff-face. Half-conscious, you let go of the talons and slide down into the bleak, rocky land (deduct 3 points from your STAMINA). Turn to **275**.

95

Suddenly a Minotaur leaps out. He swings his club at you and misses, crashing it into the wall. Next, he tries to gore you with his horns.

MINOTAUR   SKILL 9   STAMINA 9

If you win, you see two tunnels before you: one to the west (turn to **355**) and one to the south (turn to **380**). Which do you choose?

96

You run as fast as you can in the snow. Soon you
hear the sound of approaching riders. The ground
trembles with their hoofbeats as you rush to a
nearby cave and hide. Eventually four riders
appear; they stop and examine your tracks in the
snow. One of them, swathed in a large black cloak,
directs the search; the others are all Orcs. They
dismount and follow your footprints. You know
that you will be able to defend the narrow entrance.
Do you decide to fight (turn to **201**) or do you turn
and go further into the cave (turn to **44**)?

97

You are in a room that contains a glass box standing
on an obelisk. Inside the box there is a flower the
scent of which, strangely, you can smell (add 2
points to your STAMINA), but the box is unbreakable. Return to **160** and throw a die for your next
position.

98

You enter the Street of Forty Guilds. You walk up and down and find that only four guild shops are not barred or padlocked. Choose the one you wish to enter; afterwards you may come back to this paragraph and choose another shop. Once visited, do not re-enter a guild. Do you choose:

Cross Keys?	Turn to 341
Frying Pan?	Turn to 26
Hammer and Anvil?	Turn to 246
Prancing Pony?	Turn to 185

99

You manage to take the evil enchantress by surprise with your ability. She takes a step back and holds out her staff; it sprouts a series of jagged-edged daggers. Use your Necromancer fighting level as your SKILL score for this fight.

NECROMANCER   SKILL 9   STAMINA 10

If you win, the evil creature's body disappears and the staff burrows, worm-like, into the ground. You run off and stumble down the mountain for many hours (mark off 2 Poison units on the *Adventure Sheet*). The path you are following divides. Which route do you choose to take: the one to the left (turn to 379) or to the right (turn to 122)?

There is only one accessible corridor, to the north; all the other exits are blocked by sealed metal doors. Ahead, in the gleam of distant daylight, you see a grey stone horse. As you approach, it comes to life in a creaking, crumbling manner. Suddenly metal poles with spikes sticking out in all directions shoot out of the walls and block the tunnel ahead. You cannot climb over this barrier for you would be torn to pieces on the spikes. Your only hope is to jump the stone horse over the obstacle. You mount the horse, dig your heels into its sides, and it charges at the poles. Throw 2 dice for the height of the poles, then throw 2 dice again for the jump of the horse. If the jump is greater than or equal to the height of the poles, you have cleared them successfully. If not, then the horse hits the metal poles and begins to fall to pieces. You crash into the spikes and are killed instantly. Your quest is over.

If you clear the poles, the horse solidifies again; you dismount and stagger out. Turn to **295**.

101

You don't trust anyone on this road – but walking is fatiguing (deduct 2 points from your STAMINA). At one point you pass two large stone bulls set on either side of the road and you notice large herds of long-horned bulls grazing. Suddenly a storm begins to blow up; sand, stones and dust are whipped up all around you. As you stagger on you hear evil laughter and you lose all sense of direction. When finally the storm dies down, you can no longer see the road and you find yourself facing a mountain slope. You are completely lost. Turn to **397**.

102

You are just able to move your left hand to touch the Talon, but the effort exhausts you (deduct 2 points from your STAMINA). You scan the horizon as another undead being slices at a piece of your cloak. Suddenly, you are lifted up high into the sky by something. The Necromancer screams in frustration and unleashes a bolt of lightning at you. She misses, however.

Nighthawk Swoop, the Boulyanthrop who is holding you, tells you that, following the orders of Eleonora, he has been finding out what is happening in Sharrabbas. 'The city has been tainted by a poisonous evil, and the pure-hearted are being killed and driven out.' He must travel back with the news, so he sets you down in a thickly forested region and soon disappears into the low clouds. Turn to **167**.

103

You go through a door that closes behind you. You find yourself in a tunnel with a row of stone bulls on either side. They may be made of stone – but you are sure that they are moving slightly as you pass. Suddenly they all come to life and charge at you. You run flat out until you come to the junction of a tunnel heading south (turn to **50**) and the tunnel you are already in heading east (turn to **337**). Which do you choose?

104

You draw your sword. The Kazanid warrior screams a warning to you, but it is too late. The Kalamite instinctively squeezes your body and you are crushed to death. Your quest is over.

105

To screams of 'No, no' from the old woman you reach in and scoop up some gold coins in your hands. Suddenly, something stirs among the glistening treasure. Before you can withdraw your hand, a golden snake rears up and, hissing, bites your finger. The hag shakes her head and looks at you pityingly. 'You have forfeited my trust . . . but I will not let you die.' She pulls some crushed leaves out of her apron and rubs them on your bitten finger. 'You will feel weaker for some time' – deduct 1 point from your SKILL and 2 points from your STAMINA. Mark off 2 Poison units – 'but nevertheless I will not let you go empty-handed. Here . . .' She hands you 5 gold coins, then hobbles off with the chest on her back. Add the gold coins to your *Adventure Sheet* and turn to **115**.

106

The Trolls pocket your bribe and let you pass. The cart-driver has seen everything. He asks if you want to ride with him. You climb aboard and, as he flicks the reins and you set off, he starts complaining. 'Chingiz again! Imposing tolls on a road that used to be free when Segrek was alive. Pray the gods send us a true monarch who will rid us of this scum.' Turn to **155**.

107

You join a small crowd surrounding a man who is leaning over a box. It is a dice game; he pits his throw against any challenger and pays back double the stake if he loses, plus your stake-money, of course. Do you wish to risk your one remaining gold coin on the throw of the dice (turn to **125**), or do you turn your back on the dice game and continue wandering around (turn to **213**)?

108

The hurdy-gurdy man straightens up and pulls out a shortsword. His fake peg-leg is kicked away and he rushes at you in his real identity: that of a Mamlik Assassin.

MAMLIK ASSASSIN   SKILL 8   STAMINA 10

If you win, you see a cart coming towards you. You rush over and ask the driver the price for carrying you away from Korkut. He smiles and tells you that he will accept you for the pleasure of your company and the security of an extra sword. 'The lands ahead are full of thieves, brigands and villainous creatures,' he comments. Turn to **286**.

109

You cut his bonds with your sword. He gets up, pulls a battered wizard's cap out of a pocket and begins chattering. 'Yes, yes, you're the one I've been waiting for. Let's go!' He takes you to the far corner of the room and lifts a trap-door. Following him into it, you find another tunnel. In the gloom you can hear a breathy rumbling sound; the wizard suddenly stops, then runs round to a position behind you. In front of you appear two vicious black panthers. 'Ah yes, the beasts,' the wizard murmurs behind you. 'Er, would you mind?' You pull out your sword. Fight each in turn.

	SKILL	STAMINA
First PANTHER	6	5
Second PANTHER	6	6

If you survive (mark off 1 Poison unit on the *Adventure Sheet*), the wizard cuts one claw off each beast, just before they disappear in a cloud of pungent smoke. 'Could come in useful,' he comments cheerfully, 'come on!' Just then his legs collapse under him and he asks you to carry him. Do you comply (turn to **144**) or do you give up on him as a waste of energy and carry on alone (turn to **222**)?

110

You seek out Chogum, explain the situation to him and set up the deal. He agrees to give you 20 gold coins for negotiating the transaction (add 20 gold coins to your *Adventure Sheet*). Well satisfied, you wander out of town and back on to the road. Turn to **280**.

111

You can hear crashing and the splintering of wood behind you. You dart and weave your way through the undergrowth – but suddenly you come face to face with Skrutch. He looks embarrassed, then turns away. You run off and find a tall tree to hide in. You decide to get down only when you are sure your pursuers have lost the scent. Turn to **391**.

112

The singing is accompanied by the sound of hammering on an anvil. Suddenly, the Dwarf notices you; he stands squarely in front of you, hammer raised above his shoulder. He is naturally suspicious and asks you what is your business here. Politely, you ask him to direct you to the correct path for Sharrabbas. He muses on the question. 'So, you avoid the main roads, do you? You must have something to hide – and therefore you're an enemy of Chingiz. Good.' He seems to be pleased with the result of his reasoning; he brightens up and begins hammering at a small metal object. 'Yes, I know the least frequented route,' he goes on. 'But you will need this.' He gives you a small but heavy metal ball, attached to a coil of thin wire rope. He wants no payment for it, and directs you back up the path. Turn to **245**.

113

When you bend down to stroke it, other similar little creatures appear and rush towards you. However, they stop as the one you are stroking begins to trill with pleasure. They all begin to purr, and then retire into their holes. Add 1 point to your LUCK. Walking on, you go through a metal door that shuts behind you with a soft clunking sound. Turn to **342**.

114

You sit down and put your boots on. Then you stand up and take a look at the tree in front of you. It has what look like the heads and bodies of warriors attached to it, and you notice that two separate branches are moving towards you. You chop at one of the branches as it tries to grab you, but fail to observe that the other is encircling your ankle. Other branches move out menacingly towards you.

GNARLED OAK   SKILL 7   STAMINA 8

If you survive (mark off 1 Poison unit on the *Adventure Sheet*), you find yourself completely lost in the forest gloom. You are sure you can hear Impish laughter in the distance. You pick out two possible paths at random. Which one do you take: the route leading straight ahead (turn to **311**) or the one to the right (turn to **257**)?

115

The path slopes gently down for some way. Eventually you walk round a huge boulder and come upon a strange sight: a large, hideous, fanged worm with something bird-like struggling in its mouth. Around it flutter and squawk strange beings with golden wings. They are trying to help one of their number release himself from the worm before it can drag its prey into the ground. Do you decide to help (turn to **374**) or do you prefer to keep a low profile and not get involved (turn to **18**)?

116

You walk for many hours and the ground begins to get steeper. The track eventually peters out; gazing around in the clear light, you see, far below, a line of riders. You cannot know who they are, but decide to press on. You reach the snowline and, turning, see the riders release a message hawk. You come to an area of very thick snow; your legs sink in up to your knees and progress becomes very slow and tiring (deduct 1 point from your STAMINA and mark off 1 Poison unit). Suddenly, rounding a bend, you come up against a deep chasm. There are two snow-bridges across it. Which do you risk using for your crossing: the one on the left (turn to **27**) or the one on the right (turn to **226**)?

117

You enter the Dead Man's Chest Tavern. It is full of old salts, Kazanids, seafaring Dwarfs, and Goblin deck-hands. You sit and rest (eat some Provisions if you have any left; otherwise your only option is to pay 1 gold coin for a meal. Add 4 points to your STAMINA). In a corner of the inn you see a group of sailors crowding round a one-eyed individual. They are playing Snakes' Eyes. Do you wish to gamble (turn to **354**) or do you just leave (turn to **168**)?

118

You elect to stay close to your new companions. As you mount your horse you hear the swish of arrows. *Test your Luck*. If you are Lucky, the arrows miss and you ride into the fray. If you are Unlucky, one arrow wounds you in the thigh. You pull it out (deduct 3 points from your STAMINA) and join the others.

You face two Orcs holding long spiked spears. Fight each in turn.

	SKILL	STAMINA
First ORC	6	5
Second ORC	7	6

If you survive (mark off 2 Poison units on the *Adventure Sheet*), you become separated from the others in the dark. You listen carefully for sounds of your companions. You can hear a noise to your left (turn to **11**) and something going on straight ahead (turn to **272**). In which direction do you choose to ride?

119

You find yourself in a room on the edge of a precipice. A frail wooden bridge spans the chasm. At your feet lie two heavy stone blocks. A compelling voice tells you to carry the blocks across to the other side. You may not refuse. Throw 2 dice to determine the weight of the blocks; next throw 2 dice to determine the strength of the bridge. If the weight of the blocks is greater than the strength of the bridge, it will collapse and you will fall into the bottomless pit. Your quest ends here. If the bridge holds, add 1 point to your LUCK, return to **160** and throw the magic die to continue through the Maze.

120

You trudge through the snow for a long time. The wind is cold and cuts chillingly into your skin. Eventually it stops snowing, the wind dies down and you hear the sound of hoofbeats on the soft snow . . . they are getting nearer. Do you decide to hide behind some rocks (turn to **353**) or stand your ground (turn to **30**)?

121

You pull out your sword and attack. Fight each Goblin in turn.

	SKILL	STAMINA
First GOBLIN	5	5
Second GOBLIN	5	6

If you win (mark off 2 Poison units on the *Adventure Sheet*), you hear a strange, distant voice. 'Brave adventurer, you have defended the tomb of Segrek,' it says. 'You are the last of the Select. Take the horn, it will help you find the True Path to the Throne.' The voice fades and a small curved horn appears on the tomb. You pick it up. Add the horn to your *Adventure Sheet*.

You leave the room and enter another that has a large fireplace in the middle of one wall. Light is coming down the chimney, and you notice a series of steps cut into the sooty blocks of stone, leading upwards. In the far corner of the room is a spiral staircase, also going upwards. Which route do you choose: the chimney (turn to **82**) or the staircase (turn to **260**)?

122

You press on. The ground becomes broken and large crevices appear, so that you have to jump across the wider gaps. The occasional black bird flies over, and eventually a thick mist clears momentarily to reveal the distant towers of Sharrabbas across a desolate-looking plain. The mist closes in again and at last you reach a rushing river. There is a small boat tied to a stake on the bank – but there are no oars. Do you get into the boat (turn to 51) or do you prefer to walk along the riverbank (turn to 229)?

123

The Bogomils ride hard and fast. Eventually you reach a settlement of stone buildings in the shape of a rough circle. Horns are sounded, and many other riders appear. You are told to dismount and are made to stand in a clearing in the middle. Then the crowd parts to let in a large white stallion which has obviously not been tamed: it bucks, kicks, jumps and twists. One of the riders announces: 'Bucephax.' You must ride this creature for as long as you can. Two horsemen lean down and catch you by the upper arms; they lift you up between them and drop you on to the horse's saddle. Throw 1 die. If you throw a 1 or a 2, you are unseated and crash to the ground (deduct 2 points from your STAMINA). You are then remounted in the same way. Repeat this procedure *four* more times. If you are unseated a total of three times, the third time you are winded by the fall and cannot move; the horse kills you with a blow from its hoof. Your quest is over. If you survive (mark off 1 Poison unit), you are dusted off and led to a large gate. Turn to **20**.

124

Turn to **361**.

125

You push your way to the front and challenge the dice gambler. Throw 2 dice for your turn and 2 dice for his. If your total is the greater, you double the stake and throw again. If the throws are equal, throw again. If you lose, you lose all. Continue until you lose your stake or win a maximum of 9 gold coins (mark the changes on the *Adventure Sheet*). Turn to **213**.

126

As the holder of two Medallions, you have the right to choose two Powers that will aid you when you sit on the throne of Kazan. Choose *two* from the following list, then go to the relevant paragraphs: **93**; **166**; **330**; **356**; **376**; **384**. Note down which Powers you now have (they are listed in capitals at the start of the appropriate paragraphs) – but do not read any further into those paragraphs. When you have chosen two Powers, turn to **74**.

127

The leader of the bandits stands in front of you and questions you. You see no reason to deny the real nature of your quest. Upon hearing your story, he raises his visor and smiles. 'You see, I was formerly one of the Select, but I gave up the quest: Chingiz is too strong. However, you are brave to carry on. Do you wish to purchase information? Ten gold coins to a fellow adventurer.' If you would like to buy information, turn to **279**. If you have no gold, or do not wish to spend it, turn to **383**.

128

You approach a rough-looking sailor lounging on the gangplank and ask him how much passage to Kazilik would cost. He rubs his stubble with his fingers and looks you up and down. 'Twenty gold coins, all found – and as many ship's biscuits you can eat.' Some of the sailors nearby look up and laugh. If you can afford it, do you accept (deduct 20 gold coins on your *Adventure Sheet* and turn to **299**), or give up the idea of travelling by boat and walk on along the harbour (turn to **339**)?

129

The route described by the Dwarf is long, but there is less likelihood of meeting Mamliks or Orcs on it. You follow the city walls for a long time. They are not well guarded and there are occasional breaches; as you pass one of the larger holes, you hear a yapping, growling sound and see a pack of white wolfhounds racing towards you. Three choose to attack you. Fight each in turn.

	SKILL	STAMINA
First WOLFHOUND	7	6
Second WOLFHOUND	6	6
Third WOLFHOUND	6	7

If you survive (mark off 2 Poison units on the *Adventure Sheet*), you press on. The directions given are perfect, and eventually you stand at the entrance to the Street of the Forty Guilds. Turn to **98**.

You support the old crone through the forest. She tells you that her name is Mayaka and that you are taking her to Brassino-Dendro, in the north of the forest. Eventually you arrive at a clearing where you find three figures, just like Mayaka, grouped around a boiling cauldron. Mayaka tells them how you helped her escape from the huntresses and of your quest, and they agree to help you. They give you six sprigs of prime Treffilli, and Mayaka explains the spells that go with them.

'You may use the herb only when you feel it vibrate. Crush one sprig and whisper "*By Ash and Bird*", and your adversary will fall asleep. Crush two sprigs and whisper "*By Ash and Bird and Crust*", and you will become invisible to all senses for several minutes.' She warns you to be frugal in the use of these spells since they are harmful: you must deduct 3 points from your STAMINA for every sprig you use. Mark the Treffilli on the *Adventure Sheet*. Mayaka shows you the path out of the forest on to the Kazanid plain.

After many hours' walking, you reach a fork in the road. A carved-stone obelisk points in two possible directions. Which way do you choose: the way of the Bull (turn to **278**) or the way of the Horse (turn to **225**)?

131

You elect to roll away, but the dagger is at the point of striking you. *Test your Luck*. If you are Lucky, the blade cuts through your cloak and breaks on the hard wooden board. The Assassin makes a swift exit through the half-open door. If you are Unlucky, the dagger grazes your ribs. Deduct 2 points from your STAMINA and henceforth mark off *double* the Poison units on your *Adventure Sheet*.

You find no trace of the beggar and, if you had them, 5 gold coins are missing from your purse (deduct these from the *Adventure Sheet*). You go outside, wondering whether to trust the beggar's advice. Turn to **150**.

132

You are in a gloomy chamber. You cannot move and your hands are Spellbound. Suddenly, a Mamlik Assassin appears, raises a Dagger of Darkness and plunges it into your chest. The illusion fades (deduct 2 points from your STAMINA). Return to **160** and throw the magic die for your next position.

133

When you get close to the statues, they begin to creak, then start crashing their hoofs down. *Test your Luck.* If you are Unlucky, you are struck (deduct 3 points from your STAMINA) and you lose all potions, rings or gems you may have in your possession (make the appropriate adjustments on the *Adventure Sheet*). If you are Lucky, the hoofs miss you. In either case, mark off 1 Poison unit. You rush out of the maze (turn to **295**).

134

The Yigenik then accompany you to a large wooden gate. The walls of the Maze beyond it are composed of thick poisonous bushes. The old woman orders three Fangtigers to be released into the maze; however, as she is wishing you good luck, a disturbance is heard from within and a large Grypvulture is seen flying off, carrying a small Orc in its talons. The Yigenik elders notice with horror that the Orc is holding their Medallion. 'It is taken by one not of the Select. Recover it at once or we are doomed,' they cry. The warriors shoot volleys of arrows at the Orc. One arrow pierces his thick hide and he falls into a nearby street. You give chase on foot through the narrow lanes. You observe a trail of blood and see on your left a door to a house being shut. You enter the building and glimpse the Orc running upstairs. Do you rush after the Orc (turn to **46**) or do you proceed carefully and cautiously (turn to **218**)?

135

The hut is gloomy and you melt into its darkest recesses. The Mamlik appears at the door, pulls out a dagger and slowly enters; he seems to sense your presence, so you attack him. If you have the ability of Darkfight, fight as normal; otherwise deduct 2 points from your SKILL for this combat only.

MAMLIK   SKILL 6   STAMINA 10

If you win (mark off 1 Poison unit on the *Adventure Sheet*), you hide the body and quietly slip back out. Turn to **319**.

136

You come to a door which you push open and enter another tunnel. The door closes silently behind you, and you follow the tunnel which turns a corner and then heads east. In the torchlight you see a small figure. It is a Dwarf who, when he sees you, rushes over and begs: 'Please help me, for I lack the strength to open these doors.' He looks at you with pleading eyes which you cannot resist, so you agree to help him. He claps his hands with joy, then walks to the door with you. You push at the door then, suddenly looking around, see the Dwarf transformed into a hideous monster that fills the width of the whole tunnel. Long-clawed hands reach out to grab you.

DUNGEON DELVER   SKILL 7   STAMINA 8

If you win, you push the door open. Turn to **292**.

137

The screen prevents your hearing most of the words spoken and although the chanting goes on, you can't tell what is happening. Occasionally, the room is lit by multi-coloured flashes, and odd pieces of broken glass fly past you. The commotion slowly dies down, until you deem it safe to escape. As you creep out on all fours, you come across a Red Gem on the floor. If you wish to take it, mark it on your *Adventure Sheet*. Thankfully, you leave this lair of magic-making and find yourself in the open air once more. Turn to **70**.

138

Adana-Broussah is pleased. She tells you that Beshbalik has been away, making final preparations to carry out a small job: an attack upon a large group of bandit Trolls who are preying on a local village. A horn-blast greets the arrival of Beshbalik who comes charging across the shallow river, riding two Fangtigers and with a Grypfalcon perched on his shoulder. He enters the camp at an incredible speed.

The attack is prepared; there is no spare mount for you, so you must join the rabble who run behind the horses (deduct 1 point from your STAMINA). By the time you reach the others, the Marauders have already engaged the Trolls in battle. Arriving at the scene of battle, you walk straight into a huge, wounded Troll who swings a giant scimitar at you.

BANDIT TROLL   SKILL 9   STAMINA 9

If you win (mark off 1 Poison unit on the *Adventure Sheet*), do you join a large group who seem to be dividing the spoils among themselves (turn to **67**) or will you stay in the shadows of the Troll huts (turn to **319**)?

139

You search the body. You find a Blue Gem and a box marked 'Treffilli', with two sprigs of a green plant inside it. If you wish to keep either of these, mark them on your *Adventure Sheet*.

On getting up, you find yourself facing two Bone-crusher Beasts. Fight each in turn.

	SKILL	STAMINA
First BONECRUSHER	7	8
Second BONECRUSHER	8	6

If you survive (mark off 2 Poison units on the *Adventure Sheet*), you rush out through the door. Turn to **295**.

140

You crawl through the hole in the wall, to find yourself on top of a smelly mound of rubbish. Something falls on to your shoulder and joins the rotting mess; it looks like an animal's carcass. Just then, you hear a scrabbling sound and see three huge rats. They are blind and have no tails; one of them begins to sniff at your boots, then pulls at one of the straps; then it vanishes into a very large hole. Looking around, you spot a ladder. Do you wish to climb up the ladder (turn to 57) or follow the rat into the hole (turn to 378)?

141

You crawl along the narrow tunnel. It is old and parts of it are collapsing. Something scuttles along the ground and bites you (deduct 1 point from your STAMINA). The roof of the tunnel begins to shake – and then collapses on top of you. You are covered in dirt and rubble; holding your breath, you try to dig your way out. Throw 2 dice for the amount of air in your lungs, then throw 2 dice for the amount of air you will need to escape from the cave-in. If the air in your lungs is equal to or greater than the air needed, then you have made it to another tunnel (turn to 377). Otherwise, you suffocate; your quest is over.

142

You have drunk the fatal mixture of the Luckless. Fortune has not favoured you in your quest for the throne. You suffer an agonizing death.

143

You are in a room with a large trapdoor set in the floor. The walls of the room begin to close in and the trapdoor swings open to reveal a snakepit. You drop down into the pit. Throw 1 die for the number of snakes that bite you as you rush towards the door leading to safety. Deduct 2 points from your STAMINA for each bite. You open the door – and everything blacks out. Return to **160** and throw the magic die to continue.

144

You pick him up and carry him on your back. Fortunately, he is very light. While you trudge on, he continues to mutter. 'Look out for that flagstone, make sure you jump over it – Orc trick, every thirty-third pace . . .' You do as he bids. He tells you his name is Saxifragus, then he mumbles the name of Astragal. 'Oh yes, you're lucky you ran into me,' he goes on (add 1 point to your LUCK), 'I believe you are the last of the Select.'

You pass rooms and tunnels with the dust and cobwebs of centuries on them. Finally, you come up against a giant sticky web. The wizard tells you to cut through it with your sword and adds that you'd better hurry up about it. You must cut 24 thick strands. Throw 2 dice four times for the number of strands you manage to cut. If you throw 24 or over, turn to **277**. If you throw less than 24, turn to **29**.

145

You stagger along the rocky path as it drops down into a valley. Ahead, you make out a small wisp of black cloud that takes on the shape of a face and you hear a female voice: 'Forget your quest. Kazan will have its ruler from the line of Chingiz.' The mountain begins to rumble and shake, and rocks start to roll and slide down towards you. You rush for cover. Throw 1 die six times and mark the sequence of numbers you throw on the *Adventure Sheet*: this represents the random fall of rocks. Now throw 1 die six times to mark your run for cover. If a number in the second sequence matches its counterpart in the first, a rock has hit you and you are severely injured (deduct 4 points from your STAMINA and 1 point from your SKILL. Mark off 1 Poison unit). If you make it unscathed, add 1 point to your LUCK.

You carry on down a dry river valley, and eventually your route divides into two paths. Which do you follow: the left-hand path (turn to **7**) or the right-hand path (turn to **81**)?

146

The sprigs of Treffilli vibrate in your pocket. You can just move your hand with great pain and effort. You reach two sprigs of Treffilli, crush them and recite the formula: 'By Ash and Bird and Crust'. Deduct the two sprigs from your *Adventure Sheet* and 6 points from your STAMINA. If you are still alive, the Necromancer is startled as you disappear, Spell-binding control is released, and you are free to walk away from the hideous scene.

You follow a winding, twisting path for many hours, then stop to eat some Provisions (add 4 points to your STAMINA). Turn to **122**.

147

You walk along the corridor and go through another metal door. You are beginning to feel tired, and the air is stifling (deduct 1 point from your STAMINA). You are faced with tunnels running west (turn to **232**) and north (turn to **305**). Which do you choose?

148

The horse is very fast over the rough ground. There are shouts behind you and you hear the swish as an arrow passes over your left shoulder. You ride at full gallop for many miles until at last you find yourself faced with a huge felled tree-trunk lying across your path. You press your horse on, it jumps high, clears the obstacle and lands on the other side with a jolt that snaps the saddle-girth. The saddle slides off and you are thrown to the ground. *Test your Luck.* If you are Unlucky, you fall badly (deduct 2 points from your STAMINA). If you are Lucky, you land on soft turf. The horse canters off into the distance. You get up, shake yourself down and walk on until you come to a good place for a rest. Turn to **399**.

149

The Dragon brew slips down your throat very easily. You feel good and your body begins to warm up from the inside (add 4 points to your STAMINA). Alkis returns, sniffs the tankard and is agreeably surprised that you have chosen his favourite brew. 'Don't on any account try the Scimitar dregs unless you're a Khomatad from the northern wastes,' he advises. Turn to **210**.

150

You trudge on through the snow until the path you are on begins to feel firmer underfoot and you realize that you must be on some sort of highway. You walk on cautiously until you reach a place where the road forks. A small obelisk marks the left-hand way with the carving of a horse. Do you choose this route (turn to **391**) or do you prefer to take the right-hand fork (turn to **275**)?

151

You approach the evil Mage and pull out your sword. He smiles and stands, stock still, with staff upraised. Your sword strikes his staff, and the smile is wiped from his hideous face. Use your Necromancer fighting ability level as your SKILL score for this fight.

NECROMANCER   SKILL 9   STAMINA 10

If you win (mark off 1 Poison unit on the *Adventure Sheet*), the body disappears in a cloud of pungent smoke and the staff burrows, worm-like, into the ground. A great cheer goes up from the Marauders, and Beshbalik brings you two Fangtigers to ride, as the horde prepare for another rampage. Turn to **197**.

152

You enter a chamber containing sculptures of Fang-tigers. Before your very eyes, two of the carvings come to life; they prowl around, sniffing, then they spot you and attack. Fight each in turn.

	SKILL	STAMINA
First FANGTIGER	6	8
Second FANGTIGER	7	10

If you survive (mark off 2 Poison units on the *Adventure Sheet*), the bodies turn to stone again. You find yourself in front of two doors. Which do you choose: a door to the left (turn to **254**) or a door to the right (turn to **392**)?

153

You are at a crossroads: tunnels lead north and west, but there are shut and sealed doors to the south and east. The northern passage is short and at the end of it you can see an open door leading to some more tunnels. If you choose to go north, you pass through the door, which shuts softly behind you (turn to **221**). If you choose to go west, turn to **240**.

154

You will not draw a weapon in the shadow of the Throne of Kazan. You walk past the Ogres, who suddenly stop in their tracks and turn to stone. You sit on the Throne and watch, horrified, as Meghan-na-Durr, daughter of Chingiz, collapses and turns to dust. A slight breeze blows her ashes out through an open window. Turn to **400**.

155

The cart climbs over a rise and you get your first clear view of Sharrabbas: a city dominated by its Fortress. Flaxwort, the driver, has guessed that you are one of the Select, and decides to help you get into the city. To that end, he disguises you as his assistant. 'They're looking for lone adventurers, so if you put this apron and cap on and cover up that blade, there . . .' It being market-day, the city is crowded with carts. The Orcs at the gate only give you a brief glance before putting a small chalk-mark on the side of the cart. The road forks and Flaxwort asks you which way you wish to go: to the left (turn to 343) or the right (turn to 249).

156

You walk down the tunnel and are amazed to see a number of sparks shooting out of a small pebble that is lying on the floor. A black, foul-smelling smoke rises from the pebble; it takes the shape of a man wearing a hooded cloak and carrying a staff inscribed with a black panther. With an ironic bow he declaims gratingly, 'I am Sigismuh, from my Lord Chingiz's cohort of Necromancers. I am here to destroy YOU.' At once you pull out your sword and strike at him. The blade passes clean through his body, with no effect. He laughs and strikes the ground with his staff. Immediately, the roof begins to cave in and you are forced to run for the next door. Throw 1 die three times for a series of falling blocks and then throw 1 die three times for your run to the door. If any numbers match in the first and second sequences, you are hit (deduct 4 points from your STAMINA). If you survive, you go through the door and it shuts behind you. Turn to **264**.

157

You are in a room with a long table in the middle. Scrawled on the table is the legend, 'The Fiend Loves Flowers'. Return to **160** and throw the magic die for your next position.

158

You open the door to a room containing three Gremlins; they comprise Chingiz's personal body-guard. Suddenly, a fourth, which had been hiding behind the door, strikes you in the side with a shortsword, then runs off as the others attack. If you have the Power of Invulnerability to Sword-Strike, fight as normal. If not, then deduct 1 point from your SKILL. Fight each in turn.

	SKILL	STAMINA
First GREMLIN	4	4
Second GREMLIN	4	6
Third GREMLIN	4	6

If you win (mark off 2 Poison units on the *Adventure Sheet*), the fourth Gremlin has busied himself, lock-ing a great door with a massive key and then, with difficulty, managing to swallow it. He now stands with his back to the door. If you have the Power of Persuasion, turn to **347**. If not, then turn to **54**.

159

You slip behind a tree and work your way towards cover behind some rocks. Suddenly you become aware of a large Grypvulture that is sweeping down above you. It screeches and attacks you with iron-lined spike-talons. You pull out your sword just in time.

GRYPVULTURE   SKILL 6   STAMINA 6

If you survive, *Test your Luck*. If you are Unlucky, you find yourself surrounded by Orcs, one of whom throws a large net over you (turn to **92**). If you are Lucky, you manage to slip back into the milling crowd on the roadway just before the Orcs arrive. Turn to **308**.

You are escorted to the next chamber. 'The Maze has 24 chambers,' you are told, 'and you move around it by throwing the magic die and moving the number of squares indicated by the throw. Mark your position on the chart below. There are many dangers and you will probably experience them again and again.'

Make a note of the number of this paragraph. You are at Start. Throw the die and move in the direction indicated by the arrows. (For example, if you first throw a 4, count 4 squares and move on to **73**. Turn to that paragraph and, when instructed, return here, throw the magic die again, and continue your progress through the Maze.)

If you encounter a Serpent's head or a Stairway, you will be told to move straight away into another chamber. Mark your new position on the chart before throwing the next die. If you throw a die that would take you beyond 398, go to **398**.

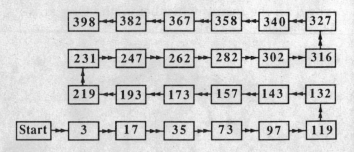

161

You walk along the path for many hours. The mountains behind you recede, the path grows less steep and the countryside becomes much greener. You cross several small streams and you notice more and more trees, until at last you find yourself at the edge of a huge forest. Within, you can hear strange creatures screaming and calling to one another. All this walking has made you tired; do you stop now to rest (turn to **86**), or do you wish to carry on quickly into the dark forest (turn to **368**)?

162

You walk over to the obelisk. The woman is young and strong, and you notice a sheathed dagger under her cloak. She asks you if you wish to enter the Fortress, adding that she doesn't want to know why, but she knows people who could help, 'for a price'. You ask how much and she replies, 'Twenty-five gold coins.' Have you got this much, and do you think you can trust her anyway (turn to **375**) or do you prefer to carry on alone (turn to **276**)?

163

The Eagle grasps an iron rod between its talons, and Geronicus invites you to take a firm hold on the rod. The huge bird flaps its wings and lifts you up with a judder. It has great strength but your arms tire (deduct 1 point from your STAMINA), and you are glad when it puts you down on a path and then flies away. Turn to **391**.

164

You are in the Street of the Stonemasons. In front of you a group of Kazanids are hauling blocks of stone up into a cart. One of them calls you over and asks if you want to earn 2 gold coins. You can see the shadowy figure of a Mamlik standing at the street corner. Do you help the stonemasons (turn to **296**) or refuse the offer of work and carry on walking (turn to **350**)?

165

You stride along the tunnel. The torches burn brightly and you examine the wall-carvings. At one point you make out the word 'THE' engraved on a wall, but this makes no sense to you. You come to a door that opens easily but shuts firmly behind you. You have a choice of continuing west (turn to **75**) or following a tunnel north (turn to **273**). Which do you choose?

166

GREAT WISDOM

You have drunk the mixture that gives you this Power. Mark this ability on your *Adventure Sheet*. If this is your first choice, return to **45** and choose again; otherwise, turn to **74**.

167

You walk on through the forest, and after many hours you stop to rest (add 4 points to your STAMINA). Just as you are getting up to go, you suddenly notice a foot poking out from behind a boulder. Creeping round with sword drawn, you come upon a scene of carnage: two Orcs and two Trolls lie dead, sprawled around a lone adventurer. You count yourself lucky that you didn't arrive here earlier (add 1 point to your LUCK). You search through the hapless adventurer's pockets and find a crumpled-up parchment. You flatten it out to read: 'The Wolfsbane at the Street of the Forty Guilds . . .' The rest is torn away. You salute the body and walk quickly away.

Eventually the path splits into two; either could be the correct way to Sharrabbas, so which do you choose: the left-hand path (turn to **23**) or the one to the right (turn to **4**)?

168

You stand in the road and watch a cart passing, pulled by four large horses. You know that you must make all speed upon your mission; the poison in your body will not let you dawdle. Do you choose to approach the cart-driver (turn to **13**) or would you rather head down to the harbour to seek other forms of transport (turn to **239**)?

You force yourself to crawl on, knowing that if you stop for just a moment to lie down, you will find it impossible to get up again (deduct 1 point from your STAMINA). As your will strengthens, the storm loses its intensity. You wander from the track you were following, and stumble on as best you can. Just then, you see a strange rippling effect moving under the snow ahead of you; something is moving fast and it is heading towards you. Suddenly you experience a sharp pain in your left ankle (mark off 2 Poison units). You lunge with your sword at the spot where you think the creature is lurking under the snow; something shrieks and nips you on the right ankle. You will have to fight it.

SNOW LEECH   SKILL 5   STAMINA 7

If you survive, you can find no trace of the creature. Turn to **370**.

170

You make for the door as fast as possible, but you can hear a strange beast just behind you. It grabs you and squeezes, trying to crush the life out of you. You shake yourself free and pull out your sword.

BONECRUSHER BEAST SKILL 6 STAMINA 8

If you survive, you rush out through the door. Turn to **295**.

171

You wait to ambush them. When they arrive, you notice that one is a Goblin. You leap out, and he orders the Sniffer Orcs to attack. Fight each in turn.

	SKILL	STAMINA
First SNIFFER ORC	7	6
Second SNIFFER ORC	7	6

If you survive (mark off 2 Poison units on the *Adventure Sheet*), the Goblin has disappeared during the fight, and you make good your escape. After many hours' walking, you find a place to rest. Turn to **399**.

When you confide in him, the Boulyanthrop, whose name is Greyfeather, decides that you must go with them back to the eyrie. They flap their great wings and lift you up. You fly over a great forest until you eventually reach a strange cliff from where you can see other Boulyanthrops flying out to greet you. You are carried in through one of the rectangular holes in the cliff and are greeted there by a bird-woman called Eleonora. She listens patiently to your tale, then speaks. 'You are in great danger. Chingiz has allied all the forces of evil against the Select. We ourselves do not possess either a Maze or a Medallion – but I will present you with the Grey Talon of Sakar' – mark this on your *Adventure Sheet*, 'If ever you need help from a winged creature, hold this in your hand and call for assistance.' Eleonora also tells you that the Grey Talon will help if you get to the Maze at Uruz: 'Two Wings, Three Talons and Seven Lives: the magic Spell will help you.' This is all the help the birdpeople can offer you. She bids you farewell and you are flown out of the eyrie. Greyfeather, your carrier, asks you which land you wish to head for first: the land of the Bogomil (turn to 225) or the land of the Uruz (turn to 278). You tell him which you have chosen, and he sets you down on the correct path, then flies off.

173

You are in a room full of flowers which give off no smell and are protected by cruel thorns. You may choose whether to pick a flower and place it in your backpack (mark a flower on your *Adventure Sheet*). If you do so, then the thorns prick you badly (deduct 2 points from your STAMINA). Return to **160** and throw another die to carry on.

174

Inside the room, torches are blazing and a cauldron is bubbling over a green flame. You plunge your hands into the chest to take one of the rings. *Test your Luck*. If you are Unlucky, a snake lying coiled beneath the treasures rears up and bites you, injecting a vile poison into your body. Henceforth, whenever you are instructed to mark off Poison units, you must *double* the number given in the text. If you are Lucky, the snake strikes at you but misses. Suddenly you become aware of an eerie chanting sound: you must hide. Do you rush behind a large screen in the far corner of the room (turn to **137**) or dive behind a padded chair to your left (turn to **394**)?

175

You enter the enclosure, spit on your hands for luck and pick up a large hammer. Many of the people in the crowd are making bets on the outcome. Throw 2 dice – this is the strength needed to ring the bell. If the total is equal to or less than your current STAMINA, then you have succeeded in hitting the bell.

You are immediately showered with daggers. *Test your Luck* again. If you are Unlucky, some of the daggers wound you (deduct 4 points from your STAMINA and mark off 2 Poison units). If you are Lucky, you escape without a scratch. Add 10 gold coins to the total on your *Adventure Sheet*.

You leave the fair and manage to find the main road to Uruz. Turn to **280**.

176

You wake up to find yourself lying on a bed of stretched hides; before you stands a woman holding a lamp made from a large crystal. 'Well met! Uruz magic is not strong but we are able to recognize one of Segrek's Select.' She points to the glowing crystal: 'We have revived you, but the rest is up to you. Do you wish to undergo the Test of Uruz for the honour of entering the Maze and seeking the Medallion?' If you agree, turn to **258**. If you refuse, you lose consciousness and awaken to find yourself lying by the side of a path. You shake yourself and get up. Turn to **225**.

177

You trudge through the snow, stumbling over the rocks. The path is level and seems to weave through the mountain pass. Ahead, you see a snow-covered mound from one side of which steam seems to be rising. You must pass it; as you do so, you sense something within the mound. Do you walk on and leave it alone (turn to **329**) or do you decide to investigate (turn to **58**)?

178

You lie quietly, thinking that if the storm persists you will find a better opportunity later. Suddenly in walks a Mamlik Assassin. He scowls and sniffs at you, before stabbing his lethal dagger into your chest. Your quest is over.

179

You crush one sprig of Treffilli (remove one sprig from your *Adventure Sheet* and deduct 1 point from your STAMINA) and mutter the spell: 'By Ash and Bird.' The Assassin immediately falls asleep. You leave him lying there and go through a metal door that closes tight behind you. Turn to **95**.

180

You walk over and help with their running repairs. Afterwards, the knights offer you a ride in to watch the joust. They are Yigenik warriors and are heading for the tournament which is to be held in a small town just outside the city of Sharrabbas. You join them and they head back on to the road. When a group of Orcs try to stop them at a road-block, they laugh and simply ride through them. On the road, one of the knights' horses stumbles and falls on his master's leg. It is obvious that he cannot now enter the joust, but the others need a fourth entrant. Do you decide to enter the tournament (turn to 42) or do you thank them for the ride and carry on, on your own, when they leave the main road (turn to 4)?

181

You stand proudly before them and announce that you are one of Segrek's Select. They circle round you and the leader orders one of them to approach you. This man dismounts, comes close and throws some bones to the ground while the others make the sign of a triangle with their fingertips. He gazes at the bones then mutters something to the leader, who urges his horse towards you. 'I am Gromarshk. You will accompany us to the Test that awaits you. Choose your horse.' He has two horses brought forward. Which do you choose to ride: the white stallion (turn to 290) or the grey mare (turn to 41)?

182

You agree to take him on, and he stands there, determined to have his money in advance. You get out your bag of gold coins, when suddenly another small boy runs past you and grabs it; they both disappear into the crowd. Deduct all the gold coins you have, except your lucky piece. Turn to **318**.

183

You tell your tale, then you can only watch as a wizened old man on a pony trots up to you, staring into a crystal. 'Huh, he lies!' he snorts. Bhoriss takes a club and hits you on the shoulder so that you fall down (deduct 1 point from your STAMINA). 'Now, tell the truth. No one lies to the Bogomils.' Turn to **91**.

184

You have chosen the wrong Medallion! *Test your Luck*. If you are Unlucky, the fiery power of the magic frizzles you up . . . your quest is over. If you are Lucky, you manage to divert the full blast – but you are blown across the Spell-plane to another part of the Maze (deduct 4 points from your STAMINA, 1 point from your SKILL and mark off 2 Poison units on the *Adventure Sheet*). Turn to **293**.

185

You are in a horse-trader's premises. There is no one about, so you take a good look around. You find a document, closing a deal with Chingiz to mount an army of Orcs to subdue the native Kazanids. Just then a fat rat waddles towards you. As you step back its shape changes to a black mist and then to that of a Necromancer. Before you can move, his staff emits snake-like coils that encircle you and form a net that begins to squeeze. You black out. Turn to **321**.

186

You enter a room full of stone blocks and snake carvings. Three snakes on three of the stone blocks suddenly come to life. At the same time, the room is filled with boiling-hot water, and you are forced to jump up on to one of the blocks. You must make your way, stepping from block to block, across the room to the door. Throw 1 die three times for the locations of the snakes, then throw 1 die three times for your leaps across from stone to stone. If any of the numbers in the two sequences match, you land on a block containing one or more snakes and are bitten; deduct 4 points from your STAMINA and mark off 1 Poison unit for every snake-bite you incur. If you survive, turn to **359**.

187

You are just in time to see the Orc disappearing into the tower opposite. In front of you, however, is a narrow bridge to which a Goblin is clinging, ready to stab you. Below, Kazanids from Chingiz's slave-guard are firing arrows at you. You rush over the bridge. *Test your Luck*. If you are Unlucky, the Goblin stabs you in the foot. Deduct 3 points from your STAMINA and mark off 2 Poison units. If you are Lucky, he misses. Throw 2 dice for the speed of the Orc you are chasing, then throw 2 dice for your own speed. If your speed is greater than or equal to the speed of the Orc, turn to **94**. If you are not fast enough, you watch, frustrated, as a Grypvulture takes off with the Medallion in its beak. You are too late.

You return to the street and leave the town. Do you wish to head down into the forested valley (turn to **257**) or up on to a mountain track (turn to **275**)?

188

The Eagle holds an iron rod which Geronicus invites you to hold on to. The huge bird flaps its wings and lifts you up. It flies fast and high until your arms tire (deduct 1 point from your STAMINA) and you ask to be put down on a path below. Turn to **278**.

189

If you have paid for your passage, you have a good rest (add 4 points to your STAMINA). If you have not paid for your passage, you are made to work hard scrubbing decks. You pass a group of sailors who are pointing at something flying out from the coast. You look closely: two fire-breathing Kazilik Dragons are flying towards the ship. There is a large cross-bow mounted at either end of the ship and you decide to help fight them off. Do you decide to man one of the crossbows (turn to 204) or do you climb up to the crow's nest with your sword at the ready (turn to 313)?

190

The tunnel is very long. By the side of a blazing torch you see a row of three carved medallions with a cross inscribed under the third one from the left. You trudge on wearily until you come across a bush with sprigs made up of triangular leaves set in a circular pattern. Above it is carved the legend 'Treffilli'. Do you pick any of the sprigs (turn to 248) or do you leave the bush alone and pass through the next door (turn to 393)?

191

You throw down your gauntlet and everyone stares at you in disbelief. The riders wager among themselves on how long you will last. Urgenj appears; he towers above you and carries a sword that you could never hope to lift. Fight until the STAMINA of one of you drops to 4 points.

URGENJ   SKILL 10   STAMINA 12

If you lose, you are on your last legs, but no death-blow is struck. If you win, you spare the warrior from death. Turn to 31.

192

Nonchalantly you carry on walking as the rider gets nearer. Eventually a cloaked figure on a steaming horse passes you and then stops. 'Who are you, stranger?' asks a woman's voice. You are debating in your mind whether or not to trust her when you spot a Dagger of Darkness revealed by a sudden gust of wind that blows aside her cloak. She realizes that you've seen the weapon, scowls and gallops off. Now you will have to decide whether to stay on the road (turn to 53) or travel on the plain (turn to 333)?

193

You are in a smoke-filled room. Through the haze, you dimly make out a fully armed warrior. You step forward and he springs to life.

MAZE WARRIOR   SKILL 7   STAMINA 9

If you win, return to **160** and throw the magic die to continue.

194

The galloping horse does not stop, but continues to charge. Fear overwhelms you (deduct 1 point from your STAMINA). Then it passes straight through you! You realize that it is only an illusion, and you continue north through another door. Turn to **349**.

195

You play dead. The wooden hand of the Kalamite closes around you and lifts you up a little way. The temptation to move is great but the female warrior's eyes implore you to keep completely still. Suddenly she leaps up and strikes out at the hand of the creature, cutting the hand off in one blow. From high above comes a distant scream, as a thick sappy liquid oozes from the severed limb. You are free. You run after the sure-footed warrior as she weaves in and out among the tall reeds. Eventually she stops; you are exhausted (mark off 1 Poison unit), but she is not even out of breath. All at once she announces that she knows you are one of Segrek's Select and that she has something to tell you – but it is up to you to trust her. Do you decide to stay and hear her out (turn to **49**) or would you rather bid her a hasty farewell and carry on alone, until you find somewhere to rest (turn to **399**)?

196

Walking along the corridor, you notice the words 'GOLD COINS' carved on the wall. On the floor below the legend is a small bag that contains 5 gold coins. You pick these up (add them to your *Adventure Sheet*). You go through another door. Turn to **72**.

You ride the Fangtigers at the head of the yelling horde, Beshbalik at your side. During your progress, you come upon an Orc road-block: a large group of them are subjecting several individuals to the test of the Crystal. Beshbalik and his Marauders take no notice of shouted orders to stop; they plough through the Orcs, divesting them of various pieces of armour and their weapons. You get your first view of Sharrabbas when the horde finally stops. Adana-Broussah takes you to one side. 'Beshbalik will not enter Sharrabbas,' she confides. 'He knows that Chingiz is too powerful there. You have breached the first blockade, now you must travel on your own. Astragal entreats you to seek out the Wolfsbane, I know not what he means.' When the horde sets off again, they take a different route, away from the city; you drop back and jump off the Fangtigers. When all is quiet once more, you have to decide whether to stay on the road (turn to **85**) or take to the rough, wooded ground and follow the less obvious paths (turn to **167**).

198

You leave the Dead Man's Chest Tavern and walk straight into another Goblin who is leading two Orcs down the small back alleyway. He stops, points at you and screams in guttural Goblin style – and the Orcs leap to attack you. Fight each Orc in turn.

	SKILL	STAMINA
First ORC	7	6
Second ORC	7	6

If you survive, you can see no trace of the Goblin. You leave the alleyway and round a corner into the main street. You feel a distinct throb from the poison in your blood (mark off 2 Poison units). Turn to **168**.

199

Taking the Medallion, you replace it with a bag containing 10 gold coins (deduct the gold from your *Adventure Sheet*). You hold your breath, but nothing untoward happens. You have chosen the correct weight! Add 1 point to your LUCK. You look carefully at the back of the Medallion and see that it is marked with the number '1000'. You stumble out of the Maze and into the daylight. Turn to **295**.

200

Adana-Broussah leads the way to the camp of Besh-balik's Marauders. 'The path to Sharrabbas is full of dangers,' she says. 'One way will be to go as one of the horde. They are always picking up lone adventurers who can prove themselves.' You reach the camp, where you find the Marauders huddled round a camp fire. They are suspicious of you at first, but Adana-Broussah calms them and proposes that you be tested. They discuss the idea for a while and finally agree. You are thrown a large club and then, without warning, two of them attack you. Fight each in turn until the STAMINA of either combatant drops to 4.

	SKILL	STAMINA
First MARAUDER	7	8
Second MARAUDER	8	8

If you win (mark off 1 Poison unit on the *Adventure Sheet*), you are accepted (turn to **138**). If you lose, you are taken away and left at a lonely roadside (turn to **116**).

201

You stand, your sword raised, ready to hold your ground. At first the Orcs are chary of attacking until a peremptory scream, emitted by the remaining mounted figure, makes them shudder and impels their attack. Fight each Orc in turn.

	SKILL	STAMINA
First ORC	6	5
Second ORC	6	5
Third ORC	7	6

If you survive (mark off 2 Poison units on the *Adventure Sheet*), you suddenly become aware of a distinct draught, and you catch a gleam of daylight at the back of the cave. Do you decide to try and find a rear exit (turn to 44) or would you prefer to go out by the way you entered (turn to 34)?

202

Deciding to take no chances, you lie flat out in the grass with your cloak over you. You hear the rider pass by, then stop. After a short time you hear the horse trotting away. You get up, with no idea whether or not the rider saw you. Do you wish to carry on along the road (turn to 53) or do you prefer to keep off the road and travel on the plain (turn to 333)?

203

You know that this fight is not yours and that you must conserve your energies for greater things. You steal away and pass a shadowy figure that is looking in another direction.

You walk for many hours; the ground begins to slope down and now you can see more trees and bushes. Eventually, with daylight, you find yourself walking on a track. After a few hours, this track forks, becoming two well-made paths. Beside one path stands an obelisk with a stallion carved on its side; an obelisk with a Fangtiger stands beside the other. Which way do you choose to follow: the way of the Stallion (turn to **391**) or the way of the Tiger (turn to **209**)?

204

Both the Kazilik Dragons are small, but they are breathing fire in the direction of the ship. You take up position and swing the crossbow, aiming at the leading beast which is heading straight for you.

Throw 1 die for the position of the Dragon, then throw 1 die for your shot. If the two numbers match, you have hit the creature. Turn to **16**. If you miss, then it's too late for a second shot. You are enveloped in white-hot fire and fall into the sea (deduct 4 points from your STAMINA). Near exhaustion, you swim towards the coast (mark off 2 Poison units on the *Adventure Sheet*). Turn to **348**.

205

You walk on slowly. Suddenly a door in front of you swings open and out charges a long-horned bull. It lunges and heaves its huge head at you. *Test your Luck.* If you are Unlucky, one of its horns smashes through your armour and breaks several ribs (deduct 4 points from your STAMINA and mark off 2 Poison units). If you are Lucky, the bull lifts you between its horns. It then rushes off, with you lying across its neck. You manage to pull out your sword as it runs straight through the next wall and emerges in another part of the Maze. At last you are able to plunge your sword between its shoulder-blades. The bull collapses to its knees, then disappears with a foul stench into the ground. You look around and find a solitary door which you must push open. Turn to **95**.

206

The huntresses all line up as their leader, Omorphina by name, explains the task. You must cut three logs and a taut piece of leather below them, before a candle has burnt through a piece of twine and released a spray of poisonous darts. She seems to relish giving the explanation and the agonizing death you can expect.

Throw 2 dice; this is the time it will take the candle to burn through the twine. Throw 2 dice; this is the time it will take you to cut through the three logs. If your axe-wielding time is equal to or less than the time it takes the twine to break, then you are successful. You are bound once again and taken to a hut which is already occupied by another prisoner, an old woman dressed in rags. Turn to **303**. If you fail, there is a great cheer as you are peppered with darts. You die an agonizing death.

207

You can see an exit to the south and one to the east. To the south you can hear a crashing sound. To the east you see flashes of colour. Which way will you go: south (turn to **66**) or east (turn to **283**)?

208

Walking down a dark lane, you step on something shiny. You stop to look and pick up a Dagger of Darkness, just like the one you hope to return to Chingiz's hand. Suddenly, the dagger bends and wraps itself around your wrists, and a Necromancer rises out of the dust in front of you. 'One of the virtuous Select, I see. My Lord Chingiz wants to meet you before you die. You have survived longer than we expected.' He stretches out a long bony finger and touches your forehead. You lose consciousness as you feel the poison throb in your body (mark off 2 Poison units). Turn to **321**.

209

The track leads down into a forested valley. Soon the trees blot out the sun and you have to stumble through a murky gloom. Feeling tired, you stop for a rest and some sleep (add 4 points to your STAMINA).

When you awaken, you are covered in leaves. Looking up, you see a little Imp running off with your boots. You get up and give chase across the forest floor of fallen pine-needles (deduct 1 point from your STAMINA). Eventually the Imp drops the boots and disappears up a tree. Do you put your boots on straight away (turn to **114**) or do you decide to run across the prickly ground with them in your hand (turn to **33**)?

You relax as Alkis recounts tales from the deep, dark chasms. All at once, he stands up and pulls out his sword, as a horde of warriors bursts into the inn. Heavy, weighted nets are thrown in which you manage to entangle yourself. Suddenly you are hit over the head (deduct 1 point from your STAMINA) and lose consciousness.

You come to in a cart, tied up with many others. Feeling about, you realize that all your possessions are still with you. There is no sign of Fearslicer. The cart is followed by riders and at one point you hear them talking: 'Aye, they'll be fine for the Korkut Slave Battalions. That one even has his own sword.'

The journey is long. Eventually you reach the land of Korkut and are forced to climb down from the cart. Dismounting, one of the riders stands before you and shouts: 'You are all battle-slaves now – but if you wish to fight for your freedom, choose now and you may fight Urgenj.' Do you elect to fight for your freedom (turn to **191**), or do you reveal to your captors that you are one of Segrek's Select (turn to **385**)?

211

You draw your sword. The riders are pleased that you have chosen this course of action; they form a circle and prepare to enjoy some good sport. The Yigenik scimitar-wielder spits, makes the sign of a triangle, then bears down on you.

YIGENIK RIDER   SKILL 7   STAMINA 8

If you win (mark off 1 Poison unit on the *Adventure Sheet*), you are told by the other riders that you are free to go, in spite of having killed one of their number. They ride off, screaming and bellowing their enjoyment of the recent fight. Turn to **18**.

212

You throw open the left-hand door. Behind it is a Dark Elf holding a dagger. He stabs you (deduct 4 points from your STAMINA). Nevertheless, you attack.

DARK ELF   SKILL 8   STAMINA 6

If you win (mark off 2 Poison units on the *Adventure Sheet*), you race through the right-hand door. Turn to **187**.

213

You come upon a stall that boasts a 'Test of Strength and Bravery'. It involves hitting a lever that shoots a wooden block up a pole. If you get it to the top, the block rings a bell and also releases a shower of daggers. You have to ring the bell and then jump clear of the area before the weapons land. The prize is 10 gold coins. Do you want to risk entering this test (turn to **175**) or do you prefer wandering about the market (turn to **344**)?

214

You know that running is the most sensible option; your quest is too important for distractions. You run fast; the poison in your blood makes your legs throb (mark off 2 Poison units). You continue climbing through the long night, until after sunrise, when you find a pathway (turn to **275**).

215

You walk northwards, suspicious of the woman. She is surrounded by a pile of rubble on the ground, as if she has fallen through the roof. Suddenly she stirs. You get nearer and she begs you to help. Then you notice that half her face has peeled off, to reveal the demonic visage of a Mamlik Assassin. The Assassin realizes that his disguise has been torn away and leaps to the attack.

MAMLIK ASSASSIN   SKILL 8   STAMINA 10

If you win (mark off 2 Poison units on the *Adventure Sheet*), you walk on past an elaborately carved wall with the word 'TEN' inscribed on its centre. You go through a door that shuts behind you. Turn to **64**.

216

You continue to wait until the door crashes open and two killer Ogres rush in, swinging double-headed axes. Fight each Ogre in turn.

	SKILL	STAMINA
First OGRE	8	10
Second OGRE	8	10

If you win (mark off 2 Poison units on the *Adventure Sheet*), you dash out, but by this time there is no sign of Vetch. You are not sure where you are. Do you venture down a dark lane straight away (turn to **271**) or enter a larger, busier street to your left (turn to **328**)?

217

You worm your way out through the large hole. You are now in the open, away from the town. Beyond a low hillock, you can see smoke rising and hear the sound of battering-rams smashing the Maze. You can also make out screams and orders shouted in guttural Orc accents, and you guess that the Uruz are defending their Maze stoutly. You creep away and in a small hollow you come across a bored-looking Orc guarding the raiding party's horses. Do you attack the Orc in order to take one of the horses (turn to **331**) or creep past (turn to **21**)?

218

You listen for the footsteps to stop, but, as soon as you are ready to follow, without warning a shadow appears in front of you. You are astounded as it takes the form of a dark, shrouded figure holding a staff. It speaks in a hoarse whisper: 'You are too late. The Medallion is taken by my Lord Chingiz's servants.' You strike at the figure, but your sword passes clean through it. The Necromancer laughs. 'So, you want to play games . . .' Turn to **56**.

219

You are in an empty room. Before you stands a Fiend who at once begins to rush towards you. If you have any flowers in your backpack, you can present one of them to the Fiend (make the appropriate adjustment on your *Adventure Sheet*). If you have no flowers, you will have to fight.

MAZE FIEND   SKILL 6   STAMINA 8

If you win, or if you have bribed the Fiend with flowers, return to **160** and throw the magic die for your next position.

220

The horse-trader invites you into the shack. You ask him the cost of hiring a sturdy steed. He fusses around and cannot seem to make up his mind. He tells you to wait while he consults his partner. Do you sit down on a bench and wait (turn to **14**) or do you get suspicious and leave (turn to **388**)?

221

Tunnels open up to the north and west. To the north, in a glimmer of daylight you see what appears to be a body lying in the middle of the path. To the west is a figure standing stock-still. Which tunnel do you choose: north (turn to **351**) or west (turn to **268**)?

222

You leave the poor demented wretch and walk on carefully alone. Suddenly the floor beneath you gives way and you drop on to a bed of spiked stakes where you die instantly. Your quest is over.

223

You enter another chamber, this one full of carvings of birds. You look on, astounded, as two Greyeagles of Kazan come to life and attack you. Fight each in turn.

	SKILL	STAMINA
First GREYEAGLE	6	11
Second GREYEAGLE	6	11

If you survive, you have a choice of two more doors. Do you choose the door on the right (turn to **254**) or the door on the left (turn to **186**)?

224

You have rightly been wary of anyone you may have met in this land; but it is obvious that he knows that what you told him was a pack of lies. He thanks you politely and crosses the bridge. When he is safely across, it collapses. You suspect Goblin Spell-casting. You cast around until you find another path, one that leads down the Ilkhan mountains. Turn to **278**.

225

The path is long and the way arduous. Stopping for a moment to get a stone out of your boot, you shake the stone out, only to discover it is a Yellow Gem (mark the Gem on your *Adventure Sheet*). By sheer chance (add 1 point to your LUCK), your path leads to a stone hut with a dirty sign tacked above it: 'Honest Gimcrak's Trading Post'. Do you choose to go inside in order to trade something (turn to **12**) or do you prefer to carry on along the road (turn to **391**)?

226

You step on to the perilous bridge of snow and walk hesitantly across. Throw 2 dice for your weight, and add 2 if you are carrying more than 10 gold coins. Throw 2 dice for the strength of the bridge. If your weight is greater than the strength of the bridge, it collapses and you fall to your doom in the snowy chasm. If your weight is less than or equal to the strength of the bridge, you cross safely. Turn to 310.

227

The pain in your shoulder is agonizing. Suddenly an arrow flies past the bird, followed by another. Drukkah must be firing at the bird! A third arrow slams into the Grypvulture's wing and it plummets out of control, releasing its hold on you. Luckily, you land on your back in stagnant water (add 1 point to your LUCK). You pick yourself up but can see nothing but reeds surrounding the pond. Turn to 322.

228

You dislodge the true Medallion of the Uruz from the wall. You examine it carefully and see the number '1000' inscribed on the reverse of the Medallion. Suddenly the figure of Agellatha appears and speaks. 'Your efforts have been crowned with success. Now you must find the true path out of the Maze.' The vision fades. At that moment, something drops from the ceiling on to your back: it is a Mamlik Assassin, his dagger raised, ready to strike. Luckily, the dagger fails to penetrate your armour; it glances off and breaks; meanwhile you roll over and throw the Assassin off. If you have some Treffilli and know how to use it, you can now feel it vibrating. If you wish to use it in order to escape, turn to **179**. Otherwise, you will have to fight.

MAMLIK ASSASSIN   SKILL 9   STAMINA 10

If you win (mark off 2 Poison units on the *Adventure Sheet*), you rush through a metal door that slams shut behind you. Turn to **95**.

229

The mist seems to cover everything. Ahead, you can just make out three shadowy figures. They get closer and you see a Necromancer with two Mamliks. Do you dive into the water (turn to **32**) or rush back to the boat (turn to **51**)?

230

You lose yourself in the crowd but keep a wary eye on the Necromancer. A Mamlik appears, throws off the guise of a beggar, and shakes his head. The Necromancer goes into a towering rage. 'I *know* there is one of them here, I can smell the purity. I will kill them all!' She strikes the ground with her staff; you feel the earth tremble and then you hear the noise of rushing water. A great tidal wave crashes through the crowd and sweeps up everybody. You find it difficult to swim as you are swept away through the river valley. Throw 2 dice for the strength you need to swim to safety, then compare this with your STAMINA. If your STAMINA is greater than or equal to the strength needed, you make it to safety, get out of the torrent and dry yourself off (deduct 2 points from your STAMINA). You set off again and soon find a road. Turn to **23**.

If your STAMINA is less than the strength you need to swim ashore, you are dragged under by the weight of your sopping-wet clothing and you drown. Your quest ends here.

231

You stand in a room with water trickling down its walls. In front of you is a large staircase, and you feel compelled to climb it. Turn to **382** and mark your new position on the chart.

232

You walk along the corridor to the sound of echoing footsteps. Ahead, you can see a large number of metal spikes on the roof of the tunnel. If you wish to retrace your steps back to the tunnel going north, then turn to **305**. If you decide to continue, the tunnel turns a corner and you head north. Suddenly, the spikes begin to break off and drive into the ground. *Test your Luck* twice. If you are Unlucky, you are hit by a spike (deduct 4 points from your STAMINA, 1 point from your SKILL and mark off 1 Poison unit). If you are Lucky, you make it safely to the next door. You go through the door and it shuts behind you. Turn to **100**.

233

You stoop down to pick up a scroll. It falls apart in your hand. At the same time, you hear a sigh coming from the body as it also begins to disintegrate. All the objects lying around disappear in clouds of pungent, yellow smoke. The snow begins to fall heavily, and you know that you cannot stay there much longer. There are two distinct paths that lead away from Drago's Gate. Will you take the one on the left (turn to **177**) or the one on the right (turn to **314**)?

234

You have no way of stopping or controlling the plank-sled as it hurtles ever downwards. Eventually, however, you crash into a grassy bank at the bottom. A Kazanid is standing in front of you, holding a spear. He picks up the plank, puts it on a cart with a pile of others and then starts moaning to you. 'Somebody just kicked one of the tobaks down the chute. I'm not saying you did it – but it's dangerous standing here collecting tobaks all day long . . . Hey, who are you?' You draw your sword and step towards him. At this threatening gesture, he faints, so you make good your escape into the grassland. The land here is flatter and more open. The path you are following divides. Which way do you take: the left fork (turn to 379) or the right fork (turn to 122)?

235

You walk carefully towards the obelisk. It is intricately carved with galloping horses – and there, on the top, you see the Medallion! You examine the area carefully, fearing one last test. There are holes in the ground and in the walls; peering into the holes, you can see arrowheads poking out. You suspect that it is the weight of the Medallion that is keeping the arrows from firing, and you will have to replace it with exactly the equivalent weight. If you have sufficient gold coins, how much do you think the Medallion weighs: 5 gold coins (turn to 307) or 10 gold coins (turn to 199)? If you have no gold coins, or you just wish to grab the Medallion, turn to 291.

236

You walk along the tunnel and notice some odd-looking holes in the walls. Suddenly a small furry creature rolls out of one of the holes. You watch it carefully as it stretches itself and begins to purr; it looks very sweet. Do you decide to stroke it (turn to **113**) or, opting for discretion rather than valour, do you avoid it (turn to **362**)?

237

You hold the Grey Talon tight. A ghost figure of the hawk flutters on to your shoulder. All else is still and time has no meaning. The bird speaks in your ear in a chirruping squawk: 'See the pattern I stand on, there, is the secret for the true path through the Maze. The top is the entrance to the north, and the bottom is the exit to the south. Follow the true path and you shall have the Medallion.' The spirit of the hawk returns to its body, and you walk towards the entrance. Turn to **366**.

238

You drink deeply from the cool, sweet water. You feel refreshed and in good heart for the tasks and perils to come (add 4 points to your STAMINA and do *not* mark off the next Poison unit you come to). You push the door open and enter; it closes behind you with a strong thud. Turn to **292**.

239

You walk down to the harbour. You see a ship that seems to be ready to set sail. Kazanid sailors, thieves, beggars, Dwarfs, and all manner of folk are milling round it. You ask a passer-by where the ship is bound and he replies: 'The Dragon coast of Kazilik.' You know that the Kazilik possess a Maze and that they have a Medallion. Do you wish to ask about getting passage on the ship (turn to **128**) or do you carry on along the harbour (turn to **339**)?

240

You walk purposefully along the corridor and then notice two blocks of stone with dice-markings, suspended from the ceiling. As you pass, they fall to the ground. Throw 2 dice. If you throw 9–12, add 1 point to your LUCK. In front of a door before you, you observe the word 'WEIGHS' carved on the wall. You push open the door and it shuts behind you. Turn to **349**.

241

You allow the old woman to gloat over her treasure-chest. Finally, she whispers a spell and a golden snake rises out of the chest. Crooning to it, she strokes its head and slips it into her pocket. Then she hands you 15 gold coins (mark the coins on your *Adventure Sheet*), and makes the following speech: 'You have helped me, brave adventurer; now I may be of help to you. I am the repository of many secrets, what do you wish to know?' You decide to reveal to her some details of your quest for the throne. 'Ah, Segrek's Select, you are in great danger. Chingiz is overturning the great traditions. To achieve ultimate success, you must seek the Medallions. Follow this path to Uruz. When you stand before the entrance to the great Maze, look to the top left for the pattern that is the key to the Maze. Remember, you must enter from the top or the north. I know the Maze well, for I helped fashion it when I was young, and my powers then were keen.' Without another word she picks up the chest and disappears down the path.

You set off in the opposite direction. The path you are taking is difficult and rough; to your left lies an easier, flatter route that leads in the direction of some birds circling in the sky. Do you take the left-hand path (turn to **115**) or keep on the path indicated by the old woman (turn to **161**)?

242

You do not think it wise to enter without first checking where you are, so you edge along the wall. Suddenly you feel a coldness in your bones and the mist swirls apart to reveal a Necromancer. If you have not achieved Necromancer fighting ability, you are immediately put under a spell. You cannot see, hear, or touch and your quest ends here.

If you have the ability to fight Necromancers, use the level you reached as your SKILL score for this combat.

NECROMANCER   SKILL 9   STAMINA 8

If you win (mark off 2 Poison units on the *Adventure Sheet*), you decide after all to go back and jump in through the window. Turn to **174**.

243

Adana-Broussah throws a startled glance in your direction as the Necromancer announces that there is one in the horde whom he wants and is willing to pay dearly for. Beshbalik is tempted by the bag of gold held up by the evil creature. Adana-Broussah tells you to make yourself scarce. Do you ride off (turn to **60**) or do you have, and know how to use, two sprigs of Treffilli to make yourself invisible (turn to **10**)?

244

You drop like a lead weight from the tower. Suddenly, a strange force surges out of the stone; it has the likeness of a great hand that catches you and draws you safely to an overhanging stone block. You cannot understand how or why this has happened (add 1 point to your LUCK). Turn to **381**.

245

You continue on the upward path for a long time. It is difficult and partially blocked here and there with landslides and minor avalanches. Eventually you come to a great icy chasm. On the far side is a raised drawbridge, guarded by what looks like an ice warrior. Further scrutiny reveals an obelisk with a hole in the top of it: obviously you have to throw something into the hole to get the bridge to lower. If you have a metal ball, turn to **315**. Otherwise, there is no way across the chasm. You will have to turn back and waste time going down the mountain and into the forest: mark off 2 Poison units, deduct 4 points from your STAMINA and turn to **88**.

246

You enter a smithy. The first thing you see is a small Dwarf crouched, shivering, in the corner. Then you notice a Mamlik and two Orcs who are trying to listen to something through one of the house-walls. They do not sense you, and the Dwarf motions for you to get out quick. You go back into the street. Turn to **98**.

247

You stand in a room that has stone walls full of small niches. The floor is covered with little darts and the skeletons of three human beings are lying on the ground. Suddenly little poisoned darts shoot out through the holes in the walls. *Test your Luck.* If you are Lucky, you are hit only once (deduct 1 point from your STAMINA). If you are Unlucky, throw 2 dice and deduct the resulting total from your STA-MINA. Mark off 1 Poison unit. If you are still alive, return to **160** and throw the magic die to determine where you go next.

248

You carefully pick three sprigs – and the plant then begins to wither and die. Add the sprigs to your *Adventure Sheet*. You enter another door which seals tight behind you. Turn to **393**.

249

Flaxwort turns to the right and, after a short distance, drops you off and wishes you good luck. You find yourself in a small square that is teeming with people. Just then you see two Dwarfs being force-marched to the centre of the square and chained up by four Orcs. From what you overhear in the crowd, this is one of their regular executions held for disloyalty. Next a horn is sounded, and three Gargoyles swoop down from the tower above. They tear the first Dwarf to pieces but, in so doing, they accidentally break the bonds of the second. He hares off into the crowd and passes close to you, with one of the Orcs in hot pursuit. Do you want to help the Dwarf (turn to **6**) or do you keep a low profile and walk away (turn to **208**)?

250

The riders line up in front of you. 'Who are you, stranger? Why do you not bow to your Yigenik masters? You forfeit your life if you do not speak.' One of them dismounts and, drawing a scimitar, makes several cuts in the air with it. 'Bow down, slave. Your life is mine.' Do you speak up and tell them that you are one of Segrek's Select (turn to **181**), bow down and mutely take the consequences (turn to **304**), or prepare to fight the warrior (turn to **211**)?

251

You stay in the middle of the group of Marauders, knowing that there will be a confusion of smells. The Mamlik passes by you, and returns to Besh-balik. They start an argument, but eventually the Mamlik, fuming, rides off on his black steed. Turn to **319**.

252

You have to pass close by two Orcs who are sitting on a rock. The falling snow has built up into two pointed cones on their heads. They are eating strange yellow fruit and spitting out the pips, betting on which of them can spit the pips the furthest. They ignore you, so you decide to stroll quietly past them. Just then one of them spots you and calls out: 'Hey you, come over here.' You go over to them and they explain that they want you to stand ten paces away so that they can have a competition to find out which will be the first to land a pip on your hat. Do you agree to do this (turn to **24**) or do you draw your sword and attack them (turn to **320**)?

253

He rubs his hands gleefully as you count out the money (deduct 5 coins from your *Adventure Sheet*). Then he leads you to a stone hut that is well protected against the elements, with windows that are all heavily barred. Inside, it is warm and cosy. 'I think that you are one of the Select,' he tells you, hugely pleased at his own cleverness. 'Chingiz wants to kill you, but I know the secret of the Maze at Bogomil . . . yes, you must have a medallion.' He stops talking and then looks at you, as though for the first time, 'I *will* tell you . . . when first you enter, turn west, then north, then west, and so on until you get out. It's simple.' He seems vastly satisfied with himself and asks you if you wish to rest. You may rest in the hut (turn to **84**) or, if you prefer, go out straight away (turn to **150**).

254

You are in a room filled with the statues of stallions. Suddenly three of them come to life; they stamp their feet and snort, crashing their hoofs down on the stone floor. Throw 1 die six times to show the path you take between the stallions. List the result on your *Adventure Sheet*. Then throw 1 die to show where the stallions stamp. If this number matches the first number in the sequence you have written down, you are hit (deduct 4 points from your STAMINA). Repeat the process five more times and compare throws. If you survive, you succeed in reaching another door. Turn to **359**.

255

The crowd on the road spills out into the market-place of the small town of Torrez. Here are game-sters, jugglers and acrobats, as well as market stalls. If you are carrying any gold, you feel for your purse. It has gone! Someone has stolen *all* your gold except the coin that you sensibly keep in your boot. Deduct all gold coins but 1 from your *Adventure Sheet*.

You take out your one coin, knowing that you will need gold in order to succeed in your quest. You wander round the market in a daze. Do you go to the left (turn to **107**) or do you go right (turn to **213**)?

256

Geronicus hands you the phial, which you drink while they lead you through various back-streets to the Fortress. You feel a stabbing pain in your shoulder as you are pulled against your will towards a sheer rock-face. You pass through the rock, but when you reach the other side you fall to your knees in agony (deduct 2 points from your STAMINA, 1 point from your SKILL and mark off 2 Poison units). You realize that something is dreadfully wrong. Suddenly a Necromancer stands before you, staff in hand. He speaks to you in a hoarse, rough voice: 'Yes, we have found this entrance and tainted it with the Black Poison of Lisz. Now, proud adventurer, you DIE!' If you do not have Necromancer fighting ability, your quest ends here in dreadful agony and death. If you have the skill to fight the shadowy beings, turn to 365.

257

Making progress through the forest is very arduous. You have to cut your way through a mass of undergrowth (deduct 2 points from your STAMINA). Turn to 86.

258

You are taken out of the hut. You hear a horn being blown, and a crowd gathers, forming a circle. The woman, who is called Agellatha, stands in the middle and raises her hands for silence. Two fierce black bulls are led in; however, they move as though they were in a trance. A cord is tied to the neck of each of the bulls; the other ends are looped around your forearms tightly and the last foot or so of loose cord hangs from your hands. 'You must use all your strength to pull the two bulls together and tie a knot in the two cords,' Agellatha explains. 'If you fail, you will be torn asunder.' Throw 3 dice to discover the strength of the bulls. Throw 2 dice and add the result to your current STAMINA to find out the power of your attempt. Your strength must be greater than that of the bulls for you to succeed. If you fail, your quest ends here. If you succeed, turn to **28**.

259

You sneak out and walk along a corridor. Ahead is another door that is partly open. You peek in, to see Vetch with an Orc; they are unchaining a hideous Gargoyle. The Gargoyle senses your presence, screams then rushes out after you. You run into a dead-end, turn and pull out your sword.

GARGOYLE   SKILL 9   STAMINA 10

If you win (mark off 1 Poison unit on the *Adventure Sheet*), the others by now have fled, so cautiously you leave the building. You now have a choice: a dark lane which lies in front of you (turn to **271**) or a busier, well-lit street to the left (turn to **328**).

260

You rush up the staircase, past a small open window. Just then, you hear the sound of someone coming down the stairs, so you decide to climb out on to the window-ledge. Outside, you find a narrow walkway and, as you edge along, three Gargoyles appear and start screaming at you. You try to ward them off with your sword, but they make such a noise, fluttering and squawking, that you are not surprised to see one of Chingiz's Kazanid guards follow you out on to the ledge. He tells you that being found in this part of the Fortress means you have forfeited your life and he pulls out a scimitar.

KAZANID GUARD   SKILL 7   STAMINA 10

If you survive (mark off 1 Poison unit on the *Adventure Sheet*), you watch the Gargoyles flutter down after the body of your opponent, as it falls to the cliffs below. You climb back in through the window and, on hearing some more footsteps, run into another room and clamber up the wide chimney of an empty fireplace. Turn to **82**.

261

You find a good place to hide beneath a pile of loose turfs, and stay there until you think any potential danger will be past. You feel better after the rest (add 2 points to your STAMINA). When you get up, you find yourself surrounded by a group of silent horsemen. A miserable-looking Orc is chained to one of the horses and there are Gryphawks circling above the group. One of the riders moves forward and introduces himself formally as Bhoriss Canterstrike; he demands to know your business 'in these lands of the Bogomils'. Do you reveal that you are one of Segrek's Select (turn to **91**) or do you tell them you are a travelling merchant (turn to **183**)?

262

You stand in a room which contains the corpse of a Mamlik Assassin. His neck is encircled by a large snake. Even in death he clutches his deadly dagger in a grip of iron. Add 1 point to your LUCK. Return to **160** and throw the magic die for your next position.

263

You approach the Troll warily; his strength is formidable. He bows and introduces himself as Skrutch, of the Vizier's Own Trollfighter Cohorts. He stands to attention, salutes and then ruefully has to admit that he's lost. 'I'm due on guard at the Bogomil road and I'm already late.' You agree to accompany him. You are surprised – and pleased – that he possesses a map. However, he holds it upside down, and it's obvious that he cannot read. The map is very accurate and you are able to lead him out of the forest and on to the start of the Bogomil road. Suddenly, you are confronted by two Trolls who, on seeing you, pull out their short-swords. At the same time they hurl abuse at Skrutch and call out to him to kill you. Do you make a dash to the right (turn to **8**) or do you attempt to escape to the left (turn to **111**)?

264

Smoke and dust are swirling around you, and through the haze you can see that large stone blocks have collapsed from the walls and roof of the Maze. You hear footsteps approaching and dive behind some fallen blocks.

'Captain Snapskull, have you the Medallion?' The voice is that of an Orc. 'No, sir,' comes the reply, 'but we have found two of them dead. And there is another one close by.' He sniffs. 'Lord Chingiz wants them all dead,' says the first voice. 'None must appear at the Fortress with a Medallion: the power of the Throne is still too strong.'

You see two possible ways out of the crumbling Maze. Which do you choose: to prise loose a block on the left (turn to **78**) or to scramble through a large hole straight ahead (turn to **217**)?

265

You stumble around the chamber in the dark and find another door. It opens easily, then seals tight behind you. You feel an intense heat and see a white-hot glow ahead. You are passing the Cauldron, the force that powers the Heart of the Throne. You run quickly past the Cauldron. Throw 1 die and deduct the result from your STAMINA score. You cannot avoid being affected by the intense heat. Mark off 2 Poison units on your *Adventure Sheet*. You enter another tunnel. Turn to **360**.

266

The old man does not seem to touch the branches of the bushes; they merely part as he passes. You, however, have to fight your way through. Suddenly he stops and turns; he has remembered something. 'Chingiz has summoned the demonic Necromancers, beware of them. Geronicus, er, that's me, will help you attain a level of fighting ability against them. If you can achieve level six, seven or eight, you will be able to fight them in the flesh.' Geronicus proceeds to summon up a magical pattern:

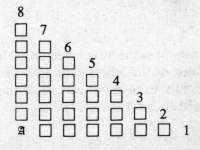

You have to stand at A and throw a die as many times as it takes to reach numbers that denote the different SKILL levels. On a throw of 5–6, you move up one block; on a throw of 2–4, you move one block to the right; on a throw of 1, you must deduct 1 point from your STAMINA, and you do not move. You may make *two* attempts overall, but must deduct 1 point from your LUCK if you decide to make the second attempt. If you reach level six, seven or eight, mark Necromancer Fighting Skill in the Abilities Box of your *Adventure Sheet*.

Geronicus summons three eagles. He tells you that they will help you find the correct paths in order to seek the six Medallions Of Kazan. Which bird do you pick: the Black Eagle (turn to **163**), the White Eagle (turn to **188**) or the Golden Eagle (turn to **2**)?

267

You run to help. The figure – a woman – sees you and tries to draw her sword, but she hardly has the strength pull it out of its scabbard. She lies back and you offer her a mouthful of water. As she sips it, you see that an arrowhead is lodged in her neck and that her leather armour is scuffed and torn. She raises her head and speaks in a whisper: 'I am Barabba of the West Moor . . . I must get to Sharrabbas, I am one of the Select of Segrek.' You see the pallor of death rising in her face. You try to quieten her, but she begins to rave: 'The Medallion . . . no . . . you shall not . . .' Then she recovers slightly and you tell her of your own status. She smiles. 'I am done for, I know. Take the Hulugu Medallion, I bequeath it to you.' From a pocket she takes out the Medallion and hands it to you. 'At Sharrabbas, seek the Wolfsbane at the Cross Keys . . . he will . . .' She shudders, then gasps and dies in your arms. You gaze at the Eagle etched on the Medallion; on the reverse is the number '1000'. Add 2 points to your LUCK and list the Medallion on your *Adventure Sheet*. You salute your brave comrade and set off again. Turn to **81**.

268

You head westwards. You get close to the figure, but still it does not move; you even poke it with your sword, but it seems to be made of rock. Shrugging, you pass by – then your ears are assaulted by a strange wailing noise which gets louder and louder until it begins to numb your mind. You pound at the figure with the flat of your sword, and that seems to have some effect in lessening the racket. Fight the Screecher as in normal combat.

SCREECHER   SKILL 7   STAMINA 8

If you win, the noise stops and you pass through a door that shuts behind you. Turn to **64**.

269

The corridor comes to a corner and you peek round, to see a room filled with a gaggle of Dungeon Beasts. They scuttle up to you and block your progress. You cannot fight them all. There is a large open window to one side of the room. If you have the Power of Storm-bringing, turn to **47**. Otherwise, you must turn back and go the other way: turn to **369**.

270

You take hold of the rod. Suddenly, leather thongs spring out from it and encircle your wrists. You are unable to let go as the line pulls you down into the pool. You hold your breath as you are dragged to the bottom and a strange creature, half-man half-fish, dives into the water after you. It is an Elkiem! Quickly you loosen the thongs but, before you can reach the surface, the monster grabs you. Deduct 1 point from your SKILL for the duration of this combat only. If you throw double-1 in your Attack Round, you have drowned.

ELKIEM   SKILL 7   STAMINA 8

If you survive (mark off 1 Poison unit on the *Adventure Sheet*), you haul yourself out of the pool and take a deep breath; then you walk on, shuddering and shivering. Turn to **167**.

271

You walk towards the Fortress. The only visible way in seems to entail climbing a long staircase of stone steps that are guarded by a dozen bored-looking Orcs with a Mamlik captain. You know immediately that you cannot attempt *this* route. You look around and notice a woman standing by a tall obelisk and carrying a large basket of flowers. She waves to you. Do you approach her (turn to **162**) or carry on looking for another way into the stronghold (turn to **276**)?

272

You find yourself back among the Yigenik. They have taken care of all the opposition and are now in the process of stripping their enemies' bodies of weapons and valuables. Eventually, the whole party sets off and rides for a long time until below you you see a large settlement in a mountain valley. Here you are brought before an old woman who asks you if you feel strong enough to undertake the Test of the Yigenik. Do you reply that you wish to undergo the Test (turn to **346**) or do you decide to leave now in order to build up your powers and abilities (turn to **209**)?

273

You continue to the north. In the torchlight, you see a word carved on the stone wall: 'MEDALLION'. You pass a metal grille and breathe in a waft of fresh air; you feel strangely energetic (add 3 points to your STAMINA). You go through a door that seals behind you. Turn to **153**.

274

Thwarted, the Trolls decide to arrest you. You pull out your sword with one swift move. Fight each Troll in turn.

	SKILL	STAMINA
First TROLL	8	9
Second TROLL	9	10

If you win (mark off 2 Poison units on the *Adventure Sheet*), the cart-driver spits in the direction of the dead bodies, takes back the gold he had been forced to hand over and offers you a ride on the cart. 'Scum! Chingiz's lackeys making us pay illegal tolls. Pray the gods send us a true ruler soon.' He looks at you sideways, and you believe you can detect a twinkle in his eye. Turn to **155**.

275

The land is very mountainous. The snow has begun to whip up, and you find the going difficult. The wind seems to shriek in your ears. You feel very tired (deduct 2 points from your STAMINA); before you, you see a figure whispering to you to sit and rest. Do you choose to obey the soothing voice (turn to **15**) or do you force yourself to go on through the storm (turn to **169**)?

276

You set off behind a cart, trying to look as much as possible like one of the locals. There are numerous Orc patrols and you pass the occasional Mamlik. Suddenly, a small bird lands on your shoulder, then hops to the ground and into a quiet alley. You follow it and stare as it scrawls the 'A' rune, the sign for Astragal, in the dirt. You watch in amazement as the bird proceeds to write a complete message from the wizard.

'I hope this winged messenger reaches you in time. If you have not already done so, contact one Mandrake Wolfsbane and no other. He is usually to be found smoking a large smelly pipe at the Dragon's Wings Tavern – where my absent-minded brother wizard, Geronicus, will be signalling unceasingly from its chimney with puffs of smoke.' The bird then hops over to the message, erases it with its wings and flies away.

You stay and rest in the shadows for a few hours, before setting out to follow the trail of smoky puffs and find the tavern. Turn to 298.

277

You pass through the remains of the web which begins to reseal itself almost immediately, just as a Giant Spider drops down from the roof behind you. You rush away from the hideous beast. Turn to 76.

278

You follow a track that leads towards an open plain. Occasionally you pass clumps of trees and bushes, and you can hear rushing water. The track begins to get busy with other people: travellers on foot, on horseback and in carts. Everyone is heading in the same direction; from what you overhear, it is market-day in the local town of Torrez. You merge into the crowd and feel safe – until you see a road-block ahead. A large group of Orcs is inspecting everyone who passes. Do you decide to get off the road (turn to **159**) or do you stay and take your chances with the crowd (turn to **308**)?

279

You hand over the 10 gold coins (deduct 10 gold coins from your *Adventure Sheet*). The bandit leader smiles and pockets the money. 'Head for the lands of the Bogomil. This road is the quickest and the guards upon it are not crack troops. If you pass the Test, the Maze is not complex: turn west when you first enter, then north and west alternately, until you reach the Medallion.' He makes it sound so simple, but warns that others may be there already: 'The Medallion may already have been taken.' Add 1 LUCK point and turn to **383**.

280

You walk along the road to Uruz among a crowd of Kazanids who are also leaving the fair. Carts pass the walkers and some offer rides 'for a price'. You ask one that stops, 'How much?' and he replies. 'Two gold coins.' If you can afford it, do you agree to ride on the cart (turn to 364)? If you have no money or you prefer to walk anyway, turn to 101.

281

Cautiously you make your way along the dusty corridor. Just as you are turning a corner to the north, you trip over a skeleton slumped in the shadows; it is wearing the remains of ancient leather armour and you stare as a large worm pops out of the skull's eye-socket. Suddenly there is a screech from above you and a tall, gangly creature lands on your back, knocking you down. You roll away and pull out your sword in one swift move. The creature has sword-like arms and long pointed fangs.

LIFESUCKER   SKILL 7   STAMINA 8

If you survive (mark off 2 Poison units on the *Adventure Sheet*), you continue north until the passage turns to the west. You reach an open metal door and pass through; it clangs shut behind you. Turn to 342.

282

You find yourself in a room that has a Medallion, etched with a snake motif, strung up in front of you on a length of fine cord. Suddenly, the ground beneath you opens up and you fall into the mouth of a huge Serpent (deduct 2 points from your STAMINA). Turn to 97 and mark your new position on the chart.

283

You make your way cautiously, but the lights that are coming from panels in the walls seem to have little effect on you (deduct 1 point from your STAMINA). You turn a corner and head south (deduct 2 more points from your STAMINA). You begin to feel weak and realize that the lights are sapping your strength. You run towards the far door. Throw 2 dice for your speed, then 2 dice for the speed with which the magic takes effect on you. If your speed is equal to or greater than the effect of the magic, you get safely through the door. Turn to 393. Otherwise, all your STAMINA is sapped, and you collapse and die. Your quest is over.

284

You have drunk the potion of the exploding death. Your insides make a conscious decision to leave your body and you die an agonizing death. Your quest ends here.

285

You open the next door, to find a woman sitting on the Throne of Sharrabbas, surrounded by four chained Ogres. The woman smiles. 'Welcome, brave adventurer. My father and his Mamliks found you a difficult foe, but you shall not take possession of the Throne – it is *mine*! He wouldn't let me have it, so I had to kill him. Now, I must kill YOU.' She rushes towards you, dagger raised. You stop her arm and squeeze her wrist; the dagger drops to the floor and begins to burn. She collapses in a heap and calls out, 'Go on then, sit on the Throne – and let my Ogres tear you limb from limb.' The Ogres are suddenly released from their chains and leap forward to attack. Do you fight them (turn to **335**) or put your sword away and walk straight to the Throne (turn to **154**)?

286

The cart creaks along and Drukkah, the driver, doesn't ask you any questions. The trail is long and he explains that he is heading for a large trading-post in central Kazan. In the long hours he tells you tales of when Segrek was strong and the badlands were well policed. At one point he stops the cart, stands up and, head cocked to one side, looks around the reedy landscape. You follow his example and draw your sword in readiness. Suddenly, two Grypvultures come skimming across the reeds and attack. Drukkah drops the first with a swipe; however, you miss, and the huge bird sinks its claw into your shoulder, lifts you off the cart and carries you high over the reeds. Do you risk stabbing it (turn to **309**) or do you choose to wait for it to put you down (turn to **227**)?

287

As you ride, Zaranj explains that the Korkut are strong believers in luck, chance and good and bad fortune. 'The Test and the Maze are like no other, but a strong and brave adventurer attracts good fortune,' he declaims. Eventually, after a long ride, you reach the heights above Korkut. You see that the region is a port, with several ships in the harbour. Zaranj leads you through the twisting streets to the fortress; here he informs the Elders and Mages that you aspire to the Throne. There is much fuss and preparation. You are rested and fed (add 4 points to your STAMINA) and finally you are called to the Chamber of Chance. Turn to **77**.

288

The Goblin has pulled out a large scimitar and stands his ground. He sneers at you: 'I know your smell, you have the scent of the Select. You will die.'

GOBLIN   SKILL 5   STAMINA 5

If you survive, you begin to worry about the bird he has released; you realize that it must be a signal. You decide to make a run for it. Turn to **96**.

289

When you wake up, your first thoughts are for your belongings. Although you are tied up and cannot move, you believe that nothing has been taken from you. A young Kazanid girl enters and feeds you some nourishing broth (add 1 point to your STAMINA). Reluctantly, she answers some of your questions: 'Yes, you are wanted by the Lowlanders. They did say "All who pass towards Sharrabbas, all lone travellers." They asked that nothing should be removed and they are coming for you when the storm dies down. The message hawks have been dispatched.' Then she leaves. For a precious moment before the other guards return, you are alone. Do you roll over towards the fire and burn off your bonds (turn to 371) or do you prefer not to risk an escape attempt yet (turn to 178)?

290

The stallion has a fiery temperament and is difficult to ride over the rough ground. You suffer from the fast pace and, by the time you stop to camp, you are shattered (deduct 2 points from your STAMINA). Turn to 372.

291

You grab the Medallion and are instantly sprayed by a volley of arrows. You stagger along the passage. Throw 1 die for the number of hits you suffer and deduct 3 points from your STAMINA for each hit. If you survive (mark off 2 Poison units), you look at the Medallion: on the reverse is the number '1000'. You crawl out of the Maze into the bright sunlight. Turn to **295**.

292

You are faced with a choice: a tunnel to the east (turn to **25**) or one to the south (turn to **205**). Which route do you take?

293

You are in a smoky tunnel. Slowly the smoke clears and you see a black-cloaked figure holding a staff. He lifts it and strikes the ground. Huge fanged worms shoot out of the earth and block your way. You run back up the tunnel as the walls begin to collapse all round you. You are sure that you can hear chanting over the rumble of collapsing structures. Turn to **264**.

294

You scramble ashore and look around. It is very misty and you cannot see where you are treading, so you step carefully until you come upon a high stone wall. You walk along the side of it until you find an open window. Inside are a lot of phials, bottles and jars; there are magical paintings on the walls, and in the middle of the room is a large open chest, full of jewels, rings and coins. Do you climb in through the window (turn to **174**) or carry on along the side of the wall (turn to **242**)?

295

You are standing in a stone trench; bemused, you watch a wisp of smoke transform itself into a figure that greets you. 'Brave adventurer, you have traversed the Maze of the Bogomil, a great feat. If you do not have the Medallion, good luck to you in your search. If you do have the Medallion, good luck in your quest for the Throne. Fare thee well.' The figure disappears and you climb out of the trench. You are in open country. You walk on for many hours and eventually find a good place to rest. Turn to **399**.

296

You join the other labourers. It is very hard work; it appears that they are busy rebuilding the outer defences of the city. It's obvious that Chingiz expects war from the clans if he becomes the ruler of Kazan. When the work is done, you are exhausted (deduct 2 points from your STAMINA, mark off 1 Poison unit and add 2 gold coins on your *Adventure Sheet*). The workers disperse and you carry on walking. Turn to **350**.

297

The path you take leads in the direction of a range of very high mountains. At one point you see a possible track leading down into a heavily forested valley. Which path do you wish to follow: up into the mountains (turn to **37**) or down into the forest (turn to **88**)?

298

The Dragon's Wings Tavern is packed. Several fires are blazing, but the smokiest corner is that part of the room where an old man is sitting with a box on his lap. By his side is another, puffing at a smelly pipe. You head for the pair of them. If you have not met them before, the man with the pipe looks at you carefully then holds out a small crystal that glows red. He introduces himself as Mandrake Wolfsbane and his companion as Geronicus. (If you have met the absent-minded Mage before, he does not recognize you now.)

You sit down and Mandrake begins to brief you. 'Chingiz has tried to spellbreak the ancient secret entrances to the Fortress. Geronicus alone possesses a set of the phials that point the way and open the hidden gates for the Select. All the others have been taken by the devilish Necromancers who are trying to discover the secrets of the Throne. *You* are the last hope of the Kazanids; you must enter the Fortress, with Medallion or without, and sit on the Throne, in order to rid us of the evil of Chingiz and his deadly daughter, Meghan-na-Durr. Now, look into your heart and choose a phial.'

Which phial do you choose:

The Dagger?	Turn to 361
The Half-Moon?	Turn to 338
The Cross?	Turn to 256
The Holy Triangle?	Turn to 124

299

Captain Sneerblood shows you to a cabin with a hammock already slung, then gives you four large, foul-smelling, unbreakable ship's biscuits. You get into the hammock just as the ship begins to heave and pitch. You decide you are fairly comfortable (add 1 point to your SKILL and 4 points to your STAMINA). Turn to **189**.

300

You run, looking for good cover, but then see a Grypvulture swooping down from above. You turn round, pull out your sword and swipe at the bird.

GRYPVULTURE   SKILL 6   STAMINA 8

If you win, you find that while you have been busy slaying the Grypvulture, three Orc guards have caught up with you. Fight each one in turn.

	SKILL	STAMINA
First ORC	7	6
Second ORC	7	6
Third ORC	7	6

If you survive (mark off 3 Poison units on the *Adventure Sheet*), you decide to stay off the road and hide for a while. Turn to **261**.

301

There is no time to roll away. You manage to stay the assassin's hand and a ring falls from his gloved finger. He gives up the struggle and leaps out through the door. You peer out through the barred window and see him release a small Gryphawk, then ride off. You pick up the ring (mark it on your *Adventure Sheet*). You cannot find the beggar, so you go outside. Turn to **150**.

302

You enter a room that has a huge beam suspended in the middle of it. Above the beam is a glass bowl containing 10 gold coins. You walk under it. Check your STAMINA. If it is an *odd* number, you upset the balance and get the coins (add them to your *Adventure Sheet*). If it is an *even* number, nothing happens. Return to **160** and throw the magic die.

303

The ragged bundle stirs. She is not bound but appears quite weak. She looks at you and tells you that you will be lucky if they decide to kill you straight away. 'The huntresses of Owlshriek believe that they gain power from inflicting pain and torture.' Suddenly the old woman stares at your shoulder where some bits of greenery are lodged in the joints of your armour. 'Treffilli! You've brought me Treffilli.' At first jubilant, she becomes suspicious. 'Who are you that bring me Treffilli?' You explain your quest to her. She smiles and tells you that she will help you now. She picks up the sprigs and crushes them while muttering some words in a foreign tongue . . . both of you at once become invisible. She unties you and together you walk past the guards. You collect your sword from another hut, and she chuckles as that also disappears. Just as you become visible again you enter the forest, and the old woman invites you to accompany her. Do you accept her offer (turn to **130**) or leave her and carry on alone (turn to **368**)?

304

You know that you cannot fight them all and that it might prejudice your chances of eventual success to reveal your status. You drop down on your knees. They all laugh. 'You are lucky, fellow, we have had good hunting today, so get up.' The riders think this a terrific joke – but the smile is quickly wiped off their faces when they spot a large bird hovering in the distance. They ride off in pursuit. Turn to **18**.

305

You set off northwards. Some way behind you, a portcullis suddenly slams down, then another a little nearer. You realize that the gates behind you are getting closer and dropping quicker each time. You manage to run past one before it crashes to the ground, then sprint off for the next one by the final door. *Test your Luck.* If you are Unlucky, you are trapped by the portcullis; your quest is over – you have no means of stopping the poison from spreading through your body (mark off all the remaining Poison units). If you are Lucky, you make it, racing through a doorway just before the portcullis slams down behind you. Turn to **72**.

306

You brave the thieves' quarter. The Dwarf has given you excellent directions and you negotiate the busy streets easily with your possessions and pack strapped down, and one hand on your sword. As you are passing a small girl, a Gryphawk swoops down and attacks her; she screams and blood drips from her neck. Do you stop to help her (turn to **55**) or take no notice (turn to **373**)?

307

You take the Medallion and place the bag holding 5 gold coins down at the same time (deduct the gold from your *Adventure Sheet*). The bag sinks and, as you rush away, arrows fire at you. Throw 1 die. This is the number of arrows that hit you. Deduct 3 points from your STAMINA for each arrow that strikes. If you survive, you stagger out of the Maze. Looking at the Medallion, you see on its reverse the number '1000'. Turn to **295**.

308

The Orcs are standing in the middle of the road, letting the crowd filter through. At your side, a merchant carrying several large bags starts complaining to you: 'Searches, searches, always searches. This is what we'll have to look forward to if Chingiz becomes king. Me, I've got truffles here, from Gorak. You'd think ten gold coins a kazan-weight was a reasonable price to ask, I paid six. But no one seems to like them in this land. My name's Chogum, by the way, and I've got 110 kazanweights of the stuff.' You help the merchant carry his bags, thinking that the smell of the truffles will disguise any scent the Orcs may be trying to pick up from you. *Test your Luck*. If you are Lucky, the Orcs let you pass. Turn to **255**. If you are Unlucky, they look and sniff at you suspiciously, then grab you. Turn to **92**.

309

You stab at the Grypvulture. It screams and drops you. *Test your Luck*. If you are Unlucky, you fall badly (deduct 2 points from your SKILL and 4 points from your STAMINA. Mark off 2 Poison units). If you are Lucky, your fall is cushioned by reeds. Turn to **322**.

310

You take just a few steps on the other side of the chasm when you feel the ground begin to vibrate. Both snow-bridges collapse behind you. You stagger forward – but are stunned to see two Kazanid horsemen and one of the legendary Tusker Mammoths. The beast lurches heavily forward and stamps on the ice. Its rider draws an arrow aimed at your heart. You stand stock-still. The Tusker trumpets and suddenly encircles your waist with its trunk. Everything blacks out. Turn to **289**.

311

You cut your way through the forest until you come to a clearing. Sitting under an oak tree is an old man wearing wizard's robes; he is watching acorns fall, burrow into the ground, then appear as saplings. This seems to amuse him; he is chuckling and sniggering. Then he notices you standing there watching. 'Ah, I've been waiting for you,' he mumbles. 'Now . . . what was it I was to tell you? Astragal said not to forget.' He fingers a knot in his long beard fretfully, mutters to himself and wanders off among the thick bushes. Do you follow him (turn to **266**) or do you prefer to carry on alone (turn to **257**)?

312

Turn to **184**.

313

You climb the rigging and draw your sword. The first Dragon has been furiously breathing fire; however, when it sees you, its forces are spent and it can only snort. It flaps about as you strike at it.

KAZILIK DRAGON   SKILL 10   STAMINA 12

If you survive, the other Dragon has meanwhile set fire to the ship, seized several sailors in its talons and swooped away. The burning ship begins to sink. Striking out in the oily water, you grab a piece of driftwood and float to the coast. Turn to **348**.

314

You walk along the path, keeping one eye on some large birds circling overhead. The snow has stopped and the track begins to slope downwards. Soon you find yourself walking by a fast-flowing stream. As you bend over to drink some water, you see a shadow looming over you: it is a wizened old crone, dressed in tatters that might once have been finery. She introduces herself as Gehlehna and asks if you would like to earn some gold. She wants you to do a little job for her. Do you agree to help her (turn to **22**) or decide to ignore her request and carry on alone (turn to **115**)?

315

You take out the metal ball and swing it up over your head, aiming for the top of the obelisk. Throw 1 die, then throw 1 die again; if the numbers on the two dice match, you have succeeded first time. If they don't match, then deduct 1 point from your STAMINA and try again . . . as many times as it takes until you succeed. If you give up, you have to take a much longer route (turn to 88). If you succeed, the drawbridge is lowered over the chasm and the Frozen Warrior speaks: 'Pass, stranger.' You cross over and follow a path that slopes downwards until, eventually, it forks. Which way do you go now: to the right (turn to 81) or to the left (turn to 145)?

316

You are in a room of ice. The ice is increasing all the time and you have to hack at it to keep yourself from being enveloped. Throw 2 dice for the speed at which the ice grows and 2 dice for your speed at hacking it down. If the speed of ice build-up is greater than the speed of hacking, you are suffocated and frozen. Your quest is over. Otherwise, deduct 2 points from your STAMINA, return to 160 and throw the magic die.

317

You swing your sword and strike at a metal object. There is a gruff laugh and you feel a sword touch your back. 'So you think you can fight me in the dark? Well, good luck.'

If you have the ability of Darkfight, fight as normal; otherwise, deduct 2 points from your SKILL for this combat only.

DARK WARRIOR   SKILL 6   STAMINA 8

If you win, you stumble off in the dark. Turn to **214**.

318

There is a large crowd of people in front of you watching a procession, but you cannot see anything where you are standing. Do you push through the crowd (turn to **396**) or ignore it and head for the Fortress (turn to **271**)?

319

Adana-Broussah joins you. While she wipes the blood from her sword, she chatters animatedly to you. 'There has been some dispute with Chingiz about the cost of a proposed operation. Beshbalik is determined to continue rampaging around as a free agent. I'm afraid it won't be as easy as I had thought to approach Sharrabbas.' Do you now wish to slip away and travel on your own (turn to **88**) or stay with the Marauders (turn to **386**)?

320

You know that you dare not hang around while they play their stupid games; their commander will be along soon. You pull out your sword, and they are not slow in drawing theirs. Fight each in turn.

	SKILL	STAMINA
First ORC	7	6
Second ORC	7	6

If you win (mark off 2 Poison units on the *Adventure Sheet*), you manage to dash out of sight just as you hear someone approaching. You make your way down the mountain. Turn to **122**.

321

You awaken to find the hideous face of a Necromancer staring into yours. She is licking her lips, displaying her long pointed fangs. You are Spellbound and cannot move. Looking around, you can see other figures nearby, and you realize that you are at the top of one of the towers of the Fortress. Just then, trumpets sound and in marches Chingiz, surrounded by his bodyguard and with a woman in tow. 'So, this is the last of the Select,' he sneers. 'Well, how do you propose to kill this brave being?' The Necromancer points to a cauldron of boiling oil and some heavy boulders. 'Boiled and crushed,' she replies with a snigger. 'Too elaborate – throw the last of the Select over the edge of the tower.' With these damning words, he marches out. You are dragged over to the parapet, the spell upon you is broken and you are thrown into space. If you possess the Grey Talon of Sakar, you may turn to **43**; if you possess at least one Medallion, you may turn to **244**. However, if you have neither of these, turn to **83**.

322

You wade through the reeds for a long time. Eventually, you become aware of a peculiar cracking sound. A strange wooden creature suddenly rises up out of the reeds; it expands its limbs at a fantastic rate, towering over the land, and it seems to be looking for something. As quick as a flash, you drop down into the reeds – where you come face to face with a Kazanid woman. She motions for you to keep still and silent. The creature, a Kalamite, rattles about until it finds you; then it encircles your body with its giant hand, prior to lifting you up. Do you go for your sword now (turn to **104**) or do you play dead (turn to **195**)?

323

You turn to face the Elf. He looks a little the worse for wear. He leads you to a bench and you both sit down. 'Look, I know they're after you, I have the Sight, I can help you. I used to be in the court of Segrek, a High Elf no less!' You agree to let him help you and he hands you a small black bottle. 'Drink this. It's the only way to get past the senses of the mad Necromancer. The brew blots out all his mind-delving, we just pretend we're drunk.' You drink the mixture, which tastes awful (deduct 1 point from your STAMINA). You pass easily through the road-block and the Elf, who calls himself Lightfinger, tells you he has important information to sell you for 10 gold coins. If you have this much gold on your *Adventure Sheet* and wish to pay, turn to **71**. If you don't have the money, or you don't want to buy the information, you thank the Elf politely for his help and carry on along the road. Turn to **23**.

324

You stand facing a Minotaur who is holding a huge club and straddling the corpse of a Mamlik. The Minotaur attacks.

URUZ MINOTAUR   SKILL 9   STAMINA 9

If you win, the body of the Minotaur sinks into the ground. You look around and see two tunnels. Which do you choose: the one leading south (turn to **156**) or the other heading east (turn to **190**)?

325

You walk through the door and find yourself staring at a scene of carnage. Mamliks, Knights, Trolls and Goblins all lie dead in front of a Necromancer who is laughing wildly. He spins round, sees you and hurls a mass of small knives at you. *Test your Luck.* If you are Unlucky, throw 2 dice for the number of knives that hit you, then reduce your STAMINA by that amount. If you are Lucky, all the knives miss.

This is Zizzadek, the mad master of the undead beings. He turns himself into a Dragon of substance and lumbers forward to attack.

ZIZZADEK   SKILL 11   STAMINA 14

If you win (mark off 2 Poison units on the *Adventure Sheet*), the body decays to the accompaniment of an unworldly scream. You step over the other bodies to find two doors facing you. Which do you opt to go through: the left-hand one (turn to **158**) or the right-hand one (turn to **54**)?

326

There are too many of them for you to fight and hope to win, so you rush off up the mountainside. Suddenly, you are tripped and fall as a weighted thong, thrown by one of your pursuers, wraps itself around your ankles (deduct 1 point from your STAMINA). You are surrounded by evil, grinning faces. Jeering, they release you from the thong. Turn to **127**.

327

You stand in a room full of mirrors. Suddenly, the head of a serpent appears through the mirror on the floor and you fall down through its mouth into the darkness (deduct 2 points from your STAMINA). Turn to 157 and mark your new position on the chart.

328

You are in the Street of the Swordsmiths. One of the doors suddenly flies open and a group of Elves are marched out by a squad of armed Orcs. One of the Orcs hammers a notice on the wooden door. You walk over and read: 'Anyone caught helping or harbouring strangers: the penalty will be death. A reward of 30 gold coins will be paid for any stranger turned over to the authorities.' You turn round to find two Orcs looking thoughtfully at you. You run to the door. *Test your Luck*. If you are Unlucky, the door is locked and you are surrounded by a squad of Orcs. One of them hits you over the head. Turn to 321.

If you are Lucky, the door is open. You enter, lock and bolt it, run through the workshop, replacing your blade with a Kazan Surefighter (add 1 point to your SKILL) and go out through a back door. Turn to 65.

329

You hurry on by, but when you look back the nature of the bundle reveals itself. A large leather covering has been thrown off, and you see a Goblin in the act of releasing a Gryphawk. The bird flies off and disappears over the mountain. Do you return to attack the Goblin (turn to **288**) or continue your journey (turn to **96**)?

330
POWER TO CHANGE METAL OBJECTS

You have drunk the mixture that gives you this Power. Note the fact on your *Adventure Sheet*. If this is your first choice, return to **45** and choose again. If this is your second choice, turn to **74**.

331

You descend upon the Orc, but he moves with surprising swiftness.

GUARDIAN ORC   SKILL 7   STAMINA 6

If you win (mark off 1 Poison unit on the *Adventure Sheet*), tether one horse, cause the others to scatter, then ride off on your chosen mount. Turn to **148**.

332

You stand in front of a torchlit panel showing six circles with, on each, the drawing of an animal: the Bull of Uruz; the Eagle of Hulugu; the Fangtiger of Yigenik; the Snake of Korkut; the Horse of Bogomil and the Dragon of Kazilik. If you do not possess a Medallion, turn to **61**. If you have one or more Medallions, choose one and place it in the appropriate niche. Then deduct the number 641 from the number on the back of the Medallion you have chosen, and go to the paragraph with that number.

333

You think the plain will be safer. Unfortunately, the land grows boggy and you are forced to weave your way around the marshy patches until you find it difficult to stay travelling in the right direction. A large bird flies overhead, sees you, and flies off. In the distance you hear the sound of digging and, as you breast a slight rise, you come upon a Marsh Goblin burying something; nearby lies a dead body. The creature senses you, screams that you shall not have his gold, and attacks.

MARSH GOBLIN   SKILL 6   STAMINA 6

If you win (mark off 2 Poison units on the *Adventure Sheet*), you drag out the half-buried chest and find 25 gold coins in it (mark these on your *Adventure Sheet*). Suddenly, from the direction of the deep marshes, you hear riders. Do you hide until they have passed (turn to **261**) or run back to the road (turn to **53**)?

334

You are powerless. Two Orcs are ordered to grab you . . . and you remember nothing more until you come to in a graveyard. The Necromancer speaks: 'You are mine to do with as I please, and I please to see you suffer . . . slowly.' She strikes the ground with her staff and the tombs begin to open. Decayed bodies and skeletons emerge clutching new daggers, and some begin slashing at you. You are in great danger, your quest will be at an end unless you have the Grey Talon of Sakar (turn to 102) or at least two sprigs of Treffilli and you know how to use them (turn to 146). If you have neither of these, you die the death of One Thousand Cuts. You have failed.

335

You pull your sword out. However, it falls from your grasp, and you are left defenceless. The Ogres attack you, and you hear a voice from the Throne announce that no weapon may be drawn or used near the Throne of Kazan, on pain of instant death. Turning, you see Meghan-na-Durr; she is still clutching the dagger, but her face collapses to reveal the skeleton underneath. She falls over and dies. You, alas, will suffer a similar fate. You needed greater wisdom, and your quest has ended, in sight of the great Throne.

336

You sit down on the wooden plank and shove yourself off. The speed is tremendous as you bank, turn and sweep down the ice chute. Turn to **234**.

337

You run at full speed, then stop and press yourself against a wall. *Test your Luck*. If you are Lucky, you have survived with a little bruising from the passing bulls (deduct 2 points from your STAMINA). If you are Unlucky, throw 2 dice for the number of times you are struck by the bulls and deduct *double* that number from your STAMINA. The bulls charge on through a wall and disappear. The tunnel you are in turns south and then leads to a door which you push open. Turn to **207**.

338

Turn to **361**.

339

You walk along the quay. No other ships seem to be leaving at this time. Just then, you spot a horse-trader; he is sitting on a fence holding the reins of a selection of horses. Do you wish to try and hire a horse (turn to **220**) or do you decide to leave Korkut on foot (turn to **388**)?

340

You are in a room with a giant Grypvulture. It flutters about, crashing into the walls. *Test your Luck.* If you are Lucky, it does you no damage. If you are Unlucky, throw 1 die and reduce your STAMINA by that number. Return to **160** and throw the magic die to continue through the Maze.

341

You enter the guild. Inside there is a sign: 'Mandrake Wolfsbane – Locksmith (and Saddlemaker)'. You walk through another doorway and find a large man, puffing at a pipe, humming and filing at a key. He asks you what you want. You reply in a whisper that you are one of Segrek's Select and a friend of Astragal. He stares at you and then admits that he doesn't know what you are talking about. He puffs a smoke ring at you; it encircles you and turns red, then makes the 'A' rune shape. 'But if you're looking for somewhere to stay, why not try the Dragon's Wings Tavern?' He picks up some chalk and writes, 'Welcome, but beware! There are eyes and ears everywhere. Keep to the shadows. I will see you at the inn in a few hours.'

You leave by a back door and enter a narrow alley. Do you choose to turn left (turn to **65**) or right (turn to **276**)?

342

You are faced with two corridors, running north and west, and two doors that will not open in the south and the east. You notice footprints heading north and you can hear shrieks coming from the western tunnel. Which do you choose: north (turn to 87) or west (turn to 36)?

343

Flaxwort drops you off in a busy lane, close to a small trading-post. He wishes you success and drives off. You look around, conscious of the fact that Chingiz must have many paid informers. You set off, trying to look purposeful, but the lane you are following soon divides. Do you head for the trading-post (turn to 52), carry straight on down the lane (turn to 208) or turn left into another road (turn to 318)?

344

You are walking past a group of wealthy merchants when you suddenly hear the familiar Gorak accent, 'What I'd give for some truffles right now. No one seems to like them here, so no one bothers to import them.' Do you know anyone who has truffles to trade? Go to the paragraph which is the same as the number of kazanweights he possesses. If you don't know any truffle importers, you make your way out of the town of Torrez. Turn to **280**.

345

The Boulyanthrop swoops down, lands and stands before you. She cannot carry you far because she is wounded: an arrow-shaft protrudes from her side. At first you refuse her offer of help, but she insists; she lifts you off the scrubby hill, flies with you for several miles and finally deposits you upon another hillside. You thank her deeply and she flies off. This would be a good place for a rest, you decide. Turn to **399**.

346

The preparations are swiftly made. You are placed at the end of a row of warriors who stand on either side of a trench of burning coals. The old woman announces this to be the Test of the Yigenik, the key to the Maze. 'You must race over the hot coals as fast as you can and at the same time try to ward off the blows of the warriors.' Throw 1 die for your speed and another die for a blow. If the two totals match, deduct 2 points from your STAMINA. Repeat the Test ten times. If you survive, turn to **134**.

347

You speak to the Gremlin with a silken tongue that worms itself into his mind. Slowly his face lights up, as he realizes that he *should* open the door for you. He turns his back and, after a few convulsions, produces the key and opens the door for you, a broad smile on his face. Turn to **363**.

348

You haul yourself out of the water and stagger inland. Expecting more Dragons, you clutch your sword tightly to you. Nothing appears. You have to walk for many hours until you find a place that can be easily defended while you rest. Turn to **399**.

349

There are two sealed doors, to the south and east, and corridors north and west. You hear a strange sniffing in the stillness to the north and see a woman sitting on the floor. Do you head for her (turn to **215**) or choose to go west (turn to **147**)?

350

You are walking along a narrow lane when you are stopped by a warty Troll, holding a small cage; he demands to see your identity scroll. You search about in your pack, then pull out your sword. The Troll opens the cage and a small bird flies out.

TROLL   SKILL 6   STAMINA 9

If you win (mark off 1 Poison unit on the *Adventure Sheet*), you cannot see the messenger bird anywhere. You know there is little time left before it brings reinforcements. In front of you there are two lanes; which do you take: the one to the left (turn to **65**) or the one on the right (turn to **276**)?

351

You approach the body; it is that of a woman, dressed like a fellow adventurer and probably one of Segrek's Select. You can see no wounds on her, but she seems to have no bones left in her body. There is a brighter gleam of daylight here. Do you start to search the body to see if she has a Medallion (turn to **139**), run to the door outside (turn to **170**) or head back to the tunnel leading west (turn to **268**)?

352

You accept the stranger's offer, pay the money (deduct 2 gold coins from your *Adventure Sheet*), and climb up on to the spare horse. The rider leads and you follow. Suddenly you are set upon by six Orcs and a Mamlik who rush out from the bushes. Your horse will not move and you seem to be glued, spellbound, to the stirrups and saddle. The Mamlik smiles a terrible smile, walks round and stabs you in the back. Your quest is over.

353

You are well hidden behind a large boulder by the time the riders approach. They pass by and you breathe a sigh of relief. Suddenly, however, they return and gaze at the footprints in the snow. They know where you are! They release a large Gryphawk that flutters up into the air, then dives at you and attacks your back and neck (deduct 2 points from your STAMINA). You rush out and stand in a defensive attitude before the riders. Turn to **250**.

354

Snakes' Eyes is a dice game. You place a stake in gold coins on the table and make three attempts to throw a double. If you do throw a double, you get back double your original stake and that particular game ends. If you throw double-1 (snakes' eyes) you get back three times your stake. There is a maximum stake of 5 gold coins and you may play only three times. Play the game and make the appropriate adjustments on your *Adventure Sheet*.

You finish playing, gather up your winnings (if any) and then you notice a Goblin who is scrutinizing you carefully. Do you go outside through the front door (turn to **168**) or do you prefer to leave through a small back door (turn to **198**)?

355

As you walk along, you hear rumbling, shaking and screaming noises close by. You stop to read an inscription: 'This is the True Path out of the Maze; here, brave adventurer, you will be safe.' Suddenly, two Orcs rush at you, yelling and brandishing their shortswords. Fight each in turn.

	SKILL	STAMINA
First ORC	7	6
Second ORC	7	6

If you survive (mark off 2 Poison units on the *Adventure Sheet*), you push open a door which then shuts behind you. Turn to **264**.

356
THE POWER OF PERSUASION
You have drunk the mixture that gives you this Power. Mark this on your *Adventure Sheet*. If this is your first choice, return to 45 and choose again. If it is your second choice, turn to 74.

357
The Scimitar brew slips down your throat very easily. You feel a warm glow – but suddenly you start to see black circles and your insides want to change places with your outside. Alkis comes back, smells the brew and knocks the mug from your hand. You feel terrible (deduct 1 point from your SKILL and 2 points from your STAMINA). Turn to 210.

358

You are standing in a dungeon, facing a Fiend. You can see the Medallion lying on an obelisk in front of you. Suddenly, the Fiend splits in two. If you have flowers to placate the Fiends, take two and hand them over. If you have only one flower, you will have to fight the first Fiend. If you have no flowers at all, you will have to fight both Fiends in turn.

	SKILL	STAMINA
First MAZE FIEND	6	8
Second MAZE FIEND	7	7

Mark off 2 Poison units on the *Adventure Sheet*. If you win, you are able to pick up the Medallion. You look at the snake motif on it, then turn it over and see the number '1000'. Turn to **69**.

359

A door in front of you slides open. You walk into an antique chamber, full of tombs bearing carvings of skeletons. The voice of the Heart of the Throne speaks: 'You have passed the first barrier to the Throne of Kazan. Now, do you possess a second Medallion? If you do, place it here.' An obelisk rises out of the stone floor. If you have a second Medallion, deduct the number 874 from the number inscribed on the Medallion's reverse side and go to that paragraph. If you do not, then a door opens in the wall in front of you and you have to enter a strange room, full of jars and bottles. Turn to **45**.

360

You walk on through the echoing corridor. You enter a large doorway and see Segrek's tomb in the room in front of you. Two Goblins are trying to Spellbreak the sarcophagus. Do you attack them (turn to **121**) or sneak out again (turn to **38**)?

361

All three of you leave the Dragon's Wings by a back door. Through various back-streets you approach ever closer to the Fortress. Geronicus hands over the phial you have chosen and you drink it, feeling it do you good. Standing in front of a rock-face, you are drawn through the stone. Unseen forces then lead you down an ancient corridor until eventually you come to a halt. Turn to **332**.

362

Cautiously you try to pass the small creature. Angered at being ignored, it begins to shriek and several others roll out of the holes in the walls. One of them gets close to you and bites your ankle (deduct 2 points from your STAMINA). Throw 2 dice for the number of small furry creatures that attack you, then throw 2 dice again: this is the number you manage to ward off by waving your sword at them. If more creatures attack you than you can ward off, then you are bitten: deduct 2 points from your STAMINA for each bite. You dash to a metal door, push it open and go through. It shuts behind you. Turn to **342**.

363

You open the door to a plush bedchamber. Sitting in the middle of a large fourposter bed is Chingiz. There is no one else in the room. With rather a strange look on his face, he murmurs in a weak voice: 'So, you have made it, Select of Segrek . . . I suppose you want to know where the Throne is?' He starts to keel over and puts out a hand to steady himself. Quick as a flash, you draw the Dagger of Darkness from your boot, where it has been safely hidden throughout your journey, and put it in his hand! He looks at you and smiles. 'You are clever . . . if you can defeat my deadly daughter, then . . .' He tips over and you see a large dagger sticking out of his back. He is dead. You suddenly feel much better (add 4 points to your STAMINA and do not mark off any more Poison units). Turn to 285.

364

You hand over the 2 gold coins. The old man looks you over carefully and sniggers. You climb on the cart and he urges the horses on. You are relieved that you won't have to wait for a while. The driver asks you if you would like some fruit and, as you turn round to get an apple, you see the shadow of a raised dagger in his hand. Twisting round, you knock the dagger from his hand and, locked together, you struggle as the horses bolt and the cart careers, out of control, down the road.

MAMLIK ASSASSIN   SKILL 7   STAMINA 8

The loser in this unarmed combat falls off the cart and is crushed under its wheels. If you are the survivor (mark off 1 Poison unit on the *Adventure Sheet*), you have to get off the cart somehow. Do you leap to the left (turn to **19**) or to the right (turn to **90**)?

365

You draw your sword and strike at the evil being, tearing his cloak. He is surprised at your ability and runs back into the darkness. Two Mamliks, holding scimitars, appear in front of you and the Necromancer orders them to attack you while he is changing shape to that of a panther. Fight each in turn.

	SKILL	STAMINA
First MAMLIK	8	10
Second MAMLIK	9	10
PANTHER	8	9

If you survive (mark off 2 Poison units on the *Adventure Sheet*), the dead Necromancer's staff weaves around your ankles like a snake, and then bites you. You lose consciousness. Turn to 321.

366

You enter the great Maze and walk south into the darkness as the doors slam shut behind you. Faintly, you hear Agellatha's voice: 'Now we are releasing the two Minotaurs of the Maze who will pursue you throughout your quest for the Medallion.' You come to a tunnel that heads east. Do you take this (turn to 103) or do you continue south (turn to 136)?

367

You are in a room with jewel-encrusted walls. Before you can move to examine them, a giant Serpent's head appears and you are sucked down into its mouth (deduct 2 points from your STAMINA). Turn to **17** and mark your new position on the chart.

368

You move fast through the undergrowth, but the path is difficult to follow and soon you become lost. Trying to find a way out, you stagger on in the dark forest. Suddenly you emerge into a clearing. In front of you stands a large, heavily armed Troll, who is gazing at a tree. Do you circle round past the Troll (turn to **79**) or do you approach him (turn to **263**)?

369

You walk along until you come to a halt in front of four Orcs guarding a door. If you have the Power to change metal objects, you change their spears to look like gold; the Orcs forget about you and begin to fight among themselves. If you have the Power of Persuasion, you whisper softly to them that their whole aim in life is to let you pass, and they do.

If you have neither of these Powers, fight each Orc in turn.

	SKILL	STAMINA
First ORC	7	6
Second ORC	7	6
Third ORC	7	6
Fourth ORC	7	6

Whatever your Power, if you have survived (mark off 3 Poison units on the *Adventure Sheet*) you pass into another room. Turn to **325**.

The storm continues and you struggle on for many hours. Suddenly you see ahead a warrior being attacked by six hideous Goblins which are preventing him from crossing a bridge across a chasm. Although the warrior shows supreme fighting skill, one of the Goblins has crept behind him and is about to stab him in the back. You come instantly to the aid of the warrior.

GOBLIN   SKILL 5   STAMINA 5

If you survive, add 1 point to your LUCK; the Goblins' attack is beaten off. The warrior turns to face you and you realize that he is blind. Formally, he introduces himself as Alkis Fearslicer, from the ranks of the legendary blind Sensewarriors who live in the deep Chasms below Gorak. He tells you that he is in pursuit of an escaped criminal who has come to Kazan to ally himself with Chingiz. He then asks you your business. Do you trust him and tell all (turn to **62**) or do you mumble a few lies (turn to **224**)?

371

You roll in the dark towards the fire and thrust your bound wrists close to the flames (deduct 2 points from your STAMINA and mark off 1 Poison unit). Your bonds burn through and you just have time to pull out your sword before the guard returns.

KAZANID GUARD   SKILL 6   STAMINA 7

If you win, you hurry out into the snowstorm and run round to the back of the hut. Here, you find a pile of arrow-shaped planks and an icy track that leads down the mountain. You kick one of the planks and it shoots off down the track. This looks like a quick means of escape. Do you want to try it (turn to 336) or do you think it too risky (turn to 59)?

372

The Yigeniks make camp and water their horses, then they feed themselves. The horses stay, grazing, very close to the warriors. You manage to get some sleep (add 1 point to your STAMINA). You are awakened by the whinnying and stamping horses – they seem very nervous. In seconds the Yigeniks are mounted as a large phalanx of Orcs charges out of the trees. Do you stay and fight (turn to 118) or do you escape into the darkness (turn to 203)?

373

You ignore the incident and keep well away from the girl. The Gryphawk stops pretending to attack her and settles on her shoulder. The girl pokes her tongue out at you and wipes the red dye from her neck. You take care to avoid any other tricks. At last you find the Street of the Forty Guilds. Turn to 98.

374

You approach the worm with care, but it does not see you because it is preoccupied with the others flying around above it. You pull out your sword and slash at it. It turns to face you, dropping its birdman prey.

SKULUGGI   SKILL 6   STAMINA 8

If you survive (mark off 1 Poison unit and add 2 points to your LUCK), you are carried by the birdmen to the top of a mountain, where they thank you profusely for saving the young birdman. They call themselves Boulyanthrops and, by way of reward, they ask if there is any way they can be of aid to you. Do you tell them that you are one of Segrek's Select (turn to 172) or do you ask them to carry you back down to the road, and then watch them fly away (turn to 161)?

375

She orders you to follow her. She makes a tour of the numerous guilds, giving each of them a small bunch of flowers in return for a large purse of gold coins. When one guild-master refuses to accept her flowers, two large Kazanids suddenly appear and proceed to smash up most of the shop. Eventually, you are led down into a cellar full of beggars, thieves and criminal types. You peer around and see a Mamlik standing in the crowd, watching you. Do you run away, up the stairs and out (turn to **65**) or will you face up to the Mamlik (turn to **80**)?

376
THE POWER OF STORMBRINGING

You have drunk the mixture that gives you this Power. Note this on your *Adventure Sheet*. If this is your first choice, return to **45** and choose again. If it is your second choice, turn to **74**.

377

You walk along the tunnel. Suddenly, you stumble over the burnt-up body of someone or something. You look at the wall above the body and see two bulls' heads with gleaming green eyes. You step closer, and fire belches from their nostrils, lighting up three Medallions set in a row between the bulls' heads. Which Medallion do you choose to take:

The first?	Turn to 184
The second?	Turn to 312
The third?	Turn to 228

378

The giant, tail-less rat scampers off in front of you. You hear a booming voice: 'Yes, follow the rat, it will conduct you to the entrance.' It leads you through ancient dusty tunnels for a long time, then stops and scrabbles on the floor. Looking carefully, you can make out the inscription of a horn. If you possess Segrek's horn, blow it now. The ground shimmers and opens up for a moment under your feet. You fall in: turn to 332.

If you do not possess the horn, you must dig with your sword (deduct 3 points from your STAMINA and mark off 1 Poison unit) until you succeed in breaking through; then you jump into the hole. Turn to 332.

379

The path you are following drops down into a dry river valley and then opens out on to a flat plain. You are overtaken by several carts, and can see and hear yelping dogs and a crowd in the distance; all the people seem to be making for a market. Just ahead there is a road-block, commanded by six Orcs who are searching everyone who passes. To one side stands an evil-looking, black-cloaked figure: a Necromancer. All you can do is stand there, wondering what to do. Just then you notice an Elf staring at you. You move away, but he follows and calls out to you. Do you stop and turn round to talk to him (turn to 323), or would you rather hide yourself among the milling throng (turn to 230)?

380

The ground shakes and chunks of stone drop down out of the ceiling, to reveal sunlight streaming in from above. *Test your Luck*. If you are Unlucky, you are hit by a stone block (deduct 2 points from your STAMINA). If you are Lucky, they all miss.

There is much noise and smoke. An armoured Orc rushes past but fails to see you. You walk over to an open doorway; the door that was there has been knocked off its hinges. You go through – and bump into another Orc.

ORC   SKILL 7   STAMINA 6

If you win (mark off 1 Poison unit on the *Adventure Sheet*), the only clear exit is to the north. Turn to **264**.

381

You look up to see some Orcs and a knight looking down at you. They balance the cauldron of boiling oil on the tower wall as one of the Orcs throws a boulder at you. Throw 1 die for your position, then throw 1 die for the place where the boulder hits. If the two numbers match, you are hit, fall off and die. Your quest ends here.

If the rock misses you, the boiling oil is then poured down at you. Throw 1 die for the number of places on your body that are splashed with oil and deduct this number from your STAMINA.

You press close to the wall as another boulder smashes against the side of the tower, loosening a few stones. You launch a kick at the stone blocks and a section of the wall caves in. You dive in, head first, as another shower of oil comes hurtling down. Inside, you land on a pile of smelly rubbish that breaks your fall. In the dim light you can see an entrance to a chamber on the left (turn to **265**) and one on the right (turn to **40**). Which room do you enter?

382

You are in a room containing jars full of herbs. All are impossible to open except the one marked 'Treffilli'. You have time to take only two sprigs before the jar seals itself again. If you want them, take the sprigs and mark them on your *Adventure Sheet*. Turn to **398**.

383

'You are fortunate that I have a strong regard for the Select. Farewell, brave adventurer, and good luck.'

The bandits fade into the mountainside and you carry on down the sloping track until the land becomes less bleak. Eventually the path before you divides. One way is marked by an obelisk bearing a carving of a stallion (turn to **391**) and the other by a similar obelisk with the carving of a Fangtiger (turn to **209**). Which do you choose?

384
THE POWER OF FORTUNE

You have drunk the mixture that gives you this Power (in any situation that depends on LUCK, you will be Lucky). Mark this on your *Adventure Sheet*. If this is your first choice, return to **45** and choose again. If it is your second choice, turn to **74**.

385

You select the guard standing next to you to explain your situation to. He looks you up and down, smiles confidentially and tells you to speak to no one else. He cuts through your bonds and tells you to walk behind the cart. You do as he orders. Suddenly he sets upon you from behind, screaming that you have tried to escape. You spin round and attack him.

KAZANID GUARD   SKILL 7   STAMINA 8

If you survive (mark off 1 Poison unit on the *Adventure Sheet*), the other Kazanids have had time to group around you and one prepares to fire an arrow into your heart. Turn to **31**.

386

The Marauders ride off. This time you ride with them as you have been given a horse in payment for your part in the battle with the Trolls. The horde moves at a fast gallop. At a crossroads the leading group is stopped by a black-cloaked man holding up a staff. Two of them try to hack him to pieces but their swords pass clean through him. From this, you recognize that the figure is that of a Necromancer. If you have achieved Necromancer fighting skill level, do you urge your horse forward (turn to **151**)? If you do not have the ability or choose to remain where you are, turn to **243**.

387

You approach the figure and it holds out a thin bony hand, pleading for money. You slip the beggar a few iron coins of little value. He gazes at the head of Tancred on the coins and then looks you up and down. He tells you that, if you have five gold coins, he will help you. If you have the money, do you accept the offer (turn to **253**) or do you refuse his help (turn to **150**)? If you have no gold, you must refuse.

388

You wander through a maze of alleyways until finally you leave Korkut. There is only one road out of the town, and you trudge along it, feeling hot and tired (deduct 1 point from your STAMINA). Just then, you become aware of someone following you: he has a patch over one eye, he stumps along on a wooden peg-leg and he carries on his back a hurdy-gurdy music-box. He catches up with you and asks if you would like to hear a tune for the price of a crust of bread or a few iron coins. He looks desperate. Do you agree to let him play for you (turn to **9**) or do you refuse (turn to **108**)?

389

You rush over to the obelisk. There is a Medallion on the top! You grab it and it crumbles to dust in your hands. There is the sound of muffled laughter as a clawed hand bursts out of the obelisk and grabs your wrist. The hand belongs to a Dungeon Delver; it breaks out of the obelisk and attacks you.

DUNGEON DELVER SKILL 7 STAMINA 6

If you survive, you rush through another door. Turn to **100**.

390

The tunnel leads to a small iron-barred window. Outside, you can see the hideous features of a Gargoyle. Suddenly, a door you have passed without noticing it opens outwards. A Goblin emerges, carrying a bucket, and limps off down the corridor. Cautiously, you look inside; all manner of folk are chained up, or strapped to instruments of torture. You hear a weak call coming from a corner by the rack: 'Come here and release me.' You walk over, to find a thin wretch smiling at you. A demented Dwarf screams, 'No, don't do it, don't do it!' Do you decide to release the prisoner (turn to **109**) or do you leave the room and go south (turn to **360**)?

391

You set off along the track which soon becomes a good solid road. After many hours of walking, the land has flattened out to a grassy plain. You meet no one during all this time. Eventually, you hear the sound of a rider on the road behind you. There is little cover on this grassy plain. Do you decide to lie down in the grass and hope that no one will see you (turn to **202**) or do you carry on like a normal traveller (turn to **192**)?

392

You step into a room that is full of statues and carvings of dragons. Horrified, you watch three of them begin to move and thrash about. They are small Kazilik Dragons which, you know, can be placated with gems. If you have three gems in your possession, you may pass without a fight (make the necessary adjustments on the *Adventure Sheet*). If you have two gems, you will have to fight the first Dragon. Similarly, if you have just one, you will have to fight the first and second Dragons.

	SKILL	STAMINA
First KAZILIK DRAGON	10	12
Second KAZILIK DRAGON	10	14
Third KAZILIK DRAGON	11	16

If you pass through or survive the fight, turn to **359**.

393

You are faced with two tunnels. Which do you take: the one heading east (turn to **205**) or the other heading south (turn to **377**)?

394

You hear shuffling footsteps. You peep out and see four Necromancers entering the room. One is carrying a box that contains four phials, each with a distinctive marking. One of them says to the others: 'We have been charged by Chingiz to discover the secret entrances to the Heart of the Throne that the Select will take if they reach the Fortress. In one month we have Spellbroken only the entrance of the

Cross – we must work harder.' They begin to chant a demonic spell and you hear the sound of breaking glass and the roll of thunder. In the turmoil you sneak out through the window.

Outside, you can discern through the mist two main paths away from the building. Do you follow the left-hand path (turn to **23**) or the path to the right (turn to **70**)?

395

You are bound with leather thongs that seem to get tighter the more you struggle. Nothing is taken from you, however, and you are led through the dark forest until you reach a small settlement in a clearing. The silent figures now reveal themselves, by removing their hoods. There are no men in the group. One of them speaks to you. 'Intruder, you have trespassed into Owlshriek, the penalty for which is death – unless you can prove yourself both strong and fit to live. The choice is yours. Do you wish to Run the Arrow, or undertake the Test of the Three Cuts?' Which do you reluctantly agree to try: the Run (turn to **48**) or the Test (turn to **206**)?

396

You force your way through to get a better view of
the procession. A Kazanid beside you is describing
what is going on to a blind companion. 'There he is
now, that Chingiz filth, I'm not surprised he doesn't
trust anyone. If I was Vetch, I'd kill him now. Vetch
is standing over there, a little to our right, with
Mandrake Wolfsbane who's smoking his infernal
pipe.' You look across: Vetch is well clad in fighting
armour, while Wolfsbane is dressed like a black-
smith. The procession ends and the two men separate. Do you wish to follow either of them? If so, do
you choose Vetch (turn to **68**) or Wolfsbane (turn to
5)? Or would you prefer to carry on to the Fortress
(turn to **271**)?

397

You stagger up the mountain slope. Suddenly, a small Gryphawk swoops down and lands in front of you. It begins to squawk . . . and then changes its shape to that of an old wizard. 'I am Icaricus, well met. I have sought you for many hours. I bring a message from Astragal . . .' He stops and puts his finger in his mouth; he cannot remember it. He kicks a rock, which explodes. 'Ah, yes: "Beware the Necromancers, they have been unleashed by Chingiz who is now delving in the evil arts. To help you in your struggle, I have empowered . . ." Er, I can't remember the rest. Well, never mind, which way are you heading? I suggest the lands of the Bogomil. Come.' He changes into a large eagle, gets you to grip his talons and takes you a long way; then he absent-mindedly drops you on to a path and flies off. Turn to **391**.

398

Zaranj stands before you. 'You are brave and have passed successfully through the Maze, but fortune has not favoured you with the Medallion. You must try elsewhere.' Your mind goes blank. Turn to **69**.

399

You build a sheltered camp, eat some Provisions and settle down to sleep (add 4 points to your STAMINA). You are awakened by a small green-and-red bird that flutters about and lands in front of you. It picks up some charcoal from the fire in its claw and scratches the 'A' rune on a rock. You know now that it is a messenger from Astragal. Speaking in a high-pitched whistling tone, it says: 'Greetings, friend. Speed is now of the essence. The Medallions are all taken; make for Sharrabbas as fast as you can. You *must* enter the Fortress, by fair means or foul. If you already have a Medallion, the task will be easier. For help, you must go to . . . Mmm . . . Vetch . . . on no account . . .' The bird stops, drops the charcoal and flies away.

You set off immediately; after many hours, you come to a fork in the road. Both paths look likely, but which will you take: the one on the left (turn to **297**) or the one on the right (turn to **116**)?

You have defeated the evil Vizier Chingiz and his deadly daughter, Meghan-na-Durr, in their attempt to seize the throne of Kazan. Through your bravery, wisdom and skill, you yourself have sat upon the legendary throne at Sharrabbas. The Six Clans will now support you, both by dint of tradition and because you have proved to them that you are the greatest warrior in the land. The Necromancers, Mamliks and all the other fell creatures summoned by Chingiz slink away into the shadows and crawl back into their holes. You set up a strong force to police the land and protect the weak. Trade between Kazan and the rest of Khul flourishes and the land experiences an era of peace and prosperity. You are hailed by many as a worthy successor to the great Segrek.

After one year and one day of your reign, you must declare your own Select. Once you have died, they will strive to sit upon the throne of Kazan; thus the traditions continue.

E. Hin.

"I thought there m̲ ̲ ̲ ̲ ̲ ̲ ̲ ̲ ̲ you wanted to te̲ ̲ ̲ ̲ ̲ ̲ ̲ ̲ ̲ ̲ you're so scared and what you're running away from."

Seth laid his hand gently over hers. "Maybe I can help you."

Marie shook her head. "Just fix my car so Patty and I can get out of this town," she said with a quiver in her voice. "Believe me, you don't want to get involved."

"I'm already involved," Seth countered. "Let me help."

"How?"

"I don't know. But I can't help unless you let me in on your secrets."

"Either you read a lot of mystery novels or you've had personal experience with this kind of thing."

When he didn't answer, Marie studied his face. She didn't want to place anyone else in jeopardy, but she desperately needed an ally.

"All right," she finally said. "But the less you know, the better off you'll be...."

Books by Valerie Hansen

Love Inspired Suspense

Her Brother's Keeper
The Danger Within
Out of the Depths
Deadly Payoff
Shadow of Turning
Nowhere to Run

*Serenity, Arkansas

Love Inspired Historical

Frontier Courtship
Wilderness Courtship

Love Inspired

The Wedding Arbor
The Troublesome Angel
The Perfect Couple
Second Chances
Love One Another
Blessings of the Heart
Samantha's Gift
Everlasting Love
The Hamilton Heir
A Treasure of the Heart

VALERIE HANSEN

was thirty when she awoke to the presence of the Lord in her life and turned to Jesus. In the years that followed she worked with young children, both in church and secular environments. She also raised a family of her own and played foster mother to a wide assortment of furred and feathered critters.

Married to her high school sweetheart since age seventeen, she now lives in an old farmhouse she and her husband renovated with their own hands. She loves to hike the wooded hills behind the house and reflect on the marvelous turn her life has taken. Not only is she privileged to reside among the loving, accepting folks in the breathtakingly beautiful Ozark mountains of Arkansas, she also gets to share her personal faith by telling the stories of her heart for Steeple Hill Books.

Life doesn't get much better than that!

Love Inspired
SUSPENSE

TITLES AVAILABLE NEXT MONTH

Don't miss these four stories in November

THE GOOD NEIGHBOR by Sharon Mignerey

Detective Wade Prescott has his prime suspect:
Megan Burke. He found her in the yard beside the
body of her neighbor's grandson, didn't he? Case closed.
Yet Megan's sweet demeanor has Wade believing
in her innocence. And if she is innocent, a murderer
is still at large....

THE PROTECTOR'S PROMISE by Shirlee McCoy
The Sinclair Brothers

Who could be after his widowed neighbor and
her little girl? Grayson Sinclair vows to find out—*without*
getting emotionally involved. He won't let anyone hurt
Honor Malone, or her daughter. But the threat is closer to
home than anyone realizes.

SHIELD OF REFUGE by Carol Steward
In the Line of Fire

No evidence, no other witnesses—no wonder Officer
Garrett Matthews doubts Amber Scott's claims that
she saw a kidnapping. Then someone begins tailing Amber,
and Garrett starts to suspect that she's telling the truth.
And that means that the danger she's in is real.

HOLIDAY ILLUSION by Lynette Eason

Little Paulo desperately needs a new heart. But for the
surgery, orphanage director Anna Freeman must take him
to the city she fled in fear years ago. And she finally has to
tell Dr. Lucas Freeman about her secrets. Her past. And the
danger stalking them all.

LISCNM1008

VALERIE HANSEN

NOWHERE TO RUN

Steeple
Hill®

Published by Steeple Hill Books™

STEEPLE HILL BOOKS

**Steeple
Hill®**

ISBN-13: 978-0-373-44312-3
ISBN-10:   0-373-44312-9

NOWHERE TO RUN

The Lord holds victory in store for the upright,
he is a shield to those whose walk is blameless,
for he guards the course of the just and protects
the way of his faithful ones.
                                    —*Proverbs* 2:7-8

This book is dedicated to computer gurus and dear friends, Judy and Larry Vierstra, and to others in their family who also advised me regarding the Internet.

Left to my own devices, I'd still be writing with a pencil and using two tin cans with a string stretched between them to communicate!

ONE

It took a lot to frighten Marie Parnell—unless the perceived danger affected her five-year-old daughter, Patty. That changed everything.

Trembling, she peered out the front window of her Baton Rouge apartment to see who was pounding on the door and shouting her name. It hadn't been her imagination. Roy Jenkins was back. Her nightmares had come to life.

Marie froze, her brown eyes wide. She could hardly breathe. The tone of Roy's voice had risen until he'd started to sound more afraid than irate. That was puzzling. It wasn't like him to show weakness. Not at all.

She chanced another quick peek out the window, hoping and praying he was alone. The last thing she wanted was to expose Patty to the low-life types who had always been Roy's cohorts.

Keeping her voice as calm as she could, she answered him through the closed door. "Go away."

His fist slammed against the wood so hard it made

her jump. "Not this time, Marie. If you don't let me in I'll break this door down. Don't make me do it."

Don't make me do it. The familiar phrase sent chills zinging up her spine and turned her stomach. That was what Roy always used to say before he hit her. As if it were her fault and she deserved being punished. It had taken her a long time to realize that the problem was Roy's temper, not her behavior, and she thanked God daily that she had not been fool enough to marry him, even though she had not been a Christian during the time they were together.

"Hush. You'll wake the neighbors," she warned. In her mind she added, *and you'll wake Patty.* That mustn't happen. The little girl had finally gotten to the place where she'd stopped asking for him, and Marie didn't want to have to start that healing process all over again.

Outside, Roy pleaded more softly, "Marie, darlin'. You have to listen to me. If you won't let me in, at least talk to me face-to-face."

She knew better than to open the door. Experience had taught her well. Yet, there was something in Roy's tone that tugged at her heart, made her remember the few good times they'd had before he'd turned to crime and begun to physically abuse her when she'd objected.

Twisting the dead bolt, she eased the door open a crack. Roy hit it with his shoulder and shoved her out of the way as he burst in, followed by a gust of humid air.

Marie staggered back, her hands raised in self-defense.

Roy gave a cynical snort. "Simmer down. I got no beef with you. I got worse problems. And so do you. That's why I'm here."

"I don't believe you." She sent a concerned glance toward the hallway leading to the bedroom, then realized immediately that she'd given away Patty's location.

"I came to warn you," Roy insisted. He began trying to edge past her toward the room where his daughter slept.

"Leave her alone," Marie said, standing firmly in his way. "You haven't bothered to even write her or send any support for over two years."

"She's my kid. I got a right to see her."

"You have no rights. We were never legally married, and I have a restraining order against you."

"Yeah, yeah. That piece of paper is only good if I pay attention to it. Tonight, I have other things on my mind." He paused, shaking his head. "If you weren't so stubborn you'd listen to me."

"I stopped listening to you years ago," Marie said.

"I know." Roy began to pace. "Look, Marie, I'm in trouble. I'm going to have to leave town. And after I'm gone, there are some old buddies of mine who're going to be royally teed off."

"What does that have to do with me?"

"Plenty. They're bound to come looking for me. You and the kid are my only ties to this area. If you were them, what would you do?"

She folded her arms and faced him as he continued to walk back and forth. "You don't want to know what

I'd like to do," she said candidly. "And I refuse to lie for you, so don't tell me where you're going."

"That's not the problem," he said. "You're dumber than dirt, aren't you? Look. This is serious. You have to leave town, too."

"Not on your life, Roy. Patty and I are finally happy. I have a good job, she's starting school in the fall, and we've even joined a church. We're not going anywhere, especially not with you."

He laughed coarsely. "Not *with* me, you idiot. That's the last place I'd want my kid to be, considering the jam I'm in. But you can't stay here. It's not safe."

"Sure, Roy. Tell me another fairy tale." She tucked strands of her cinnamon-brown hair behind her ears with trembling fingers. "Patty and I aren't going anywhere. Understand?"

"Yeah, I get it. Just don't say I didn't warn you." He began to back away.

Marie followed him to the door, locked it as soon as he'd stepped outside and leaned her forehead against it. She hadn't wanted Roy to see how deeply his anxiety had affected her, but she was terribly concerned. Could he have been telling the truth for once? He had certainly seemed sincere.

And he hadn't forced her to let him see Patty, either. That, too, was totally out of character for Roy.

She shut off the inside lights so she couldn't be seen as she peered out the window to watch him leave.

Suddenly, two shadowy figures appeared on either

side of Roy. They grabbed him and held his arms as he squirmed.

Marie pressed her fingertips to her lips to stifle a gasp. The larger men easily dragged him to a waiting car, shoved him inside and sped away.

Immediately reaching for the phone, Marie dialed 911. The police might not be her ex-boyfriend's first choice for a rescue, but the way she saw it, Roy was out of options. It never occurred to her that her story about his abduction wouldn't be believed.

Seth Whitfield, the thirty-two-year-old garage mechanic who lived and worked in Serenity, Arkansas, didn't exist. At least not in the normal sense.

Stepping out of his weathered barn into the spring sunshine, Seth removed his ball cap and raked his fingers through his thick, prematurely graying hair. Alice had always insisted he keep his hair dyed dark, so he had—until she'd been taken from him by the same men who had driven him into hiding.

After Alice's death nothing had mattered, least of all his appearance, and with the addition of a bit of necessary plastic surgery and his farmer's tan, he hardly recognized the face he shaved every morning.

He blew out a sigh. Looking across the unspoiled valley always made him a bit wistful. This morning was no exception. He could smell the fresh green grass and appreciate the balmy wind from the west that often brought showers to nourish the groves of oak, hickory and cedar dotting the rocky, gently sloping hills.

Alice would have loved it here, he thought absently, then realized the opposite was true. His late wife had been a city girl. She'd never have agreed to visit the Ozarks, let alone move there to live. That was one of the reasons he had chosen this spot for his relocation. He had had absolutely no ties there.

"And I couldn't have picked a place that I liked better," he told himself.

The black-and-white border collie at his side nudged the leg of his jeans, panting and begging for attention in response to his mellow voice.

He bent to stroke the dog's head. "That's right, Babe, you and I love this place, don't we?"

Excited, she wagged her tail and spun in a circle, making Seth smile in spite of his earlier melancholy. As long as he continued to take one day at a time, the same way this smart dog did, and stop brooding over a past that couldn't be changed, he'd do fine. Regrets were for fools and dreamers, neither of which was an apt description of him. He was intelligent. A survivor. A fighter.

And if he didn't get a move on he'd be late for work, he added, glancing at his watch.

He patted his thigh. "Come on, old girl. Hop in the truck. We're heading to town."

The herding dog took off at a run, bounded through the open window of the cab of the old green pickup and turned to look back at him as if to say, "Hurry up, slow poke."

Seth squared his Serenity Repair Shop ball cap on his head and slid behind the wheel. There were times,

like now, when he could almost feel free, almost forget that he was still in jeopardy in spite of his secure niche in the rural community. If the time ever came that his enemies did locate him, he knew it was going to be harder to pack up and leave these friendly folks than it had been to relinquish his highly paid, undercover, security job and abandon his luxurious residence outside Philadelphia.

The one thing that spoiled his fond memories of that house, of the life he had once led, was the image of his late wife, Alice, prostrate on the kitchen floor with a note of warning pinned to her night gown.

Marie had not rested since she'd witnessed Roy's abduction. The police had been no help; nor had they offered to guard her, as she had hoped. Consequently, she had followed Roy's advice, taken Patty and fled.

Before she'd reached the Louisiana border, she was certain she'd spotted a car in pursuit. It was only after night fell again that she'd managed to elude whoever was after her. Then, she'd turned and headed northwest.

If she had been traveling alone, she never would have visited fast-food places or lingered in gas stations and truck stops. Keeping her curious, excited five-year-old cooped up in the car all the time, however, was next to impossible. When Patty wasn't napping, she was wiggling and asking scads of questions.

In response to the child's latest demand for food, Marie pulled into the drive-thru lane of a familiar hamburger chain. "Okay. Here we are. What do you want?"

"That!" Patty said, pointing to the colorful, inside play area.

"I thought you were hungry."

"I am. I'll eat, too. I just wanna have some fun."

"We're on vacation, honey. Seeing all these new places is fun, isn't it?" The pout on the little girl's face made Marie smile. "Okay. You win. I guess I can use a short break, too."

She parked her overloaded blue sedan where she was certain she could watch it through the plate glass windows, then helped Patty unfasten her seatbelt and climb down from her booster seat. "Hold my hand," Marie cautioned.

"I'm a big girl. I can walk by myself."

"I know you can. But Mommy gets worried when there are lots of cars around." Matching coffee-colored gazes met and held in a battle of wills. Marie won by arching her eyebrows and giving her daughter a silent, no-nonsense warning.

"I'll get you a child's meal," Marie said as they entered the fast-food restaurant. "Stay in the play area where I can watch you." She bent down to reinforce her admonition with a serious look. "This is important. If you can see me, then that means I can see you, too. Okay?"

Barely nodding, the child grinned and skipped off toward the play area.

Marie knew there would be a place for her to sit and eat near Patty and the other children. She cringed at the thought of all those sticky little fingers touching the same play surfaces, but this time she'd make an excep-

tion. Considering the fact that Patty had been dragged away from home in the middle of the night, the poor little thing was coping pretty well. Too bad her mama was such a nervous wreck.

As usual, it was hard to convince Patty to slow down long enough to eat. Marie had consumed her own meal long before the excited child was half-finished.

Running out of patience, Marie again gazed out the window toward her car. One of those big, boxy, delivery trucks had stopped sideways in the parking lot and was blocking her view.

She immediately got to her feet and started to gather up their trash. Trucks like that were common, yet there was something about the situation that set her nerves on edge. Then again, since Roy had been kidnapped, *everything* made her nervous.

"Come on, Patty. We're leaving," she called.

"Aw, Mom. Do we have to?"

"Patricia Anne. Now." Marie knew her raised voice was attracting undue attention but she didn't care. As long as she couldn't see her car, there was no guarantee it was all right. Not only was that vehicle their current means of escape, but also practically everything they owned was crammed into it.

Dragging the reluctant little girl by the hand and praying silently, Marie hurried toward the exit. Something made her stop in the small entryway and look up just before she pushed through the glass outer door.

A muscular man in jeans and a sleeveless T-shirt was preparing to climb into the box truck. He had one

booted foot planted on the step, his hand on the open driver's door. Nothing about the scene would have bothered Marie if the trucker hadn't paused to stare straight at her—and kept on staring.

She stood very still, wondering if she'd be able to make her feet move if she had to. Seconds crept by. A group of noisy, jostling teenagers piled out of a yellow school bus and filed between Marie and the menacing truck driver, temporarily distracting her and blocking her view.

She had to step back and pull Patty close to allow the rowdy teens to squeeze by in the confining space of the entryway. When she looked back at the parking lot, she was relieved to note that the worrisome truck was slowly pulling away.

Her relief was short-lived. As the unmarked vehicle passed, the menace in the driver's piercing gaze gave Marie chills all the way to her toes.

Marie's car didn't begin to run badly until later that afternoon. At first it just stuttered and missed a few times. Then it began to falter as if it wasn't getting enough fuel.

Marie nursed the car into a filling station and garage off Highway 62. Was it was possible she was out of gas? She was trying to figure the distances in her head and make an educated guess when a tall, broad-shouldered man came toward her.

"That engine sounds like you have a problem," he said amiably.

If he hadn't been wearing a baseball cap with a repair service logo on it and wiping black grease off his hands as he spoke, Marie might have been worried by his approach.

She nervously combed her fingers through her cinnamon-colored hair and tucked the longer side tresses behind her ears out of habit. "I don't know what's wrong with it. It was running fine until a little while ago."

"You from around here?" the man asked.

She tensed. "Why?"

"Just wondered," he said, still smiling. "Want me to have a look at it for you?"

"I don't know. I …"

"No charge," he said. "I promise."

Her eyes narrowed as she studied him, looking for hidden motives behind the magnanimous offer. Maybe the good Lord was looking out for her after all, she reasoned, feeling guilty for being so suspicious. If God chose to use this man to bless her, who was she to refuse or to doubt?

"I'm just being neighborly," he said. "The name's Seth Whitfield."

"Pleased to meet you. If you think you can tell anything about my car by looking, go for it. Just don't start taking things apart. I can't afford expensive repairs."

"It's a deal." He raised the hood, propped it up and leaned in.

Marie got Patty out of the car and stood with her in the shade of the service station bay while the man

tinkered with her car. If she'd had the slightest warning that she'd need to make a cross-country trip she'd at least have had the car serviced first.

Penitent, she took a moment to thank God that she'd managed to escape the same fate that had befallen poor Roy. It seemed odd that she didn't feel much connection to him other than simple concern, but she supposed the intervening years of separation had deadened her emotions. Roy had chosen to continue his illegal activities in spite of her pleas for him to stop, and the last time she had tried to discuss it with him he'd gotten drunk and given her a brutal beating. That had been the final straw. She'd left him that night and never looked back.

Marie smiled down at her daughter. The child was her joy, her whole life, and she wasn't a bit sorry that she'd finally had the courage to distance herself from Roy. She was just sad that the little girl would grow up without the love of a decent father figure.

She sighed, remembering her own childhood. She'd managed to survive without the moral support of either parent and she'd turned out okay. Well, sort of, if you didn't count her unwise alliance with Roy when she was only seventeen. He had promised her the moon, and for a while she'd been able to fool herself into believing him, to put up with his terrible temper no matter how much he hurt her.

Patty's birth had changed everything. It had placed an innocent life in Marie's hands, and for the first time in her life she knew what it was like to really love and

be loved. The realization that there could be so much more to living had been such a shock she could still hardly believe it.

And it was concern for her little girl's welfare that had drawn her into church, had brought her to acknowledge a faith she'd only glimpsed before circumstances had led her to make that choice. When she'd decided that Patty needed exposure to Sunday school, Marie had attended, too, and had found solace and acceptance there, as well as soul mates, when she'd finally turned to Christ.

Leaving her church family behind in Louisiana without so much as a goodbye had been hard for Marie. Those wonderful people cared about her, truly cared. And they would be so worried when they realized she had left town without a single parting word.

Sighing, Marie watched the mechanic move from side to side and tap on parts of her car's motor. She had no idea what was wrong, nor did she care. All that mattered was getting the car fixed and being on her way again.

If the man hadn't acted so friendly to begin with, she might have been put off by his rustic looks and grease-streaked clothing. She didn't expect a garage worker to wear a suit, of course, but the employees of the place where she went to have her oil changed dressed in neat coveralls. This man's tattered jeans and short-sleeved shirt looked anything but professional.

"Are you sure you know what you're doing?" she finally asked.

He straightened, grinning, and wiped his hands on

an already dirty rag. "The boss thinks I do. But if you want to go on down the road, you're welcome to."

"Do you think my car will make it very far?"

"Honestly? No. I suspect you got some dirty gas the last time you filled up. Where was that?"

She wanted to snap at him, to tell him it was none of his business, but she stifled the urge. He wasn't asking anything that a normal person wouldn't be glad to answer. Rather than admit that her trip was far from typical, she shrugged. "Beats me. I didn't pay much attention. We've just been kind of rambling across the country."

"I see. I noticed the Louisiana plates and figured you were probably headed north."

The license plates! She'd been so upset she hadn't thought of that. "I—I borrowed the car from a friend," Marie alibied. "She lives down there. I'm actually from Texas."

Her daughter tugged on her hand and looked up at her. "Mama? No, we're…"

"That's enough, Patty," Marie said, purposely interrupting. "You and I will go get an ice cream while this man works on our car. How does that sound?"

"Chocolate," the five-year-old said. "Two scoops."

"Fine." She turned back to the mechanic. "I'll trust you to do whatever the car needs, within reason. Can you have it running soon?"

"I can try," Seth answered. He pointed. "There's a café on the square that has good food. And Hickory Station, about half a block that way, sells ice cream and snacks."

"Thanks."

Hesitant to leave her belongings unattended, Marie nevertheless grabbed her purse from the front seat and walked off. She figured it was best to get Patty away from the service station before the child revealed too much. She knew it was wrong to lie, let alone to ask an innocent child to do so, but in this situation she was certain the good Lord would forgive them. After all, He was the one who now had their lives in His hands, the one who had promised to look after His children.

Marie started to smile in spite of all her worries. If that rough-looking guy with the sandy-gray hair was supposed to be a Heaven-sent guardian in disguise, his masquerade was working. He surely didn't look the part.

He'd had nice eyes, though, she mused. Blue, like the summer sky, with tinges of gray to match his hair and little smile wrinkles at the outer corners. He didn't appear to be very old, but she supposed it was possible for a man to be turning gray in his thirties, which was roughly what she estimated his age to be.

Pausing and waiting for passing cars before crossing the peaceful, tree-lined street, she glanced back at the service station.

Instead of working on her car as he'd promised, the man was standing beside it with his hands fisted on his hips. His eyes were shaded by his ball cap, but she could tell he was looking directly at her.

She stared back at him. He didn't flinch. His intense, unwavering concentration gave her the shivers from her nape to her toes.

Grabbing Patty's hand, she half dragged the little girl as she hurried across the street. The sooner they were back on the road and heading for parts unknown, the happier she'd be.

The only question now was how she could either change cars or find another license plate that wouldn't reveal her origin. If she'd been a thief like Roy, she'd have simply stolen one. Being an honest person could be difficult at times, couldn't it?

She glanced Heavenward. "Father, how about leaving a discarded license plate along the road somewhere, huh? I know it's a lot to ask, but…"

"Mama?"

"Yes, honey?"

"Are you praying?"

"Yes, Patty," Marie said with a nod. "I sure am."

"Good," the little girl answered, hurrying to keep pace with her mother's rapid strides, "'cause you lied and I don't want God to be mad at you."

TWO

Seth frowned. He had an uneasy feeling about that woman. Oh, she'd seemed innocent enough at first, but she'd definitely wanted to hide where she'd come from, so there was no telling what else about her story was false.

The real question was, why not tell the truth? Was she the stranded motorist she pretended to be, or was there a more sinister reason for her supposed breakdown? He hadn't thought his enemies would use a child to get to him, but that woman looked enough like his late wife to be her younger sister. Same light reddish-brown hair, same few freckles, same long lashes and beautiful brown eyes.

That uncanny resemblance gave him pause. If someone was trying to send him a message or make sure his real identity was exposed, what better way to do it than through a pretty woman pretending to be in distress?

He turned back to the car. If she was a planted informant and he let her go, there was no telling how long it would be before someone else followed. Perhaps someone more lethal. If he kept her in town for

a few more days and checked her background, however, he'd have a better idea whether or not his real identity had been discovered.

It made sense to know his foes up front, he told himself. And it looked as if it wasn't going to be easy to repair the woman's car without disassembling the fuel system, so that would give him overnight, at least.

He slipped into the passenger's seat and popped open the glove box. The car was registered to a Marie Parnell. If the driver had actually borrowed this vehicle from a friend, that friend must be named Parnell. That, or the woman had fibbed about where she'd gotten the car.

Either way, it looked as if he'd offered to be a good Samaritan for a bald-faced liar. He just hoped he hadn't made a big, big mistake. Then again, it wouldn't be his first.

He huffed in self-disgust. One mistake had cost him dearly. He just wished he'd recognized the looming danger in time to have saved Alice's life. Perhaps, if he hadn't been so caught up in his work, he'd have realized that she was planning to file for divorce and he could have made the news public. Then, the men who were trying to frame him might have changed their minds about eliminating her.

Or, they might have gone ahead and killed her anyway so they'd have even more to blame him for, he argued. Corporate espionage could be just as dirty and just as deadly as covert government operations. In his case, he had been pegged as the fall guy because he'd

been doing deep undercover work for Corp. Inc. and hadn't been able to prove his innocence. If he hadn't had friends who had warned him, he'd probably either be buried beside poor Alice or serving time for her murder, along with a conviction for corporate theft.

Seth shuddered at the thought, then turned back to the car he'd been working on. Reliving the past was counterproductive. As long as he kept his guard up and didn't let a good-looking woman like this car's driver get too close to him, he'd survive. At this point in his life, that was all he could ask for.

By the time Marie and Patty returned from their ice cream quest, Seth had put the compact car up on a rack in the garage and was poking around under it.

"What do you think?" Marie asked, holding tightly to her daughter's hand.

He shrugged as he continued to work. "Beats me. I disconnected a plugged fuel line, and it looked as if somebody had dumped sawdust into your gas tank. Did you tick someone off?"

"No, I..." The memory of the incident in the fast-food restaurant parking lot flashed into her mind. If anyone had been tampering with her car, she couldn't have seen the individual doing it because the van had blocked her view. And if that was where her gas tank had been fouled, that meant her instincts had been correct: she hadn't shaken her pursuers after all. The conclusion made her shiver in spite of the warmth of the afternoon.

Seth turned to look at her as he pushed a button that lowered the car to the ground. "What?"

"Nothing," she said quickly. "Nothing. I have no idea who might have done such a thing."

"Well, it won't be an easy fix. The fuel filter is inside your gas tank. That means I'll have to drain the gas and drop the tank in order to flush it out, clean the lines and change filters."

"How long will that take?" She noted the lack of his usually warm smile.

"Depends. If I can pick up a new filter here in town, probably a day or two. If I have to wait for parts, maybe a week or more."

"No. That's impossible. I can't stay here that long."

"You don't really have much choice," he said. "I'm good at my job, but if you don't let me replace the filter, I can't guarantee that you'll get very far."

She peered past him at the quaint little town. "I don't even know where I am. Is this Missouri?"

"Not yet. You're about twenty miles shy of the border." He pointed north. "Missouri's that way. This is Serenity, Arkansas."

"Where can I rent a car?"

Seth laughed. "Here? Lady, you're lucky there's any place that can even repair your car, let alone rent you another one. I suppose if you've got enough money, you might be able to trade for a different vehicle down at Tony's sales lot."

"I'd love to," Marie replied. "Unfortunately, I'm

not rich." She gave a wry chuckle. "But I guess you figured that out from the car I'm driving."

"Never can tell about folks around here," Seth said. "Some of the people who look as if they can't even afford their next meal could buy and sell this garage and have change left over."

"Are you the owner?"

"Nope. I just work here. You'll need a place to stay. We have a nice family motel close by. Maybe you noticed it when you drove past."

"I'm afraid not. I was too concerned about the way my car was running. Or I should say, *not* running."

"That makes sense. Look, I'll be glad to give you and your daughter a lift to the motel, as long as you have no objection to sharing the truck seat with a friendly dog."

"A dog?"

Seth pointed toward the corner of the service bay where his black-and-white border collie was napping on an old blanket. "That's Babe. She never lets me out of her sight, and I wouldn't want her to get hurt trying to follow us on foot." He smiled benevolently, easing Marie's mind.

She looked down and saw an eager expression on the little girl's face. "Patty loves animals. She's always asking for a pet. I'm sure she'd love to meet Babe. Wouldn't you, honey?"

"Yeah!"

"I thought so. All right. We'll accept a ride that far. And thanks."

"You're welcome. Just give me a sec to tell the boss where I'm going. I'll be right back."

Marie reached her free hand toward him, barely touching his sleeve to stop him. "One more thing," she said soberly, quietly. "I need to ask a favor."

"Sure. What?"

"If anyone should come by looking for us, promise me you won't tell them where we are?"

"Why not? What'd you do, rob a bank?"

She frowned. "That's not funny. Will you do as I ask, or not?"

"Of course," Seth said with a casual shrug. "I don't even know your name so I can hardly blab all your secrets, can I?"

"It's Marie. Marie Smith. And this is Patty."

"Pleased to meet you, ma'am. Pick out whatever luggage you'll need from your car and go wait by that green pickup truck over there. Babe and I'll join you in a minute."

As he hurried away, Marie felt Patty's tug on her hand. When she looked down, she saw the child's lips pressed into a thin, thoughtful line. "What, honey?"

"You did it again, Mama."

"I know I did. And I'm sorry to be setting such a bad example for you, but sometimes grown-ups have to make up stories."

"Why?"

"To keep our wonderful children safe," Marie said. "Someday, when you're older, I'll explain everything. I promise."

"'Cause that man's a stranger?" Patty asked.

"That's right. He is a stranger. And you know how I've warned you not to talk to strangers."

"But *you* talked to him."

"Only because I had no other choice," Marie said.

"I think he's nice. And his dog is real pretty," the child said with a smile. "Maybe if I'm good, he'll let me play with her."

"Don't count on it. We aren't going to stay here one minute longer than we absolutely have to. As soon as our car is running again, we're leaving."

"Aw, Mama. I like it here."

"Why?"

"I dunno. 'Cause everybody's friendly?"

As Marie scanned the almost deserted street, looking for evidence of another nemesis, she saw nothing but a peaceful place of safety. It was future hidden dangers that she knew she must fear. If she allowed herself to be lulled into unquestioning acceptance of the rural Ozark town and didn't remain alert, she'd be an easy target. And so would Patty. That must never happen.

The white truck cruised slowly along the stretch of highway that passed through Serenity. Its driver peered out the windshield. He didn't know what could have happened to the Parnell woman. He'd been so sure he'd find her car broken down along the road because of the way he'd doctored her fuel tank that he hadn't felt it was necessary to actually keep her in sight. Now it looked as if he'd miscalculated.

Not that he wouldn't eventually pick up her trail again, he told himself. He'd better. His partners did not take kindly to failure.

There was a lot more at stake here than just lives, too, he added. Roy had made off with enough money to make anybody drool. Even if he hadn't passed the cash to his old girlfriend for safekeeping, they figured to use the kid as a bargaining tool. Old Roy didn't have much that he cared about except his little girl. Once they got their hands on her, they knew he'd reveal where he'd hidden the ransom money.

The driver smiled to himself. And then they'd kill him. With pleasure.

Seth delivered his passengers to the redbrick, Hilltop Motel, followed them into the small, sparsely furnished lobby and lingered near the front desk to see if the woman produced a credit card. She didn't.

The clerk looked concerned. "I'm sorry, ma'am. We prefer you pay by charge card."

"All I have is cash," Marie said. "Surely, you don't mind taking real money."

"Well, I don't know. Most people…"

Seth spoke up. "It's okay, Clarence. We have her car down at the station. She's not going anywhere till it's fixed. And I promise to give you time to count the towels before I let her leave town."

"If you say so, that's good enough for me," the clerk replied with a smile. He programmed a key card and

handed it to Marie. "Your room is around back, by the pool. Ground floor. I trust that's satisfactory."

She nodded and managed to return his grin. "That will be fine, thanks."

"Can I hug the dog goodbye?" Patty asked her.

"That's up to Mr. Whitfield."

"How about we both walk you to your door?" Seth suggested. "I need to deliver your suitcases for you, anyway."

He could tell by the reluctance in the woman's movements that she wasn't keen on letting him help, so he gave her no options. As soon as they left the office, he whistled to his dog and swung the heavy bags out of the back of the truck.

Marie was crouching to join her daughter in petting the joyful border collie when she suddenly froze in that position.

Seth followed her line of sight to the street. There was nothing about the passing traffic that he saw as threatening, but the woman sure seemed to.

He paused. "Are you okay?"

"Fine. Fine," she answered, grabbing the child's hand and hurrying her around the side of the motel building.

Babe bounded along beside her new playmate and Seth followed. As soon as Marie had unlocked the door, the dog ran into the room ahead of everyone, much to Patty's delight.

"Look, Mama! She wants to stay and play with me."

"Well, she can't." Marie practically yanked her bag from Seth's grip. "Thank you for your help."

He bowed slightly and smiled, placing Patty's smaller suitcase at the foot of the closest bed before backing toward the open door. "My pleasure. C'mon, Babe. I think we've overstayed our welcome."

When the door slammed behind him, he was certain he heard the deadbolt click into place, too. Something had sure spooked Marie, although he had no idea what.

Sauntering back to his truck, he motioned to the dog to jump in ahead of him, then scanned the street as he pulled out of the driveway. There were more pickups passing than there were cars, which was normal for a place like Serenity. A slow delivery van was partially blocking traffic halfway up the block. The driver was probably lost, which was not unusual either, since so many of the outlying streets were unmarked, dirt roads.

When Seth had eased up even with the idling van, he leaned across his truck seat, past Babe, to peer at the driver. "Can I help you?"

The man's "No" was followed by a curse that caused Seth to recoil. Folks in the South were so well known for their amiability that this kind of response stood out like a red flag. If the stranger truly was an innocent delivery man, there was no earthly reason why he should act so inhospitably.

Pulling ahead and back into the line of traffic, Seth raced for the service station. He wasn't sure that any of this pertained to Marie, but he wasn't about to take the chance that it might. Something had frightened her when she'd stared at the street a few minutes ago, and

as far as he could tell, there were no strangers in the area except the foul-mouthed guy in the delivery truck.

Therefore, Seth was going to do all he could to hide her car from prying eyes until he found out exactly what was going on.

And he *was* going to find out.

One way or another.

Marie was beside herself. She immediately drew the heavy, maroon drapes together and peeked through a thin slit where they met in the center of the motel room window.

Had the van's driver spied her? She didn't think so. But what about her car? Although it was parked inside the repair shop for the present, Seth would probably move it out of the way until he was able to get the necessary replacement parts. If he did so, the man in the white van would surely spot it. And then it would only be a matter of time before Roy's enemies were able to track her down.

Hands trembling, she picked up the thin local phone book and looked up the number of the garage. She didn't want to involve Seth in her problems but saw no alternative.

The pleasant-sounding man who answered the telephone quickly put the mechanic on the line when Marie requested to speak with him.

"Where is my car?" she blurted.

"Marie? I mean, Mrs. Smith?"

"Yes. Where did you put my car?"

"I left it inside," he answered calmly. "Where nobody can see it if they drive by."

She was taken aback. "You did? Why?"

"Beats me. It just seemed like the best thing to do. Would you care to tell me what's going on?"

"Not really."

"I didn't think so."

"It's better if you don't know."

"Is it? That remains to be seen. How can I help you if you won't confide in me?"

"All you have to do is keep my car out of sight, like you already have, and everything will be fine," she said.

"What are you afraid of?"

"Nothing."

"Don't you know it's a sin to lie?" he asked.

"That's what Patty keeps telling me."

She heard him chuckle before he said, "Smart kid. What was your response to that?"

"I told her it was probably okay if it was absolutely necessary."

"Can't argue with you there, although I imagine my pastor would," Seth said. "Look, I'll be off duty in a couple of hours. How about if I stop by and pick you both up for supper? I know a couple of great little places to eat. Patty likes pizza, right?"

"We aren't going anywhere with you," Marie said flatly. "We don't even know you."

"Do you want your car left in the garage or shall I move it outside, tonight?"

"That's blackmail." She didn't want to give in to his demands but saw no easy way to avoid capitulating.

"Not exactly. Let's just call it Southern hospitality in an extreme form. Be ready at seven. I'll pull around back, and you won't have to show your face until we're out of town if you don't want to."

"We're leaving town?"

"Just as far as Gumption. It's about five miles away."

"All right," she said, although every instinct told her to stand her ground. "But the dog comes, too. I want an impartial chaperone."

Seth's resulting laugh sounded warm and not at all threatening. "It's a deal. Babe loves pizza almost as much as I do. And it's going to be a warm evening. We can make it a picnic in the park—totally public—if you're worried about being alone with me."

"I'm a lot more worried about being out in public, with or without you," Marie admitted ruefully. "We'll be waiting."

THREE

Marie had showered, washed and dried her hair and changed into lightweight slacks and a casual top long before it was time for Seth to pick them up. It had occurred to her that perhaps it would be wise for both her and Patty to dye or bleach their hair, but she couldn't bring herself to alter the child's beautiful, natural coloring.

Besides, the way she saw it, as long as they were driving that old blue car of hers, there was no way a changed physical appearance was going to help much. What she needed to do was ditch the car, the way pursued victims always did in the movies. Unfortunately, she had barely enough cash to continue running away, let alone buy a different vehicle.

Another problem was Patty's insistence that her mother always tell the absolute truth in spite of the danger of doing so. Smiling, Marie recalled being the same kind of stubborn, exasperating child she was now raising. Except in her case, her mother had simply given up. And her father? He had been gone so much

that, although Marie had an overall impression of his being rather handsome and suave, she could barely envision his face.

Marie promised herself that she was not going to make that kind of mistake in regard to Patty. With the blessing of having a child came serious responsibility, not only for that child's physical needs but for the spiritual, as well.

A knock on the door brought her back to the present and made her heart leap. Instead of answering verbally, she hurried to peer out the peephole.

It was Seth. He had picked up Babe and was moving the dog's foreleg so that it looked as if she was waving hello.

Relieved, Marie opened the door. "Hi. You're early."

"I figured you two might be hungry, so I hurried," he said with a smile. The minute he released the dog, she bounded through the door and jumped onto the bed, trying to kiss her new buddy.

Giggling, Patty pushed her away and ran back to the door, with Babe in pursuit.

Marie gathered up her purse and jackets for her and Patty in case the evening turned chilly, made sure she had her key card and closed the door behind them before remarking, "You clean up pretty nicely, mister."

"Thanks. These are my best jeans and a new shirt. Are you surprised?"

"I wasn't referring to your clothes," she explained, feeling her cheeks warming. "I just didn't think you'd ever be able to get all that grease off your hands."

"Sandpaper does it every time," he quipped.

She arched an eyebrow and played along. "Must be painful."

"Not if I use a fine-enough grain."

The deadpan way he delivered the silly explanation made Marie laugh. She'd had serious misgivings about going anywhere with Seth—or with anyone else—and it helped to find humor in the situation. There had certainly been little to laugh about in the past few days.

"How about if I hold Patty on my lap and we let Babe have the window seat?" she suggested as Seth opened the truck door for her.

"Sorry. Seat belts for everybody. It's a rule of mine."

"We didn't use belts when you drove us up here," Marie argued.

"No, and we should have." He pointed into the truck. "I took the liberty of pulling Patty's booster seat out of your car. She can sit in the middle." He began to grin. "I suppose you could hold Babe on your lap if you want, but you're liable to get covered with dog hair if you try it."

"Then I guess I should have worn something black and white instead of light blue," Marie said, making a face. "All right. You win. I'll sit by the door and use my seat belt."

"Good decision. We don't want to set a bad example for your little girl." He was grinning. "I'll fasten Babe in the truck bed so she won't fall out and we'll have more room up front for people."

"Really, I…"

"I know. You want to hide behind the dog."

Marie was astounded that he'd deduced the truth so easily. "Well…"

"Don't worry. Your secret is safe with me, whatever it is. Here." He held out a dark blue ball cap similar to the one he'd been wearing when she'd first seen him. "It's brand-new. No grease or anything on it, honest. Tuck your hair underneath, pull down the brim to shade your face, and your own mother wouldn't recognize you."

"That's the truth," Marie replied, accepting the cap and doing as he'd suggested. "The color almost matches my jacket."

"I suppose I should say I did that on purpose, but to be perfectly honest it was accidental."

As Patty crawled into the booster seat, Marie held her side of the seat belt while Seth pulled the opposite end into place.

When their hands brushed, she jerked away. His fingers had felt a bit calloused, yet warm and gentle at the same time. The mystery was, why had she noticed? After all, she had sworn off men for good, thanks to Roy, and nothing had happened since then to make her change her mind. Perhaps someday she'd feel free to seek happiness other than in her role as Patty's mother, but right now she had plenty of problems without inviting more.

She took her place beside the little girl, drew her own belt over her shoulder and snapped it shut. It would pay her to remember that this trip to the pizza parlor

was not her idea. She had been coerced into going, and she was *not,* repeat not, going to enjoy herself.

Glancing sidelong at Seth, she was able to observe him without being too obvious. He looked awfully pleased, didn't he? That was off-putting. Distressing. When he had first insisted on this trip, she had assumed he was simply playing a macho role. Now that she'd had a chance to judge his reactions more closely, however, she was beginning to wonder if there was a deeper reason behind his behavior.

Of course, he might just be a nice, friendly guy who felt sorry for a stranded mother and daughter, Marie thought.

She huffed quietly. Yeah, right. And Roy Jenkins was just a misunderstood bad boy who had accidentally gone afoul of the law. If she had learned anything from her lonely childhood and disastrous time with Roy, it was that men could not be trusted or relied upon. Especially not good-looking, seemingly nice ones.

Seth drove toward Gumption on back roads, careful to avoid what little late evening traffic there was on a week night. His adult passenger had scooted down in her seat and was hiding her face with her raised hand. Therefore, as he pulled up to the pizza parlor, he chose a parking place as far away from the rest of the cars as possible.

"Here we are. How's this?" he asked, taking care to keep his tone light and easygoing.

"Fine. It doesn't look crowded at all."

"That's because this is early in the week. Friday and Saturday nights are much busier. Some places around here don't even stay open in the evenings except on those two days."

"Wow. That's amazing. Back home the restaurants are busy all the time."

Seth circled the truck to open her door for her. "And where would that be?" he asked nonchalantly.

"Alaska," Marie quipped. "Fairbanks."

Patty's eyes widened. "Mama…"

She smiled. "I know, I know, honey. It's not true. It was just a joke, okay?"

Seth didn't think the child looked convinced, but he let the moment pass. Sooner or later, one of them would slip and reveal the truth. Until that happened, he couldn't let down his guard for an instant. His heart told him that Marie and her little girl were innocent of any wrongdoing, but that wasn't enough to satisfy him. He'd been careless in the past, and it had cost him dearly. This time, he was determined to root out the truth before he permitted "Mrs. Smith" to leave Serenity.

Marie had decided that it would be best to remain inside the restaurant to eat, rather than take their meal to the city park, as Seth had suggested earlier. She was hungry and the pizza smelled delicious, but she was so nervous that she could hardly choke it down.

Worse, Seth and Patty were chatting away and seemed to be becoming fast friends. The child's trusting nature was very worrisome, especially where that

enigmatic man was concerned. On the surface, he seemed perfectly normal, yet there was something about him that made Marie's nerves tingle with unexplained warning.

She had tried repeatedly to pray for the Lord's guidance and had found it impossible to keep her mind from wandering with unanswered questions and baffling suspicions. Had she been so traumatized that she was unable to trust even the most casual acquaintance? Or was God warning her to stay alert despite a seemingly innocent situation?

Either alternative was possible, she finally decided. And until her car was repaired and she was free to continue her flight, there wasn't a thing she could do about it except cope as best she knew how.

"You're not eating much," Seth remarked with a smile.

"I'm not all that hungry, I guess."

"Well, Patty and I are," he replied. "We're saving our crusts for Babe. See?"

"I'm sure she'll enjoy them," Marie said, glancing at her daughter with a wistful smile. "We probably should be getting back to the motel. Patty's up way past her usual bedtime."

Seth stifled a yawn. "Yeah. So am I. But then, I get up at dawn and work hard all day, so I need my beauty sleep."

"Where do you live?" Marie asked. "In Serenity?"

"Sort of. I have a place out in the country, near Heart. It used to be a bustling town, even after Serenity was named the county seat back in the 1800s. Later, as

people got cars and began to move around more easily, the heart of Heart kind of withered and died."

"That's too bad."

"Times change. Places change. It's just the way things are." He paused and Marie noticed how seriously he was looking at her before he added, "Take you and Patty, for instance. I get the idea that you're not going back to wherever you came from."

"Really? Why would you think that?"

"Mainly because you have so much stuff crammed into your car. It looks more like you're making a permanent move than taking a simple vacation."

"Maybe." She stared at her half-eaten slice of pizza rather than look at him and take the chance he could read her thoughts. "I haven't decided."

"What made you head this way?" Seth asked quietly.

She shrugged. "I don't know. It seemed sensible."

"Yes. Especially if you're running away from someone or something down south."

Her head snapped up, her gaze locking with his. "I don't know what you're talking about."

"Really? Well, if it's not that, then why are you so afraid of being seen? And why did you practically beg me to hide your car while it's in the garage?"

"I did no such thing."

His grin was lopsided and his eyes bored into hers as if he was positive he was right and was gloating about it.

"Don't look so smug," she added. "You don't know anything about me."

"No, I don't. But I'd like to. If I'm going to stash your car for you, don't you think you owe me an explanation for why it needs to be kept out of sight?"

"Absolutely not."

Seth's eyebrows arched. "Okay. But if I had some idea of why you were in such a hurry to leave town, I might be more inclined to hurry the repairs."

"Are you threatening me?"

With a nonchalant shake of his head he shrugged off her question. "Not in the least. I already told you it might take a few days to get the parts. Remember?"

"Yes, but now that I think about it, you didn't say you'd install them right away. Promise me you will."

"Why?"

"Because I'm asking you to. And because there's no reason why you shouldn't." Her eyes narrowed. "Is there?"

"Of course not. We at Serenity Repair are always prompt and efficient. You can ask anybody."

"I'd rather ask you. Will you do the work in a timely manner, or are you going to stall?"

"Now, why would I do that?" he asked, sobering and staring back at her as if he had suddenly discovered she had three heads or something equally as bizarre.

Marie's lips were pressed into a thin line. "I can see no reason why you should," she answered. "I'm not looking for romance or a meal ticket, so if you're trying to court me, you can forget it."

When he chuckled, she was taken aback.

"*Court* you? Lady, that's the last thing on my mind."

"Then why take us out to eat? And why all the questions?"

"Maybe I'm just trying to be friendly."

She huffed in self-derision. "In that case, I apologize for misjudging you. I'm not used to men paying me this much attention for no reason. Just so you understand, a pizza and a little repair work on my car won't get you anywhere with me."

Seth laughed again, this time more loudly and with evident glee.

"I hardly think it's *that* funny," Marie insisted, scowling across the table at him.

He managed to get control of his high humor and reduce his laughter to a wide grin before he said, "Forgive me. If you knew what I've been thinking you'd probably be laughing, too."

"Are you going to tell me?"

"Nope," Seth said, still smiling. "You'll just have to trust me the way you want me to trust you. I have no amorous intentions. I promise."

She wasn't sure whether to be relieved or not, considering the fact that he was practically insisting he didn't find her attractive.

Well, that was what she had wanted, wasn't it? And since she'd had the opportunity to state her views implicitly, there was no way he could misconstrue her reasons for agreeing to let him treat her to supper.

Still, there was something odd about the man, a hidden part of his psyche she'd only glimpsed in an

occasional unguarded instant that came and went in a flash. Whatever that ominous-feeling insight was, it was too brief for her to interpret.

Seth's constant probing of her background was nevertheless unsettling. Granted, he might be no more than an interested bystander, yet he asked questions like a professional inquisitor, never missing the opportunity to slip in another query and never taking his eyes off her face when she answered. It was almost as if he knew more than he was letting on.

Her breath caught. There was no way this man could be in cahoots with the people who were pursuing her, was there? Of course not. He might be nosey, but he wasn't a dangerous criminal the way those other men were. No one could possibly have known she'd break down in Serenity and end up stopping at that very garage for assistance.

She shivered as more of the truth settled in her befuddled brain. If someone had sabotaged her car, as Seth surmised, they had known she would have car trouble. It was only by the grace of God, literally, that she had made it as far as Serenity and had managed to find temporary sanctuary.

Peering at Seth from beneath the brim of her cap, she studied him carefully. There was a hard edge to his personality, an undefined cautiousness, a strength that lay behind those smoky blue eyes no matter how wide his smile was or how casual his conversation might be.

Was she imagining things because she was so tense?

she wondered. Or was the good Lord enabling her to glimpse reality in order to know how best to proceed?

She had trusted Roy once, and look where that had gotten her. She'd be twice the fool if she placed her future in the hands of a stranger like Seth. Then again, he did seem to care what happened to her, or he wouldn't have taken it upon himself to keep her car where it couldn't be seen in passing.

The fact that he had done that, before she had asked, was the biggest puzzle of all. It was as if he had been on his guard all along.

That was why she had felt such an immediate affinity for him, she concluded, shocked by the turn her thoughts had taken.

Her eyes widened and she stared across the table. *Of course.* It was suddenly all too clear. Seth had empathized with her plight because he, too, was deathly afraid of someone or something.

FOUR

Roy's head was spinning and his whole body throbbed from the beating he'd received. Drifting in and out of consciousness, he thought of Marie and his darling daughter. He must hold out long enough to allow them sufficient time to get away. If he was going to die—and he was pretty sure that he was—he wanted his death to be for a good cause.

He wished he'd given Marie some of the stolen ransom so she'd have had traveling money. But it was too late now. He would probably never see Patty again. That was his punishment for trying to double-cross his three partners in crime, for hiding the whole ransom and trying to make them believe he'd never collected it. How was he to know they'd had a cohort on the inside who knew the truth? If he had it to do over again…

Someone yanked his hair to raise his head. Through swollen eyes, Roy peered at Frank, the largest of his captors, while Earl stood back out of the fray, nervously cleaning his thick eyeglasses.

"You might as well spill it," Frank said. "Al's

already closing in on your girlfriend and her brat. If you don't want this same thing to happen to them, you'd better tell us what you and she did with our money."

The portent of the beefy man's words hit Roy in the gut like a sucker punch. It had never occurred to him that his former partners would think he actually had passed the ransom to Marie. His silence had not protected her, as he'd hoped; it had made her a target!

The only thing to do was confess, he reasoned. Even if they killed him as a result, at least it would call the wolves off his little girl and Marie.

Through split, bleeding lips he managed to croak, "I—I…"

His response apparently wasn't fast or lucid enough to suit his abuser. Frank's meaty hand smacked him on the temple. His head snapped back and he doubled over. Blackness encroached. Flashes of colored light obscured his already blurry vision.

Roy stayed conscious long enough to hear Frank begin to laugh while Earl's squealing voice berated him for being so rough.

Then, picturing his darling little girl, Roy smiled, let go and sank into the peace of oblivion.

Seth was disappointed that his questioning of Marie had been so unproductive. He'd thought about trying again as he drove her back to the motel but had decided to back off and let the woman relax in the hope that that tactic would loosen her tongue. He had plenty of time. As long as her car was broken down,

she wasn't going to leave town before he was ready for her to go.

Marie entered her motel room, turned and blocked the door with her body, shielding her little girl and making it clear she did not intend to invite Seth in. "Thanks for the pizza," she said flatly as she doubled the front sides of her lightweight, navy blue jacket across her body and held them in place like a shield.

"My pleasure."

"About my car…"

"I told you I'd fix it and I will. Whoever dumped sawdust in your gas tank didn't intend for you to get very far, you know. You're lucky you made it to the station."

He saw her shiver and grow pale. "I know. I'm so glad I didn't stall along the highway."

Nodding, Seth agreed. "Exactly. There are some pretty isolated stretches between here and the major cities like Little Rock or Memphis. You'd have been much more vulnerable if you'd broken down way out there."

He watched as his statement sank in. Clearly, she was afraid. And given the circumstances of sabotage to her vehicle, that reaction made sense. What remained a mystery was why she was so frightened and what had driven her from her home in the first place.

"Well, good night," Seth said, politely touching the brim of his cap. "Stop by the garage tomorrow afternoon. I should be able to give you an idea of the time frame for repairs by then."

The look on her face was unreadable as she shut the door. Seth knew she was desperate to be on her

way, and he didn't intend to keep her in Serenity one minute more than necessary. But he wasn't going to let her leave until he made sure that she wasn't a plant sent there to unmask him.

Yes, his appearance had changed. And, yes, he had made a secure place for himself in the little town in the past three years. But that didn't mean that his enemies had given up searching for him. It only meant that they had not yet found his trail.

Leaving the motel, he drove straight to his farmstead. As he pulled into the darkened yard, he carefully scanned the shadows before getting out of the truck. While he'd been at supper with the woman and child, he'd left his short-barreled .38 locked in the glove compartment instead of carrying it, as was his usual practice. Now, he stuck it into his belt.

No matter how much time passed, Seth was never totally at ease. Hunted men who got careless were the ones who died. There had been some dark days in his past when he'd almost wished for the solace of death, but his Christian faith had kept him from giving up. Rather than alienating him from God, as was sometimes the case during difficult times, his trials had brought him closer to the Almighty than ever before, and for that he was thankful. The way Seth saw it, if the Lord wasn't ready to call him home, there must be a good reason.

He climbed out of the truck. Babe followed and ran her usual pattern of wide circles around the yard, sniffing and checking the territory. Seth had gotten her

for a companion rather than a watchdog, but as it had turned out, she was both. If Babe indicated that the place was secure, that was good enough for him.

Slapping his leg and calling to her, he entered the house and flipped on the lights. It was late and he was tired, but he had some work to do on the computer before he'd be able to sleep.

It had been a long time since he'd checked in with his old acquaintances at Corp. Inc.—for very good reason. However, since he needed inside information on the woman calling herself Marie Smith and their database was the best place he knew of to get it, he'd make a one-time exception. As long as he routed his access through a couple of anonymizer sites and kept his query time short so no one had time to actively trace him, Seth didn't see much threat to himself—or to her.

He brewed a cup of coffee and carried it from the large farm kitchen to the computer desk in his bedroom. His fingers hovered over the keyboard. Contact with those involved in his former life, even via false identities, held a risk, yes, but if that was the only way to find out what Marie was hiding, he'd have to chance it.

First, though, he'd try a search of common, open databases and see what those turned up. *Smith* was too generic to be useful but *Parnell,* the name he'd found on the car's registration, might lead to some answers.

With Babe curled up at his feet, Seth checked the

telephone listings for Louisiana and quickly located a Marie Parnell in Baton Rouge.

"Got her!" he said aloud, causing the dog to open one eye and blink up at him. Seth chuckled. "Sorry, girl. Didn't mean to disturb you. This is turning out to be a lot easier than I'd thought."

From there he checked local Louisiana newspapers online and found nothing of note. He did, however, see that crime was at its usual level and that law enforcement seemed to be struggling. In other words, everything was normal and other men like him were probably working undercover to do what the regular officials could not openly condone.

That conclusion brought his thoughts back to his former colleagues at Corp. Inc. They had access to a covert information network second to none. If there was anything about Marie Parnell that he should know, it would be found on that well-guarded database.

Seth cracked his knuckles, took a deep breath and started hiding his tracks through one site after another, eventually coming to the point where he could enter Corp. Inc.'s system through a "backdoor" by using the access code he'd been given before he'd gone into hiding.

It still worked! He was in. Seth's eyes widened as the information about Marie appeared below her photograph. Not only was she tied to the disappearance of a known criminal named Roy Jenkins, but also she was suspected of having been involved in a

kidnapping that had occurred several months before. The ransom had been paid and the victim released, but the perpetrators were still at large.

Seth sighed and sat back. "Well, well, Mrs. Smith," he said softly. "What have you been up to?"

Marie hadn't expected to sleep well that night and her expectations unfortunately had been fulfilled. Patty, on the other hand, slept like the carefree child she was and awoke full of energy and enthusiasm.

Choosing the most nondescript outfits she could put together, Marie dressed herself and Patty, added their jackets against the morning chill and went to the motel office.

"Good morning," she said with a smile. "You're Clarence, right?"

"Yes, ma'am." His Adam's apple bobbed.

"Is there a nearby café where we can get breakfast?"

The desk clerk gestured with a thin arm and a wide grin. "No need, ma'am. We have free coffee and juice and donuts right in there. And you're in luck. I just bought a fresh box of 'em from down at Hickory Station."

Marie stifled a giggle as her vivid imagination suggested a very long shelf life for the previous batch of donuts. She would have preferred something more nutritious for Patty, but under the circumstances she was willing to settle for just about anything she didn't have to venture out to fetch.

"Thank you," she said, "and while I think of it, I

need to pay you again. Mr. Whitfield says he won't be able to get the parts for my car for another day or so."

"So he told me," the clerk replied. "Don't you worry none. Seth vouches for you, that's good enough for me."

"Thanks." Marie led Patty into the anteroom where the coffee and juice bar were set up and got her settled with milk, juice and a donut before pouring herself a cup of coffee. Clarence was lounging in the doorway, so she took the opportunity to quiz him. "Have you lived here long?"

"All my life. I was born over in Camp, but my folks moved to Serenity when I was little. Dad worked at the feed mill and Ma sewed at the shirt factory till it shut down in the '90s."

"I suppose Seth, Mr. Whitfield, has been here all his life, too."

"Nope. He's a flatlander, I reckon. Leastwise that's what folks say. He's never talked much about where he came from."

Marie raised an eyebrow. "Really? Why not?"

"Some folks don't, that's all. We just let 'em be."

"So, you don't know anything about his past?"

Clarence chuckled and shook his head. "Around these parts, a man's past don't count near as much as how he behaves every day. Seth's a right regular fella. You can trust him not to cheat you when he fixes your car, if that's what you're worried about."

Concentrating on her coffee cup instead of making eye contact with the amiable clerk, Marie chose

to let Clarence assume that her concerns were financial. She did have some worries about the size of her repair bill, but money wasn't the most important thing. Safety was. And as long as she stayed in one place, the chances that her pursuer would locate her were probably greater than if she was once again on the road.

As she pondered the possibilities, she began to wonder if the Lord had not used her breakdown for something good. Yes, she was stuck in Serenity. But she was also in contact with a man who seemed almost as wary as she was. That could be to her advantage, especially since Seth had already taken it upon himself to try to protect her.

It was his hidden motives that were worrisome. He had not said or done one thing out of place, yet she could sense that he was hiding something. Her time with Roy had taught her to spot a practiced liar, and she was almost certain that Seth Whitfield was cut from the same cloth, no matter how popular he happened to be with the townspeople.

Al, the truck-driving criminal who had been trailing Marie, stopped in a little café on the square in Gumption. The place looked as if it had been caught in a time warp and had never left the 1950s.

He crossed the checkerboard floor, chose a stool at the counter and listened to the conversation going on around him as he wolfed down his breakfast and sipped strong coffee. These hayseeds were incredible.

All they seemed to care about were crops and cows and hunting and fishing. Didn't they have *real* lives?

Taking advantage of a lull in the conversation, Al nodded toward an older man on his right. "Morning."

The local eyed him warily from beneath the brim of his sweat-stained ball cap. "Morning. You're not from around here, are you?"

"Nope. Just passing through. Been having trouble with my truck, though. Can you recommend a good mechanic?"

He noted how the man was studying his crudely tattooed forearms, so he added, "I'd be obliged if you could help me out. I want to hit the road again as soon as I can."

That seemed to satisfy the farmer because he loosened up. "Well, let's see. There's Butch's place. It's up the road toward Moko, on the way to West Plains. And if you're headed south, there's the Serenity Repair shop just off the highway."

"Thanks," Al said. "I'll check those out."

"Which way you goin'?"

Instead of answering, Al slapped some bills on the counter, turned and walked out. This job was getting too confusing for one man to handle. The first thing he was going to do was get on the phone and recruit some help. If there were two or three of them searching, they could spread out and cover more territory. The way he saw it, that was the only way they'd be sure of nabbing the Parnell woman before she got too far away to track.

He pulled his cell phone from his pocket and punched in a number.

"Frank? This is Al," he said as soon as he was connected. "No, I don't have her yet. But I know I'm close."

Frank began to curse loudly. Al held the phone away from his ear till the shouting stopped.

"Yeah, yeah. You don't have to rub it in," he finally said. "I know I screwed up. What I need is a little help here. The woman can't have gone far. I just can't be in more than one place at a time, and I need to check all the local garages before she gets her car fixed and takes off again."

As he listened to Frank's reply, his countenance darkened. "Roy's dead? Well, what did he say?"

The answer didn't do anything to elevate his mood, and he spoke before censoring his words. "And you say *I'm* stupid? How could you let that happen? I mean, what if the woman gets away and we never find our money?"

His cohort's reply was anything but understanding.

"Yeah, I know," Al said. "I'll find her. You and Earl just get up here and help me, will you? I can't be everywhere at once."

When he'd hung up, he sat in the cab of the truck and stared out the windshield. Things were getting worse fast. There was no telling what would happen to the lost ransom money. And if somebody didn't manage to find Roy's kid and use her to make her mama cough up the dough, he'd be in as much trouble with his partners as Roy had been.

FIVE

Unbelievably antsy, Marie started to walk toward the garage just after noon. There were no sidewalks and very little room for pedestrians on the shoulder of the road, so she decided to cut across some lawns and detour through a used-car lot.

Judging by the prices painted in white on the windows of the vehicles, she could tell there was no chance she'd be able to trade her sedan for one of these trucks or cars without putting up additional money—that she couldn't spare. Every cent had to count and it was only a matter of time before she'd have to stop and get a job to finance their continued escape. The thought of having to settle anywhere, even temporarily, was so unnerving it made her tremble.

"Please, God," she whispered, "tell me what to do?"

Patty tugged on her hand. "You don't need to pray, Mama. I already did."

Marie smiled down at her. "Thank you, honey."

"You're welcome. And you know what? God said

we should stay right here so I can play with Babe some more."

Grinning, Marie shook her head. "I'm afraid you're imagining things, Patty. I know you like that dog, but we can't stay."

"Why not?"

"Because."

"Because why?"

"Just because," Marie said. "When you're older, you'll understand."

"Aw, you always say that."

Although the child began to pout, Marie didn't elaborate. All along she had told Patty as much of the truth as possible, withholding troublesome details such as Roy's background and the fact that she and he had never been married. It was bad enough that that was true and that there was nothing Marie could do about it. Her pastor had assured her that all her prior sins had been forgiven when she'd given her life to Christ. Still, there were times when she wished mightily that she could go back and relive her earlier days. Do things differently.

Except that if she hadn't gotten mixed up with Roy and conceived a child with him, Patty wouldn't exist. That scenario was unthinkable. In retrospect, she wondered if the Lord had not purposely used her mistakes to create the wonder that was her little girl, knowing that someday Marie would need someone special to love the way she loved Patty. It was certainly a possibility.

Now, her sole responsibility was to protect her child, she reminded herself. That was her most important task, her God-given assignment. And she was determined to succeed.

Wending her way across the used-car lot separating her from the repair garage, she took her time while enjoying the warmth of the sun. The farther north she'd driven, the more she'd missed the Louisiana heat. At home there was pretty much one season—hot and humid—except for occasional dips in temperature during the winter months. Up here in northern Arkansas the weather was definitely less predictable, as she was quickly learning, and she hoped she'd packed enough warm clothing for the chilly evenings.

For Marie, there was no respite from worry about anything and everything. Her stomach had been in a knot for days, and it wasn't feeling any better. Yes, she knew she should be praying and trusting God, which she was, but that didn't mean He wasn't expecting her to use her head, too.

Arriving at her destination, she sidled past the east wall of the repair shop and paused in the shade of the service bay to look for Seth. He wasn't immediately visible. Babe was. Patty gave a whoop, pulled her hand free from her mother's grasp and ran to the dog.

The wiggly welcome the border collie gave the little girl made Marie grin in spite of her other concerns. Patty fell to her knees to hug the dog, while Babe did her best to lick every inch of the little girl's face. Though it wasn't a sanitary greeting, it was comforting to watch.

Still smiling, Marie looked up as Seth joined her.

"I see they remember each other," he said pleasantly.

"You might say that. I could hardly keep Patty from racing down here first thing this morning."

"That would have been all right with me."

"I know," Marie replied, "but we'd have been pretty bored just standing around all day." She eyed her car where it was parked in the opposite bay with the overhead doors closed. "Any word on the parts?"

"Not yet. Most days we get a delivery at about two in the afternoon. If you're looking for something to do, there's a preschool class at my church. Patty may be a little old for it though."

"Your church? I don't think…

"It isn't far. Only a mile or two. I could drive you over there if you want."

"No, thanks. I wouldn't want to take you away from your work."

"I get an afternoon break," Seth said. "Bob's an understanding boss. He won't care if I take it a little early today."

It seemed to Marie that Seth's gaze was boring right into her, as if he were expecting her to say something earth-shattering. She wasn't particularly eager to meet any more new people, but now that he'd mentioned it, she couldn't think of a better place to hide from whoever was pursuing her. It might be nice to be among believers again, too. She didn't miss the city of Baton Rouge, with its chemical plants and oil refineries and traffic jams, but she certainly did miss the Christian friends she'd left behind there.

"Well, all right," she said with a sigh. "I guess we could go see the preschool. Actually, I used to…" Realizing that she was about to reveal one of the jobs she'd held in the past, she stopped herself.

Seth's eyebrow arched. "Yes?"

"Nothing. Nothing. If you take me to the church, at least I won't be stuck staring at the four walls of that little motel room all day."

And I'll be safer than I am on the street, she added to herself. Every time she poked her head outside, she knew she was taking a terrible chance. It would be comforting to visit the church, even if she was going to have to fib to those people, too. There were scriptural precedents that allowed deception, such as Rahab's hiding of the spies Joshua sent into Jerico. Surely the Lord wouldn't hold it against her if she was less than truthful now, especially since she'd be doing it solely to protect an innocent little girl.

Seth knew he hadn't spent enough time on his computer to find out everything there was to learn about Marie. He was, however, certain she was in trouble. And if it turned out that she really was a guilty fugitive, he knew he'd eventually have to turn her in to the law.

How he might do that while still protecting his own anonymity was a concern. If he went to the local law enforcement folks with his suspicions, they'd ask him how he'd gotten his information and he wouldn't dare explain. If he notified the Louisiana authorities anony-

mously, they'd be swarming all over Serenity, along with the FBI because Marie had crossed state lines, and he'd be in jeopardy from that investigation, too.

As it stood, he figured he was better off just letting Marie drive away. If his conscience hadn't kept getting in his way, that's exactly what he'd have done.

It seemed to Seth that the wisest course of action was the stalling tactic he was already employing. There was something about the Parnell woman that had gotten under his skin. His mind told him she was guilty, as the computer files had claimed, while his gut insisted she could not have committed any crime, let alone a felony as heinous as kidnapping.

His instincts had been nearly infallible in the past. Now he wasn't sure he could trust them. The more he got to know Marie, the less she looked like Alice, yet there was still that lingering resemblance. Plus, there was the presence of the child, who was the spitting image of her mother. If he and his late wife had ever had a child…

"Thank God we didn't," Seth concluded prayerfully. With Alice dead, there was no way he could have fled and lost himself in rural Arkansas, not if he'd had a young son or daughter to look after. Successfully hiding himself had been hard enough.

Which brought him back to Marie's obvious dilemma. She did have a child. And she was clearly on the run, whether from the law or for another reason. He couldn't help feeling empathetic. He just wished she'd confide in him so he could be certain what course to take.

Marie was waiting when he returned from the office. As before, she had tucked her silky, cinnamon-colored hair up under the Serenity Repair Shop baseball cap and was standing on the inside of the open truck door as if shielding Patty from whatever nemesis might lurk nearby.

"I left the booster seat, as you can see," Seth said.

"I noticed. What I should do is retrieve more of our things from my car so we have them in our room."

"I really don't have much time right now. Suppose I help you do that this evening, after work?"

"You don't have to," Marie insisted.

"I know I don't."

"Then why are you offering?" she asked, frowning and staring at him.

Letting himself grin, Seth shrugged as nonchalantly as possible. "Beats me. Guess I have a soft spot for Babe's buddies. She's always been able to sort out the good guys from the bad guys, and I trust her judgment."

When Marie suddenly looked away as if unwilling or unable to honestly meet his gaze, Seth was disappointed. That was not the reaction of an innocent person. If she wouldn't talk to him about her problems, he'd have to probe deeper via his computer. His conscience insisted.

There was a red alert flashing on one of the Corp. Inc. computer screens when section leader Eccles returned from a coffee break. He snorted. "Well, well,

well. It's about time you made a little noise. Now, let's see what you've been up to, buddy boy."

His fingers flew over the keys. He began to scowl as he realized it wasn't going to be easy to trace the source of the contact. Seth was evidently smarter than anyone had given him credit for. That figured. After all, he had been the only investigator who had managed to make sense of the inside information that had nearly exposed the entire corporate espionage operation. And for that, Seth had been expertly framed. Why he hadn't stuck around to try to clear his name was the only puzzling thing. Then again, his disappearance had kept him alive.

But now—now they were finally getting somewhere. "I'll find you," Eccles grumbled. "Maybe not this time, but I will figure out where you went. And when I do, I'll see that you pay for all the trouble you've caused me."

He glanced over his shoulder as another agent joined him. "Look who just popped up on my screen. Our old pal Seth."

"You're kidding."

"No, not a bit. He did a good job of routing his connection to hide his tracks, but I'm going to put McCormick on his trail."

"Do you think Mac can trace this back to its source?"

"If his new software is as good as he claims it is, yes," Eccles said. "He tells me it's only a matter of catching the connection while it's active and then hacking into the proxy server systems, one after the other."

"Whoa. If we do find Seth, he can cause plenty of trouble for us."

"Who said anything about bringing him in? He's a wife-killer, remember? He's sure to resist arrest and that can be fatal."

"I don't know if I like that idea. He was always a pretty decent guy."

"That was his trouble," Eccles answered. "He was far too honest for this job. And in the end, his high-and-mighty principles are bound to get him killed."

Serenity Chapel sat near the crest of a ridge, where it could be readily viewed from the road below. It was a large, gray stone edifice backed by the dark green of the forested hills, which made it stand out even more.

Marie was taken aback as they approached. "Oh, my. It's so *big*."

"Just like the hearts of the people inside," Seth answered. "You'll see. Don't let the imposing building put you off."

He parked next to a side door, out of sight of the street, patted Babe on the head and told her to stay as he passed the bed of the truck, then opened the passenger door for Marie and Patty.

"Maybe this isn't such a good idea, after all," Marie said, holding her daughter's hand and lagging back.

"Nonsense. It's the perfect answer to your boredom. And if you stop to think about it, it'll give you the kind of anonymity you seem to want."

"I beg your pardon?"

"Never mind." Chuckling quietly, Seth led the way into the church building and shepherded his guests down a long hallway to the recreation room, where the preschool was located.

"Here we are. I'll pick you up about five," he said matter-of-factly. "Then we'll go get the stuff out of your car, load it in my truck and haul it up to the motel."

"You're awfully bossy, you know that?" To his relief, she was smiling enough to soften her statement.

"Just being sensible. Your car is out of commission, you need your things and toting them up to the motel by hand would be silly."

Marie made a face at him. "When you're right, you're right."

"Glad you see it my way."

"Do I have a choice?"

That made Seth laugh again. "Yes. You could always refuse to let me help you and *walk* to wherever you wanted to go. I think you're smarter than that."

"Let's hope so." Marie sobered as they stood outside the door to the rec room. "I also hope I'm not in the way here. I wouldn't want to put anybody out."

"Trust me. My pastor's wife, Becky Malloy, started this preschool program after their son Timmy was born. It's become very popular. They're always begging for volunteers. I'm sure you'll be more than welcome, even for a few hours."

He saw Marie's shoulders relax a tiny bit. She sighed. "Okay. I'm convinced," she said. "C'mon, Patty. Let's find some nice kids for you to play with."

Seth accompanied her and made the necessary introductions, then headed back to the garage. He'd been more edgy than usual of late and couldn't seem to shake a building sense of foreboding.

As he wheeled into the drive to the garage, his breath caught. Marie's car was outside!

He hit the ground running, gesturing and shouting to his boss. "What happened, Bob? Did the parking brake fail?"

"Naw. We got a lube job and needed the room, so I just gave that other car a shove. We can push it back inside for the night if we need to. Those parts you sent for were backordered anyway."

Seth was already rummaging through the storage area looking for a large tarp. When he found what he needed, he ran back outside, gave it a flip and unfurled it like a bedsheet. He was just pulling the outer corners into place to cover the blue sedan when he saw that familiar white delivery van cruising slowly by. The driver had an elbow out the window and was shading his eyes, staring at the garage.

Seth's breath caught. He doubled his efforts to fully hide Marie's car, then straightened and looked back toward the highway as soon as he was satisfied.

The van had stopped across the road. Its driver wasn't getting out and appeared to be talking on a cell phone. Who was he? Had he seen Marie's car? Did it matter one way or the other?

If only she'd have confided in him, Seth reasoned.

If she had, he'd know how to react. As it was, he felt as frustrated as if he were blindfolded and swinging a bat at fastballs thrown by a major league pitcher. His chances of hitting a home run were nil.

Turning back to his work, Seth continued to watch the van. It remained parked on the shoulder for another fifteen minutes or so, then slowly pulled away.

Seth immediately jogged to the edge of the garage's parking lot and peered after the disappearing van, hoping to be able to get a license number.

His fists balled. Nobody could have read that plate. It was conveniently smeared with enough mud to not only obscure the letters and numbers but also blur the state of origin, although the dark blue border was right for Louisiana. For all he knew, that van might have followed Marie all the way from her home state.

Clearly, there was more Internet research ahead for Seth that evening. As soon as he'd gotten Marie and her belongings safely moved to the motel and had made certain they hadn't been observed by the truck driver—or by anyone else—he'd go to work digging up more answers.

In the meantime, he had a normal job to do. Getting fired wasn't on his agenda.

Seth glanced along the street, satisfying himself that the departing van had not turned up the driveway to the Hilltop Motel. That was good enough for now. If his gut feelings were right about that driver, Marie would be safe where she was at present. That kind of

guy was not the type to casually drop in at a church. Chances were very good that no one had seen him take Marie to Serenity Chapel, either. As long as she stayed put and waited for him, she'd be fine. For now.

SIX

It wasn't that Marie felt unwelcome at the church pre-school. She was simply so used to being on her guard that she found it impossible to relax and open up to the other women the way she had hoped she could.

The children were another story. Patty had taken to the group of three- to five-year-olds as if they'd been lifelong friends. As she chattered away and told her new acquaintances tall tales about imaginary pets, Marie smiled benevolently. It was no wonder that the Bible instructed believers to come as a little child. There was a pure trust and innocence in childhood that Marie wished she could still feel and share with her daughter.

Would we ever be a normal family again? she wondered. Were they ever normal? In the strictest sense, no. Without a daddy, Patty had missed a lot. And without a reliable spouse, Marie had, too. Poor Roy. There were times when she'd fooled herself into believing that he could change, that he'd actually wanted to reform. But that had been a foolish dream.

Though she had continued to pray for him over the years, Marie had long ago given up hope that he'd become the kind of reliable, good example of a father that Patty needed. She figured it was better for them to be a little lonely than to live with a man whose temper could explode into violence at the slightest provocation, not to mention the negative influence of his life of crime.

Shivering from the disturbing memories, Marie looked up at the clock on the wall. It was nearly five—time for Seth to arrive. To her chagrin, she felt a quickening of her pulse, a tremor of anticipation.

She blinked in surprise. That kind of juvenile reaction was ridiculous. She was overwrought, that was all. And weary. So weary. If only she could rest, could sleep as she had before Roy's latest crimes had put them all in danger.

Becky Malloy and the other women had begun to help the children pick up their toys, so Marie joined them.

"You don't have to do that," Becky said with a grin. "You're our guest."

"I want to help," Marie replied, continuing to urge Patty to follow her example.

"Will we see you tomorrow?" the young, red-haired pastor's wife asked.

"I don't know. I suppose that depends on whether or not Seth can fix my car."

"Well, you're most welcome to come back if you'd like. We'd love to have you and your daughter visit.

One of our older members is baking her famous chocolate chip cookies for our snack."

"In that case," Marie said with a smile and warming cheeks, "I'll certainly do my best to be here."

That brought mutual laughter from all the adults and smiles from some of the children.

Suddenly, the hair on the back of Marie's neck prickled and she felt a shiver skitter over her skin. She whipped around. Seth was here! Even having come straight from work, he was a sight for sore eyes.

The warmth already infusing her cheeks increased until she was certain she must be beet-red. She smiled at him. "Hi, there."

"Hi yourself. Ready to go?"

"I think so." She looked to Becky. "Is this part of the room clean enough, Mrs. Malloy?"

"It's just fine. You two scat. And we hope to see you again tomorrow."

Falling into step beside Seth, Marie watched Patty skip down the hall a few paces in front of them.

When the little girl reached the outer door, however, Seth ordered, "Wait! Don't go out yet," and lunged to grab the door so she couldn't open it.

Wide-eyed, Patty immediately flew to her mother's side, hid behind her leg and clung to her.

Seth was clearly taken aback by the child's unusual show of fear. He apologized. "Sorry. I just didn't want her running outside ahead of us."

"Why? What's wrong?" Marie was stroking Patty's

hair to comfort her. Now she frowned and laid her other hand on Seth's forearm.

"Nothing, I hope," he said.

By the way he cleared his throat and hesitated, Marie could tell he was searching for just the right words. Her grip tightened. "Go on."

"I think the same white box truck I'd seen before was parked by the station when I got back there after my break. Do you know anything about it?"

She felt the high color draining from her cheeks. "Why?"

"Because…Bob, my boss, took in another job while I was gone and pushed your car outside to make room in the shop. I covered it with a tarp, but that truck seemed to be hanging around just the same. I thought there might be something you wanted to tell me."

"Like what?"

"Like why you're so scared and what you're running away from." He laid his hand gently over hers where it was still resting on his arm. "Maybe I can help you."

Marie shook her head. "Just fix my car so Patty and I can get out of this town," she said with a telltale quaver in her voice. "Believe me, you don't want to get involved."

"I'm already involved," Seth countered. "Let me help."

"How?"

"I don't know. I made sure no one was following me when I drove up here, but I can't tell what else to do if you don't let me in on your secrets."

Scowling, she stared at him. "Either you read a lot of mystery novels or you've had personal experience with this kind of thing."

When he didn't answer or comment, Marie studied his face. There was a hardness, a seriousness in his expression that would have frightened her if she hadn't considered him a friend.

That was the best way to take him, she decided easily. Only a friend would have warned her, would have gone out of his way to cover her car and hide it. And only a friend would have offered to continue to protect her.

She didn't want to place anyone else in jeopardy but she desperately needed an ally. Since the Lord had obviously placed her in Serenity and in the care of Seth Whitfield, she was going to accept the assistance he offered and worry about the consequences later, if at all. Seth would be safe enough once she was on her way north again. In the meantime, she was going to let him help her. She could see no other option.

"All right," she finally said. "As soon as it gets dark, you can drive me back to the garage and we'll get a few things out of my car the way we'd planned. Okay?"

"Okay." He was scowling. "Is that all?"

"Yes," Marie said flatly. "The less you know, the better off you'll be. In the meantime, how about taking us back to that pizza place? This time, the meal's on me."

She saw him glance at his clothing and scowl. "If

I'd known you'd want to go out again, I'd have stopped to change before I picked you up," he said.

"You look fine to me. Besides, if we were too dressed up, we'd stand out from the crowd and folks would be more likely to notice us."

"You wouldn't like that, would you?"

"No," she said, sobering and boldly meeting his inquiring gaze. "I wouldn't like that one bit."

Several hours later, headlights off, Seth coasted into the darkest portion of the parking area at the rear of the repair shop. His tires made quiet, crunching sounds on the loose gravel apron while thunder rumbled in the background, highlighted by distant flashes of lightning.

Now that it had gotten dark, Marie was no longer wearing the cap he'd given her to disguise herself. She had also scooted down and was holding Patty close rather than having her use the booster seat. Seth chose to allow the breach of rules this time, in spite of his safety concerns.

"Looks like it's about to pour," he said, peering out the windshield at the thick cloud cover. "Do you want me to go get your stuff for you so you don't get wet?"

"No, thanks. I have my jacket. There's no way I can tell you what to bring and what to leave in the car. It'll only take me a second to pick out a few things."

"Okay. What about Patty?"

"I'll keep her with me."

"Fine, as long as the lightning doesn't get any closer or we don't meet up with your buddy from the van."

"Then you stay here and watch her. I'll go alone."

"No way. I'm not letting you out of my sight until you tell me what's going on."

"Then I guess we have an impasse."

"Not necessarily. Why don't we put Babe up here in the cab with Patty? That dog can protect her better than we can. And they'll both be warm, dry and safe." Seth could tell from Marie's frown that she wasn't convinced.

"Will she do that?"

"Oh, yeah," Seth assured her. "Babe is all business when it comes to guarding her flock." He smiled to try to lessen the tension, hoping the dim streetlamp and ever-increasing flashes of lightning would reveal his expression well enough to make a positive impression on the anxious mother. "And Patty is definitely one of her favorite sheep."

Although she still didn't look fully persuaded, Marie finally said, "Okay. You're probably right. It's not like we're going very far. We'll only be away a minute or two, and I don't want Patty to get all wet and catch cold." She pointed. "Besides, my car is right there."

Slipping out of the truck, she waited at the door while Seth brought his dog from the rear and commanded her to jump in beside the little girl.

"Patty, you stay right there and take care of Babe," Marie cautioned. "You're the doggie's babysitter. Don't you let anyone bother her, you hear?"

Patty nodded sagely as she wrapped her arms around the dog's thick ruff.

"It's a good thing the dome light in your truck is

broken so nobody could see what we were doing just now," Marie said as she pulled her jacket closer and joined Seth in the shadows next to the building.

"It's not broken. It's disconnected," he replied.

"Did you do that for my benefit?"

"No. I always keep it that way." He knew he was probably sounding too alarmist, but he thought it was best to let Marie know how cautious he could be.

Bent low, they skirted the brightest circle of illumination from the streetlights and approached her tarp-covered car. Louder thunder heralded the quickly approaching storm, and the wind had started to pick up.

"Care to tell me why that is?" she asked, pushing her windblown hair out of her face and trying to tuck it behind her ears the way she always did.

Seth avoided answering. Instead, he lifted the edge of the tattered blue tarp, handed her the car's keys and changed the subject. "Trunk or back door?"

"Both. Some of Patty's toys are in the backseat, but a lot of stuff is in the trunk, too."

As Marie fingered the key ring, looking for the right key, headlights swept the station yard like the rotating beacon of a lighthouse.

Seth instantly grabbed her and pulled her into a crouch beside him, one arm around her shoulders, the other hand cupping her head. He hadn't intended to touch her, let alone embrace her, but circumstances had dictated a faster, more sure response than she'd made and his survival instincts had taken over.

Barely breathing, he held very still. The scent of her hair was like vanilla, its silkiness even finer than he'd imagined. She was trembling as if the nighttime temperature was icy cold.

"You all right?" Seth whispered.

Her head nodded slightly. "Was that him?"

"I don't know. It could have been anybody. Even if it wasn't that van, we don't want to attract attention and make folks think we're robbing your car."

"Good point." She shifted her weight away from him so she was no longer leaning against his chest and pushed back her blowing hair once again. "I think they're gone."

"Yeah." Seth was reluctant to release her even though he knew there was no reason to continue to hide.

He straightened and took her hand to help her up. "I'll hold the edge of the tarp and you sneak underneath. If another car comes by, I'll drop the flap down and you can hide under there till it's safe again."

"Gotcha." She hesitated and smiled at him. "Thanks. For everything."

"My pleasure, ma'am." His gaze shifted to the nearly deserted street before he looked back toward his truck. "Just make it snappy. The sooner we're done and out of here, the better it'll be."

All Marie said in response was a fervent, "Amen."

Marie had gathered up some of the plastic grocery sacks in which she'd hurriedly crammed so many of their belongings. Their departure from home hadn't

been organized the way she'd have preferred, but cramming things into sacks and pillowcases still beat leaving their personal possessions behind merely because they'd lacked adequate luggage.

She ducked out from under the tarp and handed Seth the plastic bags she'd chosen. Clearly he was standing guard in spite of the large raindrops that had begun to dot the landscape.

"Is this all?" His head swiveled from side to side.

"Almost. One more peek in the trunk and I'll be done."

"Well, hurry it up. I'm about to get soaked standing out here."

"You don't have to snap at me."

Although his reply was muffled as she ducked back beneath the tarp, she was certain it was gruff.

Terrific. She made a face. It wasn't that she didn't want Seth to take her plight seriously; it was just that she didn't need him or anyone else ordering her around. She had enough problems without adding a taciturn stranger to the mix.

But he wasn't really a stranger, was he? She'd only known him for a couple of days, yet he was already such a necessary element of her life that she didn't know what she'd do if she couldn't rely on his expert assistance.

Except for the increasing wind and thunder, the country night was quiet, especially when compared with the constant city background noise she was used to in Baton Rouge. Here the air smelled fresh and there

were no sirens, no constant drone of traffic, no shouts or shots in the distance to spoil the ambience.

Consequently, when she heard a sharp, yipping bark, Marie froze and took notice. She closed the trunk with a soft slam and peeked out from under the tarp. The instant her gaze locked with Seth's, she knew the bark had to have been Babe's.

Seth laid a finger against his lips and shook his head when she opened her mouth to speak. "Shush."

Moving slowly, deliberately, he lowered the grocery sacks to the pavement and stepped away from them as their handles fluttered in the wind. When Marie started to follow him, he used his arm to block her. "No. Stay here."

"In a pig's eye." She had expected an argument. Instead, all she got was a momentary look of irritation before Seth turned away and headed toward the rear of the garage at a trot.

By this time, Babe was starting to sound really upset. Her bark had deepened and become louder, more frequent.

Marie was already so nervous she could hardly breathe, hardly make her wobbly legs work well enough to race after Seth. She never should have let him talk her into leaving Patty with the dog, not even for a few short minutes, she thought, panicking. *Never.* How could she have agreed to such a stupid plan? What kind of mother was she?

A frightened, lost one, she answered, using up her

last shred of confidence and self-control as tears filled her eyes and clouded her vision.

All she could do was cry out to God in her mind. Beg Him to help her, to help them all. Her body might not be on her knees before the Lord, but her heart certainly was. That would have to be good enough.

"Oh, please, oh, please, oh, please," she mouthed, barely speaking. This couldn't be happening. Not after all she'd done to escape.

As she passed the corner of the building, she saw Seth whip around the far side of the truck, shout, and dive out of sight.

Patty screamed.

Marie's heart was in her throat. The child was right where she'd left her, but it took Marie's mind an instant to process that critical fact.

"Patty!" she shouted, jerking open the passenger door.

"Mama." The frantic little girl held out her arms to her mother and Marie swept her up an a tight embrace as a gust of wind slammed the truck door with a bang.

Patty's arms gripped her neck. "Mama. Babe's gone. I tried to stop her but…" She began to sob inconsolably.

"It's okay, honey. It's okay," Marie said. "Where did she go?"

Pointing to the opposite side of the truck, Patty was crying too much to speak.

Still holding her child close and shielding her with her own torso, Marie edged around the old pickup.

There was nothing there. Not only was the dog missing, but also so was Seth. That was the last place Marie had seen him, just before he'd yelled and made a leap for someone or something. Now he'd disappeared. And so had Babe.

She froze, straining to listen. A dog was barking in the distance, but, even allowing for the distortion of the wind, it sounded much too far away to possibly be the border collie.

There were no lights nearby except those illuminating the used-car lot, and there was no sign of movement in that direction other than the fluttering of the rows of multicolored plastic triangles strung high from pole to pole to attract the attention of prospective customers.

Glancing at the stormy heavens, Marie watched the flashes behind the rapidly moving clouds and felt a few huge drops hit her face as she sent up another wordless prayer. Where was Seth? Would he just run off and leave her if he could help it? Of course not. Either something had drawn him away or he'd been forcibly taken the same way Roy had been. Neither notion was acceptable.

More important, she couldn't simply stand there, exposed and vulnerable, and continue to make herself an easy target for both her enemies and the lightning, which was now illuminating the entire sky.

But what could she do? Where could she go? It was at least half a mile to their motel, and if they tried to

walk to their room, they'd be totally defenseless and probably also get soaked before they arrived.

At her wit's end, Marie held Patty close and looked around again, hoping for ideas. Seth's pickup. Her refuge was right under her nose! She'd climb into that truck with Patty, lock the doors, hunker down and wait for Seth and Babe to return.

Satisfied that she'd chosen the only logical course of action, she grasped the nearest door handle.

It didn't budge.

Neither did the one on the other side.

In all the confusion, both doors had somehow gotten locked!

SEVEN

Al was wiry and agile, but he was running out of steam by the time he reached the car where his two partners waited. He dove into the backseat, then quickly slammed the door.

Frank was behind the wheel. Startled, he jumped and swiveled his thick neck. "Did you check out that blue car? Is it them?"

"I think so," Al answered, looking from Frank to Earl. "I was about to get a closer look when the guy that works there showed up."

Earl's already furrowed brow squeezed tighter, and he peered at Al through thick glasses. "At this time of night? In this rotten weather? Why?"

"Beats me. But he had a woman and a kid with him."

It was Frank's turn again. "Roy's woman?"

"Couldn't tell. And don't you two go gangin' up on me. I was about to grab the kid, just in case, but when I opened the door to his truck, a stupid dog almost took my arm off."

"So, what now?"

"Floor it and let's get out of here," Al said, still breathless. "The guy from the garage was on my tail till I crossed the street and lost him."

"Then what's the hurry? We can just wait till he gives up, then go back to check that car the way you should have in the first place," Frank said.

"Not if that lousy dog has managed to track me." Al raised up enough to peek through the rain-streaked window. "We know where the car is. If it does belong to the Parnell woman, it's not going anywhere. I saw to that when I fouled her gas tank."

He suddenly ducked. "They're coming this way. I saw the dog. Just floor it, will you, before this turns into an even bigger mess than it already is."

Seth and Babe had pursued the fleeing man as far as Hickory Station, where the dog had lost his trail. Though she'd circled, nose to the now damp pavement, she'd returned to Seth looking totally befuddled.

"It's okay, girl," he said, slapping his thigh to draw her closer. "Come on. We'd better get back to Marie and Patty. They're probably frantic by now, and I'm not looking forward to getting any wetter, either."

He had realized, as he'd chased the prowler through the night, that he might very well be on a wild-goose chase. If he hadn't seen that strange man trying to get into his truck, he might have been more in doubt. As it was, he was virtually certain that the individual he was pursuing had been after the child. Babe cer-

tainly thought so. The mild-mannered border collie had never sounded that angry and protective in all the time he'd owned her. If Babe believed that the prowler was someone to distrust and fear, that was good enough for Seth.

He started to jog back to the garage, Babe at his heels. As he approached, he slowed and scanned the shadows while his dog circled, clearly searching as well. Large raindrops were now falling in far greater numbers, and Seth knew it would soon pour, probably spoiling any trail his dog might otherwise find.

"Marie?" he called over the whistling wind. "Marie? Patty?"

There was no answer. Seth peered into his truck, hoping he'd find them huddled there, together. It was empty.

As soon as he tried the handle of the driver's door, he realized that someone had accidentally locked it! Could he have instinctively done so to safeguard the child after Babe had taken off? He didn't remember doing that but anything was possible.

Muttering, he started around to the front of the garage. "Marie? Marie, honey, it's me," he called, not wanting to actually shout. "Where are you?"

Still, there was no reply. The hair on Seth's neck and arms prickled as water began to collect and drip off the brim of his cap. He shivered. He prayed. His fists clenched. Could she have headed back to the motel? He supposed it was possible, but he didn't think she'd have chanced it. Not all alone and on foot.

And certainly not when they were facing an impending downpour. So where could she have gone? More important, were she and Patty safe?

He paused, watching his dog continue to sniff the area. Since he and Marie had been right there only minutes before, it was natural for Babe to have picked up their trail.

The dog stopped next to the hidden car and began to whine.

"I know, girl," he whispered, settling her with a pat on the head. "We were here. What I need to know is where Marie and Patty are now."

Babe took a tentative step and stuck her nose beneath the fluttering edge of the tarp. Seth's heart leaped. Was it possible that they had taken refuge in the car? It made perfect sense to him, but was Marie that rational under fire? He sure hoped so.

Slowly, methodically, Seth scanned the street below the garage's front lot to be certain it was safe before he did anything else. No one seemed to be paying the slightest attention to him or to the repair business. The few cars and trucks that were still over at Hickory Station were half a block away, and those that were passing on the two-lane highway were traveling too fast to be able to see anything well, especially through the rain and in the dark.

He noticed that his hand was shaking as he reached for the edge of the tarp, unsure of what he might discover. Painful visions of finding Alice's body flashed into his mind.

No. Dear, God, no, he thought. His heart clenched. His mouth felt as though it had been stuffed with the same kind of dry, dusty sawdust he'd found in Marie's gas tank.

He decided to chance another softly spoken query; he bent and lifted the side of the tarp as he said, "Marie?"

The car door burst open, hitting his shoulder and momentarily knocking him off-balance. He staggered and braced himself. Before he could blink, Marie was in his arms and clinging to him as if she were drowning and he was her life preserver.

Seth embraced her in return, patting her shoulder and soothing her with his voice. "Easy. I've got you. It's over."

"No, it's not," she said with a shuddering sob as she reached down and drew Patty into the group hug. "It'll never be over. We'll never be safe again."

What Seth would have liked to have done was take Marie and her little girl to his pastor, Logan Malloy, tell him everything and ask for advice. He knew that Logan had been involved in law enforcement back in Chicago, before he'd become a clergyman, which meant Marie would be in good hands.

However, there was now Logan's family's safety to consider. Seth didn't want to do anything that might endanger Becky or little Timmy, nor was he willing to unburden his own soul to the pastor. Someday he would. But this was definitely not the time for un-

necessary confessions. Logan was an honorable man, and if he knew that Seth was a fugitive, guilty or not, he'd probably feel honor bound to act. The same went for Marie's trouble with the law.

So, what could Seth do? Deliver her back to the motel? That didn't seem wise, yet he couldn't see what other course was available to them. He certainly wasn't going to suggest they go home with him and have Marie think he was making an indecent proposal. She'd made it clear what kind of woman she was, and he respected her for her high moral principles.

He eased away from her, gathered up the plastic shopping bags they'd dropped and began to shepherd everyone toward his truck while Babe circled the group, tail wagging.

"Let's get out of this rain and talk," Seth said, unlocking the door and helping with Patty before handing Marie the sacks containing their meager possessions.

He circled the truck and slid behind the wheel. "So, do you want to go back to the motel?"

"I don't know what else we can do." Marie shivered. "Is there any place else around here where we can stay?"

"Not another motel, no. I did think of asking Pastor Malloy to take you in but..."

Marie's head snapped around. "No. Absolutely not. I'm not going to involve that nice woman and her family in my problems. Period. Understand?"

"Perfectly. Would you care to tell me what kind of problems you're talking about?"

"Not really."

"I think you should reconsider," Seth urged. "Who-ever bothered us tonight is probably part of the overall situation. The more I know, the better I'll be able to counter their moves."

Pausing, she scowled at him. "Who *are* you?"

"Just an ol' country boy trying to be a gentleman."

"Phooey. First of all, you haven't lived here in Serenity for very long. And second, nobody seems to know anything about your past, so don't give me that *aw-shucks* act."

"My, my," he said, flashing a lopsided smile. "You've been poking into my business, haven't you?"

"Just curious to find out what makes you so protec-tive."

Seth sobered. "All right. I'll tell you a little about myself while we drive." He eyed Patty. "Is it all right to talk in front of her?"

"Is it bad?" Marie asked.

When he nodded, she said, "Then wait till we get back to our room and I've put her to bed. We can sit right outside in the truck and talk afterwards."

Agreeing, Seth peered through the sheets of driving rain as he took them up the road toward the motel. Once again, this woman had impressed him with her genuine concern for her child and her willingness to put Patty, and others, first. Given his background and experience, he knew that was not easy to do.

Marie kissed Patty good-night and tucked her into bed. "I'll be right outside, talking with Mr. Whit-field," she assured her. "I'll leave the curtains open a little so you can see his truck."

"Can I say my prayers before I go to sleep?"

"Of course. Do you want me to help you?"

The child shook her head sheepishly. "Don't be mad, okay? I'm gonna tell God I want to stay here and I don't want you to tell Him no."

Marie was still grinning broadly when she eased out the door onto the narrow sidewalk that bordered the bank of rooms and made a dash for the warmth of Seth's truck.

He was waiting, as promised, leaning back with his arms raised and his fingers laced behind his head in a nonchalant pose.

"You look pleased," he said, watching her hurriedly scoot onto the seat and slam the door. "Is Patty all right? I know she was pretty scared tonight."

"We both were. She's fine now. She wanted me to leave so she could have privacy while she tries to convince God we're supposed to stay in Serenity."

He huffed with evident derision and lowered his arms. "Where did she get that idea?"

"From being around your dog, I guess. She's always wanted a pet and with my working all the time, it just wasn't practical."

"You're raising her by yourself?"

"Yes." Chin up, she raked her damp hair back with her fingers and let her gaze meet his boldly, defiantly. "I was never married to her father."

"I won't judge you for that or anything else," Seth said.

She could see he was sincere. "Good. Now what

was it you were going to tell me that we decided not to let Patty hear?"

"I forget."

"Oh, no, you don't. You were about to explain why you're so protective."

She folded her arms across her chest and sat sideways on the bench seat, one leg tucked beneath her, while the rain smacked against the outside of the truck and sheeted over the windows. In the illumination from the motel lights, the drops sparkled like thousands of falling stars.

When Seth didn't speak right away she added, "Go ahead. Talk. I'm all ears."

She could sense his capitulation by the shrug of his broad shoulders and the slow, steady nod of his head.

"All right," Seth finally began. "Once, a long time ago, I came home and found my wife lying dead on the kitchen floor. She'd been murdered."

Marie's jaw dropped. Although she'd imagined many possible scenarios, the murder of the poor man's wife had not been one of them. Not even close.

She reached out to him, gently patted his forearm through his jacket, and left her hand resting there to offer ongoing comfort. "I'm so sorry."

"It was a long time ago. But you can see why I'd be extra nervous about your problems, can't you?"

"In a way, maybe." She withdrew her hand and folded her arms once again. "I just don't understand how you got so good at all this clandestine stuff. Hanging around with you feels like I've been dropped into

a spy movie, only I came in at the middle and have no idea why things are happening or who is who."

She began to grin in spite of the seriousness of the situation. "Come to think of it, my whole life is starting to feel like that." Lightning flashed bright and thunder immediately rattled the truck windows, making her flinch. "Complete with really scary sound effects."

"Then maybe it's time you told me a little more. For instance, why Patty had such a strong fear reaction when I raised my voice to keep her from running out of the church ahead of us."

"It was probably partly because I've been so upset lately," Marie said. "That, and she may remember more about her father's temper than I'd thought, at least subconsciously."

"He was abusive?"

Marie could tell that Seth had tensed, because his jaw muscles were visibly clenching. Though she wanted to blurt out everything, she took a deep breath and stifled that urge before she began, "I was seventeen when I ran away from home. Roy was older, a man of the world at twenty-two. I thought he was special because he was so interested in me, took such good care of me." She breathed a heavy sigh. "Compared to what my home life had been while I was growing up, that was true."

She had been watching Seth's expression. When she judged that he was accepting her story as he'd promised, she went on. "Roy kept assuring me we'd get married, but even after we knew I was expecting Patty, he dragged his feet. Now that I can look back on

those years more objectively, I'm glad he balked. If I was married to Roy, I'd have even worse problems."

"Where is he now?" Seth asked softly.

"I don't really know." A shudder of remembrance skittered up her spine as she pictured the way Roy had struggled against his captors when they'd dragged him off to who-knows-where. "The last time we spoke, he told me he was in trouble and warned me to get out of town."

"Baton Rouge?"

Marie's eyes narrowed. "How do you know that?"

"From the registration in your car. I had a responsibility to my job to be sure you hadn't stolen it."

The air whooshed out of her lungs, and she sagged against the seat back. "Oh. You scared me."

"Sorry. Like I keep telling you, if you continue to hide the truth, it's going to be a lot harder for me, or anyone else, to help you."

"There's really nothing you can do," Marie said. "I've probably told you too much already."

"One more thing I need to know," Seth said, pinning her with his steady stare.

"All right. I'll tell you if I can."

"It's about Roy. That's his name, right?"

"Yes…"

His voice low, his words clipped, Seth asked, "Were you ever, or are you now, involved with him in any crimes?"

Marie could feel herself bristle at the implication. "Of course not. Never. That was why I left him. I gave

him an ultimatum. It was either his buddies and their life of crime or Patty and me. He chose them."

"What about the physical abuse? I don't know you very well, but I can't picture you staying with him under those circumstances."

Giving another loud sigh, Marie nodded. "You're right. When I told Roy he had to choose, he got drunk and hit me. More than once. That was the last straw. As soon as he passed out, I left and went straight to a shelter for battered women and children. Even if I'd been willing to give him more chances to reform, I knew I couldn't leave Patty in that situation one more minute."

"All right. That's good enough for me. You say you're innocent and I believe you."

She blinked back tears of thankfulness. "You really do, don't you?"

"Yes," Seth said flatly. "I really do."

EIGHT

Now that he knew Marie's side of the story, at least part of it, he decided to compare her version with that in Corp. Inc.'s files and see if he could figure an easy way out for her.

Yes, a second contact with his former agency was more risky than his initial foray into its computer system had been, but he decided to chance it. At least he no longer suspected that Marie had been sent to unmask him, which was a big relief. So was her explanation of her prior connections to Roy Jenkins. The woman was a victim, not a coconspirator and, as he'd thought from the moment he'd met her, she desperately needed professional assistance.

He closed his eyes and took a deep, settling breath before connecting to the first of the three anonymizer Web sites he'd used the last time. His mind kept insisting he was a fool to be doing this again, while his heart and soul argued the opposite.

"Father," he whispered prayerfully, "tell me what to do, what not to do, how far to pursue this."

All his adult life Seth had believed in the triumph of righteousness over evil and had fought to do good, no matter what the cost. Lately, though, he'd wondered if he'd been kidding himself all along. Perhaps he had. But that didn't mean he wasn't duty-bound to help the helpless when it was within his power to do so.

Reassured, he connected to the last proxy site and used it to begin to once again tap into the agency's secret files.

To his relief, there had been no law enforcement update on Marie Parnell or on Roy Jenkins, although there had been an unidentified body found that was suspected of being that of Jenkins. Tests were pending.

Seth printed the information, then sat back and pondered his next move. There had to be some way to get the authorities to realize that Marie was not the criminal they thought she was. But how? If he'd still been on the inside at Corp. Inc., he'd have had little trouble dropping the right hints to the right people and seeing that enough doubt arose to trigger a more thorough investigation into Roy's past.

Now, however, his hands were tied. He was as far outside the system as Marie was, and his word carried no more weight than that of any fugitive from justice.

Perhaps he should have stuck around and let them try him for Alice's murder, he thought, then quickly disagreed. The frame-up had been complete. His enemies had planted evidence that had made him look guilty of both Alice's death and the embezzlement of hundreds of thousands of dollars worth of industrial

secrets that had been shown to have ended up in the hands of foreign mercenaries.

For the evidence to have been that perfect, that co-ordinated, it had to have been planted by some of the men Seth had considered his close friends and allies. There had been no one left whom he could trust back then. No one in whose hands he'd dared place his future. No one except Jonathan Biggs, the man who just before his own tragic death had given him the secret access code he was now using.

Seth's jaw clenched. Friends like Jonathan were rare. Now that he was gone, there was no one within the agency or its affiliates who could be relied upon to help.

He was sitting there, staring at the computer screen and reminiscing, when a familiar icon popped up.

Seth's eyes widened. His heart started to race. That little bluebird was Jonathan's, and his personal ID was one that they used only for private communications. It couldn't be his old friend. Or could it?

Cautious, Seth watched as a sentence appeared. "That you, buddy?" was all it said.

He had a choice now: either respond or immediately break the connection and pretend he didn't know what was going on. If Jonathan was alive and trying to contact him, he wanted to know. He had to know. If it was a trick and he answered, however, he might be giving a lot away.

In the end, he decided to play the game.

"Who's your buddy?" Seth typed.

"A guy from Wonderland," came the answer.

Seth's gut twisted and his breathing grew shallow, rapid. Jonathan had always teased him about his late wife's connection to the fairy tale, because of her first name. Did anyone else know about that private joke? Maybe. Maybe not. If his old friend really was still alive...

"Wonderland?" Seth typed.

"Yeah. Sorry about Alice."

Seth stared at the screen for long seconds before answering. "Thanks."

"How've you been?"

"Lonesome."

As soon as he'd sent that reply, Seth realized that although it had been true to some extent at first, he was actually quite content now. At least he had been until Marie had dropped into his life a few days ago.

"Mama and all us kids would love to have you come home," the screen flashed.

"No way."

"Same time tomorrow, then," the screen said before the icon of the bluebird faded.

Seth sat very still and stared as his mind ran in convoluted circles. Was it possible? Sure it was. Jonathan had been just as good at subterfuge as any other agent. If he'd wanted to falsify his own death, he could have managed it beautifully.

The real question was, had he? And if so, how had he gotten access to the agency's system when he was no longer affiliated with it? Or was this new contact a ruse?

Seth didn't know those answers, nor did he have to

find them out right away. If his old friend was alive and kicking, he'd be a valuable ally. If not, no harm had been done. Yet. And Seth wasn't about to let himself be suckered in by some wet-behind-the-ears agent with an advanced degree in computer science.

Tomorrow he'd log on again and start asking more questions, ones that only Jonathan could answer, to see where their conversation went.

Until then, he was going to do the only thing he could. Lie low. And pray for more wisdom.

Marie hardly slept a wink all night. By dawn she felt as if she'd spent her night running a marathon. When she peered at her reflection in the morning, she wished she hadn't looked.

"Oh, ugh." Her hair was a mess, partly thanks to the effects of having been out in the wind and rain, and the skin below her eyes was darker than usual, leaving no doubt that she was sleep-deprived.

Hoping it would help, she splashed warm water on her face. Patty came into the bathroom as she was toweling it dry.

"What's the matter, mama?"

"Nothing, honey. I'm just trying to wake up. How are you this morning?"

"Fine." She brightened. "Can we go see Babe?"

"Maybe later," Marie said wearily.

"How about church school? Are we going there? You said—"

"I know what I said," Marie answered. "Just be

patient, will you. I'm so tired I can hardly think straight." She leaned closer to the mirror and blinked at her image. "I'll feel better if I shower and wash my hair. You go get dressed and watch cartoons for a while, okay? Just don't turn the TV up too loud. We don't want to disturb the guests in the rooms next door."

Seeing the child's mood plummet, Marie felt more than a twinge of guilt. She was trying to be a good mother, but her senses were on overload owing to continuous tension, not to mention the negative effect prolonged sleeplessness was having on her body and brain.

Someday she'd make all this up to Patty, she vowed, stepping beneath the soothing spray of the shower and letting it knead the tension out of her shoulders and neck.

She closed her eyes, turned and let the water wash away her tears of frustration and apprehension. Would this nightmare ever end? Would she survive to keep her promises to Patty? To God?

Lifting her face to the spray, she sent up a silent, wordless prayer, asking for the only thing she could think of that might help: superhuman stamina.

It wasn't fair. She'd mended her ways, had become a Christian and was living the most honorable life she knew how. So why was everything going so terribly wrong? Why, instead of getting better, did her life seem to have taken a turn for the worse?

She remembered what her pastor had told her when she'd gone to him for counseling after leaving the shelter. Being a Christian didn't mean that there would be no more trials, nor did coming to the Lord negate

her past mistakes. Yes, she was forgiven. And, yes, she could start over. What she couldn't expect to do was avoid the consequences of her former sins, any more than Roy could have turned over a new leaf and had his prior crimes erased without having had to face punishment.

Put in those terms, Marie could understand the spiritual concept, but that didn't mean she liked it.

When Marie finally finished her shower, she could hear the television playing in the other room. Patty was such a good girl. Always obedient. Even if she did sometimes argue, she never actually balked. What a joy it was to be the mother of a sweet child like that.

Humming, Marie slipped her robe on and stood in front of the mirror to blow-dry her hair. The shower had helped. A lot. So would getting out of that tiny rented room and at least going for a walk. Too bad they had to be so cautious, yet she might even consider taking Patty to the park she'd seen just down the road and letting her play there, providing the ground wasn't all muddy after last night's storm. The poor little girl had been cooped up a lot more than usual since they'd left home, and she had to be getting antsy.

"I'll make it up to her soon," Marie vowed. Smiling, she opened the bathroom door as she said, "That's a little loud, honey. I told you to keep it quieter, remember?"

No one answered.

Marie glanced at the bed, fully expecting to see Patty lounging there on her tummy, chin in her hands and feet in the air, watching her favorite cartoon show.

"Patty?" The air suddenly seemed to drain from the room. "Patty? Don't hide from Mama, okay? It's not funny."

Still, there was no answer.

Frantic, Marie threw the bedclothes into a heap on the floor so she could view the entire mattress. Patty wasn't hiding there, nor was she in the closet or behind the bathroom door.

Marie fell to her knees, hoping to spot the impish child under the bed, but found that it was resting on a solid platform. There was no place down there to conceal anyone or anything.

Throwing on clean clothes as fast as she could, Marie blinked back unshed tears. Her mind was racing. Her hands shook. This couldn't be happening. It was too much. Too terrible to even contemplate.

"Get a grip," she cautioned, struggling to remain functionally calm. "Nobody knows we're here except Seth and Clarence. And the door was locked, so…"

Her gaze shot to the heavy door. Every ounce of strength left her. At first glance it had appeared to be closed—but it wasn't. It was standing ever so slightly ajar.

Seth wasn't too surprised to see Marie approaching until he noted her wide eyes and semi-hysterical expression. He started to run toward her.

She met him, faltered and fell into his arms.

"What is it? What's wrong?" he demanded.

"Patty."

"What about Patty?" He glanced past Marie's shoulder. "Where is she?"

"I don't know. I don't know."

Guiding her aside, he sat her down on an old, steel-framed chair that they kept handy for customers.

Seth crouched at her feet and took both her hands in his. "Calm down. Take a deep breath and tell me exactly what happened."

"I—I don't know. I was taking a shower and Patty was supposed to be watching TV. I wasn't in the shower long. When I came out, she was gone."

"You searched your room?"

"Yes. And the motel lobby. I thought she might have gone there to get a donut, but Clarence said he hadn't seen her." She took a shuddering breath. "Is he trustworthy?"

"Very. If he said she wasn't around, she wasn't." He straightened and scanned the car lot as well as the nearby yards. "She could be anywhere. Do you want me to call the sheriff?"

Marie leaped up. "No! We can't do that."

"What if she's been kidnapped?"

"She can't be. God wouldn't have allowed it. I know He wouldn't."

Sobering, Seth once again grasped her hands and held them tightly. "I don't know that and neither do you, Marie. I learned a long time ago that I couldn't predict the future or prevent bad things from happening. If I could have, my wife would still be alive."

He realized immediately that he'd made an error by mentioning Alice. "I didn't mean something terrible

has happened to Patty," he quickly added. "I just thought that we needed more help. That's why I suggested calling the sheriff."

"I can't." Near tears, she took a shuddering breath. "I can't tell you why—I just can't let anybody know where I am."

"Not even the good guys?" Seth asked.

"Nobody. I can't trust anybody, anywhere."

"You can trust me," he said, willing her to do just that. "I promise you."

"Then *do* something. Find my little girl." Marie was nearly shouting.

"We will. We will." He left her long enough to stick his head into the office and tell Bob what was going on, then grabbed a cell phone out of his truck.

"We've got a problem down here at the garage, Brother Logan," Seth said as soon as someone answered his call. "A missing five-year-old child named Patty. Becky knows all about her. I took her and her mother to the preschool yesterday."

He could hear the pastor conversing in the background.

"That's right. Patty," Seth affirmed. "She apparently wandered off a couple of minutes ago, so she can't have gone far. Can you get a few others together and cover the ground between the motel and the garage? Good. Thanks. We'll be right here."

"No. I can't stay here," Marie argued. "I have to go look for her, too."

"We will. We'll work back the way you came and

see if we can turn up any clues, maybe see some foot-prints in the wet ground. I can't believe you didn't call me in the first place to save time."

"I never thought of it."

"Do you have a cell phone?"

She shook her head. "No. I didn't want…"

"I know. You didn't want to be traced because of it. The kind I have is simple. It doesn't allow tracing, because you buy the minutes up front instead of hav-ing an account, and if you don't give out the number or leave the phone turned on all the time, it can't be located." He handed his to her. "Here. Take this for now. I'll buy you another one the next time I'm in Ash Flat."

"I can't do that."

"Yes, you can. You have to," Seth said firmly. "It's already programmed with the garage number, so you can call me for help with the push of a button."

"Well…"

"Smart woman. Now, come on, stick that phone in your pocket and let's go."

Watching Marie's reactions, he was satisfied that he'd given her enough other things to think about to keep her from falling apart, at least for now. When they found the child, she'd have plenty of time to weep.

If they found her, he added, gritting his teeth. The prospect of failing in this instance was unacceptable. Because they were beginning their search so quickly, their chances of success were greater, yes, but there was also the possibility that Patty had been taken by

the same man who had tried to steal her from the truck the night before.

Seth knew Marie was well aware of that. He just hoped and prayed that wasn't what had actually happened.

The way he saw it, there was a fair chance of it going either way.

NINE

Marie spotted Becky Malloy first. The pastor's wife was toting Timmy on her hip and walking slowly through the used-car lot next to the garage, stopping every few yards to call Patty's name.

That meant only one thing. No one from the church had found Patty, either.

"I will not cry," Marie insisted quietly to herself. "I will not lose control when my daughter needs me to keep my wits about me."

She waved to Becky as she quickly joined her. "Any luck?"

Becky smiled benevolently. "Not yet. And luck isn't something I like to count on. We've been praying for you and Patty since the moment we heard."

Marie wanted to accept the reassurance the other woman was offering, but searching her deepest heart, she found unreasoning fear. Trepidation. Feelings of guilt and failure.

"I never should have let her out of my sight," Marie lamented. "Never. I know better."

"We can't keep our children with us 24-7," Becky said wisely. "That would make emotional cripples of them. Besides, they belong to the Lord. We're just watching them for Him."

"And I haven't been doing a good job of it, have I?" Marie was fighting tears and barely able to speak.

Becky laid a comforting hand on her shoulder and nodded. "I know how you feel. I wasn't always a pastor's wife. My life wasn't easy while I was growing up, or later, for that matter. But I think the longer we're Christians and keep following Jesus, the more instances we have to look back on where we can see God's handiwork and learn to trust Him."

"I don't know," Marie said. Her voice cracked. "I don't know anything anymore."

"We'll find Patty," Becky said firmly. "I know we will." She smiled. "Here. Why don't you carry Timmy for me for a little while so he doesn't get his new tennies muddy? He's getting heavier every day. It's hard to believe he's almost two."

Marie started to refuse, then relented. She knew the other woman was simply trying to distract her, but at the moment that didn't sound like a bad idea. As she drew the child into her arms, she was struck by his warmth, the trusting way his little arms went around her neck and he snuggled closer. She could almost imagine herself safe in God's comforting arms, instead of the child's. That comparison took her by surprise.

"Oh, Father," she whispered. "Help us."

Timmy's grip tightened and he laid his head on

her shoulder as if the Lord was using him to directly answer Marie's plea. She could barely see through her tears.

Suddenly, there was a shout from up the road. Everyone froze except Marie. She passed Timmy back to his mother as fast as she could and started to run toward the sound of the yelling.

Someone was emerging from one of the private backyards there. It was Seth. And he had Patty!

Seth was beaming. He released Patty's hand as Marie barreled up to them and fell to her knees, oblivious to the damp grass, to hug her little girl. She was weeping and laughing at the same time.

Finally, she regained enough control to hold the child at arm's length and ask, "Where were you? Where did you go?"

"I'm—I'm sorry, Mama," Patty said through her own tears. "I didn't mean to scare you. I was gonna get us some donuts, but I couldn't get the office door open by myself and there was this really pretty kitty next door and…"

"You followed the cat?"

"Uh-huh." She sniffled. "I'm sorry you were worried."

As Seth watched, Marie smoothed back the child's hair and cupped her cheeks in her hands so she couldn't look away. "I don't want you to ever go off on your own like that again, do you understand?"

Patty nodded.

Giving the child one more all-encompassing hug,

Marie finally let go and got to her feet. "Thank you. Again," she said, swiping tears from her cheeks, sniffling and gazing up at Seth.

"You're most welcome."

He assumed, judging by the serious way Marie was looking at him, that she wanted to say more, but their brief opportunity for a private conversation had passed. They were now surrounded by many of the other searchers and were being bombarded by congratulations and expressions of delight and praise.

"What now?" he asked aside. "Are you going back to the motel, or would you like another ride to church?"

"The motel," Marie said without pause. "I need to pull myself together and have a long talk with my daughter before we do anything else."

"Okay. If it's any consolation, no one has seen any sign of that white truck that we thought might be a problem. Chances are, whoever was in it has left town."

"I certainly hope so," Marie said.

Seth agreed. "Yeah. Me, too."

"What about my car? Will it be ready soon?"

"The parts may come in today's shipment," he said. "If they do, I can probably work overtime to get them installed, providing I don't run into any glitches." He paused, concentrating on her and starting to scowl. "The question is, are you sure you want to leave Serenity?"

"Of course I am."

"It might be better to stay here a while longer." He could tell his logical suggestion did not sit well with her, so he explained his reasoning. "Think about it,

Marie. Here, you have people who care about you and want to help you. Whatever your past may have been, you're among friends here. We'll stand by you."

"No." She grabbed Patty's hand and began to edge away from him. "Leave us alone. We'll be fine. Just fix my car and don't interfere."

"You're in trouble, Marie. Let me help you."

"No. You don't know a thing about me."

As Seth watched her turn on her heel and hurry away, he wished she was right, that he didn't know why she was on the run. Not knowing the truth would make it much easier for him to bid her goodbye and not worry about what might become of her.

As it was, however, he knew enough to be certain she was in for much more trouble. If the authorities overtook her before her unnamed nemesis did, they'd surely arrest her and assume legal custody of Patty. If the body that had been found recently turned out to be Roy's, that was an even worse scenario. The question then became, who had killed him and why?

Seth's hands fisted. That wasn't the only problem, was it? The most important element was the unknown. If, as Marie thought, she was actually being pursued, there could be danger around every corner, behind every rock and tree.

He couldn't just let her drive away and face that alone. Until he'd figured out who was who and what was really going on, he was not going to permit her to leave town. He'd already buried one special woman. He was not going to do it again.

Holding his breath for an instant, Seth realized the perilous direction his thoughts had taken and accepted them, although with reservations.

Yes, he agreed, he was beginning to truly care for Marie. And for Patty. But he was also not in a position to act on his feelings or reveal them, no matter how tender or genuine they might be. He was also a fugitive and therefore could never offer Marie a safe haven or the kind of normal life she deserved.

Seth snorted in self-derision. They were a fine pair, weren't they? Two innocent people who had had to go into hiding because the bad guys had gotten the upper hand. What irony.

His jaw clenched as he turned and headed back toward the garage. It wasn't fair. None of this was. Yet for the life of him, he couldn't see a clear way out for either of them. All he could hope for, at this point, was to find out who was chasing Marie and...

And then what? he asked himself. He couldn't just have them killed the way his enemies had eliminated Alice, nor did he have Corp. Inc.'s clout with which to scare them off. If he was totally honest, he'd admit he was as powerless to help Marie as he'd been to help himself.

So why get involved? Why even try?

Because he had to. He didn't know why that perception was so strong, so positive, but he knew he must follow through.

He wasn't about to credit his decision to God's leading and make himself out to be some kind of divine

avenger. He did, however, feel as strongly about attaining his current goal as he ever had about his job, his marriage or anything else.

"Well, what do you think, Mac?" agent Eccles asked his computer-savvy cohort. "Is it him?"

McCormick swiveled the chair away from the keyboard. "Beats me. He used to work with you, right?"

"Used to."

"Then you'd know him better than I would."

"Not exactly. I was sure he'd stick around and face the music. He dropped out of sight, instead. You never can tell about a guy like Seth."

"Well, my part is done. I put you in touch with him and made him think you were Jonathan Biggs. That's it. I'm through."

"I thought you were a team player," Eccles said with a sneer.

"When I know what team I'm on," McCormick replied.

"What's that supposed to mean?"

Mac turned and started to walk away. "Nothing. Forget it. I've got to get back to my station. The work is really piling up."

"You do that." Eccles's dark eyebrows arched as he watched the computer tech walk away. If he hadn't figured that he'd need Mac again, he might have been tempted to eliminate him. It was just as well he didn't have that option, he reasoned. After all, he'd gotten away

with a couple of murders, including that of Seth's wife, with no difficulty. There was no sense pushing his luck.

Marie was so exhausted when her extra adrenaline wore off that she felt as if it had to be nine at night instead of nine in the morning. She had never, ever, been that frightened. Not even when Roy was beating her.

She and Patty had stopped at the motel office to tell Clarence that all was well and to pick up a light breakfast to eat in their room.

Patty dug in as if she were starved. Marie took one bite and pushed the donut aside.

"Can I have yours, too?" Patty asked.

"No. You need good food, not junk."

"It's good. I like donuts."

"That's not what I mean," Marie explained. "Too much sugar isn't good for you. Or for your teeth. You need something else, like maybe scrambled eggs."

"Okay." The child looked puzzled. "Where can we get some?"

"There's that café on the square that Mr. Whitfield mentioned. Maybe they deliver."

"Why can't we go?" Patty began to pout.

"Because we just can't, that's all."

"But…"

"No buts, Patty. We're not going out again and that's final."

She reached for the telephone on the nightstand,

then remembered the little, folding phone Seth had given her. Flipping it open, she quickly found his work number on it and called the garage.

He answered on the first ring and immediately interrupted her greeting. "Marie? What's wrong?"

"Nothing," she assured him. "I was just wondering if you knew if the café you told me about would deliver breakfast to our room."

"I'm sure it can be arranged. I'll take care of it. What do you want?"

She told him, thanked him and hung up. "There," she said to Patty. "Our breakfast will be here in no time. We have to eat right to keep up our strength."

Which is more than true, she added to herself. She was already feeling run-down and lacked energy— except in dire situations. It would be more than foolish to allow herself to lose the edge that had kept them one step ahead of Roy's cronies thus far.

Sipping coffee from a foam cup she'd brought from the lobby, Marie settled herself in the only chair in the room and waited for their order to arrive.

When a knock finally came, she grabbed her wallet, then stood on tiptoe at the door to peek through the peephole. It wasn't a delivery boy. It was Seth.

Surprised and confused, she jerked open the door. "What are you doing here?"

"I brought breakfast, like you asked."

"I didn't mean for you to do it. I thought the restaurant…"

"Nope. Not unless you're a shut-in, and even then

you'd need to send a relative or friend or someone from your church to pick it up for you."

"Oh."

"So, are you going to make me stand here all day, or can I come in?"

Marie stepped back to give him room, leaving the door ajar as he passed. "I'm sorry. Bring it in. And thanks for doing this for us." She started to open her wallet. "What do I owe you?"

"Nothing. This was my pleasure, ma'am." Seth was grinning as he placed the food containers on the nightstand. "Just showing my Southern hospitality, as always."

"Uh-huh."

He laughed. "I love the way you respond to my efforts at courtesy, lady. Don't you ever just accept folks as they are?"

"Apparently not," Marie said, coloring slightly. "Sorry if I seem leery. It's been a rough week."

"Yeah, well, you aren't the only one who's been a little keyed up. Tell me, who are you so afraid of?"

"It's a long story."

"I don't doubt it. Why don't you dish up some eggs and ham for Patty while they're still hot, get her started eating and then walk me to my truck?"

Marie knew why he was urging her to step outside. He clearly intended to ask her more questions. Did he deserve straight answers? Would he keep her confidences about Roy and his troubles if she asked him to?

She almost believed he would. And it would be so, so good to talk to someone, to get a second opinion on her plans, such as they were. But was Seth the right person to trust? Might it be better to tell Becky, instead?

No, Marie decided easily. Seth was the one who had repeatedly stepped up and helped her, rescued her, tolerated her silence regarding her past. If she were to open up to anyone, he would be the sensible choice.

Following his suggestion, Marie fed Patty, picked up her now-tepid coffee, and led the way back out the open door into the parking lot.

"All right. Let's have it," she said flatly.

"What do you mean?"

"You wanted to talk to me. So, talk."

He stuffed his hands into his jacket pockets and struck a nonchalant pose. "I was kind of hoping you'd want to talk to *me*."

"You're right. I should." Taking a slow sip from her cup to stall for time and better arrange her thoughts, she said, "I do owe you some sort of explanation. I told you Roy came to see me, didn't I?"

"You said he'd warned you, yes."

"Well, it was more than that. I don't know what he was mixed up in or who he'd been working with, but I do know it was bad." She sipped again, finding it hard to swallow past the lump in her throat as she recalled Roy's abduction.

Seth nodded patiently. "Go on."

"That night, the one where he came to see me? I

was looking out the window after he left, and I watched some men grab him and drag him away. It was frightening."

"Why didn't you call the police?"

"I did! I told them everything. They didn't believe me. They didn't even offer to protect me. So I did the only other thing I could. I got in my car and started driving." She felt her lower lip quiver and tried to cover the emotional reaction with the foam cup. "I thought I'd gotten away till my car was messed with. Don't you see? The people who took Roy have to be on my trail or they'd never have been able to put anything in my gas tank."

"It could have been a prank."

"You don't actually believe that, do you?"

"No." Seth took a deep breath and released it noisily. "No, I don't. I think whoever was after Roy has to be chasing you now. What I don't understand is, why."

She thought she glimpsed something strange and off-putting in his eyes for an instant. "How should I know? All he said was that his partners were out to get him and I should take Patty and run away."

"That was all he said?"

"Yes. Why am I getting the impression that you don't believe me?"

"Beats me. I'm just an innocent bystander, remember?"

"You may be a bystander, Mr. Whitfield, but there is definitely nothing innocent about you, no matter how hard you try to convince people you are. I know better."

It didn't help her mood that Seth laughed before he said, "*Do* you?"

Marie stood firm. "Yes. I do. You're smooth and smart and I can see your mind working all the time. There is nothing simple, or terribly rural, about you except your clothing and that ridiculous, countrified act you put on."

His smile faded and he nodded slowly, cautiously. "All right. Say you're correct and I'm not exactly who I seem to be. Does that bother you?"

"I guess not. Not as long as you're on my side," she said soberly. "I can use all the help I can get."

"How do you know I'm not a crook like Roy was?"

"I don't know how or why I know that, but I do. I haven't been a Christian for very long, so I can't really say I'm experienced in telling what God is doing on my behalf. Not the way Becky does. But I do think my car made it this far before it quit so I'd have you to rely on. Does that sound crazy?"

"Not to me," Seth said. "I've been thinking along those same lines myself."

"You have?" Her jaw dropped.

"Yes, I have. And like I said before, I think you should stay right here and let it all come to a head."

"What if it's dangerous?"

When Seth said, "Good," she almost choked on her coffee.

"Good? Are you joking? Because if you are, I don't think it's funny."

"I'm very serious," Seth said. "I know this town like

the back of my hand, whereas you won't be a bit familiar with any new place where you might end up. If you were a pursuer, would you rather your victim be confused or well-oriented?"

"Confused."

"My point exactly."

"Suppose they find me here?"

When Seth countered, "Suppose they already have," Marie's hand started to shake. He was right. Suppose they already had!

TEN

The fluttering bluebird logo popped onto the corner of Seth's computer screen almost as soon as he logged on to the agency site that night. So much for anonymity, he thought; he was chagrined. Still, if this really was Jonathan trying to contact him, it meant he had an ally inside the old organization after all. That was worth a lot, both for himself and for Marie.

"How are things in your part of Wonderland?" Seth typed.

"Not so wonderful. Miss you, buddy."

"Yeah. You, too." Seth had been racking his brain, trying to think of something that only he and Jonathan had known. The references to Wonderland were all well and good except that someone else may have overheard them using that fantasy analogy in the past. There must be some other test, some indisputable proof. But what?

He tried subterfuge. "Remember that case about the missing parrot? Those were some good times we had."

Long seconds passed before the answer came. "Can't say that I do. What parrot?"

Seth typed, "In the Caribbean."

"You've got me there, old buddy. Sorry."

Satisfied, Seth took a chance and told him the truth. "Okay. You passed my test. Care to tell me how come you're not dead?" He could picture his old friend laughing at his bluntness.

"Always did have a fondness for being alive. How about you? I'd heard you were long gone. What made you get in touch now?"

"It's complicated. I need a little help."

"Glad to hear you've finally come to your senses. Want to come in?"

"No. It's not help for me. I need you to see what you can find out about a local case down in Baton Rouge. A couple of weeks ago there was a report of a man named Roy Jenkins being abducted. The woman who made the report was Marie Parnell."

"Gotcha. What do you want to know about it?"

"Everything you can turn up."

"You don't ask for much, do you?"

Seth chuckled as he typed, "You know me. I always want even the smallest details."

"Yeah. Okay. How do you want this information delivered? I'm not sure we should use this link again. Anything can be traced if you're connected long enough."

"I know," Seth typed. "I'd give you a cell number, but I just gave away my only phone and I haven't had time to buy a replacement."

"What?"

"Never mind. I'll get back in touch when I have another number to give you. Later tonight. Eleven sharp. Can you be online then?"

"I will be. Take care, buddy."

With a quick "Thanks," Seth disconnected.

He knew Jonathan was right about the danger of being in contact for too long a time, which was one of the reasons he had decided to ask him to do some of the research regarding Marie's case. And instead of giving him an address for mailing the information on paper, he'd use one of the new, untraceable cell phones he was about to purchase. In truth, he'd gotten so complacent that he'd been using his old one for far too long already. It was high time for a change of numbers for himself, too, just as a matter of personal safety and anonymity.

Grabbing his jacket and whistling to Babe, Seth headed for his truck. There was one big box store within reasonable driving distance, and it carried inexpensive, disposable phones with paid-for minutes included. Plus, the store was open all night. There were many advantages to living out in the boonies, but access to late-night shopping wasn't one of them, which was probably why those kinds of chain stores did such a good business.

At this point, Seth wouldn't have cared how much he'd have to pay or how far he'd have to drive. He needed phones. Period. In view of the urgency of obtaining them, he'd have given a month's pay and traveled all the way to Little Rock if he'd had enough time to make the round-trip.

* * *

Marie had dozed off when she was startled awake by a muffled, sing-song tone that she quickly realized was coming from her purse. Hands trembling, she retrieved the little phone Seth had given her and answered it.

To her relief, it was him on the line.

"Grab a pencil and write this number down," he said. "It's the one for the new phone I bought you. I'm charging its batteries and I'll program it tomorrow, if you want, when we switch."

"I can program it," she said, jotting down his area code and number. "I need to pay you for it, too. Are you sure it can't be traced?"

"Positive. Some of the new phones come equipped with internal navigational capabilities, but that one doesn't have it. Neither does the new one. And you don't owe me a thing. I'm planning to replace my phone as soon as the store gets more in stock, so feel free to use it as much as you like. Just don't run the battery down till I deliver your charger and we switch instruments."

"There's no one I want to call—except you," she said.

"Not even your friends?"

"I don't think I should. Not till things settle down and I know where I'm going. When I left home, I didn't let anyone know because I was afraid they'd get in trouble. It was bad enough that I was mixed up in it."

"In what?" Seth asked quietly.

"You know. Roy's abduction."

"Oh, that."

She could tell there had been a change in his voice, in the way he was responding to her, and it was worrying.

"What did you think I meant?"

"Nothing. Keep that new number handy and don't hesitate to call me if anything else goes wrong. Okay?"

"Okay." She took a deep, settling breath before she added, "I don't know how I can ever thank you."

"Always tell me the truth," he said flatly.

"I have." She felt the beginnings of a smile. "Well, except for the part about who I was and where I was from and why I was on the lam."

To her relief, Seth chuckled. "Now you're starting to sound like a bad gangster movie," he said. "Good night, Marie."

"Good night."

As soon as she heard him break their connection, she closed the little phone and took it back to bed with her, carefully tucking it next to her pillow so she'd be sure to hear the ring if Seth called again.

She still didn't know what to make of him, nor was she sure how she actually felt about him. Under less stressful circumstances she supposed she might have been personally attracted to him, but this was not a normal situation. Not even close. She couldn't trust her emotions when every second of every day had her on edge beyond belief.

Yes, she liked Seth, she admitted easily. And she knew he liked her. That much was evident. The question was, would they have even looked twice at each

other if they had not been thrown together by circumstances? Probably not. And the time would soon come when, in the absence of any threat, they drifted apart naturally.

It surprised Marie to realize how much she would miss Seth once she moved on. Staying put for more than another day or two was foolish, of course, yet the more she thought about leaving, the less she wanted to actually go.

Closing her eyes and clasping her hands, she began to whisper a prayer. It wasn't fancy or flowery or even very coherent, but she knew in her heart that the Lord was listening.

What His answer might be or where He was leading her was a lot less clear.

Eccles fidgeted as he sat by the agency computer and waited for eleven o'clock to arrive. He'd taken a risk by letting Seth disconnect, but he figured it was what the real Jonathan would have done. If he was going to continue to make Seth believe he was speaking with his old friend, he had to take some chances. The bit about the parrot had been a stroke of genius on Seth's part. And he'd almost fallen for the ploy until he'd remembered that Jonathan had never done fieldwork with Seth, so they couldn't have shared a case in the Caribbean.

Right on schedule, Seth logged on with, "Hey, Bluebird. You there?"

"Yeah, I'm here," his enemy typed. "Waiting for your contact info."

"I was going to have a phone number for you but I wasn't able to make the arrangements the way I'd hoped. Maybe tomorrow."

"Sorry. No can do. I'm taking a big chance talking to you at all. If I can't do it by cell phone from now on, I won't be available. Period."

Seth's silence made Eccles wonder if he'd pushed him too far. Then, finally, Seth said, "All right. I'll give you a number that will only be good for forty-eight hours. After that I'll have another one for you. Understood? Don't call before then unless you get something for me that won't wait."

"Understood. Fire away."

Seth typed in the number, then quickly disconnected.

In minutes, Eccles had used the area code to narrow his search and had identified the distributor of the batch of cell phones assigned that series of numbers. The manufacturers didn't keep records of individual users by name, but that didn't matter. Judging by the elapsed time, Seth had to have bought that phone locally. Therefore, he must be somewhere in north-central Arkansas. The trap was closing.

Until he could get his equipment in place for an illegal triangulation trace between cell towers, he'd slowly feed Seth bits and pieces of information about the Jenkins case to keep him interested.

It was only a matter of time before they'd know exactly where Seth was hiding out and everyone's troubles would be over.

First, he figured he'd better check to see that Seth's

phone was operational. He dialed, then waited until Seth answered to say, "One thing I forgot to tell you. They found Roy Jenkins's body."

"Are they sure it's him?" Seth asked.

"Yes. They're sure," Eccles answered, then quickly disconnected and began to grin. "Gotcha."

Marie responded to a knock on her door early the following morning. When she answered, Seth proudly displayed another hot breakfast. "Room service."

She had to laugh. "I didn't order anything."

"No, but you still have to eat. Man cannot live by donuts alone, you know."

"Neither can woman and child," she said, playing along with his misquote as she opened the door. "Come on in. Patty's watching cartoons."

"You sure you don't want to take her back to play at the preschool today? It would give you both a break."

"Not if I go along and help," Marie said, stifling a yawn. "What's the word on my car?"

"Well, I could tell you I'm still waiting for the parts, but that would be a lie. They came in yesterday afternoon, as expected."

Her heart skipped a beat. "Really? Then I can go?"

"If you insist on leaving, I supposed I can have the car ready by late today." He stared at her as if willing her to change her mind. "Are you positive that's what you should do? We'd love to have you hang around here a little longer."

"We? We who?"

Seth gave her a grin that made her tingle all the way to her toes. "Babe and me, of course. Well, and Becky and Timmy and the gang from church, too."

"Of course." She made a silly face. "I might as well start asking your dog for advice. I don't seem to be doing so hot by myself."

"That's because there are sinister forces working against you, not because you're making bad decisions."

"Sinister forces? Now who's being melodramatic?"

"I just call 'em as I see 'em," Seth said. "By the way, when were you going to tell me about the ransom?"

"What ransom?" Scowling up at him, Marie could tell he wasn't accepting her denial. "I don't know what you're talking about."

"Okay," Seth said, backing toward the open door. "Just think about it. When you're ready to tell me everything, you know where to find me."

"Wait!" She followed him out the door. "What ransom? What on earth do you mean?"

"There was a kidnapping near Baton Rouge a few weeks ago," Seth said slowly, deliberately. "Your friend Roy and three other men were involved, as nearly as I can tell. The authorities believe Roy got greedy and kept the whole ransom for himself, which is probably why he was so scared when he came to warn you."

"What does all that have to do with me?"

"You were tied to the crime as soon as you made that 911 call about Roy's abduction. The cops were already looking for him and his partners. I wouldn't be surprised if they're on your trail as we speak."

"Who? The police? Could they have been the ones in the white van?"

Seth shook his head. "I doubt it. They would have just pulled you over and arrested you, not messed with your car. Whoever did that intended to catch you unaware and…"

"And hurt me? Hurt Patty?" She knew her voice held panic but she couldn't help it.

"Maybe. Probably." He reached for her hand and grasped it gently. "Look, Marie. I don't think you were in cahoots with Roy during the commission of the crime, but somebody sure thinks you know more than you're letting on. He never mentioned a thing about some missing money?"

"No. Not even once. I know I'd remember because the minute he told me to run away, I started wondering how I was going to pay for it." She swallowed hard, willing Seth to believe her, to accept her statement as the whole truth. "Maybe they'll catch Roy and he'll tell them I'm innocent," she offered, hopeful.

Seth shook his head. His grip on her hand tightened, and she was glad for the moral support when he finally said, "Roy won't be telling anybody anything. They finally identified a body that was found a few days ago. Roy Jenkins is dead."

Although she had tried not to show it while Seth was still there, and make him feel even worse about being the bearer of bad tidings, the news about Roy had hit Marie like a blow to the heart. She wasn't mourning

his loss the way she had when she'd decided to make a clean break with him; she was sad because she had never been able to speak to him about her newfound faith without enduring his ridicule.

Her only hope, at this point, was that Roy had finally turned to the Lord in his last moments. After all, he might be a criminal and an abusive drunk, but he was nevertheless Patty's father. No matter what Marie might think of his lifestyle, she still cared about his eternal soul. And, in a roundabout way, she still loved the man she'd once thought he was.

She sank onto the edge of the bed and cradled her face in her hands. There were no tears, only emptiness. *Poor Roy.* How many times had she thought that about him? Probably hundreds of times, especially lately. And now she had no one left but Patty.

It surprised Marie when her mind immediately contradicted that conclusion with a vivid image of Seth; his smile, his concern, his wit, his tenderness toward both of them. She argued against including him in her inner circle of loved ones; yet, there he was, just the same.

That was not good. It was more than not good—it was awful. Her life was one big instability, her future as uncertain as a wisp of smoke in a gale. The last thing she needed was to become involved with anyone, let alone a man who was so secretive about his own background. That was not going to happen. She was not going to permit it.

Deciding on her next move, Marie looked to her

daughter. "Finish your eggs, Patty. As soon as you're done we're going out."

"Oh, goody! Where?"

"To the repair shop," Marie said with conviction. "You can play with Babe while I watch Mr. Whitfield work on our car."

"Lots?" the eager child asked.

"All day, if necessary. I don't want him dragging his feet, and the best way to make sure he's really working is for us to be right there watching him."

"Are we going to church school, too?"

"No," Marie said flatly.

"Why not?"

"Because…" Her first reaction had been to keep everything from the child, but after this morning's scare she was more inclined to share enough to help Patty avoid getting into more trouble. "Because, there are some bad people out there who want to catch us, and you and I are going to be really smart and get away as soon as our car is ready to go."

"Bad people?" Patty asked softly, hesitantly.

"Yes. Bad like the man who tried to steal Babe from Mr. Whitfield's truck the other night."

"I was scared," the child admitted.

Marie took her in her arms and gave her a supportive hug before she said, "Me, too, honey. But nobody will bother us again. I won't let them. I promise."

As she let go and straightened, Marie wondered how in the world she'd manage to keep that promise.

ELEVEN

"There's going to be a big celebration around the square in Serenity this coming weekend," Seth told Marie as he struggled to lift her gas tank and slide it back into place beneath her car. "It's called a town reunion, and it is, but it's also a street fair, with booths and crafts and all kinds of activities. Patty would really enjoy it."

"We won't be here," Marie told him.

He chose to delay the rest of their conversation until he'd tightened the bolts that held the tank frame in place. Wiping his hands, he ducked out from under the hydraulic lift and smiled at her. "It's too bad you'll miss it. There'll be turtle races for the kids."

"Turtle *what?*"

"Races. This part of the country is full of wild terrapins of all sizes. We collect dozens of 'em for the races, and each child is assigned one with a number on its back. Then they run heats, just like at a track meet, and have a runoff of the winners at the end. It's a hoot to watch. You should hear all the cheering."

"What about the poor turtles?"

Seth laughed. "They get released back into the woods, none the worse for wear, and live to race another day."

"Oh good. I was worried."

"I was, too, the first time I saw them set up for the races. It turned out to be a lot funnier than I'd expected it to be."

"I'll take your word for it," Marie said. She eyed her car, still up on the rack. "How soon before you're finished?"

"Not too long. The tank and fuel pump are done and I've blown out the lines. All I have left to do is install the new filters and put fresh gas in the tank."

"And bill me," she added.

Seth shook his head. "That's not necessary."

"Yes, it is. About how much do you expect it to cost?"

He watched her expression change to one of worry as he quoted a figure. "Like I said, you won't have to pay."

"I've never asked for charity," Marie insisted. "And I'm not about to start."

She paused long enough to chew on her bottom lip and Seth could tell she was pondering an important decision.

"Tell you what," she finally said. "I don't have much cash, but I can give you a credit card for the repair bill. All I ask is that you hold the charge for a week or so before you submit it. Will that be satisfactory?"

"I don't see any problem. Will a week be long enough?"

"Assuming Roy's partners have already traced me this far, I see no reason why not."

"What about the police? I suppose they're watching for credit card activity, too."

"I haven't done anything illegal."

"That won't stop them from arresting you. There's probably an APB out for your car."

"I thought of that after you noticed I was from Louisiana," Marie said. "I don't know how to change a license plate, not legally, anyway. I know what Roy would do but..."

"But you're an honest person," Seth finished for her.

"Bingo."

"Then I recommend mud," he said. "Just smear it on the plate and let it dry. That'll cover you at least until you get caught in the rain or drive through a wet-weather crossing too fast and make waves."

The way she blushed further endeared her to him. If he'd been able to figure out how to convince her to stay in Serenity, he'd have felt much better about everything. As it was, he intended to surreptitiously follow her, at least a little way, to be certain she got back on the highway without incident.

And after that? Seth gritted his teeth. Unless Jonathan came up with something helpful soon, there wasn't one more thing he could do except stand back and let her go. The notion of doing that tied his gut in a knot and left his mouth dry as cotton.

* * *

Al, Frank and Earl were sitting in Frank's car in the lot at Hickory Station. Earl was watching the repair garage through binoculars.

"He's letting the blue car down now," Earl said.

Al snorted. "Do you see the woman and kid?"

"Yeah. The woman, at least. She's been hanging around there all day."

Leaning back and closing his eyes, Al said, "This is boring. Wake me when something happens."

Frank hit Al's leg and cursed at him. "Bored? We wouldn't have to sit here at all if you'd done your job right."

"Me? I'm not the one who smacked Roy so hard he croaked."

"Shut up, both of you," Earl ordered. "What's done is done. The only way we're going to get our hands on that money now is through the woman, so I suggest you concentrate on helping me keep track of her."

"Yeah, yeah." Al made a sour face. "What if she can't help us? Huh? What if Roy never told her anything?"

"She'd better hope he did," Earl said, "or she's going to be in more trouble than she's ever imagined."

Marie signed the credit card charge after reiterating her specific instructions to Seth. She trusted him. That would have to be good enough insurance because there was no way she could have afforded the repair bill otherwise.

To her surprise he also handed her a wad of cash.

"What's this for?"

"I added a little to the charge so you'd have more traveling money and took it in small bills," Seth said. "I figured you had to be running short, and since you were using the card anyway, I didn't see how it could make things any worse. Right?"

"Right. Thanks. That was smart." She studied his nearly blank expression. "Are you ever going to tell me how you got so proficient at subterfuge?"

"Nope." A smile twitched at the corners of his mouth, and his eyes began to sparkle. "Not a chance."

"That's what I thought." Offering her hand, she waited for him to shake it. Instead, he grasped it gently, comfortingly. "Just before you leave, I want to give you the new phone."

"Why not trade now? I have the old one with me."

"It's complicated. I need to keep it for a few more hours. And I want you to promise you'll throw it away and replace it as soon as you reach a store in West Plains or Springfield that carries the same model."

"I don't want to replace it. How will I know I'm getting one that won't be traceable? Didn't you say some come with a built-in navigational system?"

"Yes, but…"

She pulled her hands free and began waving them in front of her in a gesture of surrender. "All right. Have it your way. I figured you'd need your old phone back because of all the numbers in its memory. If you want to wait to trade, that's fine with me. Just don't let me forget to give it to you."

"I won't. I left an extra mobile charger on the front seat of your car. It plugs into the cigarette lighter so you can use it while you drive.

"Thanks."

"Call me if there's anything I can do for you," Seth added. "Promise?"

"No." She blinked back unshed tears. "You've done enough. I don't know how I'll ever be able to thank you properly."

"I do," Seth said. He stepped closer, bending his head to one side until their lips were nearly touching.

Marie realized he expected a goodbye kiss. She wasn't going to give him one. No, sir. Not her. She was going to resist the urge to kiss this handsome, kind, generous, new friend, no matter what.

His warm breath tickled her cheek. His nearness made her shiver. She swayed, feeling suddenly off-balance. Seth was right there. So close. So appealing. So, so...

Raising on tiptoe, she made herself just tall enough for their lips to connect ever so briefly. She hadn't intended to even kiss him, let alone make it the best kiss of her life, but that was exactly what it had been.

Wide-eyed, she staggered back. "Uh-oh."

He was grinning. "You can say that again."

"I'd rather not," Marie countered, blushing.

Seth sobered. "You don't have to leave."

"Yes, I do." *Especially now.*

"All right. Here's what we'll do. I'll take your car for a test drive to make sure it's running right, then

bring it to your motel room later. While I'm doing that, you can drive my truck home and pack up your things. When I get there, we'll switch vehicles—and telephones."

"You don't have to go to all that trouble."

"Yes, I do."

She could tell by his stern expression that he was not going to budge, so she capitulated. "Okay. We'll do everything your way this time. When?"

"Here are my keys. You go now. And take Babe with you so Patty will have plenty of time to say goodbye to her. I'll bring your car by in a couple of hours."

Marie paused to lay her hand lightly on his forearm. "Be careful?"

"I will. You, too. Remember, that old truck drives just like a car unless you lock the hubs and put it in four-wheel drive, so don't let that scare you."

"Nothing scares me," Marie insisted. She turned away before she added softly, secretly, "Except how I'm starting to feel about you."

"The car's still parked over there, but it looks like the woman's leaving," Al said. "What're we gonna do?"

"I'll follow her," Frank said, reaching for the ignition key. "You and Earl get out, stay here, and keep your eyes on that car."

"What if it leaves, too? What then? Are we supposed to run alongside it?"

"I hadn't thought of that," Frank said, disgusted. "Okay. We'll all go. Or we'll all stay. Vote."

"I say we stick with the car or go get my truck," Al said. "We wouldn't have this problem if you hadn't insisted we all ride together."

Earl agreed. "Yeah. Look, we know that's her car. It has to be. So she'll be back. As long as we have that car, we've got her. What we can't do is tip our hand till we can catch her alone."

"Okay," Frank replied. "It's fine with me if you two want to sit here and stew all night long. I'm gonna go inside and get me a cold one."

With that, Al erupted into laughter. "Oh, yeah? Well, good luck, man. This is a dry county you've stuck us in. Can't get a beer around here if your life depends on it."

"You're kidding, right?"

Al's glee increased. "Nope. Get used to drinking soda pop. That's all they sell."

"Terrific. That's the last straw. If Roy wasn't already dead, I'd gladly kill him for this."

Seth realized that Marie was right about the personal information stored in his old phone. If the store had had two phones in stock the night before, his plans would have gone off without a hitch. Since they'd only had one, he figured he'd eventually give Marie the new instrument and keep the old one until he could replace it. His only real problem was the fact that he'd had no choice but to disclose the new number to Jonathan. He supposed he could have given him his old number, but that would have meant that Marie

might have taken the next call and have inadvertently led Jonathan to think Seth had betrayed him.

If he hadn't had the mind of a spy, keeping it all straight would have driven him crazy. As it was, he'd worked out the details of the phone exchange to his satisfaction and was merely biding his time until he could make the switch and let Jonathan know that the former number was no longer viable. Once Marie ditched that phone and bought a new one, there would be no more ties to her at all. In theory, it was a perfect plan.

If Seth hadn't had a niggling suspicion that it was too good to be true, he might not have broken down and phoned her at the motel.

She answered immediately, sounding a bit breathless. "Hello?"

"It's me, Seth," he said.

"I'm glad. You won't believe all the people who have called this number wanting to talk to you. I finally started taking notes like a secretary."

"Sorry about that."

"It's okay. How long before you bring my car?"

Seth chuckled. "Why? Are the children running you ragged?"

"Only the two-legged one. Babe is curled up on the rug and taking a nap. I think Patty wore her out."

"Okay. I have one stop to make before I deliver your car and we switch phones. Wait for me?"

"I have a choice?"

He had to laugh again. "Not really, unless you

plan to steal my truck. I wouldn't recommend it. It's pretty decrepit."

"So, are you telling me that the mechanic's truck needs repair?"

"Something like that." It was good to hear humor in her voice, to sense the lightness of her spirit for a change. Maybe leaving town was the right thing for her to do after all. She certainly seemed to think so.

Heading for her car, he backed it out of the garage and turned toward the street. The engine was running smoothly and without any sign of its previous fuel problem. That was good. Seth knew Marie would never believe him if he told her there was more tinkering needed. He'd been fortunate that she'd shown as much patience as she had.

He drove east on Highway 62 toward the cutoff to his home in Heart. It would take him only a second to transmit the other phone number to Jonathan and explain the change. If he hadn't been so befuddled by his thoughts about protecting Marie, he'd have used his head and found a way to handle the phone situation differently to begin with.

His grip tightened on the car's steering wheel as he glanced in the rearview mirror. There had been no sign of any suspicious white van in or around Serenity for several days, yet he was starting to get the impression that he was being followed. If they thought it was Marie in the car instead of him, perhaps he could turn the tables and find out who they were and why they were on his trail.

Seth started to lean toward the locked glove compartment to retrieve his .38, then realized it was in his truck. He was good in a hand-to-hand fight, but he was not foolhardy—he'd spotted at least two men in the car behind him, perhaps three; that ratio drastically cut his chances of easy, painless success.

Accelerating, Seth whipped along the dirt road, splashing muddy water from potholes as he bounced through them. He was glad he didn't have Babe with him, because his speed over the rough terrain would have tossed her around no matter how hard she'd tried to keep her balance.

He deliberately sailed on by the drive to his farmhouse. The other car, a low-slung, black Caddy or Buick, slewed wide on several corners and nearly skidded off the road into one of the drainage ditches that bordered the roadbed.

Seth smiled. Every few hundred yards the road curved and he lost sight of his pursuers. Then they'd drive back into view again. They were stubborn, that was for sure, but thankfully, whoever was driving was a novice off the pavement. That was good. If he did manage to outdistance them, they would probably not be able to catch him again.

In that case, the smartest thing he could do was head straight for the motel. Once he'd escorted Marie safely out of town, he'd return to his house, e-mail Jonathan and get the confusing cell phone situation straightened out.

Seth glanced in the rearview mirror in time to see the heavier car bounce out of a pothole, smack down crooked and career into a ditch. The driver tried to correct but the massive vehicle bottomed out, coming to a halt in a spray of brown water and rocks.

Three men clambered out. One of them started kicking the front tires as if the car were responsible for its own predicament.

Seth reached for his new cell phone and used it to call the sheriff to report the accident. That car wasn't going anywhere soon, and if law enforcement hurried, maybe its occupants wouldn't be bothersome much longer, either.

In the meantime, they were blocking the easiest, quickest way back to his house—and to his computer— so he'd have to contact Jonathan later. Right now, he had to get to Marie and see that she was on her way, ASAP, while the guys in the black car were still out of commission.

TWELVE

Marie had been packed and pacing for over an hour when she finally heard her car stop outside the motel room. Without remembering to be cautious, she jerked open the door.

Seth was climbing out of the car. He grinned. "Hi. Looks like you missed me."

"What took you so long?"

"I had to make a detour," he said, still smiling. "Sorry about all the mud."

She peered past him and began to frown. "No kidding. I thought I was only supposed to cover the license plates. What did you do, decide to plaster the whole car and make it brown?"

"No. I took a side trip on a dirt road. Since the rain, it was pretty messy. If I'd had a chance, I'd have hosed it off for you or at least run it through one of the creeks that cross the road out by my place."

"That's okay. As long as it's running well, I really don't care how bad it looks."

"It's humming like new," Seth said. "And I left the

other cell phone on the front seat, hooked to the mobile charger. It's turned off. Don't turn it on unless you absolutely have to, okay?"

"Why not?"

"Because I had to give the number to one other person and I'd rather you not use it except to make the call to activate the new one you promised to buy. Remember?"

"What's all this confusion about the phones, anyway? Isn't one as good as another?"

"In most cases, yes. Just trust me on this. Please?" He reached into his pocket, took out several bills and passed them to her. "Use this so you can save your money for other things. As soon as you've bought the new phone, I want you to destroy the one I got for you."

"That's ridiculous. It's a perfectly good phone, isn't it?"

She saw his expression harden, his eyes narrow. "Look, Marie, we don't have time to squabble. I think the men who've been following you are in town. That was how I got the mud on your car—outrunning them. So I suggest you and Patty hit the road. ASAP. Got that?"

There was no hint of the usual tenderness in Seth's gaze, nor did his demeanor leave room for argument. On the contrary, everything about his attitude had begun to make her edgy.

"All right. I'll go. We're packed. Help me put the bags in the car?"

Seth was one step ahead of her and had already started to gather her belongings while Babe ran in circles at his feet and Patty chased after the exuberant dog.

As Marie picked up her purse and followed the others out the door, she offered Seth his old cell phone. "Here. Don't forget this."

"Thanks." He loaded the suitcases into the trunk, slammed the lid and handed her the keys. "I'll follow you in my truck till I'm sure you're safely back on the highway."

"Why? I thought you said you'd lost the bad guys."

"I did. And if the sheriff gets to them before they manage to get their car out of the ditch, they won't be a problem. I'd just rather look after you for a few minutes longer."

"All right." She quickly transferred the booster seat from the truck to her car and saw that Patty was safely belted in.

Before getting behind the wheel, she turned to Seth. "I don't know how to thank you."

"Just stay safe," he said.

For a fleeting instant, Marie thought she glimpsed deeply felt sentiment in his eyes. When she paused to study him, to look beyond the external and search for hidden emotions, however, it seemed as if a shield had dropped. He was clearly, purposely shutting her out.

She took his hand. "Goodbye, Seth."

"Goodbye. Be careful out there."

"I will." Oh, how she hated to leave, to pull away from even that brief touch of his warm, steady hand. But she knew he was right. She had to go. And soon.

Blinking back unshed tears, she turned, slid behind the wheel and quickly slammed the car door.

As she started to drive away she saw Seth climbing into his truck with his wonderful dog already occupying the passenger seat. She was really going to miss that man. If only…

Setting her jaw, Marie reminded herself that she had no choice. She had to leave. She had to keep running. No matter how much her heart was breaking, she had to escape. For Patty's sake, if for no other reason.

Three unidentifiable trucks had arrived at three separate cell towers within minutes of one another. Their coordinator, seated close by in a plain, black sedan with darkly tinted windows, was in constant radio contact.

"Have you got it pegged yet, Mac?" he asked.

"Almost, Mr. Eccles. We were getting a good, strong signal from Pilot Knob before we lost it a few minutes ago. The hills were interfering to the south and west, and I need a clear, steady signal from all three points."

"Thousands of dollars worth of equipment and it won't handle a few little hills? What kind of tech are you?"

"A careful one. You want this triangulation to be accurate, don't you?"

"Yes, yes." Eccles started his car as he spoke into the microphone of the headset he was wearing. "I'm going to drive through town, see what I can see. Stay on this line so you can tell me the minute you get a signal again."

Pulling away from the curb, he cruised slowly

toward the Serenity square. All but one of its side streets had been cordoned off and groups of workers were obviously setting up some kind of a street bazaar.

"Stupid civilians," Eccles muttered to himself as he was forced to detour along side streets.

There was only one advantage that he could see— with such a big crowd milling around town and everything already disrupted, he and his men were far less likely to be noticed.

Marie drove northwest, heading out of town. She was doing her best to think clearly, but her mind kept arguing that there must be a better way to handle her predicament. Perhaps she ought to give the police another chance to help. After all, they were the good guys and she was on the same side of the law, wasn't she?

Her thoughts kept jumping back to Seth, as if he were the only important focus. She glanced at the cord running from her cigarette lighter to the new phone and something in her subconscious clicked.

"Oh, no!"

Patty's eyes widened. "What's the matter, Mama?"

"Seth's—Mr. Whitfield's messages. I forgot to give them to him."

"Can we go back?" the child asked, sounding eager to do just that.

"No, honey. We can't." Marie glanced in her rearview mirror, hoping to spot Seth's truck. The setting sun was so blinding she couldn't be sure if his green truck was part of the traffic behind her. Worse, it would

soon be so dark it would be impossible to tell one vehicle from another. If she stopped and got out here, hoping Seth would soon catch up to her, she might be unnecessarily exposing herself and Patty to danger. The only sensible thing to do was to phone him and hope he could convince Clarence to let him back into the motel room to retrieve the messages she had so carefully jotted down.

She pressed the red button on the cell phone and held it until the instrument gave its familiar jingle. The batteries were charged but the screen said it was still searching for a signal.

Once again, she contemplated pulling off the road and thought better of it. Surely she'd get a signal soon. After all, the phone had worked in the past. At least she thought it had. Truthfully, she hadn't had any previous experience with this particular instrument, but since it was supposed to be identical to the other one, there was no reason why it shouldn't function the same way.

Slowing, she skirted the square, noting that the carnival booths were already being set up. Too bad she and Patty had to leave town right away. As Seth had said, Patty would probably have enjoyed it. *And if Seth was with us, so would I,* she added, chagrined to be entertaining such consistently impossible notions.

"Get over it," she ordered herself in a near whisper.

Marie intended to make the turn from Main onto Church Street but found her way blocked by the reunion efforts and proceeded to Highway 9, instead. According to the Arkansas map she'd consulted, she

could get to West Plains via that road, too, and since she wasn't quite sure how to circumvent the Serenity square, she'd simply go to plan B.

Now that she was on the move again, she found her anxiety building as it had prior to their being stranded. Every shadow held menace, every car contained her enemies.

And every light that shone into the car made her feel exposed to more danger.

After all, she told herself, *it's only paranoia if no one is really after you.*

Marie glanced momentarily at the phone and noted that it was now indicating a strong cell signal. She hit the memory button, expecting Seth's number to appear. It didn't. Nothing did. Her eyes widened and she peered at the lighted screen. She'd put his new number into the old phone but apparently Seth hadn't thought to enter his work or home numbers into this one! What a doofus. And she was just as bad for not writing those numbers down when they'd popped up on the other phone.

Well, that couldn't be helped now. What was done was done. If he wanted his stupid messages, he'd just have to figure out where they were or pay the consequences of unreturned calls. Either way, it was none of her concern.

Laying aside the phone, she switched on her headlights, gripped the wheel with both hands, accelerated onto the winding, mountain road ahead and concentrated on putting as much distance between her and the past as she could.

* * *

"Got him," McCormick reported. "Did you hear me, Mr. Eccles? We've got him."

Eccles began to grin. "I hear you. Where is he?"

"Moving," the tech said. "According to our tracking devices, he's heading into the mountains on Highway 9. Chances are we'll lose him in about twenty miles. You'd better hurry."

"I'm on my way," Eccles replied, punching the coordinates he was given into his tracking system and setting a new course. "The rest of you hold your positions and keep tracking him until I tell you otherwise."

"Don't you want backup?"

"No," Eccles said forcefully. "I can handle this alone." *And I don't want witnesses,* he added to himself. *When I do catch up to Seth, I want to be able to deal with him my own way. Permanently.*

At the motel, Seth had paused only long enough to snap a short leash onto Babe's collar and fasten the other end to the seat belt anchor for safety. The dog didn't appreciate being tied in, but Seth knew how excited she could get when he was keyed up, and he figured it was smart to keep her under control. Right now, he was as nervous as he'd ever been in the past, even when directly involved in espionage, and his perceptive dog was bound to react to those feelings.

Above all, he wanted to keep Marie's car in sight, if only from a distance, for as long as possible. He hadn't cared this much about anyone or anything since

he'd lost Alice. Letting Marie and Patty drive away had hurt—all the way to his heart and soul. And that ache was still there. Maybe it always would be.

He'd give anything if he could call her, talk to her one last time, but he'd left the phone turned off and told her to keep it that way, so there was no way to reach her. That was just as well. The more they talked, the harder it would be for both of them to make a clean break.

Was all this as difficult for Marie as it was for him? he wondered. Perhaps. He didn't want her to agonize over it but it would be nice to think she'd had trouble leaving because she was beginning to care for him the same way he cared for her.

Passing the Serenity square and seeing the booths being assembled reminded him of how he'd hoped to show Patty and Marie the fun to be had in a small town. Part of him wanted to believe that he might one day get the chance, while a more perverse part insisted he was deluding himself.

Puzzled, he watched Marie continue on Highway 9 instead of detouring around the square. That made sense—in a convoluted way. As long as she kept to the main highway, it would take her to either Mammoth Spring or eventually West Plains. Once she got that far, she'd be able to find another phone and ditch the one he'd given her.

The more he pondered his decision in that regard, the more it concerned him. Yes, he trusted Jonathan, but Seth knew he'd feel much better after Marie had cut all her ties with him and his problems. He'd already

concluded that if he had to turn himself in to convince the authorities to help her, that was what he'd do. Eventually. Right now, however, he had to see her safely away from the pursuers in the car that had ended up in the ditch near his house. Once that was accomplished, he'd think about having Jonathan intercede so he could safely give himself up.

A sleek, dark sedan zipped past him on the narrow road, swerving to insert itself between his truck and Marie's car. Somebody was sure in a big hurry.

"Hang on, Babe," he said to the panting, excited dog. "You and I are about to play leapfrog with that idiot. Nobody's going to keep me from sticking like glue to Marie and your little friend."

Judging by the look the dog gave him, she understood *exactly* what he'd said.

Amused in spite of the tense situation, Seth glanced in his rearview mirror in preparation for passing the sedan. Another car was barreling up behind him.

His hands tightened on the wheel. In seconds he was glad he'd strapped the dog down, because the car clipped his bumper and nearly made him lose control.

Earl and Al were both screaming.

Frank just kept nudging the truck ahead. "Shut up, you two. Do you want to get him out of the way, or not?"

"Not if it kills *us*," Al shouted.

"Nobody's gonna get killed but him. I ain't about to let him make a fool of me twice in the same day."

"You sure that's the guy from the garage?"

"We saw them switch cars at the motel, didn't we? Who else could it be?"

"I don't know. And I'm starting to not care."

Frank muttered a curse and accelerated, ramming the truck again. It slewed but stayed on the road.

Suddenly, the truck pulled out and passed the sedan ahead of it, taking Frank and his cronies by surprise.

"Now what?" Earl asked in a squeal.

Frank turned the air inside his car blue with colorful epithets and pressed the gas pedal to the floor.

He hit the rear corner of the dark sedan with such force that it pushed it off the road onto the shoulder, where it slid to a stop.

Laughing maniacally, Frank sped ahead in pursuit of Seth's truck. When he glanced back, he thought he saw a man in a suit climbing out of the car and shaking his fist in the air. Stupid city slicker stood out like a sore thumb. Only a fool wore a fancy suit in these parts. Served him right that he got run off the road in the middle of nowhere.

THIRTEEN

Marie saw the erratic play of headlights behind her. She couldn't tell what was going on back there, but it didn't seem like a normal traffic pattern. If Seth was following, as he'd promised, he wasn't alone. As far as she could tell, there had been at least three vehicles behind her, hopefully including his. The only thing that worried her now was that she could see only two remaining sets of headlights.

Looking over at her dozing daughter, she prayed silently for wisdom and courage. What should she do? If one of the people behind her was Seth, why was he driving so strangely? And what had happened to the third driver? Where was he?

"I should have left in the daylight," she muttered. "I can't see a thing."

Suppose I turn off? I'll know then if I'm really being followed or just being paranoid, won't I?

She decided to start looking for a likely side road. If she saw one in time to make a safe turn, fine, if she didn't, she'd just keep heading north and figure that

was God's way of keeping her from making an error
in judgment. It seemed like a foolproof plan.

A brown-and-white forestry sign advertised an
upcoming opportunity. Marie slowed ever so slightly,
peering into the darkness to try to see the cutoff. There
it was! And it was paved. Perfect.

She entered the turn faster than she would have
normally but made it safely, with room to spare.

Her heart was pumping so fast and she was so
scared, her surging adrenaline made her feel as if she
were behind the wheel in a stockcar race.

Patty's head bobbed a little but she remained asleep.

Marie looked in the rearview mirror. Not only was
one car still following, but a second was, as well! If
one of those vehicles was Seth's, as she'd hoped, he
had company.

"God help us," she whispered. "I should never have
turned off. *Now* what do I do?"

Eccles had checked his car for damage and
maneuvered it back onto the highway in seconds. "Where
is he now?" he demanded over his headset microphone.

"Turned off, going east," came the answer. "Look for
a logging road or a forestry access. There are two
possibilities, fairly close together. It has to be one of
the two."

"I don't want guesses—I want facts," Eccles shouted.
"Which one?"

"Forestry. You should be coming up on it in about

a quarter of a mile. It'll be on your right." McCormick paused. "Hold on. Looks like the signal's slowing. He should be easy to overtake."

"Let's hope so, for your sake," Eccles said. "Have you got my location pegged, too?"

"Yes, sir. You should be approaching the correct road now. Can you see it?"

"Yes. I'm making the turn. Is it the same as he made?"

"Sure is," Mac said, sounding relieved. "You'll have him in a few hundred yards, at best."

"He's parked?"

"Not quite, but he's barely moving."

Eccles doused his lights and crept along. As soon as he spotted taillights ahead, he'd either pull off the road and continue on foot or keep driving with his headlights off.

Either way, he'd win. Seth would never see him coming.

Marie had had to cut her speed owing to the deteriorating condition of the narrowing, uneven forest track. "Some road," she muttered, furious with herself for leaving the well-maintained highway. "Seth is going to be really upset when he catches up to me."

That statement made her huff in self-deprecation. "He probably won't be nearly as mad as I am."

She was gripping the steering wheel so tightly that her hands hurt, her arms ached and the muscles in her shoulders were tied in knots.

"Okay, God, how about showing me a place to turn around or what to do next?" she said, hoping she would eventually cross another highway at the end of this back road, yet aware that the chances of that happening were slim.

What had the brown forestry sign on the highway said? Was it River Access or Campgrounds? She couldn't remember. Truth to tell, she hardly knew her own name at that moment, let alone was able to reason sensibly.

The overgrown passage narrowed even more. Branches hung low and encroached from the edges like the gnarled arms of menacing giants, forcing her to either stick to the center of the roadbed or scrape the sides of her car against the overhanging vegetation. The area reminded her a lot of the way the wilds took over in the wetlands of Louisiana.

She concentrated on forging ahead, trying to watch both the road and her pursuers. Out of the corner of her eye she glimpsed a yellow sign with squiggly lines across it, but she wasn't sure exactly what it had said.

In seconds, she knew. *Water.*

Slowing, she let her headlights illuminate the creek that was flowing across her path. The road clearly continued on the opposite side of the rapidly moving water, but was it safe to cross? It didn't look very deep. Unfortunately, there was no easy way to tell whether it had a solid, concrete bottom the way many such fords did or was simply a rough, bumpy track filled

with rocks that could damage her tires or the car's undercarriage.

She rolled down the car windows and stuck her head out her side, hoping to be able to shout back to Seth for advice if it truly was his truck coming up behind her.

Suddenly, she heard the crunch of metal against metal echoing in the distance. The headlights behind her faltered, then stopped. Another crash followed. It looked and sounded as if the second car had not only hit the first but also had backed up and done it again and was about to repeat the move a third time!

Out of options and frightened beyond sane thought, Marie put her car in low gear and started to inch across the creek.

The tires grabbed well, indicating a firm roadbed below. Praising God, she started to breathe easier.

Then, the motor coughed, sputtered and quit. She looked out the open window and gasped. Fast-flowing water was hitting and splashing against the bottom of the driver's door on the upstream side. Even if she could manage to get the opposite door open and try to escape, there was no way she could be certain she'd be able to keep her footing and carry Patty to safety. All she could do at this point was sit there.

Taking no action was against her most basic nature. But what could she do? What *should* she do? Considering how idiotic her choices had been so far that evening, she was afraid to make even the most elementary decision.

Sniffling, she gazed at the sleeping little angel beside her. "I'm so sorry, honey," she whispered. "Mommy is so, so sorry."

Seth had barely felt the first jar to his rear bumper. By the time his attacker had backed up and hit him a second time, he was braced for the blow and had his foot on the brake so that his truck barely moved.

"Come on. Hit me again," he urged, waiting and hoping the car would make hard contact at the center of his bumper where the heavy-duty trailer hitch stuck out. A few more hard hits like the last one and the menacing driver was sure to bust his own grill— if he hadn't already—leaving his radiator exposed and probably damaging it. Even if the attacker's car didn't quit immediately, that would mean it was on its last legs.

Seth was virtually positive that he'd recognized that car as the same one that had followed him earlier. As far as he was concerned, being stranded for the second time would serve those men right.

Braced, Seth took the third hit. The car behind him was starting to sputter as steam hissed from under its hood in a cloud of superheated mist.

Leaving his attackers behind to fend for themselves, Seth eased ahead far enough to see Marie's taillights in the distance. His breath caught. She was in the river! And she wasn't moving.

Forgetting everything and everyone else, Seth locked his truck's front hubs. Several hundred yards behind him, he could hear the men from the damaged car cursing and shouting at one another.

"One down, one to go," Seth muttered. He dropped his truck into four-wheel drive, put it in low gear and started for the river.

"Call 911," Marie told herself. She reached for the cell phone that lay on the seat beside her and punched in the number, praying that she'd still have a signal that far from town.

When the dispatcher answered, Marie was able to explain her position fairly well and was assured that help was on the way. Now, all she had to do was make sure Seth didn't get himself into the same situation she was in by chasing her into the water.

She leaned out the car window and waved as soon as she was certain she recognized his truck. Thankfulness and joy filled her. Seth was here. Everything was going to be fine, now.

"Stay there," she called when he clambered out and jogged toward the water's edge. "I've called for help. Rescue is on the way."

"Called? Called who? How?" He'd cupped his hands around his mouth and was shouting to be heard over the noise of the rushing water, but she could still tell from his tone and posture that he was upset.

"On the cell phone. You said it was for emergencies. I figured this qualified."

"Well, turn it off."

"Why? The 911 operator told me to leave it on and stay connected in case the volunteer fire department couldn't locate me."

"I said, turn it off," Seth ordered. He wheeled and stalked back to his truck.

"Well, thanks for your support," she muttered, not sure whether she was more disgusted with herself for getting stranded in the creek or with him for being so grumpy about it.

Watching him, her eyes widened. Not only was he not staying put on the bank, he had started to drive into the creek. Was he planning on pushing her out of the river? It sure looked like it.

She clamped her hands to the steering wheel and braced herself as his bumper made contact with the rear of her car. Her heart pounded. Seth might think he was pushing her straight, but she could tell she was starting to slide sideways!

Eccles had heard the repeated crashes ahead and had stopped where he couldn't be observed. Climbing out of the sedan, he softly eased the door closed, then pulled a pistol from his shoulder holster and started to walk down the center of the nearly deserted roadway.

Ahead, several men were standing next to their steaming car, arguing. He thought about accosting them, then changed his mind. He didn't have time to fool with civilians, let alone try to figure out why they were out there. Getting between him and his quarry was the last mistake they'd ever make.

Marie waved her left arm out the window so violently that she knew Seth couldn't mistake her panic. His truck sat a lot higher off the ground than

her small car did and was equipped with four-wheel drive, too, so maybe he hadn't noticed her plight. If he didn't wise up and back off soon, however, she was afraid her tires would lose what little traction they had left and she'd begin floating downstream.

At what seemed like the last second, Seth stopped pushing, repositioned his truck and pulled parallel to her on the upstream side, instead.

She frowned up at him. "What are you trying to do? Drown us both?"

"Not if I can help it." He boosted Babe out through the sliding rear window of the cab and into the pickup bed, where she usually rode, then reached toward Marie. "Take my hands."

"No way. I'm not leaving this car. It's got my whole life packed up in it."

"I should take Patty out first, anyway. Give her to me."

"That I will do," Marie said. She turned to unfasten the now wide awake little girl's safety belt and eased her out of the booster seat. "I want you to go to Seth, honey."

"Why?"

Marie understood the child's confusion but was short of patience just the same. "Because I said so." She pulled her across her lap and lifted her into Seth's waiting arms.

"Now you," he said flatly.

"I told you, I'm staying."

"Don't argue with me."

"Why should I leave my car?"

"Because I said so."

She huffed. "That lame answer may work with five-year-olds, but it won't work with me."

The look Seth gave her in reply held so much repressed anger that it gave her the shivers.

Eccles stepped behind a tree, took aim, and dropped the biggest of the three men easily. The other two stared at each other in confused disbelief.

"Just stand there in the lights from your car, boys, and this'll be over in no time," Eccles whispered. He smiled, aimed, and squeezed off two more shots before activating and speaking into his headset.

"All right. I'm close. Where's Seth from here?"

"Should be about twenty, thirty yards up the road," came the answer.

"I'm going to shut down this link so I can concentrate on him," Eccles said. "Don't worry if you don't hear from me for a while."

"I still think you should have backup," McCormick told him. "It's standard procedure."

"No. I know the man we're after. If I'm going to have a chance to bring him in, it has to be one-on-one."

Leaving no room for argument, he whipped off the earpiece and stuffed it into his pocket. He couldn't chance interference. Seth had always been cold and deadly in a firefight. Any unnecessary distraction could prove lethal when going against a man like that.

Sure of his stealth because of the darkness, Eccles walked on, wasting no more than a cursory glance on the men he'd just shot.

He spotted the red of taillights before he rounded the final bend and saw the watery crossing. There were two vehicles in the river and no way to tell which was Seth's. Therefore, the best way to find out was to fire at one of them and see which driver reacted in the most professional way.

Steadying his pistol in both hands, Eccles assumed a professional stance and prepared to fire.

A sharp crack echoed across the water. Marie wasn't sure that the high-pitched, zinging sound signaled danger, but one look at the way Seth was shielding Patty told her he certainly didn't believe it was an innocent noise.

She stared, her jaw agape. "What was that?"

"Another gunshot," he said.

"What do you mean *another* one?" She knew her voice reflected terror but she couldn't help it.

"There were others a few minutes ago," Seth said. "That last one was closer. Now will you come with me?"

"I *can't* leave my car. What if the firemen find it empty and think I've drowned or something?"

"Tell the dispatcher what you're doing and then let's get out of here. Pronto."

Under the circumstances, Marie could see the wisdom of his suggestion, even if he was coming across as so bossy and causing her to hate giving in.

She reluctantly did as he'd ordered, leaving the phone connection open, as the official on the other end of the line had instructed. She didn't know why Seth

had been so adamant about turning off the cell phone, but there was no more time to discuss it. Not if someone really was carelessly shooting nearby. Besides, she'd imagined feeling the car slip again, and she was growing more and more uneasy every moment that she sat there.

She unfastened her seatbelt, passed him her purse, then got onto her knees and began to wriggle her upper torso out the window. Directly below, she could see the roiling, churning blackness of the icy water, hear its roar, feel its spray as it hit the car door and splashed up at her. If anyone but Seth had been planning to catch her, she knew she'd have been so scared she wouldn't have been able to budge, let alone crawl out the window.

Extending her arms, she reached for him. Just as their fingertips touched, the car slipped. Slewed. Moved her just out of his reach.

Marie screamed. Seth lunged till his upper body was all the way out of the truck window.

"Save Patty!" she screeched.

"No. Jump."

"I can't."

"Yes, you can. Open the door if you have to."

Sliding back onto the seat, Marie put her shoulder against the door and tried to move it. "It won't budge," she shouted. "The current's too strong."

"Then crawl out the window. You can't stay there."

She pushed both feet on the brake pedal, hoping to stop her slide. It was no use. Every few seconds her car

stuttered and shifted. And every time it moved, it was farther from Seth and from the safety of the riverbank.

Once again, Marie got on her knees and stretched out the window toward Seth. Her hands were slippery from the splashing water and her whole body was trembling uncontrollably.

He lunged, every muscle taut.

Marie tried to reach him. *Almost there.* She was almost there. If only she hadn't hesitated, hadn't argued with him. "Dear God, help me," she cried.

One more monumental effort and Seth's hands clamped tightly around her slim wrists. Her fingers curled to grasp his, as well.

The car shuddered and started to swing around as it was pulled downstream.

Marie stifled a scream. "It's moving more!"

"Your weight must have been all that was keeping it there," Seth shouted. "Kick free before it takes you with it."

"What about…" She was going to argue against leaving all her possessions, when the decision was stripped from her. The car's traction broke loose. If Seth hadn't been holding her wrists so tightly she knew she would have been swept away, possibly to her death.

The side mirror jabbed her in the ribs, the window sill scraped her legs, but Seth's grip held.

As Marie was whisked out of the car she landed in the icy, rushing water, up to her knees. She recoiled, then tried to clamber into the truck as Seth lifted and pulled her.

She was almost in, almost safe, when another shot sounded. Something ricocheted off the metal of her nearby car and smashed through its rear window, shattering it into a million pieces.

Marie had no opportunity to react. Seth jerked her the rest of the way into his truck so fast that she didn't have time to breathe, let alone scream.

"Get on the floor and keep your heads down," he ordered, shoving her and the child in that direction as he slid behind the wheel.

Her voice was tremulous. "What's going on?"

"Somebody's shooting at us." Dropping the truck into low gear he added, "I hope it's Roy's old buddies."

"You do? Why?"

"Because the other alternative is worse," Seth said. "Much worse."

Eccles saw a flurry of activity as the driver of the truck pulled someone into the cab and started to speed away.

That was Seth, he concluded. It had to be him. His reaction had been too perfect, too practiced.

He fired once more at the fleeing truck, then turned and ran back to his car. He didn't know how he was going to squeeze past the other abandoned car or get across that fast-moving water, but no matter what he had to do, he wasn't going to let Seth escape. Not now. Not when he was so close to silencing him for good.

FOURTEEN

Marie was frightened out of her wits and so flustered she could hardly think, hardly function. Keeping her daughter on the floor between her feet, she slipped back onto the truck seat beside Seth as he drove.

"I told you to stay down," he yelled.

"This is as far down as I plan to get," she countered. "Patty's safe. I want to see what's going on."

"And give me more to worry about."

"That's not fair. I've told you all about Roy's partners in crime, but I'm getting the feeling there's a whole lot more to this mess than that."

All Seth said was "Yeah."

"So? Give. What else is going on?"

The force of his erratic driving was tossing her from side to side on the seat, and she was having to brace herself against the dash and side door to keep from sliding.

"Put your seat belt on," Seth ordered.

"*Then* will you explain?"

He made a sound of disgust that reminded her of a

growl. "All right. You may need to know more in order to defend yourself—and Patty—properly. Get the belt on and I'll tell you everything."

Marie managed to do as he'd said by bracing her feet on the floor on either side of the child. She hated to make Patty stay down there, but if Seth was convinced that that was the safest place, she'd do as he'd said.

She looked over at his profile as he drove. Her heart leaped. In the moonlight, his features were chiseled and his smoky blue eyes had darkened to slate, with sparks of obsidian. He was magnificent, in spite of his dour mood. Every muscle in his body seemed totally in tune. Every instinct told her that she was in good hands as long as she was with Seth.

That intense emotional reaction took her by surprise. She felt safe! Wanted! Secure in spite of everything that was going on. That was new for her. *Very* new. Even as a child she had never felt that protected, that sheltered. With Roy she had had to fantasize about being cared for and loved, but with Seth it was real. Though he had never expressed his feelings, they were evident. He was her guardian, her stalwart defender, no matter what happened.

Someday, hopefully very soon, she would tell him how much she cared for him and see if those feelings were reciprocated. There was no way she could imagine that they were not.

"Okay. The belt is fastened," Marie said. Her voice was shaky from the bouncing of the truck but strong, nevertheless. "Tell me what's going on."

"It's complicated," Seth said. "I told you my wife died."

"Yes."

"What I didn't say was that I was framed so the authorities would think I'd killed her."

Marie could hardly breathe, barely speak. "What?"

He was nodding, keeping his eyes on the winding road instead of looking at her. "I used to have a career working for a private firm that was heavily involved in corporate espionage." He paused long enough to give her a brief glance. "Basically, I was a spy."

Her jaw dropped. *A spy? Seth?* That was impossible. He was just a garage mechanic, a regular guy who worked on cars and lived in a quaint little Ozark town. How could he possibly have been a spy?

Continuing, he said, "There's more. I was good at my job. Before Alice was killed, I had uncovered an insider plot to steal and sell military-type secrets to unstable governments around the world. I was about to expose everything. That was why the men responsible had to get rid of me. I thought they had also killed Jonathan Biggs, a close friend of mine, but he's still alive. That was who I had given that new cell phone number to—and why I didn't want you to turn it on or use it unless you had to."

"You didn't trust me to talk to him?" Her voice was barely audible above the roar of the truck's engine.

"No, no. I didn't want Jonathan to think I had blown his cover. If he had called and you had answered, he might have broken all contact with me."

"Nobody called. Honest." She saw Seth's jaw clench.

"There's more," he told her. "Once that number was given out, even though I trusted my old friend, it made it possible for that particular phone to be traced whenever it was left on."

Marie was crushed. And angry. "Why didn't you *say* so? Why didn't you trust me enough to explain your reasons? Did you think I was like Roy?"

"Of course not."

"Then why not at least tell me a believable lie? Or is that what you're doing, now?"

"You wanted the whole truth and now you have it. Don't complain if you don't like what you hear."

"Complain? That's hardly what I'd call it, Mr. Whitfield. You led me on, made me trust you. Made me think you were…"

"Made you think I was what, Marie? Looking out for you? I am. That's why I had to finally tell you everything. There were two cars following you besides mine. One was Roy's buddies. I don't know who was in the other one, but I have a sneaking suspicion it was after you, because you'd turned on that new cell phone after I'd specifically warned you not to."

"Hold it. Are you saying we're running away from people who are after *you*?"

"It's highly likely. Although I can't understand how they managed to get a link to your position so quickly. You only turned on the phone to call for help, right?"

She laced her fingers together in her lap as if preparing to pray before she admitted, "No. I turned it on

back in Serenity when I was going to call you and tell you where to find your phone messages."

His head whipped around. He was scowling at her. "Then you turned it back off, didn't you?"

Marie shook her head and avoided his gaze. "I'm not positive. I think I left it on after that. It was still working when I picked it up to dial 911."

She had expected Seth to curse the way Roy always had when she'd disappointed him. Instead, he merely looked away as if dismissing her. That hurt more than it would have if he had called her every bad name in the book.

By the time Eccles reached the crossing, the blue car had slid off the road and was partially submerged in the racing water. All he had to do was watch it float downstream, bobbing like an ungainly boat.

His sedan was not only larger than the other car, but it was also armored enough to make it a lot heavier and therefore more stable. Still, he was relieved to safely reach the road on the far side of the torrent. He knew he was several minutes behind the truck he'd seen but figured he'd catch up to it eventually. According to his GPS unit, this road ended at a campground. There was only one way in and out. No one was going to get past him. Not alive, anyway.

Seth noted that Marie was shivering, which was not a surprise, since she'd been half submerged in that icy

creek. "There's a blanket behind the seat," he said. "Pull it out and wrap it around your legs."

"I'm fine."

He gritted his teeth. The woman was unreasonably stubborn, and she was obviously mad at him. Not that he blamed her. He'd never intended to get her involved in his problems; he'd simply been trying to help her. If she hadn't been so hardheaded...

"Then get it for Patty," Seth said gruffly. "We're going to run out of road soon, and we'll need to grab as much survival gear from the truck as possible."

"Wait a minute. What do you mean we'll run out of road?"

"Hey, don't complain to me. You're the one who turned off the highway and headed for the boonies. If you'd stayed your course instead of trying to be cute, you'd have been fine."

"If I'd known what I was really up against, I wouldn't have extra bad guys chasing me, either," Marie countered. "All you'd have had to do was tell me how important it was to not use that phone."

"I did tell you."

"No, you didn't. You gave me some silly excuse about switching phones that sounded like macho drivel. I'm not stupid, Seth. I'd have understood."

"No, you wouldn't," he said slowly, feigning calm. "You'd have started asking yourself if I was really innocent the way I claimed, and you'd have pushed me away so I couldn't continue to help you."

"I'm not pushing you away now, am I?"

He snorted derisively. "I don't see that you have a lot of choices for the present. Just know this, Marie. I am innocent of any crimes. Period. I did not kill my wife or steal and sell defense secrets. I was framed by people I had once trusted and had to change my identity in order to survive. The Feds are after me, and so are the men who accused me in the first place."

"Why didn't you go to the local police? Everyone in town seemed to like you."

"Actually, I was eventually going to tell Logan Malloy and see if he could help me get justice," Seth said. "He used to be a private detective."

"Your *preacher?*"

Her astonishment made Seth chuckle in spite of the dire situation. "Yes, Marie, my preacher. Logan came to Serenity to track down a missing baby and discovered she had grown up without knowing she'd been abducted. Actually, it was Becky. He ended up marrying her."

"Becky?" She stared at him. "So that's what she meant when she told me she'd had a rough life. Wow. I'd never have guessed. She seems so settled, so happy."

"Which just proves that anyone has a chance. Even us," Seth said. He held his breath, waiting for Marie to either affirm or deny his suggestion that they might one day become a couple.

When she didn't answer, he knew what her decision had been. She no longer trusted him. And he didn't blame her. Not really. He had hoped that she was different. That she would take him at face value even after finding out he'd had such a chaotic history.

I've been kidding myself, Seth thought, chagrined. *I can't expect a normal family life in the future, any more than I was able to have one in the past.*

His hands fisted on the wheel and his teeth clenched.

There was no way he was going to ask any woman, especially Marie, to put up with his former lifestyle. Nor was there much of a chance he wouldn't wind up incarcerated when this was all over, maybe for years. Given those two alternatives, it would be blatantly wrong to even tell her how he felt.

Glancing in the rearview mirror, he spotted the flash of headlights through the trees. Someone was still trailing them. It wasn't over yet.

"This one's alive," the sheriff shouted. "Get the medics over here."

Al groaned and stared up at the uniformed officer. His gaze locked on the man's badge. "If this is heaven, I hope you're not St. Peter."

"It's not heaven, son. But your friends may have gone there. What happened?"

"I don't know. We were just mindin' our own business and…"

"Don't give me that. I know better. We had several local reports of a car chase and shots being fired. Let's have the truth."

Al shook his head and groaned again.

"Look. If you want medical attention in a hurry, I suggest you tell me," the sheriff said. "Me and the boys can wait as long as we have to."

"Hey, I'm dyin' here. You gotta help me."

"We will. Just as soon as we know what we're up against. I don't want any more innocent civilians getting shot."

"That's us," Al said, grimacing. "We were just good ol' boys out having some fun. Then we had car trouble and this guy in a big black car comes along and shoots us for no reason."

"What about the other two vehicles—a car and a truck."

"You know about those?"

The sheriff nodded sagely, patiently. "We know. One was reported to be stalled in the river crossing, but it's not there now. Where'd they go."

"I don't know," Al insisted. "I was afraid to stick my head up and get it shot off." He raised a trembling hand to point. "They drove off that way. That's all I know. I swear."

"Okay." Straightening, the sheriff spoke into his radio, listened to the reply, then gestured to the paramedics. "You see to his injuries and I'll have my men take care of the other two. Tell the hospital to give this one whatever treatment he needs but keep a close eye on him afterward. I just found out that he and his friends are wanted men in Louisiana."

"What else do you want us to do?" one of the volunteer firemen asked.

"Nothing, unless that car is still stuck down in the creek somewhere. If it's gone, I'll drive a little farther to see what I can see. The rest of you fall back

and reorganize. We can take up the search again at daybreak."

"Isn't that an awful long time?" the firefighter asked.

"Not if I leave a unit to guard this road. By morning, if we haven't found hide nor hair of the rest of the folks messin' around out here, I'll order an official search. If the others involved are as dirty as these three, it'll do 'em good to spend the night with the skeeters, ticks and chiggers."

Marie was shaking so badly she couldn't even pretend to hold still. It wasn't merely because she was soaked and chilly. It was also shock. She knew the signs from the first aid training she'd been given when she'd worked at the preschool in Baton Rouge.

Finally, she gave in and tugged the blanket out from behind the seat, unfolded it, and used it to wrap around herself and Patty, trying to tuck it in to isolate the child from the clamminess of her damp jeans and sneakers.

She was secretly glad that Seth hadn't said another word to her since his disclosure about his criminal record. That revelation had floored her, had left her so befuddled she didn't know what to think, let alone what to say to him.

How foolish she'd been. How gullible. She'd run from one liar and landed in the arms of another. She sure could pick the wrong men, couldn't she? Compared with Seth, Roy had been a Boy Scout.

Yet, the signs had all been there if she'd chosen to

heed them, Marie concluded. She'd sensed that Seth was different right from their first meeting. She'd even asked him about it in a roundabout way. Of course he hadn't leveled with her. Now that she was aware of the truth—at least she thought she was—she could clearly see why he had not told her. They had been strangers then.

And now? Now, they had gone far beyond mere acquaintance, though she didn't like to admit it, even to herself. For him to have disclosed everything the way he just had meant that he trusted her. With his life and with his future. Could she do less for him? If she hadn't had Patty's well-being to consider, she might have been more willing to speak up and discuss it.

Through chattering teeth, Marie managed to ask, "How much farther can we go on this road?"

"A mile. Maybe two. Then we'll have to make a run for it on foot."

"I was afraid you were going to say that."

"Are you up to it?"

She shook her head in the negative, but said, "Sure. I can do anything when somebody is shooting at me."

"If I could be sure how many men were after us and that they'd follow me, instead of you and Patty, I'd suggest we split up. Unfortunately, there's no way to predict that."

"I'm not much of a country girl, either," Marie said. "I not only wouldn't know how to survive out here by myself, I'd probably wind up getting lost."

"And Patty may need to be carried," Seth added. "She's not going to be able to run as far or as fast as the rest of us."

"What about Babe?"

"She'll be fine. I take her on hikes in the woods all the time. If she gets lost, she just heads cross-country and goes home. We're not as far from my place as it seems by road."

"I wish…" Marie bit her lower lip. "Never mind."

Ahead she caught a glimpse of a square block building and a sign indicating that they had arrived at the isolated campground.

"Here we are," Seth said, turning the truck in an arc so his headlights would illuminate the entire area. "Thankfully, there's no one else camped up here, so we won't have to worry about collateral damage."

That was the kind of reference that had tipped her off to his unusual background in the first place. If she were honest with herself, she'd have to admit that she'd had plenty of clues to Seth's past. If only she'd listened to those niggling warnings.

Seth pulled into the farthest campsite, then doused his headlights and killed the engine. "We hike from here on," he said.

Marie wondered if her wobbly, freezing legs and feet would support her when she stepped out.

Seth had circled the truck, had called to Babe and was already opening Marie's door. She handed Patty to him before gathering up the unfolded blanket.

"Can you make it by yourself?" Seth asked.

"Yes. I'm coming. Just take her and go."

"Not on your life," he countered. "We all stick together."

In the distance, Marie could hear the steady grind of an engine, but she couldn't tell how far away, or how close, it might be. Wide-eyed, she stared at Seth, barely able to read his expression in the moonlight.

"That's him. He's getting closer," Seth said, confirming her fears. "Come on. And bring the blanket."

Balling it up in her arms, Marie staggered after him. Her feet tingled with needles of pain and her body shook more with every step, yet she kept pace with him.

"I—I wish we had a gun," she said, slightly breathless already.

To her shock, Seth answered, "We do. A rifle with a scope would be better than my .38, but at least we're not totally defenseless."

Of course he'd be armed, Marie reasoned. After all, he wasn't just a regular guy from a little Ozark town. He was a former spy.

That notion made her tremble anew. *A spy.* Here she was, running for her life through a trackless wilderness, and her guide was the kind of dangerous man most people only saw in movies or read about in thrillers.

At that moment, Marie realized she was less concerned about whoever was after them than she was for Seth's ultimate safety. He had been leading a double

life, staying out of harm's way, until he had chosen to risk his anonymity to help her. If he hadn't given her that phone, and if she hadn't disobeyed his orders and used it, perhaps his enemies wouldn't be on their trail at all. If anything bad happened to him, she'd never be able to forgive herself.

And if anything bad happened to Patty, she added, fists clenching, she would never forgive Seth.

FIFTEEN

Seth wasn't familiar with the area around the camp-ground, so he simply headed away from it and plunged into the densest portion of the forest. Behind him, he could hear Marie's rapid breathing, sense her fear.

Holding Patty close, bending down, and protecting her head with his hand, he forged through a thicket of hickory. The trees weren't large but they were flexible and resilient and thus more likely to spring back into place and mask their passage.

"You couldn't have found a worse trail, could you?" Marie complained in a hoarse whisper.

"If it's hard for us, it'll be just as hard for whoever is following," Seth replied. He halted to give her a chance to catch up. "Stay real close and let me break trail for you."

"Do you want me to carry Patty for a while?"

He snorted derisively. "You're kidding, right? You don't look like you can hardly hold yourself up, let alone carry a five-year-old."

"I can do anything if I have to," Marie countered, her temper obviously getting the better of her.

Seth eyed the wool blanket she still carried. The dark color was barely visible in the moonlight. "Tell you what," he said. "Bring that and we'll find a place for you to hide under it. If I cover you both with leaves, then make noise as I keep running, our enemy will pass you right by."

"No. I won't leave you."

"Don't be an idiot."

She huffed. "Hey, no name calling, mister. I know it's my fault you're in this awful mess, but it wouldn't be if I'd had all the facts in the first place. Besides, I already told you how inept I am in the woods. Even if you drew the bad guys away from us, chances are I'd get so lost we'd either starve or freeze to death out here before we were found."

"You probably wouldn't freeze this time of year," Seth said flatly. "But I do see your point. All right. We'll keep going for a little while longer."

He stiffened, pointing back the way they'd come. "Look. He's got a flashlight. That's to our advantage because I only see one beam. Since he's not following standard Corp. Inc. procedures, he's probably from the same bunch who wanted me out of the way in the first place."

"Is that good?"

"Yes. Because I think I know who it is," Seth answered. "And if it is Eccles, I won't hesitate to shoot him the second I get the chance."

"Kill him?" Marie's voice was barely audible.

"No." Seth shook his head. "I want him alive. He doesn't know it yet, but he's going to clear me with the law before all this is over. And when he does, I'm going to get back to Serenity as fast as I can and try to put all this behind me."

"Really? The way you talked earlier, it sounded as if you wanted to go back to spying."

"I used to think I did," Seth said. "But lately I've been toying with the idea of being just a regular guy doing a regular job."

"Would you... Would you consider taking Patty back to Serenity and looking after her for me. I don't have anyone else."

"Why would you need someone to do that?"

"Because of Roy. If the police believe I was involved in his crimes, the way you first thought I was, I'll probably go to jail."

"No, you won't. God willing, maybe neither of us will. Not if I have anything to say about it," Seth insisted, starting to believe his own words for the first time. He glanced past her at the erratic jerks of the distant flashlight. "But we have more pressing concerns right now. He's the last domino in the chain. Knocking him down has to come first. Later, we'll talk about the future."

"We will?"

"Yes. We will."

"Are you giving me orders again?"

This time, he could tell she wasn't speaking from

anger. "Sure am. Now get moving, woman. I want to be on high ground and set up a good defensive position before Eccles, or anyone else, catches up to us."

"We're going to let him *catch* us?"

"Yes." Seth felt the .38 in his belt to assure himself he was still armed. He didn't want to tell Marie that he had only the ammunition that was already loaded in the revolver. He wasn't going to have many shots with which to end this pursuit in their favor. He had to make sure he didn't waste them.

Seth's jaw clenched. He knew what a man like Eccles was capable of. He'd seen it firsthand when he'd discovered Alice's body. Only this time, no one was going to get past him and hurt those he loved.

His pulse hammered. He did love these two innocents, didn't he? Those feelings had sneaked up on his heart more subtly than any purveyor of espionage ever had. He'd been blindsided, pure and simple.

It quickly occurred to him that since Marie had asked him to look after Patty for her, she must have at least a mild affection for him, as well. That was enough to build on.

Seth gritted his teeth. If they survived.

The rocky outcropping rose out of the forest floor like a stack of colossal black pancakes, dropped there at an angle by a careless giant.

"There," Seth hissed, pointing to the rocks. "Get down behind the thickest place."

Marie complied, gladly. Her legs ached and she had

been trembling so badly that every muscle in her body ached. As Seth placed Patty beside her, she covered them both, head to foot, with the blanket and hunkered down. There was no more strength or fight left in her, not even enough to question his orders the way she was usually so prone to do.

"Mama?"

"Shush," Marie warned. "We have to be real quiet."

"Where's Babe?" the child asked. "I want Babe."

"We might not be able to keep her from barking so it's better if she's outside, helping Seth," Marie replied. "Now do as he said. Hold very still."

The little girl was sniffling but didn't argue. For that, Marie was doubly thankful. She wouldn't have known how to explain their situation if she'd had to, nor was she sure just exactly what that situation now was.

What would she do if something bad happened to Seth? That unacceptable question sat in her heart like a glacier, cold and oh, so heavy. Pulling her daughter closer, she began to silently pray with all the faith she could muster.

Outside the makeshift tent she could hear the rustling of fallen leaves from the previous winter. She hadn't noticed that much noise as the three of them had fled through the woods, so she could only imagine that Seth was purposely creating a diversion.

"Bless him, Father," she prayed in a whisper. "And keep him safe. Keep us all safe. Please, Lord."

Beside her, she heard a childish "Amen." Sweet

Patty was praying, too, and, in Marie's opinion the child was probably far more deserving of an answer than were any of the adults. There was something special about the pure faith of a child, wasn't there? Children weren't so liable to overthink things. They simply trusted.

I want to trust like that, too, Marie thought, directing her mind toward the heavenly Father she had so recently come to know. *I want to. I just don't know how.*

As suddenly as that thought came to her, it was followed by an assurance that she had all the faith she needed. Learning to employ and understand it might be another matter, but the faith was there. The Bible promised that she'd never have to face life's trials alone again, no matter how difficult her situation might seem. She did believe that. The hard part was wanting to know ahead of time how everything was going to end.

And to help, she added, chagrined. It was part of her nature to want to work things out herself, to fix other people's problems.

Her eyes popped open, seeing nothing in the darkness. Was that what God had been trying to teach her all along? Had she gotten into this mess because she'd been trying to manipulate her life, and the lives of others, and had failed to trust the Lord? The notion was chilling.

Could that also be why she'd been so attracted to Seth? she asked herself with a shiver of awareness. Her arms tightened around her little girl as she whispered, "Dear Lord, forgive me. And keep us safe. Please."

She listened to the stillness, hearing nothing. Her vivid imagination kept picturing Seth doing battle while she fervently prayed for his safety. Was the sense that he'd needed someone's help what had drawn her to him in the first place?

I didn't know he had problems when we met, Marie countered. *That can't be it.*

But I did sense his uneasiness and decide he had to be hiding something.

Setting her jaw, she made a face, seeing herself as gullible and foolish. She had done it again. She'd been subconsciously attracted to the same kind of man that Roy had been, and she'd fallen for her own form of personal subterfuge. It wasn't merely that Seth had kept things from her; it was more. She had refused to listen to her inner warnings, and here she was, in worse trouble than ever before.

The notion that she didn't know how to pick good men was more than true; it had just been proven for the second time. Was she never going to learn?

"If—when—we get out of this, I'll know better, God," she vowed in a barely audible whisper. "I'm better off staying single than letting myself get tangled up with this kind of guy, again. I may be a slow learner but I finally do understand."

Marie knew she should thank the Lord for that new enlightenment, but the idea of bidding Seth a final goodbye made her too sad to be truly grateful. If this was what the answer to her prayer was to be, she almost wished she hadn't prayed it.

* * *

Seth had taken up a defensive position twenty yards to the west of where Marie and Patty were hidden. He tried to control his breathing as he waited for Eccles, or whoever it was, to draw closer.

The beam of the flashlight seemed to be losing strength as the batteries ran down. "Come on," Seth murmured. "Just a little farther."

The light paused. A man called out, "That you, buddy?"

Seth remained mute.

"Come on. You can ID me, can't you? It's Jonathan."

For an instant, Seth hoped his pursuer was telling the truth. Then, he realized he had recognized the voice all right, and it wasn't that of his old friend.

Out of the corner of his eye, Seth thought he saw the blanket move. He had not intended to answer and thereby reveal his position, but if there was a chance that Marie was planning to show herself because she'd been fooled, he'd have to intervene.

"It's not Jonathan," Seth shouted. "It's Eccles."

All movement ceased. Someone laughed hoarsely.

"Good for you, Seth, or whatever you're calling yourself these days. Long time, no see. We've missed you. Where've you been hiding?"

Still, Seth remained silent. He'd thought about moving to another vantage point, but the woods was too quiet for that. One snap of a twig or rustle of leaves and Eccles would have his position. If his voice had

not echoed so well across the hilly terrain, it would already be too late.

The light began to move again. Seth stiffened, leaned his arm against the trunk of a sturdy oak and took aim. Almost close enough for a shot. Just a few more yards.

The light stopped. Seth's eyes narrowed. Tensing, he peered into the dimness of the forest.

Although little moonlight got through the leafy canopy, he was still able to see movement, manlike shadows, or so he thought. In a situation like this it was common for a person's imagination to take over and lead him to see things that weren't really there. During training it didn't matter. In this case, he couldn't afford to make a mistake.

Assessing the light beam, Seth soon came to the conclusion that it was too still, too stationary. Eccles was no fool. Chances were good that he had propped it in the crook of a tree branch and left it there as a diversion.

That meant he could be anywhere, creeping closer. And probably was.

Time passed at a crawl. Marie wanted to look out so badly that she could hardly contain herself. If it hadn't been for Patty, she'd have peeked as soon as someone had yelled. And if Seth hadn't broadcast that their adversary was the same man he'd predicted it would be, she might have made a serious tactical error.

She was about to change her mind for the ump-teenth time and peek anyway, when she heard noise of a scuffle begin. Instead of being far away, it sounded as if it was taking place right there, next to their hiding place.

Pushing Patty behind her, closer to the rocky over-hang, she shushed her. "Get back. Stay put, no matter what. Understand?"

"Uh-huh."

The frightened child was tugging on the back of her mother's jacket and whimpering.

Outside, men were clearly coming to blows. Marie could tell because the sounds of the punches con-necting and the resulting grunts and groans were all too audible.

Suddenly, something crashed into the other side of the blanket and knocked her backward. The men were right there! Close enough to touch. What should she do? Seth had ordered her to stay hidden, yet this changed everything. Or did it?

Of course it did. What kind of heroine stayed in hiding and let her hero take a beating when she might be able to prevent it? Seth might not be the kind of man she should spend the rest of her life with, but he was still her champion. She had to do something.

Slipping out from under the pitch dark of the blanket with a last, firm warning for Patty, she blinked to try to hurry her eyes' adjustment to the change in the amount of light.

She didn't have to see well to be awed by the intensity of the men's struggle. They were lunging, swinging, staggering around so rapidly and covering so much ground, it was impossible to tell who was who.

Marie edged cautiously out of the way, hoping she'd discover some way to help Seth. There must be something she could do, some way to tip the balance in his favor.

One of the men rose up and hit the other on the head with something small, probably a rock or the butt of a gun. The sharp, cracking noise brought bile to her throat. As she watched in horror, the victim slumped back onto the forest floor and didn't move.

Marie froze. She wasn't sure whether anyone had noticed her and didn't want to call attention to Patty's hiding place by making noise.

Squinting, she tried to see better. Both men were relatively the same size. They had both been dressed in dark clothing and were now equally camouflaged with mud and leaves from their battle.

One was standing over the other with his back to Marie. She saw the glint of a gun in the moonlight. That could be Seth, she reasoned. Or he could be the man lying prostrate on the ground. Surely, if Seth were the victor, he wouldn't shoot a man in cold blood, no matter how much he hated him.

The click of the armed man cocking his pistol sent shivers up Marie's spine. That wasn't Seth. It couldn't be. Not if he was half the man she thought he was.

A broken branch lay among the forest litter at her feet. Bending slowly, she hefted it as well as a small rock.

The fighter who had remained standing laughed maniacally and raised his pistol, affirming her conclusion.

Marie threw the rock as far as she could to one side, then grabbed the broken branch with both hands.

The man whirled and fired at the crash of the rock.

Marie lunged and brought the branch down on his head as hard as she could.

The blow wasn't enough to knock him out. Stunned, he faltered and started to swing his pistol toward her.

She reared back like a baseball player, swung with all her might and batted him out of the ballpark.

Seth regained consciousness just in time to see Marie's bravery. He could hardly fault her for leaving her hiding place when she had clearly saved his life.

He raised on one elbow. "Nice aim, lady. Remind me to recruit you for the Serenity All-Star team."

"Oh, Seth!" She fell to her knees at his side. "I was afraid he'd killed you."

"He would have, if you hadn't conked him the way you did. Where did you learn to hit like that?"

"Girls' softball in high school." She eyed their enemy with trepidation. "Did I kill him?"

"I doubt it." Seth started to rise, letting Marie assist him. "Let's get him tied up just in case he comes to. Is Patty okay?"

"She's fine," Marie said through tears of joy. "Judging by the way that blanket is moving, I think she's got your dog under there with her."

"Probably. I was afraid Eccles would shoot Babe, too."

"Then that is the man you thought it was?"

"That's him," Seth said, rubbing the knot on his head. "He's still dangerous. But now it looks like I'll be able to prove my innocence. He has to have lied to his superiors in order to have arranged this mission to kill me. That alone will give them reason to listen to my side of the story for once."

"I wish I could say the same," Marie said sadly. "Even with Roy dead, I still have those old partners of his chasing me. How am I ever going to prove I'm innocent?"

A strange voice echoed from the distance. "Tell me where you are and what the blazes is going on out here, and I'll believe anything you say."

Seth immediately pulled Marie into his arms and turned sideways to shield her.

"This is the Fulton County Sheriff," the voice explained, drawing closer. "So don't shoot. I'm one of the good guys."

"So are we," Marie shouted back at him. "So are we."

SIXTEEN

By the time the sheriff's men had hauled the stunned Eccles to a waiting ambulance and had guided Marie and the others back to the campground, it was nearly midnight.

She gladly climbed into the back of the sheriff's car with Patty and cuddled her close.

Seth leaned in. "Are you warm enough?"

"I will be," she answered, her teeth chattering. "Right now, all of me is numb, even my brain."

He nodded toward the sheriff. "Harlan here says I can drive my truck back to town myself. Do you mind?"

"No," Marie said. "Just be careful, okay?"

"I will." He started to reach for her hand, then stopped, so she tucked it beneath the blanket and he withdrew farther.

As he closed the car door, Marie was struck by an immense sense of loss, of loneliness. Had she come to rely so strongly on Seth's sustaining, strong presence that she missed him already, even though he was standing right outside the car? Apparently so.

Well, you'd better get used to it, she told herself. *All the excitement is over. He has no more reason to hang around and baby you.*

Although she had known that from the start, the thought still struck her like a dagger in her heart. It was essentially over, wasn't it? Oh, there would be plenty of details to iron out and lots of explaining to do, but if the sheriff was right about her pursuers being either dead or out of commission, she and Patty were probably quite safe. That was a relief.

Slamming the driver's door, Harlan glanced back at her. "Ready to go, ma'am?"

"As ready as I'm going to get," Marie replied. "I don't think I've ever been this cold before."

"I put the heater on high," he said amiably. "You'll warm up soon. And I'll take you and your little girl by the hospital so you can be checked out, just to make sure you're both okay."

"Is that really necessary?"

"It's standard procedure," he answered. "Sorry about your car. You were lucky you got out of it when you did."

"There's no sign of it yet?"

He shook his head as he turned the car around and started back along the muddy road to the highway. "Not yet. But we'll find it. The creek narrows about three miles out of town. It didn't sink upstream, as far as we can tell, so it's probably snagged down around there somewhere."

"I don't know how to thank you. Any of you," Marie said, fighting back tears of weariness and despair. "I

don't know what I'm going to do now. Everything I owned was packed in that old car."

"Don't you worry," Harlan said. "We take care of our own. After we finish at the hospital, I'll see that you both get clean, dry clothes."

"You will?"

"Of course." His smile was reflected in the rearview mirror. "Seth tells me you're acquainted with Becky Malloy. She's in charge of the community pantry. We keep both food and clothing available there for emergencies like this."

"I guess it is an emergency," Marie admitted. "I hate to be a bother, though."

"No bother. Serenity is like a big family. We have our local stinkers, sure, but we also have plenty of good folks who'll look out for you."

Meaning I won't need to bother Seth anymore, she added to herself. That figured. He had his own problems. Boy, did he. If that man she had hit over the head was any example of the kind of dangerous people who were after Seth, poor Roy had been a piker by comparison.

"Did—did the man you said was shot say anything about me?" she asked, dreading the answer.

Harlan nodded. "Sure did. Seems he and his buddies were chasing you because they thought you had money that belonged to them." He chuckled. "If they'd stayed in Baton Rouge a little longer, they'd have known that the ransom had been recovered. All of it. They were on a wild-goose chase. Two of them died for nothing."

"What about the other man? Is he still out to get me?"

"Nope," the sheriff said. "He's been told he made a big mistake. Besides, by the time the law gets through with him, he's going to prison for a good, long time."

Marie gave a sigh of relief. "Thank God."

"Sure enough, ma'am. Looks like the good Lord is takin' fine care of you and your little girl." Pausing, he added, "So, what are your plans from here on out?"

"I don't have a clue. I suppose I'll try to get my car repaired, providing the water hasn't ruined it, and then go back to Louisiana."

"Um, not right off, okay? I imagine I'll need your testimony, and it would be much easier if you were close by, at least for a while. If you don't mind."

"No. I don't mind." Marie was secretly relieved to have found a plausible reason to stop running, to stay in Serenity for a little longer. She was tired of feeling disconnected and homeless. It would be good to spend a few more days or weeks among the friendly folks in the little Ozark town.

And beyond that? She was so weary, so emotionally drained, that she didn't want to have to plan any further. Later, she'd make plans. Right now, all she wanted to do was cuddle up with her daughter, praise God for their deliverance and close her eyes for just an instant.

Before the sheriff's car reached the highway, she was sound asleep.

Seth was deep in contemplation as he followed Marie and the rest of the cars back to town. Eccles had

regained consciousness long enough to boast about his subterfuge, meaning that Jonathan wasn't alive after all. That had been a blow. Seth felt as if he was having to bid his friend a final goodbye for the second time. It didn't hurt as much as it had initially, but it was still painful.

And now what? he wondered. When he saw Harlan turn and lead the way to the emergency entrance of the tiny county hospital just off the highway, his breath caught. Was there something wrong with Marie? Or with Patty?

He whipped into the parking lot and leaped out of his truck, intending to follow them inside. Instead, he was grabbed and held fast by several men clad in black clothing and bulletproof vests.

"Let me go!"

"Easy, man," one of them said. "We just want to talk to you."

"Not now. I have to go inside," Seth insisted.

"In a minute. First, I'd like a few answers."

Seth's head whipped around as he recognized the man's voice. "Mac? Is that you?"

"Yeah, it's me. Now settle down and tell me what in blazes has been going on around here. Eccles has been acting like some kind of a madman."

"He *is* crazy if he thinks I'm going to let him get away with it this time," Seth said firmly. "He's been trying to kill me ever since I found out he was behind the theft of military secrets from some of our best clients."

"What about your wife?"

"He killed her, too, or had her killed," Seth insisted. "I could never prove it, but I know he was responsible. Jonathan Biggs had been trying to help me prove my innocence—until he was murdered. After that, I figured the best thing to do was go into hiding, so that's what I did. I wouldn't have tipped my hand and gotten in touch with the agency again if I hadn't felt I had to."

Mac nodded understandingly. "I figured it had to be something like that. We've had our eye on Eccles for months now, ever since there was another breach of internal security. If you hadn't come back into the picture and stirred things up, we might never have been able to pin anything on him."

"What about Alice's murder? Am I still a suspect?"

"You won't be. Not after we get all this straightened out. We will need you to come back to Philly for a bit, though. Think you can get away?"

"If it means I'll be free from then on, I'll make it happen. When?"

"As soon as possible. How about tonight?"

Seth eyed the emergency entrance, then nodded. "All right. Let me make sure the woman and child are okay first?"

"Sure." Mac stepped back. "As far as I'm concerned, you're not under arrest. Do what you have to do. We'll wait out here."

"Thanks," Seth said, smiling. "I will be back, you know."

The other agent grinned at him. "I don't doubt it for

a second, man. You always were so honest it made the rest of us look bad even when we were behaving ourselves. Just make it snappy, okay?"

The first person Seth saw when he burst through the door was Logan Malloy. Judging by the serene look on the pastor's face, all was well.

Seth shook Logan's hand. "Are they okay?"

"Fine," Logan assured him. "Only a few bruises from your little adventure. The doc wants to keep them here overnight, just to be sure, but he says there's nothing to worry about."

Shoulders sagging, Seth sighed. "Good. When I saw Harlan pull in here, I started imagining the worst."

"Speaking of worse things," the pastor said, "when were you going to tell me about your past problems with this guy Eccles? I might have been able to help you get justice, you know."

"I know. And I was going to confess everything, eventually. But after Marie came to town and I started trying to protect her, I didn't want anything to happen that might pull me away. Not when she needed me so badly."

"What about now?" Logan asked.

Seth gestured toward the parking lot. "The men who were with Eccles are out there, waiting for me."

"And?"

"And, I suppose the fairest thing to do is to go with them now and get it all over with." He glanced down the hallway, hoping to catch a glimpse of Marie. "I just wish I could talk to her before I leave."

"And tell her what?"

Shrugging, Seth shook his head. "Beats me. I'd like to be able to say I've been cleared of all charges, but I can't know that for sure until I go back to Philadelphia and face the music."

"Then maybe that's what you should do."

"But what if she leaves Serenity? What if I lose all track of her?"

Smiling, the pastor patted Seth on the shoulder. "I wouldn't worry about that. Harlan has already told her he wants her to stay in town indefinitely, as a prosecution witness. It looks to me as if the good Lord has the whole situation well in hand."

Seth's brow knit and he stared at Logan, incredulous. "Stay here? Isn't the case against Roy Jenkins's cohorts based in Baton Rouge?"

Logan's smile broadened into a grin. His eyebrows arched. "Could be. Don't you think we should obey whatever the sheriff tells us in this case instead of questioning him?"

"Yes, I do," Seth said, sharing a chuckle with his clever friend and pastor. "I always did say Harlan was the best sheriff this town has ever had. If he says Marie has to stay, then he must have a very good reason."

"I think so, too." Logan laughed. "Just hurry back, will you? If your Marie asks me directly, I'm going to have to tell her the truth, and I'd hate for you to miss your big chance to tell her you love her."

"Who said I...?" Seth's relief and good humor were

impossible to deny so he let himself laugh again. "Okay. You win. Look after her while I'm gone?"

"Like a member of my own family," Logan said. "Come to think of it, she's a believer, so she is family." He shook Seth's hand. "Keep us posted?"

"Will do." He eyed the door beyond which his former comrades waited. "Guess I'd better go before they decide I'm not as innocent as I'd claimed. Oh, and Babe is out in my truck. Will you take care of her, too? Let Patty have her if she wants."

"Sure. See you soon," Logan predicted, waving goodbye.

Seth turned and straight-armed his way through the swinging doors. He hoped with all his heart that Logan was right. Walking back into the fray and trusting Corp. Inc. to get it right this time was more frightening than ever, because this time there was someone on the outside whom he cared about. Someone who might actually be waiting for him once he was cleared.

And if he wasn't cleared? Seth gritted his teeth. If he went to jail after all, it was better that he had not had the chance to tell Marie how much he loved her. The last thing he wanted was for her to put her life on hold while he rotted in prison.

For Seth, the worst thought was not that he might be incarcerated. It was that he might never see Marie—or Patty—again.

Marie had not intended to hang around Serenity once all her legal problems were settled, but the sheriff

kept insisting that he needed her as a witness, so she had stayed. She didn't know enough about the workings of the law to argue, and since he and his staff had managed to clear her of any wrongdoing in connection with Roy and his former criminal partners, she felt she owed him her willing cooperation.

As the weeks passed, however, and no court case seemed to be pending, she began to wonder if she was being bamboozled.

Becky and Logan Malloy, and the congregation of Serenity Chapel, had found her a temporary place to live, helped her repair her car and given her a job working in the preschool. The more time Marie spent in the friendly Ozark town, the more she felt as if she truly belonged.

The hardest thing for her to deal with was the sense of loss she felt whenever she drove past the Serenity Repair garage. She hadn't seen Seth since that night in the woods, and the longer he was gone, the more worried she became in spite of Brother Logan's assurances that all was well and that Seth was planning to return.

She was at the church, straightening up the classroom, when suddenly the hair on the back of her neck prickled. She spun around. Her eyes widened. Her jaw gaped. There he was. Seth was back!

Her feet were temporarily rooted to the spot where she stood. It was the expectant, hopeful expression on Seth's handsome face that gave her enough incentive to move.

And move she did. By the time she'd crossed the

room and reached him, she was running. Without hesitation she wrapped her arms around his neck and hung on for sheer joy.

Seth absorbed her momentum by swinging her in a circle, her feet off the ground. When he finally set her back down and stepped away, he was grinning broadly. "I think you're glad to see me."

Marie playfully punched him in the shoulder. "Glad? I'll say I'm glad. But I'm mad, too. Why didn't you phone? You could have at least called me once or twice, you know."

"I thought Brother Logan was keeping you posted."

"Oh, sure." Marie pulled a face. "He kept assuring me you were fine, but that wasn't the same as hearing your voice for myself."

"You wanted to hear my voice?"

"Of course I did."

"Why?"

That stopped her. "Well, I…"

As Seth gently took her hands and held them, Marie saw only him, heard only him, in spite of the other adults and children who were watching.

"I wanted to phone you," he said. "But until I was free to tell you how I felt, I didn't think it was fair."

"How you felt?"

"Yes." He cleared his throat. "I realize we haven't known each other very long, but I think you and I have potential, Marie."

"You do?" Her voice was barely above a whisper,

and she knew her hands would soon begin to tremble within his warm grasp because the butterflies in her stomach were already in full flight.

"Yes. I do. I don't expect you to feel the same way. Not so soon. But I would like you to consider the possibility."

"The possibility of what, exactly, Seth?"

"Of us, as a couple. I can wait. Just as long as you don't leave town I figure I have a good chance to convince you that we belong together."

She began to puzzle over his statement. Her brow knit. Her eyes narrowed while she studied him, looking for answers. "Wait a minute. Was I asked to stay in Serenity because I'm needed for a witness, or are you behind it all?"

"I may have asked Harlan to use his influence to encourage you to hang around Serenity a bit longer. Is that so bad? It wasn't malicious."

"Oh? Then what was it?" The look on his handsome face was so appealing that Marie could hardly hold on to even a smidgen of her righteous anger.

"It was hopeful," Seth said.

"Hopeful? How?" Whatever he was trying to say, she was losing patience. If he didn't quit beating around the bush soon, she was going to scream.

He shrugged and reached for her hand. "I was hoping, if you got used to us, you might decide that this was a great place to live. You know it's good for Patty. We have very little crime, good churches, great schools." His grip on her fingers tightened to a gentle

squeeze. "And *very* friendly mechanics. Next year, I'll even take you to the reunion the way I promised."

"Next year? That's an awfully long time." *Just say it. If you love me, say so, so I can tell you I love you in return.* "And I don't need a friendly mechanic anymore," she added, growing more and more frustrated. "My car is fine."

"Ah, but how's your heart?" Seth asked softly. "Personally, mine is a mess. It has been ever since you showed up here that first day, all frazzled and needy."

"I'm not needy."

"No, you're not. Not now. And that's a good thing, because now you're better able to make serious decisions. That's why I haven't called you or tried to hurry you, Marie. I want you to get to know me as a friend so you'll feel totally free to decide."

"Decide *what?*" She wondered if he could feel her racing pulse through her fingertips.

"If you'll marry me," Seth finally said.

Marie held her breath as his smile faded and his eyes began to glisten. There he stood, sweet and gentle as ever, asking her to be his wife and leaving her speechless.

This was not the romantic proposal she had always dreamed of. Seth was not the kind of husband she had envisioned, either. Still, she knew without a doubt that she did love him, both as a friend and more. Was that enough? Or had she been right in the past when she'd totally rejected the idea of Seth as a husband?

"I don't know what to say," Marie whispered.

"At least you didn't turn me down flat."

She had to blink to clear her own vision because tears of thankfulness and love were filling her eyes.

Slowly, deliberately, she cupped his cheek with her free hand and smiled. "Patty is going to never let me live this down."

"Patty? Why?"

"Because she's been telling me for weeks that she's been praying we were going to stay in Serenity forever."

"And?"

Marie's smile widened. "And that you were going to be her new daddy."

"Am I?"

Marie slipped her arms around his neck and stood on tiptoe to give him a quick, tender kiss before she said, "Yes. You certainly are. I love you, Seth. I always will."

Amid applause and cheers from the others at the preschool, Marie gave Seth the best kiss of her life— and of his. So far.

EPILOGUE

The streets around the town square were festooned with colorful streamers, balloons and dozens of American flags. There was a small combo playing in the gazebo at the east end of the courthouse, while vendors in temporary booths hawked their wares to the happy reunion crowd milling around in the roped-off streets.

Marie took one of Seth's hands while Patty grasped the other. "Look, Daddy!" the child squealed, pointing. "Can I have a Sno-Kone?"

"After the turtle races," Seth said.

Marie never ceased to be amazed at what a perfect family they had become. At times, she felt as if they had always been together, always loved one another, instead of having been strangers a scant year ago.

She followed her husband and child to a part of the street that had been designated for the famous races. The makeshift track was nothing more than a few boards nailed into a grid of parallel racing lanes. The whole contraption was barely eight feet from one end of each lane to the other.

Marie giggled. "That's it? That's all there is?"

Seth met her gaze with a wink. "Hey, that's a marathon for a tortoise. Just watch. You'll see."

He maneuvered Patty into line, made sure she understood how to gently place the turtle in the proper lane when her turn came, then rejoined Marie. "Watch. And don't blink. It doesn't take long for each heat."

"No wonder." She was still laughing softly. "She's going to want to keep the turtle, you know."

"I know. I've already explained that it needs to go back to its brothers and sisters in the woods after today."

Blushing, Marie squeezed his hand. "That reminds me," she whispered. "I've been meaning to mention something to you. I just never seemed to find the right time. This probably isn't it, either, but I can't keep this to myself one more minute."

Seth slipped his arm around her shoulders and said. "What would the right time be to tell me Patty's going to have a little brother or sister?"

Marie startled. "You know? How? Surely, not by gossip. At least I hope not, or I'm never going to a local doctor again."

He laughed and pulled her closer. "Nobody told me. I guessed. When you stopped eating a decent breakfast and kept nibbling on pretzels, I happened to ask Becky if she had noticed that you weren't acting right."

"And she told you?"

"No. Actually, I'd looked up your symptoms on the computer and pretty much had it figured out already. She only confirmed my suspicions."

"You and your computers. When are you going to learn that messing with those things just gets you into trouble?"

"Never," Seth said. "I plan to keep doing anything I have to in order to take good care of my girls." He nodded toward Patty. "Now watch, Mama. Our girl is about to have her turn."

His dear, sincere words warmed Marie's heart so much she could hardly see through a mist of joy. There was no place she would rather be, no one with whom she would want to share her present and her future but the wonderful man standing beside her.

She was secretly glad she hadn't known ahead of time what she'd have to go through to bring her to this place in her life. The trials hadn't been easy. But she wouldn't change a thing. Not even if she could.

* * * * *

*If you liked NOWHERE TO RUN,
look for Valerie Hansen's next
exciting romantic suspense, set in Serenity,
coming in June 2009
only from* LOVE INSPIRED SUSPENSE.

Dear Reader,

In this story, both Marie and Seth are hiding from their pasts. Neither is guilty of doing anything against the law, yet circumstances of their lives have brought them together for good—and for personal healing. Although there can be times when we don't see how any good can come from what is happening to us, we all need to remember that we're seeing only a small part of the whole picture. If we have turned our lives over to the Lord, He may be acting on our behalf even when we're positive everything is going wrong. It's nice to be able to look back and praise Him. I highly recommend it!

My prayer for all of you is that you will find happiness, fulfillment and contentment through a belief in Jesus Christ.

I love to hear from readers, by e-mail:

VAL@ValerieHansen.com
or at P.O. Box 13, Glencoe, AR, 72539.

I'll do my best to answer as soon as I can, and www.ValerieHansen.com will take you to my Web site.

Blessings,

Valerie Hansen

QUESTIONS FOR DISCUSSION

1. When Marie found herself in an abusive relationship, she took her daughter and went to a women's shelter. Do you think she made the right decision? What would you have done in her place?

2. Marie made mistakes in her past, including not marrying the father of Patty, her daughter. Now that she is a Christian and has given her life to Jesus, should she be exempt from the consequences of her past mistakes? Why or why not?

3. Many people like to believe that there is good even in the worst villains. Do you think Roy finally understood right from wrong before he died? Was God giving him a second chance?

4. Though Seth lost his wife in a brutal crime, he seems willing to open his heart again to Marie. Do you think it's easy for him? Have you ever lost someone close to you and tried to start a new relationship? Discuss.

5. When Marie and Patty's car breaks down in Serenity, Patty notes that Marie does a lot of lying to Seth about who they are and where they're from. Was Marie justified in her lies? Are there exceptions in the Bible?

6. Seth is very close with his border collie, Babe. What do you think this says about his character? Is he trustworthy? Dependable? Stable? Discuss why these qualities would be very attractive to Marie after dealing with Roy.

7. Patty prays with the trust and certainty of a child. Have you ever wished you could be that sure that you're asking rightly? Have you ever prayed and then wanted to take it back?

8. When Marie learns that Seth has been keeping information from her, she doesn't trust him. Could her reaction be related to her turbulent past with her family and with Roy? Why or why not?

9. Both Marie and Seth are reluctant to trust law-enforcement officials. Wouldn't they have been better off to do so? Do their actions demonstrate that they also lack trust in God?

10. Like Marie, we are sometimes called on to defend ourselves. Do you think the Lord wanted Marie to remain in a place where her daughter could easily have been hurt—or worse?

11. The townspeople of Serenity open their hearts to Marie and her daughter, organizing a search when Patty goes missing. Have you ever been a

part of a community like Serenity? Would you
like to be? Why or why not?

12. At the end of the book, Marie must decide whether
to stay and make a life in Serenity or move on.
How does Serenity help her with that decision?
How does Seth? Do you think she made the right
decision?